Forgiven:
Finding a Path
Home

Richard D. Bangs

BookCrafters

Also by Richard D. Bangs:
Forsaken: Searching for God's Fingerprints

What readers have said about **Forsaken**:

"Just finished reading your book this morning, as I started it last night. It really is a great story and hard to put down. I liked it a lot and am looking forward to the sequel."

Tom B., Inverness, MT

"Read (*Forsaken*). For a person like me that is not a sci-fi fan, it was a good read - plenty of action to keep one turning the page. Enjoyed the references to Montana and Australia."

Steve L., Littleton, CO

"Just finished reading *Forsaken* and it was great!"
Linda D., Salem, OR

"Doggone you, Rich. I'm trying to finish reading a book I started over a week ago. And then I peeked at *Forsaken*. I can see it will be a few days before I get back to my other book. The first few pages are certainly compelling."

Bill W., Kilgore, TX

Acknowledgements

The encouragement of a great many people over the last few years has led to this sequel to my first novel, *Forsaken: Searching for God's Fingerprints*. My wife Susan and my daughter Ashley and her husband John encouraged me to keep writing and to tell more of this story. Many friends and acquaintances continue to ask when my next book is going to be published. Their reaction to *Forsaken* and their requests for more pushed me to finish this sequel.

Long before that my mother inspired me with her avid reading habits and her encouragement of my writing. My father was an ardent newspaper reader and a student of human nature.

Peggy Peterson, my editor, made me focus my thoughts and my writing. I must also thank all the science fiction writers I have read throughout my life, and continue to read.

I would like to thank Bruegger's Bagels & Coffee in Littleton, Colorado, for the good food and coffee, free Wi-Fi and for the table where I wrote most of *Forgiven* on my iPad.

A special recognition goes to David Grinspoon whose *Lonely Planets* was an inspiration and helped set the foundation for some of my ideas.

Chapter 1

Fear crept up on Jarrod McKinley as he looked over his shoulder and scanned the cabin of the Qantas passenger plane.

He was getting that "sense of evil" that he had learned to trust over the past twelve months. That sense had alerted him to the energy wave that destroyed the listening post he had been manning in orbit around the Saturn moon Titan.

In the two months after that, he had learned that every time he sensed evil something was waiting to leap from the shadows and attack.

It had been about eight months, last February, since he'd had that feeling; the day he and his companions had finally ripped open the conspiracy of the Forsaken project.

He was now on a flight from Sydney to Adelaide, the last leg of the fifteen-hour flight from Los Angeles. When the captain turned off the seat belt sign, McKinley stood and walked to the forward lavatory. He ran some water and brushed his short brown hair back before easing his five foot eleven inch frame back into the aisle of the plane.

He had not felt that sense of evil on the flight from LA to Sydney. But as soon as the plane touched down in Sydney, a dark cloud began to form. The feeling was just strong enough to put McKinley on edge.

Figures. This damned country seems out to get me, McKinley thought, remembering the several narrow escapes he and his friends had had while blowing the top off of The Rev. Christopher Larchmont's Forsaken scheme.

He walked slowly down the aisle, carefully studying each person. He remembered many of the passengers from the long LA flight, but there were a few new faces on this Sydney to Adelaide leg and he gave those the most attention.

In first class, a variety of business types were busy looking at documents, ordering drinks or harassing the attendants. No alarms there.

The first few rows of the economy section were occupied by a couple of families, some students, and several European travelers. None were cause for concern.

About halfway through the economy section, he spotted a likely suspect. The man was probably in his mid-forties with blonde hair cropped close. He had his head down pretending to read a magazine. McKinley couldn't remember seeing him on the LA leg of the flight. The man was sitting in the aisle seat and as McKinley walked by him he pretended to stumble and brushed hard against his shoulder.

"Oh! Excuse me," McKinley said.

The man looked up, smiled and said, "No problem, mate," and went back to reading.

No bad vibes there, McKinley thought.

Just across the aisle and two seats down, a tall, slim man with short black hair stared silently at McKinley. He was seated in a window seat and McKinley smiled at him and nodded. The man gave no response. McKinley recognized the man from the LA leg and there were no bad vibes coming from him.

McKinley continued down the aisle. When he reached the end, he still had no idea where the bad feeling was coming from, but it was much weaker now.

He wondered if he was imagining it. He didn't think so, but it had been more than eight months since he had this sensation.

He returned to his seat and settled in for the rest of the flight to Adelaide. He would be met there by Janet Brighton and Sam Filmore from Wilpena Pound, the center of the Search for Extraterrestrial Intelligence.

Wilpena Pound, in the Flinders Ranges in northern South Australia, had been chosen because the natural bowl surrounded by tall ridges had been ideal for the placement of a large radio telescope spread out across the valley of the bowl. The center itself was inconspicuous with six of its seven levels underground. Only a reception area, visitors' center and an observation deck rose above the ground level of the valley.

After a six-hour drive to the Pound, McKinley would finally get a chance to analyze and discuss the signal they had received. The message appeared to be from outer space and it asked explicitly to talk to McKinley.

The SETI team had kept the receipt of this signal secret after the fiasco of the Forsaken incident in which a fake signal was used to promote the mission of the old SETI Special Command, or SETISCOM. That conspiracy had badly stained the credibility of any SETI program and, even though public interest was now high, SETI management was being cautious. The team wanted to be sure that everything released to the public was true. After the lies of the Forsaken conspiracy, in which a signal had been shot back to Earth from a secretly launched rocket, it was going to be hard to convince anyone that another communication had been received. The old SETISCOM had tried to use the hoax to generate more interest, and cash, to keep Larchmont's private and religiously focused empire afloat.

Now, in November of 2088, SETI, renamed for the original effort begun in the 1960s, was on a tight financial string, hence the commercial flight and car trip to Wilpena Pound.

By the time McKinley had shuffled all this through his mind and reviewed background data about the new signal on his e-tab, the captain announced they were approaching Adelaide.

As the plane taxied to the gate, McKinley again started to sense evil creeping up on him. By the time the plane reached the gate and the captain turned off the seat belt sign, the feeling was strong enough that

McKinley was looking around again, searching for danger.

The blonde-haired man was busy collecting his personal items and paying no attention to McKinley. Families gathered their belongings from the overhead bins and students grabbed their backpacks and looked for their passports.

Across the aisle and down two seats, the tall, slim man was pulling a long overcoat out of the overhead bin. McKinley thought that was a bit strange. It was too hot for that kind of coat in Australia. It was November, just heading into the summer months, the hottest time of the year.

But there were no bad vibes coming from the man and he had been on the flight since Los Angeles. No, there's something about being in Australia that is causing these feelings of fear, McKinley thought.

McKinley collected his carry-on and waited as others began slowly exiting the jam-packed plane. He stepped on the walkway that connected the plane to the gate, plagued by a growing fear. As he went through the gate and entered the concourse he glanced nervously around. He could see no danger, but he knew it was there.

Brighton and Filmore would be waiting for him at the end of the concourse, just beyond the security barriers. There, down the concourse through the mass of bobbing heads and waving hands, he spotted them. He waved but they didn't notice him.

And then he ducked, but not soon enough. A fist grazed his head. Another slammed into his stomach and he buckled. Someone grabbed his wrist and put a hand over his mouth. It all happened so fast he didn't even get a look at his assailants. He was pushed roughly into a maintenance closet as a bag was placed over his head.

The whole maneuver had taken less than three seconds. He tried to yell but a strip of duct tape was slapped over his mouth. He was pushed to the floor, his hands jerked behind his back.

"If you want to live, keep quiet," a man rasped, as plastic ties were cinched tight around McKinley's wrists and ankles.

"We don't want to hurt you, but we will if you struggle," said another gruff voice. "And there are others who will be hurt if you resist. How much do you like Janet Brighton, or Laura Henning, or Sam Filmore? Or, Liza Alvarez? Yes, we know she's still in Montana on the farm with your dad."

"Are you going to behave?"

McKinley nodded yes.

"Okay, we're going to put you in this tub and wheel you out of here. There's someone who wants to talk to you. We're not going to hurt you, so don't struggle. But, just to be sure, take a whiff of this."

Before he could move an acidic odor assaulted his nose. Though he struggled, the two men pinned him firmly to the floor. His limbs quickly went limp and when he tried to talk under his gag he couldn't move his mouth or even formulate words of protest. Strangely, he could still hear. The two men dumped him in the tub and grabbed dirty towels and rugs to cover his slumped body. They grabbed a large rug and covered the tub.

"Okay, let's get out of here. We'll take the next door to the left, drop one floor down and we'll be right in front of the van."

"Righty-o. The boss says make it quick because our client wants to talk to him as soon as possible."

McKinley struggled unsuccessfully to regain control. Whatever they had given him had numbed most of his senses. He could hear and he could process what he heard, but there was no feeling in his limbs or in the rest of his body. He couldn't move his arms or legs, or even make out what he was lying on or what was covering him. He wasn't able to move his mouth, lips, or tongue.

Since he could hear, he tried to focus his mind to make sense of the noises coming through whatever material covered him. He heard the sound of a door opening and the noise of people in the airport's concourse and the public address announcements. Now, another door opened and closed. He had no sense of the direction he was traveling, as his limp body lay in the bottom of the tub. He heard another door open, then a second, and then a door close.

The next sound was a sliding door on a van. He heard the engine of a vehicle start and then accelerate. But he could not feel the van move. There was no sense of movement. No rocking back and forth or bumps up or down. The engine acceleration noise drowned out all other sounds and soon he stopped trying to determine where he was headed.

The tall man with the overcoat draped over his arm, watched intently as the two men exited the maintenance closet pushing what looked to be a covered laundry cart. He saw them move down the concourse away from the security barrier where Brighton and Filmore were stretching their necks looking for McKinley. In just a few steps the cart and the men disappeared through a door marked: *Employees Only, Secure Area.*

The tall man touched his hand to the side of his head for a few seconds as he looked at the floor and then walked toward the door.

He glanced quickly around and, when he was sure no one was watching, placed a small object on the door lock, opened the door and slipped inside.

Chapter 2

"I'M WORRIED." JANET BRIGHTON TURNED to Sam Filmore. "That was the last of the passengers. I asked the flight attendant. There's no one else on the plane."

"How can that be? We know he was on the plane. He called us after he took off from Sydney. Maybe he's in one of the restrooms."

"No. There's no men's room on this section of the concourse. Now that the crowd is gone, we can see all the way to the gate and there are only a couple of doors there, and none that a passenger can go through," Brighton explained.

"We must have just missed him."

"I doubt it. I was watching closely. He didn't pass here."

"Well he must have. Let's go down to the main terminal and look around. And, we can have him paged."

"I think we should call security," Brighton said. "Who knows what's happened to him?"

"You're being a bit hasty. He'll show up. Let's just go down to the main terminal. Try to find an information booth so we can page him."

"Sam! You're acting way too cavalier! Remember, this is Jarrod McKinley we're talking about. You know, the guy who seems to attract trouble wherever he goes. Remember Sydney? Wilpena Pound and Alice Springs? Jarrod attracts trouble like honey attracts bees."

Filmore sighed. "Now Janet, that was more than eight months ago and there hasn't been any trouble since we put Larchmont away."

"But there hadn't been any new signals either, until the one we got two days ago that was directed at Jarrod. Remember the last time there was big trouble? A signal directed at Jarrod started all of that, as I recall."

"No one but the SETI staff knows about the new signal," Filmore protested. "We haven't told a soul."

With a sense of foreboding, they stopped and looked at each other.

"Are you thinking what I'm thinking?" Brighton asked.

"A leak?"

"If the word got out, then Jarrod might be in danger. I think we need to contact airport security now and take no chances," Brighton said.

"Okay. You find an information booth and put out a page for Jarrod. I'll find a security officer and alert him that something's not right."

They both headed toward the main terminal. Filmore soon found an airport security guard and started to explain their concerns.

Brighton had to go farther to find an information booth and before she got there her cell phone rang.

"Brighton here," she said into the phone.

"Janet. It's Laura Henning," said the voice in the phone. "How's it going? Was Jarrod's plane on time?"

"Yeah, the plane came in, but, Jarrod wasn't on it."

"What happened?" Henning asked.

"Not sure. We're making some inquiries now. How are things at the Pound?"

Henning was now in charge of the signal monitoring at the SETI Wilpena Pound center. When the Forsaken conspiracy had been revealed, Sam Filmore had left that position to help Brighton with the administration of the complex. It seemed only natural that Henning should be promoted from her command position on the Titan Base to the job of monitoring controlling officer at Wilpena Pound.

With no manned listening post orbiting the Saturn moon Titan, there was less work to do and Henning's subordinate on Titan, Alan Cranston, was more than qualified to take control.

"Laura," Brighton said. "Are we still secure on this latest signal? I'm worried that if something leaked out, Jarrod might be in danger."

"That's why I called," Henning replied. "Something strange happened just after you left this morning. I didn't call earlier because I wanted to make sure it wasn't just an instrument malfunction. But Jack and I have gone over everything several times and I think we did have a data dump at about eight-thirty this morning."

"What do you mean data dump?"

"It appears that someone, or something, copied all the files we had on this new signal."

"How did they do that?" Brighton asked, "I thought our system was secure."

"We don't know for sure yet. We all thought it was secure," Henning replied. "That's what worries me most."

"What?"

"Well, there weren't any obvious intrusion traces. If someone hacked into our system and we can't trace it, they must have the most advanced hacking capabilities on the planet, or it's something off-world that we don't understand."

"Or," Henning continued, "it was an inside job. That would scare me even more. It means we have a traitor among us."

"Laura," Brighton ordered, "You and Jack lock down everything. Make sure everyone is accounted for and don't allow anyone access our systems unless you or he is present."

"Already done, Janet," Henning responded. "You forget, I've gone through this before on Titan Base."

"Sorry. I wasn't trying to get pushy and I do trust you, Laura. I just tend to be a bit paranoid."

"We all have reason to be paranoid," said Henning. "We all remember the attacks on Jarrod's life on Titan and while he was at Wilpena Pound."

"But Larchmont is in jail and his lackey Gregory Stalingwirth is still being held for investigation. They are going to be answering for the people they killed and injured for a long time."

"Yes," said Henning. "I still miss Charlie Snelling, his experience, his humor. I can't believe he's gone.

Those guys killed him when they sabotaged his plane and it crashed."

"Larchmont has already been sentenced to a long jail term and I expect Stalingwirth will get the same," Brighton said.

"I've got to go," Brighton said, "Sam's here with the security guard. We've got to find Jarrod."

Brighton quickly filled in Filmore on what had happened at Wilpena Pound.

"That means we have to assume someone outside knows about our issue," Filmore said, "and that they may be after Jarrod."

"What's your issue?" the security official asked.

"We can't reveal that," Filmore said. "Our concern now is that Jarrod McKinley was on that airplane when it left Sydney, and he didn't show up here. Where is he?"

"I have my team reviewing security tapes," the security officer said. "This whole area is covered. The entire airport is on camera. If he was on that plane, we'll have pictures and we will know where he went. Come with me."

Brighton stopped to put out the page for McKinley and then followed Filmore and the security official to a video monitoring room. As soon as the video began running, their worst fears were confirmed. Even before they finished watching the video, the security official put his team on alert and tried to block any escape from the airport's concourse area.

The scenario unfolding on the video was as much puzzling as it was terrifying. Two men could be seen pushing McKinley into the maintenance room door. A minute or two later they were pushing a cart out of the room. The cart was covered, hiding whatever they were carrying. They exited the next service door.

Just before switching camera feeds, Brighton said, "Stop. Look! Who's that?"

She was pointing to a tall, thin man with black hair who had just appeared at the edge of the scene. He was headed toward the service door.

"It looks like he's following them," Filmore said. "Let's wait and see what he does."

Sure enough, the man approached the service door, looked around once, and entered.

"He must be in charge of the abduction," said Brighton. "It doesn't look like he's trying to stop them."

"Where does that door lead?" Filmore asked.

"It goes down to the ground level, on the concourse, very close to the boarding ramp," the security official said. "There's a stair and an elevator. But those doors are all supposed to be secure. Only employees with security clearance should be able to open them."

When camera feeds were switched to the security monitors one floor below, they could see the men roll the cart into the van, close the doors and drive off.

The van was nondescript, white, with no markings and no license plate. Using several different camera feeds, they watched the van drive away from airport concourse toward a maintenance gate at the end of one of the taxiways.

"They can't get out that way," the officer said. "That gate is padlocked and guarded."

Just as he finished his sentence, an alert sounded and he picked up a phone. After a second he slammed the phone down.

"Damn. They rammed the gate and injured my guard."

"Go back to the video," Brighton said. "Let's see what our mysterious tall stranger was doing."

When they next saw the man, he appeared below the concourse and quickly moved behind a supporting column where he was out of view. But it was clear he didn't get in the van.

"Why didn't he go with them?" Filmore asked. "If he's part of the kidnapping, he should go with them."

"Not necessarily," said Brighton. "He just might be making sure his goons got away. He'll probably meet them later to grill Jarrod, or do whatever . . ." Brighton's voice trailed off.

"Try to follow him," Filmore said. "Let's see where he goes."

After switching around to various camera feeds, it was apparent the tall stranger had avoided the security cameras.

"I thought you said you film this whole airport," Brighton said.

"We do," the security chief said. "I don't understand."

He immediately was on the phone alerting his security team to lock down the boarding ramp area and to hold anyone who was not authorized or who appeared suspicious.

"We'll find him," he said. "We have a tight net on this facility."

"In the meantime," said Filmore, "can you call local and state officials? We need to find that van. I'm sure Jarrod is inside."

"It's already done," the chief said. "As soon as that van broke through the gate, this incident became something for state and federal authorities."

"Good," said Brighton. "Can you give me the contacts we'll need to keep on top of this?"

The security official was very helpful and offered not only contacts but assured them the security video would be turned over to the proper authorities.

Brighton immediately called Laura Henning at Wilpena Pound to fill her in.

"Sam and I will stay here for a while," Brighton told her. "The signal can wait. We have to find Jarrod."

"That's okay," said Henning. "I'll take care of things here. Take all the time you need."

"Laura," said Brighton, "let's keep this quiet. We don't want to have to deal with the media right now."

"I've already told Jack Simington about it," Henning said. "But, we'll stop it there. No one else will know. One more thing, bad news I'm afraid."

"Yeah? "What now?"

"Stalingwirth has been released."

"How did that happen? He was Larchmont's stooge and surely was involved in Larchmont's crimes."

"After your phone call, I just wanted to make sure," said Henning. "I called the federal prison in Sydney and a clerk said some high-powered lawyer had petitioned the court and then posted the $10 million bond for Stalingwirth."

"When?"

"Yesterday afternoon. Plenty of time for him to be behind all of this."

"Damn," said Brighton. "This smells too much like Larchmont directing something from his cell."

"I agree," said Henning. "Stalingwirth never had much initiative."

"We'll have to worry about that later, after we find Jarrod. Just try to keep a tight lid on things. We'll keep in touch."

Brighton quickly filled in Filmore. They told the security chief they wanted to wait there in case the search for the mysterious tall man bore fruit.

"Why don't you go down to the main terminal and have a cup of coffee," the chief said. "We should have him in custody within a half hour or so."

As they walked to the coffee shop, Filmore and Brighton discussed the signal that had initiated this chain of events. As soon as the new signal had been received, McKinley had rushed from his family farm in Montana where he had been vacationing with Liza Alvarez. It had been only two days since they'd received the signal at Wilpena Pound.

When the signal was decoded, it seemed very straight forward. The decoded message indicated the Forsaken event had been witnessed. It also asked for confirmation of the receipt of the signal. Finally, it contained a strange request to have a dialogue with McKinley.

The signal appeared to have come from Alpha Centauri, the three-star system closest to our solar system, but technicians at Wilpena Pound were skeptical because that was the same area where the fake signal from the Forsaken conspiracy had come from. They were doing more analysis, hoping to discover not only where the signal came from, but also who or what had sent it.

After Larchmont's scheme to keep interest high by faking the signal, thereby keeping cash flowing into SETISCOM, the current staff at SETI used large doses of cynicism and double and triple checked all data before making any proclamations about the facts of anything.

Even though the scandal had been a serious blow to search efforts, a nimble public relations effort and the conviction of Larchmont had managed to deflect most of the blame onto Larchmont and his cronies.

Now, with the news Stalingwirth had been released, Brighton worried he might be working with others who had been at the Pound. Most of the known conspirators were fired from SETI, including the whole security team and some of the scientists who had developed, tested, launched, and managed the rocket and satellite used to send the false signal.

But there were several people whose guilt or innocence could not be proven. Some of those were still working at Wilpena Pound, though they had been moved out of sensitive positions or positions of authority.

Still, there could be people working at the Pound who had sympathies, very well hidden, for the fanatical religious views of Larchmont.

Larchmont had raved on and on about how it was

vital that the human species find other intelligent life in the universe. He preached that human civilization would descend into chaos if it believed it were alone in the universe, if God's plan did not include others in the universe made in His image.

As McKinley and others exposed Larchmont, it became clear Larchmont was the biggest hypocrite of all; that he didn't believe any of what he preached and his only motive was to keep the money flowing to support his lavish lifestyle.

But, Brighton had to admit that Larchmont had followers who probably believed his message with a fanaticism that would never die. These were the kinds of people Brighton feared.

"He's gone," the security chief said, interrupting Brighton and Filmore.

"What do you mean gone?" Filmore asked.

"We lost him. That image you saw down near the boarding ramp was the last we saw of him, either on video or any of our checkpoints. He's just gone."

"Damn," Filmore said.

"We're going to stay in Adelaide until we find Jarrod," Brighton said. "We'll contact the state and federal authorities and we will stay in touch with you. We're going to be staying at the Comfort Hotel downtown. Here are our cell numbers. We'll get you our room numbers once we get settled."

"Good," said the security chief. "I apologize for this. No one has ever gotten through our security system. I'm going to do a thorough review to find out how this man got away."

"Thanks," said Filmore. "I'm sure you did all you could."

As Brighton and Filmore left the terminal to go to their car in the parking area, the bright blue sky was being eaten by a large cloud bank coming in from the north.

"Looks like a storm brewing," Filmore said.

"Great, just what we need. Let's get to the hotel and start making calls. Maybe the local authorities have a trace on that van that busted through the airfield gate."

As they passed through the parking lot gate, airport security was tight. They had to show identification and give the guards their names and contact information. They didn't protest.

"Nobody gets out of the airport without getting checked," the guard said.

"They'll catch that man," Filmore said to Brighton, trying to sound convincing.

By the time Brighton and Filmore left the airport, the tall thin man had traveled several miles from the airport and was securely tucked away where no one would find him. He took a small round device out of his long overcoat. It was time to get to work.

Chapter 3

Jarrod McKinley was coming around. As the feeling returned to his limbs he winced at the sharp pain from the ties around his wrists. He was still crammed in the laundry cart and the combination of being gagged, having a bag over his head and his knees pushed up against his chest made it difficult to breathe. His bent over neck ached.

He heard the crashing of what sounded like a metal on metal followed by a gunshot. He also heard one of his assailants curse at the other.

"Crikey," said the first man. "We weren't supposed use our guns. We weren't supposed to kill anyone."

"Relax, mate," said the other. "We bloody well would have been caught if we'd waited for the guard to let us out. I seen he was talking on the phone and lookin' at us mighty unfriendly. And I just winged him to get him out of the way. He's gonna be okay."

"So they're onto us," McKinley heard the first man say.

"Not to worry, mate," said the other. "We're makin' the switch in about two seconds and we'll be long gone before they get here."

"What about surveillance cameras?"

"None here. That's why we picked this route. The last surveillance camera was at the gate we crashed through and the windy path we've made will lose 'em."

"Don't be so sure," McKinley heard the first man say, the guy who appeared to be driving. "I ain't breaking no speed records windin' through this damn empty warehouse district."

"Quit your bitching," the second man said. "The Unit has got this well planned. For a plan put together in just a couple of days, I'd say we're doin' okay. Our job is to deliver this joker in the cart and then we're long gone. Here! Here's the drop spot. Pull into that warehouse with the broken windows and the big door up."

The cart containing McKinley swayed as the van swerved entering the warehouse and lurched as it slid to a hard stop.

He heard the van's front doors open and the kidnappers get out and go to the back of the van. The back doors swung open with a loud squeak and someone grabbed the cart and pulled it out of the van and down a small ramp to the floor of the warehouse. McKinley felt them grab the coverings in the cart and then the cart was tipped over and he rolled onto what felt like a concrete floor.

"Okay, pretty boy," said a man, "let's get you ready for the transfer. We're gonna free your legs. You should be able to stand now so you're gonna walk a few steps and sit on a chair."

Someone clipped the plastic tie around his ankles and he tried to move his legs. They were not working. He could barely move them. There was no way he was going to be able to stand.

"Come on, jerk off. Stand up," the second man said.

McKinley shook his head no and tried to motion to his legs.

"Grab him," the first man said. "Let's give our poor baby a little help."

The two men grabbed McKinley under the armpits and pulled him to his feet. They steadied him and, with them supporting most of his weight, he was able to shuffle a few meters, nearly collapsing as he went.

"Sit here," one man commanded. "The Unit should be here any minute. You're gonna need to be a little steadier when they come. They won't be so nice. That stuff we gave you should be wearin' off by now."

McKinley stamped his feet a few times bringing more feeling to his legs and feet and he began to feel much more in control. He tried to move, but a hand quickly pushed him back into the chair.

"Here they come," said the second man. "We can make the switch and get outta here."

"Be cool, mate," said the first. "This's gotta go smooth. We haven't been paid yet."

McKinley heard the squeal of tires as another vehicle drove through the warehouse door and stopped very near to him. The doors opened and closed on the vehicle and a new voice asked, "This him?"

"Sure is, bloke. You reckon we'd get the wrong guy? This is Jarrod McKinley. Guaranteed."

"Let's be sure," the new man said. "Pull that bag off slowly, but keep his eyes covered. He can't see any of us."

McKinley felt two sets of hands on him. The bag was slowly removed but a hand came under the bag and clamped down over his eyes before it was all the way off.

His head was turned back and forth.

"Yeah, okay," said the new man. "That's McKinley. Looks just like his picture.

"Put the bag back on, get him up and put him in the back seat of my car. Jason, you get in with him just to make sure he doesn't try anything stupid."

"Sure, boss," a fourth person said.

McKinley was jerked to his feet. This time he didn't stumble or begin to collapse. Nearly all of the feeling had returned to his legs and arms.

Just as he heard the car door open, he was aware of another sound, a high-pitched swooshing sound, like a floor polisher, only at a much higher and faster vibration. The four men around him shouted in fear.

A nearly soundless hiss repeated in four quick bursts. McKinley felt the grip of two men holding him relax just before he heard them fall to the floor with a short gasp.

McKinley turned to run, even though his hands were still laced behind his back and his head was covered with the bag. He bumped into something metallic, probably the car, as someone grabbed his shoulder.

"Jarrod McKinley. It is all right. You are safe now," a man's voice said. Or, at least McKinley thought it was a man's voice. It had a peculiarity to it that puzzled him. It was almost as high pitched as one might expect from a small woman, only with a deep resonance that made McKinley think it came from a larger person. It also carried a very calm but authoritative tone.

He struggled a bit, but the hand clamping his shoulder was firm.

"Calm down, Jarrod," the voice said. "You are safe and I am going to deliver you to your friends. You need not worry. It will be just a few minutes. I am sorry, but I am afraid I am going to have to leave your hands tied and the bag on. It is not safe if you see me."

McKinley felt a hand come under the bag and, with a firm jerk, remove the tape over his mouth.

"Ow!" McKinley exclaimed as the tape came off. "Who are you? What's going on? Who are those men who kidnapped me?" The questions came pouring out.

"I am a friend," said the voice. "Please come quickly and get in my vehicle. I will answer more questions later. We must leave this place now. The authorities are coming."

"Why do we have to leave?" McKinley asked. "We did nothing wrong, and I want to see who tried to kidnap me."

"I am sorry. But I cannot be here when the authorities come and you should not be either. Your appearance with these people will cast doubt on you and may jeopardize your mission at SETI," the man explained.

"How do you know about that?" McKinley responded. "That's top secret."

"I am afraid your secret leaked out, Mr. McKinley. Or these gentlemen would not be so interested in you. Now we must go!"

As McKinley started to protest he was grabbed firmly by the arm and led several meters.

"Stop here," the stranger said. "Now you must step up. It is a big step. I will guide you. Left foot up, now move to the left."

McKinley did as he was told and then a hand went under his armpit and pushed him up and in, and on to some kind of seat. He struggled to maintain his balance as the hand pushed him a little further in the vehicle and slammed the door shut.

Still with the bag over his head, and his hands laced behind his back, McKinley was now relying on his hearing to try to orient himself and figure out what was going on. Strangely, his sense of fear had left him. He was much calmer than he should have been, being pushed around and forced into another vehicle. He concentrated on the sounds.

Steps. Another door opening. A slight shake as the stranger entered the vehicle. A door closing. A quiet hum and a sense of movement. First a rotation, then a slow advancement in a straight line.

Blaring sirens and the screech of tires signaled the arrival of the police, he guessed. The vehicle he was in accelerated quickly and soon there was no sound except for a strange whispering hum.

"Did they see us?" McKinley asked.

"They did not."

"How can you be so sure? They were right on us."

"Trust me, McKinley. No one saw our vehicle."

"Okay. You said you would answer questions. I have hundreds."

"I will answer some of your questions," the stranger said. "But time is short and I will not have time to answer even one hundred questions. Chose your questions carefully."

McKinley hesitated.

"First," he said. "Why can't I see you."

"It is not important that you see me," the stranger responded.

"Who are you and who do you work for?"

"My name is not important. To you, I will be Smith. I work for someone who wants to see your mission succeed."

"What is my mission?"

"To understand and respond to the message received at Wilpena Pound two days ago."

"Will I see you . . . have contact with you again?"

"Only if necessary."

"Do you know anything about the signal?"

"I know of the signal. Nothing else is relevant."

"Why did the signal ask for me? And why am I important to the signal?"

"I cannot answer."

"Why?"

"That is something you must discover."

"How?"

"That is something you must discover."

"How?"

"Through your own efforts, Mr. McKinley. I cannot help."

"Why?"

"Mr. McKinley. We are going to be stopping soon. Do you have any other questions?"

"What is this vehicle? I can't tell how fast we've been moving and there has been very little noise."

"That is not relevant."

"Where are you taking me?"

"I am going to release you in a large city park in Adelaide just across the river from the hotel where your friends are about to check in while they look for you. The hotel is the Comfort Hotel at 31, 34 North Terrace. I also have alerted the police and after I release you they will come and deliver you to the hotel."

"What can I tell them about you, about my capture?"

"Tell them everything you know. Or tell them as much as you wish. That is up to you, Mr. McKinley."

"What do you expect me to do now?"

"Do just what you planned to do. Learn everything you can about the signal."

McKinley sensed the vehicle was slowing and coming to a stop.

"We are here. Please remain seated. I will help you exit the vehicle and move you to a safe distance."

McKinley heard a door open, then his door opened and a hand grabbed his shoulder.

"A big step," he was told. "Now move over here, please. And sit on the ground. Thank you for your cooperation. I must go."

"Wait," said McKinley, "One more question. How can I get in touch with you?"

"You cannot," the stranger said. "If necessary, I will contact you. There is one thing you can do."

"What?"

"Please try to develop, as best you can, your ability to sense danger. It could be very important to you and your friends."

"Why?'

"More dangers await, some even more complex than you have faced so far. You need to refine your sense of fear. Learn to locate the source that is causing your fear."

"How?"

"That is something you must discover. Now I must go."

Loud sirens wailed, coming fast and now very close. McKinley heard two doors close followed by that strange hum and a quiet whisk. Then there were only sirens as some type of emergency vehicle came to a gravely stop nearby.

"Mr. McKinley?" a voice asked.

"Are you all right?" an Adelaide police officer asked as he carefully removed the bag over McKinley's head and cut the ties binding his wrists.

"Yeah. I'm fine," McKinley said. "Did you see what kind a car that guy was driving? The one who dropped me here?"

"There was nothing around," the officer said. "You were alone, just sitting here with that bag over your head."

"You must have seen something," McKinley insisted. "I was talking to someone not five seconds before you pulled up."

"Nothing. There was nothing but you. We got a call telling us you would be here and that you might be in danger and needed to go to the Comfort Hotel. How did you get here?"

"Where am I?" McKinley responded.

"You're at Montefiore Hill, a large park near the Adelaide Oval. How'd you get here?"

"Forget it," McKinley said, already deciding he was going to keep to himself as much as he could. "Take me to the Comfort."

"Sir? I'm afraid I have bad news," a chubby, short man said as he approached the back of a tall chair behind a large desk. The chair had been swiveled away from the desk to give the occupant a view out a large window on a city landscape.

The chair didn't move.

"Yes," said the occupant.

"Jarrod McKinley is not in our custody."

"What happened?" the occupant responded, with no trace of emotion.

"The local team made the extraction but during the exchange to our men, someone intervened and took McKinley."

"Who?"

"They left no trace."

"I feared as much," said the figure in the chair, still staring out the window. "What about the men left at the scene?"

"Everything is secure, sir," the chubby man said. "The local team knew nothing about us and our men have been neutralized. We used—"

"Not important," the seated figure interrupted. "Leave now. I must contact my superiors."

When the assistant left, the man placed a mobile phone to his ear.

As he explained the issue, he smiled at the pleasant scene before him. Sydney was special this time of year, the harbor, the Opera House. Everyone getting ready for a summer of activity.

Chapter 4

"Okay, Jack. Let's go over security," Laura Henning said to Jack Simington as they huddled around the monitors in the control room at Wilpena Pound.

"Bloody hell," said Simington. "I thought we had flushed all the rats out of here after we brought down that Nazi Larchmont."

Simington, forty-eight, with graying hair that covered his ears and curled up over his collar had been recruited by Sam Filmore from his job as a weather observer in Darwin. His lack of formal training was offset by his skill at reading electronic signals and his expertise in computer security. His years in the Outback had given him a healthy skepticism for authority figures and strangers.

"Apparently not," said Henning. "But you would know better than anyone. I was gone for almost three years setting up the Titan Base and working there until the Forsaken scandal broke."

"I know," said Simington. "That's what bothers me. If we have an internal leak, it's someone I thought was trustworthy. And I had a hand at building our firewalls to protect us from outside intrusions. Any way you look at it, it's a big mistake on my part, and now Jarrod is in trouble."

"Janet and Sam are working on that. I'm sure everything will be okay. We've got to find out how the information was leaked, and who accessed our systems and how."

"I'd bet all the tucker in my bag that that snake Stalingwirth was involved," Simington said. "Now that he's out of the pokey, he's my number one suspect."

"If he is, he has to be working with someone," Henning responded. "He doesn't have the resources to do much on his own."

"Nor the smarts," Simington said. "He's as dumb as a galah."

"We should know in a few days who paid his bail," Henning said. "They wouldn't tell us but Ron Darling from Charles Darwin University is using the open records law to find out. They have to tell us."

"Even so," said Simington, "Stalingwirth is involved, I know it. It's probably true he didn't have a direct hand in the leak, the timing isn't right, but him getting bail after we have this new signal is just too much of a coincidence."

"Agreed. But our first task is to make sure we're secure and determine exactly what kind of a security breach we had. Any progress there?"

"Yeah, some, on the security side. Since we discovered the leak, there are only three people who have had access to the control room. You, me and

Larry Johnson. Larry is solid, I'm sure. We've been working side by side for years and I trust him more than anyone else I work with."

"Including me?" Henning asked.

"Laura, don't offend me. I wasn't including you, Sam or Janet. We were the core of the team that took down Larchmont."

"No offense intended, Jack. What have we learned about the leak?"

"Not so much progress there, I'm afraid. In fact, it's worse than we first thought."

"How so?"

"Well, it looks like we had a successful breach from the outside. Someone or something got through my fancy firewall. And we also discovered there was an unauthorized access internally."

"What do you mean, internally?"

"I mean someone downloaded information off the primary computer without prior clearance."

"Can you trace who did that?"

"We know the time and the computer. But without finding fingerprints or some other evidence, such as the storage device in someone's hands or in their locker, we don't have a clue who made the download.

"I've got our new security chief looking for fingerprints and we've begun searching lockers and desks for the storage device."

"Okay," said Henning. "Do we know exactly what was taken?"

"Yes, and no," said Simington. "On the download, we know exactly what files were taken. It's all the data on the incoming signals, but none of the diagnostics, including our analysis of where the signal came from. It would take someone with lots of talent to make much use of those files."

"And the intrusion?"

"Not so good, I'm afraid. When they got in they had free access to everything on the main frame and could have taken everything. The signals, the diagnostics, the structure and content of our immediate response, the communications with Jarrod. Everything."

"Damn," said Henning.

"Yeah," said Simington. "Our operation is an open book. Or was. We've stopped that with the restricted access on the inside. To protect us from the outside, we just unplugged us from the world. We cut all of our links with the Internet, the United Space Command and the United Nations. There are no physical links between us and the outside world."

"Good," responded Henning. "That's an extreme measure, but I think it's the right thing to do."

"And it won't last too long. As soon as we have Janet and Sam review our work and new security measures, we'll get reconnected."

"I agree. So have we had any fallout from the security breach? Has the story leaked out? Have we had any calls from anyone?"

"No inquiries," Simington said. "The only effect I can detect is the trouble Jarrod is in. Someone must have used the existence of the new signal as a reason to go after Jarrod."

"Yeah," said Henning. "To me, that means whoever

stole the information is using it for their own purposes. They don't care if the public knows or not."

"Who could benefit from the information?" wondered Simington.

"Could be a lot of people," Henning said. "Could be someone who wants to stop us from responding to the signal. The more they know about it, the easier it will be to stop any response. Could be someone who wants to control what we say in our response. Perhaps they think they can interrupt our signal and insert their own response."

"I think we can prevent that," Simington said. "We can install totally new encryption protocols that would be too hard break in the short time it's going to be before we send a signal. I'm more worried about someone trying to send their own response, trying to take over as the contact point for those sending the signal to us."

"Can't we develop a digital signature that would identify us to the source of the signal?" Henning asked.

"Sure. But we need to do it right away, before whoever hacked our system has a chance to respond."

"I agree. We can't wait for Janet, Sam, or even Jarrod to get here," Henning said. "Can you do something simple that will identify us as the primary contact, but not add any confusion to our initial reply?"

"Can do," said Simington. "We still have no response to our original reply that Jarrod formulated."

"Anything new on the signal?" Henning asked.

"No. We are still getting the signal at regular

intervals. It's the same each time. There is no indication they have received our initial reply. I don't think they know that we have received their signal."

"That's almost a laugh," Henning said. "With the security leak in our system, it's possible everyone on Earth will know we got the signal before the source of the signal knows we got it and responded."

"That's hard to say," Simington replied. "Depends where the source is. Radio waves can only travel as fast as the speed of light so there will be considerable lag time between sending and receiving. We won't know until we get a response from the source."

"I know," said Henning. "Are we agreed, though, that we need to send a digital signature?"

"Yeah," said Simington. "I'll get right on that."

"Okay. I'm going to put together a briefing on our leak, any possible suspects, the danger it might present, and what we've done to secure things. I'll need the help of Larry Johnson. Are you sure about his integrity? I have to trust him."

"If you trust me, Laura, you should trust Larry. Like I said, Larry is a rock. I've known him for years. I trust him a hundred percent."

"Can you ask Larry to join me in my office? We need to have a plan when Janet and Sam get back."

"And Jarrod."

"Yes, and Jarrod."

"Jack," Henning said, "before you go, let's review our report on the signal. I want to make sure we're ready so we can give Jarrod a full report when he gets here."

"Sure," said Simington. "Let's see. We received the first signal two days ago. That was exactly 264 days after the energy wave blasted Jarrod on the Sentinel Listing Post at Titan in January of this year. From what we translated from the data in the signal, we suspect it was in response to that event. Using that, we can figure how far the signal traveled."

"Yes," said Brighton. "Using the speed of light as a guide and figuring the signal was probably sent a day or two after the Titan event, and assuming they, whoever they are, received or observed the flash from the energy wave, we think our new signal traveled about 2.1 trillion miles to get to Earth."

"And that raises some questions," said Simington. "We know the nearest star system to us is the Alpha Centauri system, but that's 26 trillion miles away. And Pluto, the farthest planet, or dwarf planet, from the sun is about an average of 3.8 billion miles away from the Earth. And, the definable solar system is even bigger than that.

"As the Voyager missions found in 2012, the point at which the Solar System ends and interstellar space begins is about 10 billion miles away. That means, if all our assumptions are correct, the signal came from well outside our solar system but not even one-tenth of the distance from here to the Alpha Centauri system.

"In addition to that," Simington continued, "the direction it arrived from does not line up with what we would expect if the signal was from the Centauri system."

"So what we have," said Henning, "is a signal that

has come from the general direction of the Alpha Centauri system but seems to have originated from the middle of nowhere. From what seems to be empty space."

"I'm afraid so," said Simington.

"As least we think we know what the signal says," said Henning.

"Yeah. But even that raises questions, and some of them hint at some danger."

"Yes," replied Henning. "Just the fact they were asking specifically for Jarrod worries me. That means they were monitoring our communications closely enough to know his name."

"And that means they must know the names of all the major players. Most definitely you, and probably Sam, Janet, and maybe me. What do they want with Jarrod, and perhaps the rest of us?"

"I agree that's a worry," said Henning. "But what worries me more is why they said they sent the signal. Their specific words were, if we interpreted it correctly . . . ah . . . let's see here."

Henning flicked through a couple pages of the report and used her finger to trace a quote on the screen of her tablet. "Here's the part I worry about."

You are not alone. Your place is noted.

Your time is now. Take care in your actions.

Dangers can arise.

"What the bloody hell does that mean?" Simington responded. "Are they going to come here to mount an attack? Are they already here?"

"We don't know. That same message just keeps

coming over and over, along with the coordinates for a reply. Those coordinates match the same area that our analysis of the signal origination provided, not really a direct line to Alpha Centauri system. And what is meant by 'Dangers can arise'?"

"It could be that they don't want us leaving our solar system," Simington said. "Our history isn't too impressive with our continuous wars, violence and destruction."

"Maybe," said Henning. "But they could just be saying stellar travel is dangerous. We've never been outside the solar system. We haven't figured out how to get anywhere significant, how to beat the space/time barrier."

"All questions that need to be thoroughly analyzed and discussed before we send a formal reply," said Simington. "That's why I hope Jarrod shows up soon. We need everyone involved in this."

"Yes we do," said Henning. "What else is in the report?"

"Not much except the timing of the signal. It's coming regularly every hour. Same message. No change."

"Okay. You send the new digital signature. I'll put the final touches on this report. I'll also call Janet in Adelaide to see if they've found Jarrod."

As the cool change swept in from the north to freshen the air in Adelaide, the leaves on a suburban street were agitated by more than the change in weather. Besides the swirl pattern caused by the wind gusts, the leaves were being pushed apart like a mini wake being created by some unknown force.

The wake moved down the residential street and slowed at a home to turn in at a driveway. The garage door suddenly opened. A moment later, dust was blown aside as the silent wake moved inside the garage and the door closed.

Chapter 5

Jarrod McKinley was sitting in the lobby of the Comfort Hotel when Janet Brighton and Sam Filmore arrived from the Adelaide airport.

"Jarrod!" exclaimed Brighton when she saw him. "Are you okay? How did you get here? Where have you been?"

"Who snatched you?" asked Filmore, before Jarrod could say a word.

"Wait. Wait," said McKinley, holding up one hand. "I'm fine and I'll explain everything later. Now we've got to get my bags, especially my carry-on. It has my e-tab, and that's got some critical data on it."

"We're good there," said Filmore. "Airport security is holding your things at the airport. They found your carry-on in the maintenance closet that those thugs pushed you into."

"You saw that?" asked McKinley.

"Yeah," replied Brighton. "The security chief at the airport showed us the video. We saw everything up to just before the van crashed through the gate. What happened after that?"

"I'll tell you later," said McKinley. "Right now

we've got to get back to the airport and get my stuff. I don't trust anyone."

"I can't believe your abductors didn't take your carry-on," Filmore said.

"I'm not surprised," replied McKinley. "Those guys weren't too bright. Their orders probably said 'get the man' and that's just what they did."

"They won't be getting anyone else," said Brighton. "The state police found them in an abandoned warehouse with the van. They were unconscious and now they're in jail. Jarrod, what happened? The police are outside the hotel. I don't think they are going to let you leave until you talk to them. They found two others in the warehouse, and another car. Those men are dead."

"I'll talk to them later," said McKinley. "I also want to find out who did this. But I want to talk to you two first, and then there's the signal. That's got to be our number one priority."

"Well," said Brighton, "we're going to have to do some fancy footwork. As we came in we saw several state police cars outside and a trooper standing by the front door."

"Yeah. They know I'm here, I'm sure. The local police found me in the park across the river. I'm sure they reported it while they were bringing me here."

"What do you want to do?" asked Filmore.

McKinley paced a few steps, looked out the front door, paused, and turned back.

"They're still there," he said. "I want you two to know as much as I can remember about the incident before I talk to the police. One thing that happened was I sensed a strong aura of fear and danger as this was all going down, just like I was experiencing during the Forsaken scandal. Now, I don't trust anyone except our team; you two, Laura, Jack. It could be that someone in the police department is working for our enemies. You need to know everything I know, before we decide how much the police should know."

"There's something you need to know, too," said Brighton. "We've had a leak at Wilpena Pound. Someone else knows about the signal."

"Damn," said Jarrod as he was looking around the lobby. "That helps explain some of this. Let's go to the hotel restaurant and talk about this."

"Okay," said Filmore. "It's about noon. Do you think we'll be heading for the Pound today? Should I cancel our reservations here, or make another for you, Jarrod?"

"Cancel them," said McKinley. "As soon as we get a plan and I clear things up with the police, we need to head out."

McKinley and Brighton found a table in the restaurant while Filmore canceled the reservations. When they were all seated and had been served their drinks, they exchanged all the information about the abduction, the leak at Wilpena Pound and what they should share with the authorities.

"One of the things I don't want to share with the police is the details about how I got away from my abductors," McKinley said. "I'm not sure who the person was, but I have a strange feeling that letting too many people know will only complicate matters."

"Who do you think it was?" asked Brighton.

"I have no clue," replied McKinley. "But it was someone who knew more than he should. He knew about the signal. He seemed to know what was expected by the source of the signal, and he had this calm demeanor that made me trust him. I experienced no sense of fear when I was with him. Quite the contrary, there was a sense of order when he was around."

"But if he knows more than he should, he might be a danger," said Brighton.

"I don't think so," said McKinley. "But if we let the police know, they might try to find him. I'll just say I was out cold until they found me at the park."

"And I don't think we need to tell them about the signal," said Filmore. "We can say you were coming back to the Pound to review our PR campaign and plan for some new fundraising efforts."

"Yeah," said McKinley. "Okay. Let's try that. I'll try to keep the signal out of it, if I can. Let's go out front and talk to the police and then get my luggage at the airport. Oh, one thing more. I'm supposed to try to develop my sense of fear, or precognition, or whatever it is. My rescuer told me to work on developing it. I will be asking you some things from time to time that might make you wonder if I'm a bit paranoid, but I'll just be trying to gauge what I'm feeling."

"Okay," said Brighton. "Maybe you'll finally catch up to my paranoia."

"Not likely," Filmore joked.

When they got to the front door of the hotel, the numbers of police waiting had increased, and they were met by a man who seemed to be in command.

"Jarrod McKinley?" the man asked as he approached McKinley.

"Yes," said McKinley.

"Please come with me," the man said as he flashed a detective's badge. "We've got a lot of questions. We have two dead men and a major security breach at the airport."

"Sure, officer . . . ?"

"Detective," the police officer said. "Detective Rory Blackwell, with the South Australian police."

"I'm Jarrod McKinley, with SETI," McKinley said. "I have a lot questions for you, too. I was unconscious for most of the time during the abduction, and remember nothing. I would like to know more about who snatched me from the airport."

"We can get started as soon as we get back to our offices," said Blackwell. "This may take some time."

"Detective Blackwell," said McKinley, as he motioned him to come closer, "I'm afraid time is something I can't give you right now. We have a major event unfolding at Wilpena Pound and I must leave as soon as possible. It's a matter of national, no, international security."

"What's going on?" the detective asked.

"It's a top-secret matter," McKinley said. "I can only say that any delay in my getting back to the Pound might have consequences that none of us would want to face."

"Sir," Detective Blackwell protested, "I'm aware of SETI. Who wouldn't be after the Forsaken incident. But last I heard it was not a government agency. Therefore, there is no 'Top Secret' privilege here.

"The way our security at the airport was breached and the fact we have evidence that one person who breached that security is still at large, and that we have two people dead, raises the specter of grave danger to the public, not only at this airport but nationwide. No, Mr. McKinley, you are coming to headquarters and—"

McKinley cut him off. "How about this?" he said. "I have to go back to the airport to pick up my luggage. I'll ride with you and my friends will follow. If you are not satisfied with my answers, and me with yours, we can spend a little time at the airport security office."

"Sounds good to me," said Blackwell. "I've got my own car so it will be just you, me, and my driver."

All the while, McKinley was trying to gauge the safety of his situation. He could sense no danger in Blackwell, but there was a very faint sense of trouble, like a wisp of mist swirling gently over the asphalt driveway leading away from the hotel.

McKinley told Brighton and Filmore about the plan and then joined Det. Blackwell in his patrol car.

Once McKinley settled down in the back seat of the police cruiser, his sense of danger began to rise. It was not at the level he'd felt earlier in the airport, and not even what he had felt on the flight between Sydney and Adelaide. But it was there, if ever so slightly. He remembered what the mysterious stranger had told him. Try to develop his sense, refine his feelings. But how? He looked across the seat at Blackwell. Nothing. He looked at the driver who was sitting in front of him. Nothing, but he could only see the back of the driver's head.

As the car pulled away from the hotel, McKinley tried to imagine he was sitting in the front seat and looking at the driver. As he did, the sense of danger, though still very faint, seemed to coalesce somewhere in the front of the car. He was interrupted by Blackwell.

"So tell me everything you can remember about your abduction," he said, "starting from when you were grabbed on the concourse."

"I remember a hand over my mouth and a punch to the stomach," McKinley said. "Then in the maintenance closet they bound my hands with plastic ties, put tape over my mouth and told me to be quiet."

"Why didn't you yell out or something?" asked Blackwell.

"Before I could say anything they had threatened my friends and family, including my fiancé in Montana. By that time I could tell I was going to be dumped in a laundry cart."

"What happened then?"

"They put a cloth over my mouth and nose and I blacked out. That's the last thing I remember until I woke up in that park by the stadium."

"You don't remember anything about the van ride out of the airport?"

"No."

"What about the warehouse where they tried to make an exchange with two men in a limo?"

"What warehouse? What limo? I told you I was out cold."

"They took you to an abandoned warehouse where it looks like they were going to give you to two other gentlemen who were driving a large black sedan. All four of those men were just recovering from some kind of stun when our men arrived. The two that snatched you gave up without a fight. The other two tried to resist but were overpowered by our men."

"Who are they?" asked McKinley.

"The two who grabbed you are local petty thieves. They knew nothing except to grab you. They had help getting through airport security, but all of their instructions came to them from some unknown source. We're sure they haven't a clue where their orders came from."

"What about the other two?" McKinley asked.

"Don't know and we're not going to find out," Blackwell said.

"Why?"

"They're dead. On the ride back to headquarters they each popped some kind of drug, probably cyanide. They had no IDs. The car was stolen earlier in the day. Right now we have no leads on where they were from or who they were working for."

"Where was I?" McKinley asked.

"Gone," said Blackwell. "That's the part I was hoping you could help us with. Our men were there within a minute or two of when the guys in the limo arrived. There was no way another vehicle could have gotten out of there without being seen. How did you get away, McKinley?"

"I don't know," replied McKinley. "I told you I was out cold. The next thing I remember was being picked up in the park by the soccer oval."

All the while they were talking, McKinley was monitoring the sense of danger he was feeling. No matter how pointed or direct the questions from Blackwell, there was no change in the feeling. It was just a steady, faint feeling of danger softly waiting for something more. It puzzled him.

"Det. Blackwell, can you tell me anything more about who the men were or who hired them? I would like to know who's after me."

"Not yet," said Blackwell. "I'm sure we will be able to ID the men. Our first run of fingerprints was inconclusive but we've broadened the data base search and we are now running DNA, facial recognition, retina matches, and dental records."

"Please let me know," said McKinley. "Is there anything else? We're at the airport and I need to get my luggage and get back to Wilpena Pound."

"Just one more thing," said Blackwell. "It would really help our investigation if we knew more about why you are back in Australia. We know you broke off your vacation with your fiancé in Montana and got back here on the most direct flights. Something happened about two days ago that made you get here as quickly as possible. If we knew what was going on, it might help us develop a motive scenario."

"I appreciate your forthrightness, detective, so I'll just say this. I came back so quickly because there was an incident that could be handled only by me. My team told me that I alone could handle the situation. That's why I need, desperately, to get back to Wilpena Pound as soon as I can."

As McKinley finished his sentence he felt a flash of danger, a small spike in that undercurrent he had been feeling during the ride with Blackwell.

"Fair enough," said Blackwell. "But I need a direct line so we can keep in touch."

"I would like that," McKinley said. "I'd like updates on your investigation as well."

The two exchanged phone numbers and said goodbye. McKinley retrieved his luggage and a few minutes later was in the back seat of the Wilpena Pound car with Brighton in the front and Filmore driving as they headed out of the airport and worked their way through Adelaide toward Wilpena Pound.

"Well," said Sam Filmore, "did you learn anything?"

"Not really," said McKinley, as he filled them in about his conversation with Blackwell.

"We now know that whoever is behind this has a lot of money and is ruthless," said Brighton. "To have men willing to commit suicide to protect their boss is really scary."

"The other thing that worries me is that spike in my sense of danger that I felt right at the end," said McKinley.

"Blackwell?" asked Brighton.

"I don't think so," said McKinley. "But there was something in that car. Maybe a bug, a listening device."

"We're going have to be careful," said Filmore.

As the trio's car moved through the northern suburbs of Adelaide, McKinley started to look around from his rear-seat position.

"Jarrod?" asked Brighton from the front passenger seat, "Is everything okay?"

"I think so," McKinley said. "Probably just a residual effect from that ride with detective Blackwell."

Because of all the delays during the day, night was fast approaching. Brilliant red streaks painted the sky as the sun set. The colors of the countryside were turning gray.

They had another four hours on the road. They would get to Wilpena Pound some time after midnight.

Chapter 6

As Filmore drove toward Wilpena Pound, he and Brighton brought McKinley up to speed on what was happening at the Pound, the latest on the signal security breach, the release of Stalingwirth.

Two hours later, as they were crossing through the wheat fields of South Australia, McKinley began to squirm. Then he sat upright and began to look around.

"Jarrod?" Brighton asked.

"Trouble," said McKinley. "Be alert everybody. I don't like what I'm feeling. It's coming from ahead of us, I'm sure."

"How can you tell?" asked Filmore.

"When I look back, toward Adelaide, the feeling is not as strong as when I look forward, down the road toward Wilpena Pound," McKinley responded. "I've been practicing, like the stranger said. I can tell a difference, but very slight."

"How close?" asked Brighton.

"Don't know," said McKinley. "I'm just beginning to work on this. Give me some time. I think we're okay for a bit. The feeling is not too strong."

"What should we do?" asked Filmore. "We're all

alone out here. We don't really have any defenses. None of us have any weapons, do we?"

McKinley and Brighton both shook their heads no.

"That's something we need to change," McKinley said. "If this whole thing starts to look like our Forsaken trauma, we need to defend ourselves or hire some security beyond the usual stuff at the Pound."

"I can manage that," said Brighton. "I'll look at the security force we have now and assign our most trusted and experienced officers to a traveling detail. We don't want to lose you again. And I want to look at some personal weapons we can carry. I've been studying a new type of taser. It's wireless and has decent range. It's fairly accurate at close range."

"Okay, but we don't want any distractions as we respond to this signal," said Filmore. "I have a strong feeling this is the real thing and we all need to focus on our primary mission, not be worried about real and perceived threats."

"They're not just threats, Sam," Brighton responded caustically. "Jarrod was just abducted!"

"Whoa, calm down, Janet. I'm not disagreeing," said Filmore. "I'm just worried that in all this trauma we're losing sight of the historic nature of what might be. The opportunity we might have to finally make contact. You forget, both of you, that I've been doing this for some thirty years now. I don't want to blow it."

"Stop," said McKinley.

"We're okay, Jarrod," said Brighton. "We all have the same goal."

"No!" McKinley ordered. "Stop the car, now!"

Filmore slammed on the brakes and brought the car to a skidding stop on the side of the road.

"It's stronger, that sense of danger." McKinley said. "And it's definitely coming from up ahead, somewhere on the road or nearby. We need to make a plan before we drive right into a trap or something. Do we have a map?"

Brighton pulled one out of the glove compartment and spread it out to show the area along the Prince William Highway.

"Okay," said Brighton. "That last little town we went through was Carrieton, about twenty kilometers back. Cradock is next, maybe fifteen kilometers ahead. Next big town is Hawker, say another thirty-five kilometers."

"Well it's too late to get much help," said McKinley. "The only people working at this time of night would be the state patrol, and they're spread out over the whole district."

"Once we get to Hawker, we make the turn onto the Pound access road and will have only about 45 kilometers to go," said Filmore.

"What's in Hawker?" asked McKinley.

"There's a state police office there, but it's probably closed for the night," said Filmore. "There are some hotels and restaurants. A few of them should be open."

"The car is going to be our best protection," said McKinley. "If we can stay in the car and keep moving we'll be the safest. If we get stopped, I think we should separate. It's me they've been after. You two need to get back to Wilpena Pound. At all costs."

"Bad idea," said Brighton. "If we stick together, we'll be safer. They wouldn't hurt us all."

"Don't be too sure," said McKinley. "Remember those two guys at the airport who popped the suicide pills. These guys are hard core."

"I agree with Janet," said Filmore. "We need to stick together. Laura and Jack can handle the signal work at the Pound. We need to protect you, get you back to the center."

"Listen," said McKinley. "I appreciate your concern and your willingness to stick your necks out, but I won't have it. Remember the last time? Remember Charlie Snelling and Brad Johnson? They died on my watch. And Liza was nearly killed. I don't want any more lives on my conscience."

"Don't be ridiculous," said Brighton. "None of that was your fault. Those explosions couldn't be predicted. You had no way of knowing."

"Just the same," said McKinley. "It's not going to happen again. We'll stay together and in the car as long as we can. But when I think our lives are truly in danger we're going to split up. You guys stay in the car and get back to the Pound. I'll find a way to get back to you."

"Jarrod—" Brighton started to protest.

McKinley cut her off with a brisk, "Let's go, but slowly. I need to focus on that sense of danger. It's getting stronger."

A few minutes later their car passed through

the small hamlet of Cradock. A solitary streetlight provided scant illumination and the few houses along the side of the road were dark.

McKinley scanned the area and frequently stared forward holding his gaze on the darkness pierced by the headlights of the car. After a minute or two he relaxed and said, "It's okay, keep going."

Before long they were climbing up a significant ridge between Cradock and the Hawker-Stirling Road. As they reached the top of the ridge and saw the lights of Hawker in the distance they breathed a sigh of relief.

"Slow down!" said McKinley.

"What?" said Filmore as he looked up the road to the left and right.

"It's getting closer. The danger," said McKinley.

"Where?" said Brighton.

"I don't know," said McKinley. "Let's stop at this overlook."

Filmore pulled the car off the road to a scenic turnout that, in the daylight, would have given them their first good look at the Flinders Ranges, that jumble of overthrusts and valleys that held some of South Australia's most abundant wildlife and scenic places.

Across the valley they could see the lights of Hawker on the horizon.

"There!" said McKinley. "Look there, about half way to Hawker. There are car lights along the highway. Most of them seem to be moving, but, over there, see those? They're off the road and not moving."

"What are we going to do?" asked Brighton.

"Let's keep going at the normal speed," said McKinley. "When we get to that spot we have to be ready to make a run for Hawker. We might be safe there."

They drove off the ridge and turned right on to the Hawker-Stirling road. Soon they were driving parallel to a tall ridge on their left. As they came over a slight rise in the road they could see lights of a vehicle off the road some distance to the right.

As they passed, the vehicle raced to the highway and turned in their direction to follow them.

"Okay, Sam. Let's make a run for Hawker!" said McKinley.

Filmore stomped on the accelerator and soon they were hitting 120 kilometers per hour but the vehicle behind them was gaining. Spotlights on top of the vehicle behind suddenly blasted through the night and into their car.

"Faster, Sam. Faster," said Brighton.

"That's it," said Filmore. "I'm flat out!"

The vehicle behind was gaining fast and in a flash it was right on their rear bumper. Just as they were bracing for the worst, a horn sounded and a large four-wheel drive pickup truck zoomed past them. In the back of the pickup, hanging on to the spotlight bar with one hand and waving rifles in the other, were two young men shouting and laughing at them.

"Damn," said McKinley. "What the hell was that?"

"Just some young blokes hunting roos, I guess," said Filmore as he let up on the accelerator and slowed to a normal speed.

"It's not over!" shouted McKinley. "Watch out!"

Just ahead of them the pickup truck suddenly launched into the air and in what seemed like slow motion turned over in midair, bodies falling out the back, before it hit the ground and exploded in a fireball.

As they skidded to a stop, McKinley spotted a blockade in the road and shadowy figures lurking in the ditch. Just on the edge of the darkness he saw another vehicle, a large black SUV, no license plates, with a driver leaning over to start the engine.

At that moment another black SUV screeched to a stop behind their car and two men with automatic weapons jumped out and stood on each side, blocking the road.

"I'm going to make a run around the left!" yelled Filmore. "I think I can make it around the blockade."

"Go for it," said McKinley.

Filmore slammed the car in reverse and then in drive and with a screech of tires pointed the car off the road and around the left side of the blockade. The men on the road fired their guns at them and bullets shattered the rear window.

In a second they were off the pavement, around the blockade and back on the highway, past the carnage of the young men's crumpled bodies and their vehicle burning in the middle of the road. The two black SUVs were just getting back on the road after picking up men who had been in the ditches.

"Sam," said McKinley. "See that dry wash up ahead? When you get there you're going to slow just enough so I can jump. Then you gun it to Hawker and get help, or get back to the Pound."

"Jarrod," Brighton protested. But McKinley was having none of it.

"Kill the lights, Sam. Now," McKinley commanded.

Filmore flicked off the lights and slowed at the same time, and they were covered in darkness when McKinley threw open the back door of the car and jumped toward the dry wash.

He hit hard and rolled down the bank. He lay still, flattening his stomach to the ground to get as low as he could.

Now the lights flashed back on as the Wilpena Pound car raced toward Hawker. The two SUVs flew by McKinley and were gaining on Filmore and Brighton.

McKinley sat up and brushed the dirt and weeds off his clothes. The sense of danger was receding fast, but then he heard another sound. It was very slight and McKinley strained to hear. The quiet slap of a helicopter's rotor blades was coming fast from the direction of Adelaide, and he sensed a small tinge of danger.

He threw his body down again in the ditch as the helicopter circled and landed at the still burning wreckage of the young men's four-wheel drive.

He couldn't spot any markings on the helicopter though he did see two people, a man and a woman, exit the aircraft and inspect the scene. After a few gestures, they climbed back in and the helicopter lifted off and headed right toward him.

As the copter flew low over McKinley he searched again for some kind of markings, anything to identify the aircraft. He could see none.

After a few minutes of quiet, McKinley reached for his cell phone. It wasn't in his pocket. He was sure he had it when he was in the back seat of the car, but he didn't know if it was in his hand or his pocket when he jumped.

He did a quick search of his surroundings and, finding nothing, he began to walk. He wasn't sure how far he was from Hawker, or what he would do when he got there. But, with nothing but darkness around him and no way to contact anyone, he couldn't come up with a better plan. The darkness closed in on him as he moved away from the still smoldering scene on the highway.

A flash of lights in the distance grabbed his attention. They were coming from Hawker. He moved off the highway and hid behind a cluster of bushes. As the lights got closer, he could see the colored, flashing lights of an emergency vehicle. The fire-rescue vehicle sped by, apparently on its way to the accident scene. McKinley started walking again.

He had been walking for about thirty minutes when the fire-rescue vehicle approached from the direction of the accident. Instinctively, he dashed off the highway and crouched down. He could sense no fear or danger, but he didn't want to take any chances. The vehicle sped by and McKinley began to walk again. Another thirty minutes later, just as he thought he was seeing the faint glow of the lights over Hawker, he stopped.

"Damn. There it is again. Danger!"

He looked for a place to hide. This desolate spot afforded not one ditch. No bushes. He scrambled away from the road, glancing back, expecting to see approaching lights. The sound of a helicopter coming his way assaulted him. Now he could see it, following the highway with a searchlight scanning the both sides of the road.

Gasping for air, McKinley ran farther into the black night, away from the road. Then he saw it; a depression, perhaps a dry wash, or an irrigation ditch. Without looking he jumped over the bank and cursed as he started to fall.

Chapter 7

"Great view isn't it?" said the figure in the tall-backed chair, facing away, looking out the window.

Gregory Stalingwirth shifted about on his feet as he stood looking out from the sixty-fifth floor of the office building. Spread out before him was Sydney's classic view of blue sky, fluffy white clouds, the opera house, the bay bridge, the sparkling blue bay with sailboats, ferries and small watercraft buzzing about. Further out in the bay the huge cargo freighters were easing into industrial ports.

"It's beautiful," said Stalingwirth. "Much better than that cell I was in two days ago."

"Yes, I expect so," said the man with a quiet chortle as he swiveled his chair around to face Stalingwirth. "And I expect you to appreciate the effort it took to get you here."

Stalingwirth was surprised. He didn't expect the head of the Australian division of Galactic Mining Enterprises to be so young. He looked like a young twenty-something. An unblemished, smooth-shaved face with no wrinkles looked up at Stalingwirth. The twinkle in his bright blue eyes cast a cheery glow to his broad smile and his ruffled blonde hair had a friendly casual style. I'd be amazed if he's even thirty, Stalingwirth thought.

"I do appreciate it," Stalingwirth said. "I'm not sure how you got the charges dropped, but I am grateful."

"Mr. Stalingwirth. Excuse me for not introducing myself. Jason Ridgeway at your service," he said, still with a broad smile. "Please sit down."

Stalingwirth eased into the large leather chair and sank down to where he was now below the eye level of Ridgeway.

"Getting you out of jail was not easy," said Ridgeway. "We've been working on it since before your old boss, Larchmont, was convicted. It took a while to find the right judge at the right price."

"But I was innocent," said Stalingwirth. "Larchmont called all the shots, including the sabotage of the listening station and Learjet and the attacks on McKinley. I didn't even know about some of the stuff he was setting in motion."

Ridgeway leaned forward and straightened. His cheery disposition suddenly froze to something much more serious, even sinister. He seemed to age a dozen years in an instant.

"Don't feed me that innocent line, Stalingwirth," Ridgeway growled. "You were Larchmont's right-hand man for years and had to know exactly what was going on. At least you better. That's why you're here.

"When we got word of the new signal, we knew we had to get on top of the situation and you are part of that plan."

"New signal?" asked Stalingwirth.

"Yes," said Ridgeway. "Part of our efforts over the last eight months was infiltrating Wilpena Pound. Our source there sent word three days ago that a new signal had been received.

"I don't have to tell you what that could mean to our company. Whether the signal is real or not, we can't wait to find out. If it is real, and if there's going to be contact with an alien intelligence, who knows what kind of technology we would have access to.

"Even though we are using the latest, most powerful rocket engines known to man, we are still up against the barriers of space and time. It's no easy feat getting resources back from Titan, Mars, or the Asteroid Belt.

"And much of our mining technology is still from the twentieth century. Other companies are catching up. We need new science to compete, no, to dominate galactic resource harvesting."

"What do you want from me?" asked Stalingwirth.

"We want your knowledge of SETI," said Ridgeway. "You know the people there. You know the operation. We need to keep on top of the situation. No, we need to keep one step ahead.

"We have the signal. We have experts who we think can interpret the signal and we have the technology to respond to the signal. What we don't have is Jarrod McKinley."

"Jarrod McKinley?" responded Stalingwirth. "He knows little to nothing about signals or the SETI operation. He's just an overrated, low-level technician who got in over his head and lucked out in his battle with Larchmont."

"Apparently not everyone agrees with your assessment," Ridgeway smirked.

"What does that mean?"

"The senders of the signal asked for McKinley by name," Ridgeway said. "We don't know why, and our attempts to control that factor have not proven successful."

"I'm not sure what I can do to help," Stalingwirth said. "I only met McKinley a couple of times and not in the best circumstances. I don't think he liked it when I locked him in that cell at Wilpena Pound."

"We know you are not the best of friends," said Ridgeway. "But, we can turn that to our advantage."

"How?"

"We've already taken the first step by springing you from jail. That's going to raise a lot of suspicion at Wilpena Pound, especially from McKinley. He will want to find out what you are up to."

"So?"

"We think he will take a few risks just to make sure you are not up to some of your old mischief."

"You mean you want to use me as bait?"

"Now, Mr. Stalingwirth. Don't be offended. What we have in mind is not that simple."

"I'm not sure I want to be involved," said Stalingwirth. "I had enough headaches and trauma in the Forsaken incident."

"Mr. Stalingwirth," Ridgeway said as he scowled and leaned forward. "I can put you back in jail a lot faster than I got you out."

Stalingwirth dropped his head and said with a loud sigh, "Okay."

"Good," said Ridgeway. "Now here's what corporate headquarters in New York has planned for Mr. McKinley."

Stalingwirth sat silent as Ridgeway laid out the plan. The more he heard, the more he began to tremble. The people behind this plan were deadly serious. They made Larchmont look like a child in a playground. His last thoughts, as Ridgeway concluded laying out the plan, were about how many people were going to die. Most likely McKinley and others at Wilpena Pound. He wondered if he would survive.

"So much for our big secret," said Laura Henning to Jack Simington as she brushed her shoulder-length brown hair back and sipped on a cold cup of coffee while looking at the printout of a text message.

"What do you mean?" said Simington. "Our system has been isolated for the last twenty-four hours. Nothing's leaking out of Wilpena Pound."

"No. It's not that," said Henning. "We received inquiries from both the United Space Command and the China/Asia Space Consortium. They've detected the signal and want to know what's going on. I suspected the word would get out, the way the signal keeps repeating. It's not just the governments that are interested. There are thousands of independents and amateurs out there looking for signals, especially after all the fuss about the Forsaken incident and our PR campaign the last few months."

"What do they know?" asked Simington.

"I don't know," said Henning. "They don't say, just that they've detected something. I doubt they're even trying to interpret the signal. Most agencies are leaving that up to us."

"What about the Europeans?" said Simington. "Heard they've been trying to set up an analytical division since Forsaken."

"Haven't heard from them. As far as I know, nobody but us has the equipment and expertise to decode the signal."

"Wonder how long it's going to be before we're contacted by some of the world governments?" said Simington.

"Soon, I expect," said Henning. "Especially the Australians. They've been paying close attention to us since we raced around the country trying to nab Larchmont. I also expect to hear from C.R. Duncan soon, that reporter from *The Age*."

"Speaking of hearing from someone," said Simington. "Any word from Sam and his merry band of travelers?"

"Nothing," said Henning. "We last heard from them when they left Adelaide about six hours ago. They should be here by now."

"Anything could have happened," said Simington. "Maybe they got tired and stopped to sleep. Or maybe they had car trouble."

"I doubt that," said Henning. "There are three of

them. They would take turns driving if one got tired. And, it's not that long of a drive. If they had car trouble, they would have called. I worry it's something more, with what happened to Jarrod at the airport."

"Let's not borrow trouble," said Simington. "They'll be okay. They're probably pulling up to the gates right now."

Henning's mobile phone began to ring. She looked at it and sighed with relief. "It's Janet," she said as she answered the call.

"Oh, no!" said Henning. "What happened?" She was shaking her head no at Simington and grimacing. "Okay. Will do. See you soon."

"What?" said Simington when Henning clicked off.

"Jarrod is missing again." Henning told Simington of the events on the road near Hawker.

"Janet said she and Filmore just made it to Hawker and pulled up in front of a state police office before the black SUVs caught them. When they stopped, the SUVs drove past slowly, shining a spotlight on them. Then the black SUV drove back they way it came, toward where the roadblock was. She believes they were looking for Jarrod."

"What is it with that guy?" Simington said. "He seems like a trouble magnet."

"Well, when you are named specifically in a message that may have come from outer space, that will probably draw some attention."

"What about Jarrod?"

"Janet said that after reporting the incident, they,

and the police, went back to the scene but could find no trace of him.

"They contacted the state police in Adelaide and the local division is launching a search, but no luck so far. Janet wants us to get ready to send a response to our signal senders. Something along the lines of: *Jarrod is delayed and will be here soon. He is very eager to begin communications.* She doesn't want to tell them he is missing."

"So, we begin this interstellar contact with deception?" asked Simington in a caustic tone of voice.

"I don't think that's the idea," said Henning. "I just think Janet wants to reassure those sending the signal that we're being cooperative and not scheming."

"What I wonder," said Simington, "Is how long we are going to control the message? How long before some government demands that we turn over contact to them?"

"We can't worry about that right now. We just have to get ready to send the message."

"That might not be as easy as we once thought," said Simington. "Something has changed."

"What?"

"The signal is changing. It's coming in around every twenty minutes now, instead of every thirty minutes. And the source location seems to be changing."

"How can that be?" Henning asked.

"We're not sure, but we noticed that, starting early yesterday morning, each time we received a signal it came a little earlier than the last one. Over the last fourteen hours, the time between signals has shortened by almost ten minutes."

"What does that mean?"

"We're guessing that the source of the signal is coming toward Earth. And the change in the location is consistent with what we imagine might be a flight path toward Earth. All of the signals are along a line consistent with the signal's original source point, but just slightly off center, like the curving arch of an extended, very long-range flight path."

"So you think that whoever or whatever is sending the signals is planning a trip to Earth?"

"No. I'm not ready to say that. But I think we need to fully analyze these anomalies before we send our first response. And we need to be sure we keep this to ourselves. I can just see the 'Outer Space Invasion' headlines now."

"Yeah, right," said Henning. "We have to be as straight forward and as honest as we can. We don't know what is happening."

"What we really need is Jarrod," said Simington. "It's not that I think he's got all the answers. I just want to be able to comply with the request that's coming from our senders."

"Jack. What do you think we should call these senders?" asked Henning. "I'm tired of calling them 'senders.'"

"I think that's a bit premature," said Simington. "First, we still haven't proven it's from an intelligent source, although I'd be willing to bet the farm on it. And if it is, why don't we wait until we know who they are and what they call themselves?"

"There's nothing revealing in the signal," said Henning. "When will they identify themselves?"

"If you were dealing with us, I mean the human species on Earth, would you tell all your secrets before you knew if we were going to become violently destructive? We have a history of that, you know."

"Yeah, I know," said Henning. "But the last fifty years have been peaceful. There have been nothing but very isolated local conflicts."

"It may seem that way to us," said Simington. "But, who knows how they look at it. If, in fact, they know anything about us. I just know that if I was trying to reach another civilization on a planet far, far away, I'd be very careful."

"I suppose," said Henning. "I'd just like to get a little more personal with our senders."

"I'm hoping that's where Jarrod fits in," said Simington. "Why else would they ask for him?"

"I hope he's okay," said Henning. "I wouldn't want to be alone at night in the outback with some dangerous characters looking for me."

Chapter 8

Two tall, slim figures watching on a wall-sized screen saw Jarrod McKinley leap over the bank of an irrigation canal in the outback near Hawker.

"There he goes again," said the female. "Literally leaping before looking. I sometimes wonder if he is the right one."

"We believe he is, Athrena," said the male standing next to her. "And look at how far he has come in just the last few hours. All we had to tell him was to try to exercise his danger sensors. He has already expanded his range and is able to directionalize it."

"But, Conteus, do not you agree he was virtually a random choice. If it had not been for that failed plot by his former employer, he may not have come to our attention. I admit he has shown some intuitive abilities, but I fear his success is due more to accident than through skill or intellect."

"But, he has good blood lines," said Conteus. "His mother comes from good stock. She had very high intellect and exceptional intuitive abilities."

"Just the same, we are going to have to go slow. He has not faced his most serious test. There are far more dangerous matters to deal with than a few angry humans." Athrena pushed her short silver hair back. The motion highlighted her slightly oval face, accented by wide set crystal blue eyes and a long aquiline nose.

"I agree," said Conteus. "We will continue to monitor him carefully and report fully to the council and the Project Forgiven Team."

Conteus was almost as tall as the six-foot-four Athrena. His wide shoulders and slim waist were highlighted by the skin-tight two piece outfit he wore. The gray pants were offset by a light blue shirt that carried a military looking patch on the shoulder.

Athrena was dressed similarly except her pants had full-length crimson red strips on the side and a small coat of arms and imperial seal on the left side of her chest area indicated a rank above that of Conteus.

"Good. You know this project has some detractors. What about our agent in the area?"

"He has been instructed to intervene only in life or death situations and to give nothing away. He may occasionally communicate surreptitiously, to try to guide McKinley or to enhance his natural abilities."

As they watched, McKinley was clinging to the bank of the irrigation ditch he had jumped into. It was clear he was not panicking, but focusing in the direction of the road as he was inching along the embankment. He was being careful not to reveal his position while moving steadily away from the source of the danger.

"See how he moves," said Conteus. "You can tell

he is learning how to integrate his intuitive abilities while using his motor skills to alter his circumstance."

"Very well. Point taken," said Athrena. "We will give him some time. What is next?"

As Conteus began to brief Athrena on Forgiven, they moved away from the screen and sat in chairs facing a large window.

Outside, the change between the setting of Progenia and the rising of Alphine was casting a warming light on the verdant green hills and fern forests that bordered the lapping seashore. As the waves broke gently on the rocks, a seafoam green spray glistened, reflecting the darker green of the water.

"I love Alphine's rising. It casts such a gentle purple glow," said Athrena. "I find Acquaria's rising just a little too harsh; especially in season five, as we are in now."

"I am partial to Progenia rising," said Conteus. I prefer it when the light is more subdued, but still strong enough to see and to provide energy. That is more comforting to me. I do not know what I would do with total darkness, like they have on Earth."

"Yes," said Athrena. "Similar to what McKinley is dealing with right now."

Jarrod McKinley knew exactly where he was, and he didn't like it one bit. He was cold and wet, without a mobile phone, and a dozen kilometers from the nearest town—Hawker.

He had watched the black SUVs drive back down the highway and locate the spot where he'd jumped out of Filmore's moving car. He'd been traveling away from the road when he began to sense their arrival and by running and jumping into the irrigation ditch, had avoided detection.

After a few minutes of searching and using spotlights to pierce the darkness, the SUVs moved off in the direction of Adelaide. Just as he was about to relax, he heard more vehicles approaching and flattened himself against the side of the irrigation ditch. He sighed with relief as he watched Filmore and Brighton arrive with the police. He was about to climb out of the ditch when he heard, just overhead, the sound of a helicopter. Not exactly that of a helicopter. More a sound like a faint rotor wash, muffled, but close by. He could see the red dot of a laser scope flicking around the area. Someone was gunning for him. He lowered himself back into the water. If they were using heat sensing radar, that would mask his image.

By the time the hovering aircraft finished scanning the area, Brighton and Filmore and the police had driven back toward Hawker.

McKinley fumed. Great! I guess I'm getting my exercise tonight!

He waited, projecting his danger sensors outward and upward. He felt the danger above him moving away rapidly. He waited another ten minutes just to be sure, using the time to pour the water out of his shoes and wring out his socks.

The November night was warm and cloudless.

There was no moon and, even now when he was fully adjusted to the dark, he could see only a few meters in any direction. A faint glow illuminated the horizon in the direction of Hawker, but he would not go back to the road and risk the possibility of detection. He knew the road paralleled the ridge to the west and, about ten kilometers to the north, turned west through a gap in the ridge and into Hawker.

Having traveled the road several times, he was familiar with its route, but not that of the country it traversed. He would walk parallel to the road but keep at least five hundred meters away.

Moving slowly to pick his way through the darkness, he began to have the feeling he was being watched. He felt uneasy. Not exactly the kind of danger he sensed before, but something was lurking in the darkness.

He occasionally heard something scurrying away from him as he walked, probably rabbits, mice or lizards, he thought. No worries.

But he was being followed. He was sure of it. He could hear nothing, but he knew they were there. When he stopped, the followers stopped. He whirled around but could see nothing.

He walked faster, stumbling over rocks and the occasional bush. When he quickened his pace, those behind came faster too. When he stopped, they stopped.

He tried to focus his sense of danger. It was confusing. He was able to judge the direction and approximate distance, but the sense of danger was not as elevated as it had been throughout the day. Yet it was persistent.

As he was peering into the darkness behind him, a sudden noise made him whirl around. He raised his arm just in time to ward off a glancing blow. A large Australian grey slammed into him and bounded away into the night.

He was knocked to the ground and stunned. As he lay shaking his head to clear the cobwebs, his followers began to rush. He pushed himself to his feet just as two dingoes reached him.

He stood, shook his hands and shouted. The dingoes slid to a stop just inches away, then backed off slightly, snarling and barring teeth, the hair on their backs raised.

McKinley looked around desperately for something with which to defend himself. In the dark he could make out only a few scattered bushes, rocks and weeds. He moved away, shouting and shaking his hands. The dingoes could sense he was helpless and approached. He saw them clearly now. They appeared very healthy, strong and confident.

McKinley pushed harder, trying to move faster while keeping the dingoes at bay. He tripped and fell.

He felt the rip to his pant leg as he went down. His adrenalin was pumping as hit the ground. The dingoes were moving in for the attack. His hand fell on something hard and round. Still on his back, he grabbed a large rock and swung it hard toward the head of a rushing dingo. He missed and swore loudly. Then he saw next to him a steel post, part of the fence he had just tripped over. Now he had a weapon. He leapt to his feet and swung the post just as the second dingo jumped at him.

He felt the post smash into flesh and bone and heard the yelp of the dingo. He whirled again and raised the post as a spear. The first dingo stopped in mid-charge and backed off. He shook the post and yelled, watching the dingoes slink away.

When he felt safe again, McKinley tried to get his bearings. He searched for the glow of the lights of Hawker in the distance, but couldn't see them. He looked in vain for the outline of the ridge to the west.

"Damn," McKinley said out loud. He realized that while fending off the dingoes he had stumbled down a slight embankment into a depression. He couldn't see the horizons or judge the depth or width of the depression.

He focused on using his danger sensor, trying with his mind to peer through the darkness. There was nothing. Even the sense of concern he had over the dingoes was gone.

He felt safe though he had no idea which way to go. Walking slowly in a direction away from the fence he had tripped over, he felt the land sloping up slightly. Soon he spotted the horizon in the distance, discovering that he was walking away from the glow of the Hawker lights.

Correcting course, he set off again, thankful that the sky was not the inky black it had been. Sunrise was at least an hour away, he guessed, but already the landscape around him was becoming more visible, even cloaked in gray as it was.

"Ah, my friend the sun," he said, picking up his pace.

As he trekked, he thought about the dingoes, reflecting on the sense of danger he'd felt when he had first detected them. It was different than the others he had become used to. Perhaps it was because of their species. Was his sense of danger different for humans than it was for other species? He vowed to try some experiments. What was this sense of his? Was he reading some type of aura emanating from beings? Could he read the auras of inanimate objects?

Where did all of this come from? Why did he seem to have it when others around him did not? Why was he sensing the presence of species only when they were a danger? Could his senses be enhanced to detect other presences?

He needed someone to practice on. Someone who would understand what he was going through. He needed Liza. The Liza he was thinking about each day. The woman he was going to marry. He must get Liza back with him. He would send for her and get her off his father's farm in Montana as soon as he got back to Wilpena Pound.

Danger! There it was again! And it had a human signature! He scanned the countryside around him, now able to see things quite clearly. The sun was nearly over the horizon to the east.

He recognized the sound about the same time as he saw the craft. It was the same machine that had hovered over him earlier in the night. It was moving over the Hawker highway right of way, swinging in wide arcs to cover everything within a kilometer of the road. It was a few miles south of him but would be directly overhead in a minute or two.

He searched for place to hide, finding nothing but flat, rocky ground with a few bushes. He picked the largest bush and crouched as close to it as he could. No good. He lay down and squirmed under the bush as far as he could.

As the aircraft sped over him about one hundred meters off the ground, he saw it was not like most of the helicopters operating in the area. It had twin rotors housed in a wing-type cowling protruding from the top of the fuselage. The main body was shaped like a long tear drop, a stealth shape, the latest technology, McKinley thought.

Just as that thought came to mind, he remembered the heat detection he'd been concerned with a few hours before. In this cool morning, his body heat signature would stand out like a sore thumb.

Sure enough, the craft made a sharp bank and turned to come back to him. If they could read his heat signature, could they tell him from an animal?

As the craft began to come his way, it descended so it was only a few dozen meters off the ground. As it flew, animals of all kinds scattered.

"That's how they'll do it," he said out loud. "They'll flush me out!"

Hiding was not going to work. He would have to run for it. But where? There was nothing to run to and he surely could not run away from the craft. He stood up and started jogging toward where he thought Hawker would be. He wasn't sure how that would help, how he could avoid capture, but there weren't many good choices.

As the craft got closer, he could see it was smaller than he thought. It was unmanned, he realized, there was no one on board.

He was about to stop and confront the craft when a series of gunshots burst out and the dirt near him was kicked up by bullets.

He started to jog again, in the direction of Hawker. But the craft moved around to try to cut him off, releasing a burst of gunfire with bullets spraying the ground in front of him. McKinley darted to his right and the craft let him go, shadowing him.

When he tried to move to his left, toward Hawker, the craft again moved in front of him and put down a spray of bullets.

McKinley was struck with the realization that they wanted him alive, and didn't want him to get to Hawker. "Well," he said out loud. "I can play this game."

The next half hour was a lethal game of dodgeball, or dodge bullets. McKinley darted back and forth, always trying to work his way in the direction the craft did not want him to go, toward Hawker.

As he became more bold, he came closer and closer to the spray of bullets put down to herd him.

At one point, after a dodge in one direction and a dash in another, he ran right under the craft as he heard the hiss of the bullets whizzing past his head. That move angered those piloting the remote craft and this time when it circled around, it laid down a steady stream of bullets as it moved toward him.

McKinley stopped and dropped to his knees. He was exhausted. He needed to rest. Still the craft moved toward him, bullets spitting into the ground. He was showered with dirt and braced himself for the impact of the bullets.

The craft stopped just a meter in front of him. A voice emanating from the craft ordered: "Jarrod McKinley! Resistance is useless. Please move to the southwest in the direction of the oncoming vehicles."

McKinley spotted the black SUV raising a cloud of dust as it bounced over the rough outback. He saw guns protruding from the windows. He scanned his surroundings. There was nowhere to go.

He glanced up at the craft hovering in front of him as it suddenly changed shape. From a whirling, crouching black menace, it changed into an orange fireball.

McKinley threw himself down as the explosion raked over him. The force of the blast and the fireball left him senseless. He had thrown his hands over his head and they tingled from the heat. He shook his head and tried to focus. His hearing returned just as the smoke and dust cleared and he saw another craft approach in a landing glide. He rose up to his knees and watched the black SUV head away at a high speed.

He covered his eyes to shield them from the dust

raised by the long rotors of a conventional helicopter. As it landed, a state trooper jumped out and headed toward him. Janet Brighton was right behind.

"Who were those guys?" McKinley asked Brighton after they climbed into the helicopter.

"We don't know, yet," said Brighton. "The state police are looking into it. They will have investigators at this crash site in a few minutes. The highway patrol has set up roadblocks to try to stop the SUVs. Whoever did this has the deaths of those young men in the truck last night to answer for. They'll be caught."

"I wouldn't be too sure," said McKinley. "They seem to have all the latest tools. A drone copter trying to herd me across the desert? Who spends that kind of money?"

"Could be another government," said Brighton. "Now that the story of the signal has leaked, we could have all kinds trying to interfere."

"I think another government would just swoop into Wilpena Pound with its storm troopers," McKinley replied. "No. It's something else."

"Well," said Brighton, "somebody wants to have some control over what we are doing, or are about to do."

"It's a bit early for that," McKinley replied. "We haven't even confirmed the signal, much less begun to communicate with it."

"Speaking of that. We've got to get you back to Wilpena Pound. Our signal senders are getting impatient."

"How so?" asked McKinley.

Brighton explained the increased frequency and change in location of the source of the signal.

"So, they're coming," McKinley said with a worried looked on his face.

Chapter 9

"So, tell me exactly what your message to the senders said," McKinley said as he, Janet Brighton and Sam Filmore were being briefed by the Wilpena Pound team.

"We said: *Your message has been received. Jarrod McKinley on his way here and will respond. Accept no other messages as authoritative.*

"We also added our complete coordinates and the frequency we have been using, along with a digital tracking signature. We didn't want to take the chance that someone else would send a message before we did and step between us and the senders to try to hijack this whole operation. We're trying to keep control of the situation."

"I suppose you did the right thing," McKinley said. "But couldn't anyone send exactly the same message? How do the senders know it is coming from us?"

"We're hoping that the coordinates will help," said Jack Simington. "We could tell that they were aiming their signal right here, at Wilpena Pound. So, we responded from the same coordinates."

"I hope that works," said Brighton. "I hope they're friendly. Now they know exactly where to find us."

"Let's not forget," said Filmore, "that the folks who sent this are probably pretty smart. I doubt they'll be fooled by some imposter."

"Whoa, whoa," said McKinley, holding his hand in the air. "I think we're getting ahead of ourselves. We haven't even confirmed that this signal is from another intelligent species, let alone a species that has developed to the level of our intellect and can understand our communications."

"That's true," said Simington. "We have been getting the same message over and over again. There's no indication of rational thought behind what we've received so far."

"And there is still the chance this is another hoax," said Henning. "We all bought the Forsaken scam hook, line and sinker the first few weeks."

"Agreed," said McKinley. "We need to confirm the source of the signal and begin a dialogue. We need to get a conversation going."

"First part's already done," said Simington. "My team is absolutely sure of the source. We've received the repeated signal enough times now that the general location of the source is no longer in question."

"Tell me about that Jack," said McKinley. "You say the source appears to be shifting locations?"

"Yes, slightly. And the response time has been diminishing. At first we were receiving the signal every thirty minutes. Gradually, over the last two days, three now, I guess, the time has shortened and we are getting a signal every eighteen minutes and the source of the signal has shifted several times. We're still analyzing that part of it. But we think it's changed locations about twelve times. All the locations are similar, still pointing toward Alpha Centauri, just a little off line."

"And each time there is a change in location, the source is getting closer to Earth?" Brighton asked.

"Based on the time the signal took to get here, yes," said Henning.

"Let me caution everyone," said Simington. "We are making a lot of broad assumptions here. Nothing is certain."

"And the message is always the same?" asked McKinley.

"Yes."

"How long ago did you send that generic response," asked McKinley.

"About half hour ago," said Henning.

"And no response from them since that was sent?"

"Yes. One response. The same as all the rest. But that signal came to us before they would have received ours. We're assuming that because we are getting a signal every eighteen minutes, it is taking about that long for the signal to get from them to us. And ours would take eighteen minutes to get to them."

"Based on the speed of light, that means their signal is traveling more than three trillion kilometers?"

"Yes," said Simington. "And the first set of signals was traveling about 4.5 trillion kilometers."

"It's coming toward us fast," said Brighton.

"Based on our assumptions and our logic, yes," said Simington.

"We can't be sure," said McKinley. "Our assumptions, and our logic could have no meaning here. We don't know what we're dealing with. But, using those assumptions, what is the earliest we could expect a response to the generic signal you sent?"

"The next signal should be coming in . . ." Simington looked at the digital clock above the control panel, "right about now, in thirty seconds."

Everyone fixed their gazes on the clock as it clicked down to 25, 20, 15, 10, 5, and 0.

There was no signal. The small warning chime, which had been set to go off when a signal arrived, was silent.

They looked at each other mutely, no one wanting to be the first to speak. Was it over? Was that the last of the signals? Was this just another false alarm?

"See," said Simington at last. "We can't make too many assumptions here. We are flying blind, dumb as galahs, I'd say."

"Yes," said McKinley. "We can't rely on our logic here. If there is a signal, who knows what rules it is following."

"Jarrod," it was Sam Filmore this time. "I've been at this longer than any of you and I say—"

Just then the chime went off. Another signal had arrived.

"What were you going to say, Sam?" Simington chortled.

"I was going to say, give them time to read what we sent."

"How long to decode the signal?" McKinley asked.

"Based on previous experience, a couple of minutes," Henning said.

"Wait. This message is much shorter. It's coming up on the screen right now."

The screen began to flash as the message appeared.

Message
Received
Awaiting
McKinley
Will
Comm
Only
With
Authorized
Sender
Authorized by PFT

There was stunned silence in the room and some audible gasps. A technician burst in from another room.

"Jack, Jack!" the young woman called out.

"I see, Jenny. We all see!"

"Okay," said McKinley, "I'm going to take that as a positive sign. A sign of first contact. I have my response ready. Can we send it now?"

"Yes," said Henning. "I just need to type it in and the computer will translate it into the algorithms we've been using."

"Here it is. I've kept it short. I hope to get to the point but move the dialogue along."

McKinley handed Henning a short note and she began to type. The note read:

Welcome. We hope for a peaceful and thoughtful exchange of ideas. We have many questions, as I am sure you do. Our first questions: Who are you? Where are you? With all respect and curiosity, Jarrod McKinley and the SETI team.

"Well, Mr. Stalingwirth," said Jason Ridgeway. "I'm afraid our little plan will have to be implemented much sooner than I thought."

"Why? Right now?" whined Stalingwirth.

"The team sent to capture Jarrod McKinley has failed twice. I don't believe in three strikes and you're out. My players get only two strikes. That team has been terminated. It's time for Plan B. Or should I say, Plan S, for Stalingwirth," Ridgeway sneered.

"I'm not ready," said Stalingwirth. "I need more time to put everything in place. If we go now, McKinley will see right through the plan and we'll be back where we are now, with nothing."

"We don't have more time," Ridgeway said. "We've detected another set of signals from Wilpena Pound. There were two outgoing signals and one incoming that caught our attention. Those signals were different than the ones we have been monitoring for the last three days. We don't know what they said. Our team is very close to breaking the code, but not quite yet. But we know something is going on. We're running out of time. You will initiate Plan B no later than tomorrow morning, Mr. Stalingwirth. If not, you can expect to be back in jail by tomorrow night."

"But," Stalingwirth started to protest.

"Quit your whining, Stalingwirth," said Ridgeway. "You're wasting time. You're excused."

With that, Ridgeway swung his chair around to look out his wall of glass on the sixty-fourth floor of the Galactic Mining Enterprises building. Sydney was sparkling in the morning sun.

"Right now?" asked Liza Alvarez.

"Yes. I need you next to me," said Jarrod McKinley. "You understand me better than anyone and you can help me as I try to work through this."

Alvarez was in northern Montana on Jarrod's family farm. It had been four days since McKinley had flown to Australia to be at Wilpena Pound to respond to the new message.

McKinley had told her everything that had happened in that time—the encounter with the stranger after his abduction, the strange instructions to increase his sense of forewarning, and the narrow escape in the outback. He needed her, he said, to help him develop that sense of forewarning and to keep him focused on the big picture, on first contact.

Alvarez was skeptical. She had nearly been killed in the plane crash on the way to Wilpena Pound during the Forsaken scandal. A crash that killed the pilot Charlie Snelling. She also had been right next to Brad Johnson when the explosion on the listening post Sentinel had killed him. Was she bad luck? Would she get Jarrod killed or injured?

There were also reasons she did not want to leave the farm on the flat wheat fields of northern Montana. There was a sense of peace here. The isolation, the expansive sky and low horizons had a way of making her feel protected. You could see a great distance here. Dust clouds announced people coming down the roads. Storm clouds in the distance forewarned of bad weather. Farm dogs gave notice of prowling coyotes.

And there was Jarrod's father. Nearly seventy years old, he was still spry and sharp as a tack, and Liza and he were just getting to know each other. He loved telling stories about the farm, Jarrod's mother, and what Jarrod was like as a boy. The more she learned, the stronger her ties to Jarrod seemed to grow.

It wasn't that she didn't want to be near Jarrod. She missed him terribly, even though it had been just a few days. For all the dangerous encounters they had shared, she felt comfort in his strength and his growing self-confidence. They were engaged, after all. She just thought he might be safer if he didn't have to worry about her. She wanted to tell him that, but she could only say:

"If that's what you want, Jarrod. Of course I will come."

This is going be a long trip, Alvarez thought as she hung up the satellite phone. The farm was thirty kilometers from the nearest town, which was sixty kilometers from the nearest airport. The one flight a day from that airport had to connect with Denver and then Los Angeles before she could get a direct flight to Australia.

If she started now, it would be at least two days before she would see Jarrod, probably three if the connections didn't all work.

"Is this what you want?" Jarrod's father asked her when she gave him the news. "We're just getting acquainted. And there's a lot more to the story of Jarrod and his mother."

"The stories will have to wait," Alvarez replied. "Not that I haven't enjoyed them, and enjoyed this time on the farm getting to know you, but Jarrod needs me."

"Yeah," Mr. McKinley sighed. "He always seems to need someone."

"What do you mean by that?" snapped Alvarez. "Jarrod was the one who uncovered the Forsaken plot."

"Yes. But from what you tell me, he had lots of help. Wait. Wait. I don't want to upset you," said the father. "It's just that ever since his mother died, he seems to lack direction. You know the trouble he had getting through school and the career path he settled on."

"You're not upsetting me, Mr. McKinley. You're starting to make me angry. His career was my career, you know."

"It's not that." Mr. McKinley spoke in an apologetic tone. "You both have done very well. I just know Jarrod's mother had more in mind for him. She saw him as a leader. As someone who could bring people together. She wanted him to go further."

"Well, look at what's happening now," Alvarez said. "If this is first contact, he could bring worlds together."

"Perhaps. Perhaps," Mr. McKinley said with a distant look in his eyes. "His mother would know more."

"Well, he doesn't have his mother. He's got me," Alvarez said with determination. "Now can I use the sat phone to make arrangements?"

In Sydney, Gregory Stalingwirth was listening in as Liza Alvarez made her travel arrangements to meet Jarrod. After making some notes, he went to a large table covered with maps and papers. On a large map of Australia, he circled an area deep in the outback between Wilpena Pound and Alice Springs. He labeled that circle with a large red letter *A*. On another map he circled Los Angeles International Airport and labeled it *B*. He turned again to the Australian map and found the Sydney International Airport. It was labeled *B2*.

Stalingwirth sat down on a high stool next to the table and began to make notes. He checked timelines, crossed out some notations, and wrote in a new set of plans.

He was very meticulous. He had learned that from the Rev. Christopher Larchmont, the architect of the Forsaken project. After all, hadn't he and Larchmont kept that whole project secret for almost twenty years? First, there was the building of the transmitting satellite and the rocket and launch pad. And then the launch and waiting nearly five years before setting in motion the final plan of sending the fake signal. The effort had involved hundreds of people and billions of dollars and he had managed it all and kept it secret.

If it hadn't been for that one little glitch in the satellite and the work of Jarrod McKinley, Forgiven would have worked beautifully and he and Larchmont would still be in control of humankind's only search for extraterrestrial intelligence.

But, Stalingwirth sighed, it hadn't worked and now he was being hired by someone else, an interstellar mining consortium, to do one simple thing. A task, he told himself, much simpler than the Forsaken project.

All he had to do was convince one man, Jarrod McKinley, that it would be in his best interest to join forces with him and Galactic Mining Enterprises, while he made first contact.

There were many reasons to join forces with GME. The corporation had the most resources available to help make first contact. It had the latest communications systems, the fastest space ships, and the best scientists.

Hell, thought Stalingwirth, with the new stealth technology, robotics and communications platforms, GME made SETI operations look like a horse and buggy outfit. Galactic Mining could even match the resources of most countries of the world. Only the United States of North America and China came anywhere close.

Yes, if the best effort was to be put forth in making a success of first contact, GME should be part of that effort, Stalingwirth convinced himself. Now all he had to do was convince Jarrod McKinley. And he had several different methods for making his case.

But, he needed more time. There were a lot of moving parts and they were not all yet in place.

He picked up the phone and started making calls.

"What now?" asked Janet Brighton after the SETI team had sent the response to the signal coming from the direction of Alpha Centauri. "There can be no doubt we have established contact with something out there that is intelligent and can respond to us."

"Yes," replied Jarrod McKinley. "But we have no way of knowing whether the responders are extraterrestrial. What is PFT? Maybe someone is playing a hoax on us."

"That's possible," said Sam Filmore. "But we have so much more to go on this time, I think we need to tell others."

"Like whom?" asked Janet Brighton. "Last time we went public, we came out looking like fools."

"I still think our best bet is to be as honest and open as we can be," replied Filmore. "And in this case I think that means laying all our cards on the table and being an open book. Let the public see everything, each step we take."

"I'm not sure that's wise, Sam," Brighton said. "Remember all the crazies the last time? We had all kinds of weirdos crawling out from under rocks. You know, from 'The World is Doomed' folks to the 'Let's Make Love, not War,' crowd. It'll be crazy."

"I know," said Filmore. "But, if there is one thing we've learned from the last time, it's that we can't hide this for long. I'm surprise word hasn't leaked out to the public, especially because we know someone has penetrated our security, thus the attacks on Jarrod. That might be another way to keep him safe. Have the whole world know we are trying to make contact."

"The secrets. That's what's going to get us," said Jack Simington. "Look what it got for the last blokes running this place. Larchmont's in jail now."

"Jarrod, what do you think?" asked Henning. "After all, it's you who are going to be the point on this."

McKinley had been silent during the discussion. He hesitated now, even after the direction question. He stood up, moved to the side of the group and turned slowly.

"Look," said, speaking slowly and gazing in turn at each member of the group. "We've already had this discussion. We don't know what's going to happen. We don't know yet if this is real or not. If it is real, we don't know whether they are friendly or deadly.

"We discussed all of this after Forsaken. We all agreed that the worst things that happened during the

Forsaken scandal, the deaths, the near riots, serious injuries to others, all of that might have been prevented if everyone had known the truth.

"We have to be better than SETISCOM or the public will never trust us. World governments won't trust us. We won't even trust ourselves. Everything we say and do must be based on the truth. The same truths, the facts and figures, all the data that we use must be available to everyone. If we can't build a sense of trust and teamwork among ourselves, and by that I mean all of humankind, how in the world can we expect someone from another world to trust us?"

"But Jarrod," said Brighton. "What about those goons who kidnapped you? Those people who tried to grab you in the outback? Are we supposed to trust them?"

"No," said McKinley. "I'm not going to trust someone trying to harm me, but I would like to know what their motives were. If they had wanted me dead, I wouldn't be here right now. If I get the chance, I'd like to know what they want."

"Good way to get yourself killed," Simington quipped.

"Jack's right," said Brighton. "Let the authorities handle that."

"I'm willing let law enforcement do their thing," McKinley responded. "I just want to know what they want. Whoever they are."

"Jarrod," said Filmore, "stay away from them. You are our point on this. Remember, whatever is out there will only talk to you."

"Okay," said McKinley, "but, remember our plan. Once we're convinced we've made contact, we go public, and we contact others who will need to be involved. Are we agreed?"

They all said yes, or nodded in agreement.

"Sam, Janet, you start contacting the right people. We want the United Space Command in Alice Springs to know first, followed by the European Space Command and the China/Asia Space Consortium. Then the world political powers—the United States of North America, the European Union, China, and the Asian countries.

"Laura, Jack, you get ready for the publicity onslaught. Have all the data boiled down to the simplest terms. I will call C.R. Duncan at *The Age*, first. He deserves the scoop on this after his help during Forsaken. But I'll only give him a few hours before I alert the other international news organizations. I can be the spokesperson, as I was during the campaign after Forsaken, but I will need all of your support."

"You'll have it, Jarrod," Henning said. "We're all behind you on this."

"Good," said McKinley. "I want to let you all know I've called Liza. She's coming as fast as she can. She can help me with the PR."

"Jarrod?" asked Filmore. "What do we do when everyone, I'm talking Space Command, USNA, and others all want to control this operation?"

"We talk. We work together. We are honest in all our dealings. But most of all, we do what is best for humankind, in this case a successful first contact. If there are others who can do it better, we can't let our egos get in the way. This is not just for us. It's for the whole world."

"I hope everyone believes that," said Brighton. "I don't think the men behind the black helicopter would agree with you."

"There will always be some, perhaps many, who will want to take advantage of this special moment," said Filmore. "We just have to do our best to keep the big picture in mind. One of friendly contact."

The technician interrupted.

"Jack," she said, looking at Simington. "Jarrod has a call."

"Yes, Jenny, we know," Simington said. "We answered it a few minutes ago."

"No. I mean a real call. A phone call."

"Who is it?" asked McKinley.

Jenny Hastings was one of the new hires after the Forsaken scandal. She was a new graduate from Melbourne University with a degree in communications and astrophysics. She was five feet nine inches tall, with a slim build that she kept in shape by riding her bicycle all around the Wilpena Pound area. Riding the lonely roads in the outback of South Australia was much different than her competitive riding on the university cycling team but there was a peacefulness about it and it kept her fit. She wore her blonde hair in a ponytail that swished as she turned toward McKinley.

"Jarrod, he says his name is Gregory Stalingwirth."

Chapter 10

"THEY ARE NOT BEING HONEST," said Athrena, after the team leader had presented her with the message sent by Jarrod and the SETI team.

"How so?" asked Conteus.

"I believe they are very afraid. I do not believe they have thoughtfully considered how difficult and how long this communication will be. What about the other political entities on the planet? Does this small group of scientists believe they are going to speak for their world? The questions they ask, 'Who are you?' and 'Where are you?' are questions meant to be answered at a later time."

"I fully understand their questions," replied Conteus. "Their species has been looking toward the stars for answers for millennia. The questions reflect that desire to know."

"Do not patronize me," Athrena snapped back, her head jerking toward Conteus on her long slim neck. "I understand those simple emotions they might have. I just do not believe they would not use more subtle, diplomatic communications to establish whether or not we might be a danger to them and their world. The blunt questions they use are just to hide their fears while they try to think of a more appropriate set of questions. Questions that, I am sure, will try to probe our weaknesses."

"Perhaps," said Conteus. "Or, perhaps because they are all scientists, their questions are blunt and to the point. Our FPT lead technician suspects that is the case."

"I don't really care what the team leader thinks," Athrena shot back. "We developed plans for this scenario years ago and I do not see any reason to deviate. We will conform to the plans. Our response will be friendly but oblique. We will establish the procedure for contact as we have outlined. One that will build trust. One that will allow them to trust us before our final action."

"Surely we must be open to changes in the plan," suggested Conteus. "What about the unexpected?"

"Conteus?" asked Athrena, with a steady glare, "How long have we been in this situation?"

"Two thousand years?"

"More than that. Do you not believe we have studied every conceivable scenario in that time?"

"Perhaps. But I also know that, like time, the potential scenarios are infinite. It would not be possible to have studied them all."

"True," said Athrena. "That is why, during the last two hundred years, while they began to develop technology, we spent so much time narrowing the possibilities, to shorten the range of viable options a species on a planet like that would have.

"We have predicted almost all of their technological advances, their push into their own solar system, the level of communication, rocketry and weaponry they have been able to develop. The planetary defense systems. And at this point there have been no surprises and nothing that should stop our plan from working."

"We did not anticipate their attempt at sending a false signal back to their own planet," said Conteus, still trying to make his point.

"No. We did not. But we had that simple little scheme diagnosed long before anyone on their planet and after analyzing it decided this would be a good time to initiate our plan."

"But our plan was not scheduled for another one hundred fifty years," Conteus made one last effort to convince.

"As long as we stick to the plan and make them trust us, our plan will work. I am confident. But I do believe they have begun this journey too fast, otherwise they would not be asking such simple questions.

"No. We will go more slowly. We will make them take some time to consider all the implications of making contact with another world. Besides, this will give us time to insert this new data into our plan to see if changes are warranted. We have spent far too much time on the plan to see it fail now because of our eagerness to make it a success.

"There is more to consider than just the happiness of one species on a small planet."

"What should we do, then?" asked Conteus.

"Do not respond to this communication yet. Call a meeting between the Forgiven Project Team and the Council. We will discuss and consider our next action."

"Stalingwirth?" Jarrod McKinley said into the phone with a low growl. "What do you want?"

"I want to help," replied Gregory Stalingwirth.

"The last time I let you help me I ended up in a jail cell seven floors under Wilpena Pound," said McKinley. "I don't want your help, and I know I never want to see you again. I thought you'd be in jail by now."

"Jarrod, Jarrod," whined Stalingwirth. "You have me all wrong. I was never in favor of those things Larchmont did to you. I was your champion. I tried to protect you. I was the biggest supporter of the search. I want mankind to find our brothers in the universe. You must believe me."

"Never," snapped McKinley. "Like I said, what do you want?"

"I think I can help with your latest problem," Stalingwirth said, almost in a whisper.

"My only problem is that I'm talking to you. I'm going to disconnect now."

"You want to know who they are and where they are, I believe, to use your own words," Stalingwirth hissed back.

McKinley hesitated. He looked at Sam Filmore and Jenny Hasting who were also listening to the phone call.

Filmore shrugged his shoulders and put his hands in the air as if to say he didn't know what to do. Hastings had a scowl on her face and was slowly shaking her head back and forth as if to say, "no."

McKinley took a deep breath.

"I don't know what you are talking about Stalingwirth," McKinley said.

"I think you do," said Stalingwirth. "And I have some clues that will point you in the right direction."

"Again, Stalingwirth, I'm going to disconnect now," McKinley glanced at Filmore who was now gesturing that he wanted to hear more. Hastings was still shaking her head no.

"Forsaken was a big mistake, I know," Stalingwirth said. "But, we found something."

"What are you talking about?"

"On our second launch," Stalingwirth said.

"There was only one launch," said McKinley. "We looked over every inch of the launch site."

"You found what we wanted you to find, Mr. McKinley. We were very good at hiding things. Remember, Forsaken was hidden for more than twenty years before a sad chain of events let the secret out."

"What did you find?"

"Our first launch was successful but the satellite malfunctioned and we had to launch a repair mission. That's when we found it."

"Found what?"

"Someone, or something, had tampered with the satellite," Stalingwirth said.

"How did you know?" asked McKinley.

"There were markings," Stalingwirth said. "We took pictures."

"What did they look like?" McKinley quizzed, looking at Filmore and Hastings for an idea of what to do.

"I can't explain them," said Stalingwirth. "You'll have to see them."

"Okay. Send me an image. I can take it on my cell phone right now."

"I don't have them. We left them all in a secret hiding place at the launch site."

"No you didn't. We went over that place with a fine-toothed comb."

"I told you, Mr. McKinley. You missed it. We were very good at hiding things. But I can show you where they are."

"What do you mean, show me?"

"I can meet you there and show you the hiding place."

"Just tell me and we'll have someone go there and find them."

"That's impossible," said Stalingwirth. "It's too complex. But I have a map. I have to go there and connect the dots. And it has to be with you."

By this time both Filmore and Hastings were violently shaking their heads "no" and making gestures to stop McKinley.

"Why me?" McKinley asked.

"It's always been you," replied Stalingwirth. "I'm not sure why. You could probably answer that better than I. But, you're always in the middle of this."

"I'm busy right now. It will have to be someone else."

"No. If you don't agree right now, I'm going to disconnect and you will lose the chance to help solve this little mystery you have on your hands."

There was a pause while neither person spoke. Filmore and Hastings were still urging McKinley not to agree to anything.

"Okay," said Stalingwirth, "I'm disconnecting now!"

"Wait!"

McKinley gave a helpless gesture to Filmore and Hastings as he said into the phone. "When can I meet you?"

"Tomorrow morning at eight at the launch site," replied Stalingwirth. "We need the morning shadows to make this map work."

"I'll see you then," said McKinley. "This had better not be a waste of time."

"You won't regret it."

McKinley thought he detected the hint of a smirk in Stalingwirth's last words.

Liza Alvarez settled into her middle seat on the left side of the Qantas jetliner in Los Angeles when a young man with wavy straw-colored hair flowing over his ears leaned over and gave her a big smile.

"Excuse me," he said with a friendly, toothy grin, "I believe I have the window seat."

"Sure," said Alvarez with a smile. She stood in the aisle as the man stashed a small bag in the overhead bin and slid into his seat.

"First time going to Australia?" the young man asked.

Alvarez buckled her seatbelt and glanced at the man. It was hard not to notice his trim build, muscular arms and golden tan.

"No," she replied. "Been there before. How about you?"

"First time. I'm finally going to get in some real surfing. The waves in California can't compare to those at Bondi Beach."

"Bondi what?" Alvarez asked.

"Bondi Beach, near Sydney. Best surfing outside of Hawaii," the man replied with a big grin.

"Wouldn't know," said Alvarez, grabbing a magazine from the seat-back pocket in front of her.

The big Qantas jet was filling up fast with passengers, Alvarez noticed as she glanced around. The rows of four center seats were nearly full, as were most of the seats on the right and left side of the plane. There were families with fussy kids.

Oh great, Alvarez thought, fifteen hours of that.

As she watched a mother try to calm her child, she noticed a heavyset man with a short military-style haircut come down the aisle looking for his seat. When he reached Alvarez he stopped and looked directly at her without saying a word. The man continued on for two more rows and found his seat, directly behind Alvarez.

Alvarez suddenly shivered.

"Cold already?" asked the man next to her. "They haven't even turned on the air conditioning. Wait 'til we're up in the air."

"Guess I'd better find a blanket," Alvarez said with a laugh.

"Maybe you can have two if no one takes the aisle seat," the man said with a grin.

"I'm Josh. Josh Reynolds."

"Liza. Liza Alvarez."

"So, why are you going to Australia?" Reynolds said. "Got family there?"

"No. Not really," Alvarez said. "I'm going to meet my fiancé. He's working there."

"Oh . . ." Reynolds paused as if he wasn't sure his conversation was welcome.

Alvarez noticed the doubt crossing his face and decided to continue the conversation. It was a long flight to Sydney. Might as well be friendly.

"So what do you do, Mr. Reynolds? When you're not surfing, that is." Alvarez spoke with a pleasant smile on her face.

Reynolds' face brightened noticeably. "I just finished my post grad studies in astrobiology. Figured I would take a vacation before beating the airwaves for a big 'career.' " He grinned, raising the fingers of his hands to indicate quotes.

Alvarez couldn't help being reminded of Brad Johnson, her crew mate who was killed in the blast on the Sentinel listening post. Brad also had been a happy-go-lucky blonde from a California university. The thought made her frown and lower her head.

"Sorry. Didn't mean to upset you."

Alvarez shook it off, raised her head and smiled.

"Oh, it's nothing you said. I just was remembering someone I used to work with."

"Did he make you sad, too?"

"No, not at all. He was very pleasant. Cheerful in fact. We went to school together."

Alvarez could tell that Josh was going to be talkative for the whole flight and she welcomed that to a point. However, she resolved to go nowhere near her experiences with SETISCOM, Forsaken, or the new information Jarrod had given her. One could not be safe enough, given what Jarrod had said about the abduction attempts. Who knew what information was safe to talk about, what was not, and who was safe to talk to. Best just to keep it quiet.

"So, Mr. Reynolds, where were you born?"

"Please. It's going to be a long flight. Call me Josh. I was born in Idaho. Near Boise."

Thus began a pleasant conversation about each other, current events, politics, and everything in between. Alvarez found Reynolds to be quite knowledgeable about most topics. When their conversation touched on space travel, Reynolds indicated that he believed strongly there was intelligent life elsewhere in the universe, he just wasn't sure the human species would ever be able to make contact. He said he was sorry when he heard about the scandal created by SETISCOM and was afraid the search for extraterrestrial life might die.

He also had strong opinions about which country was making the most progress in space exploration. According to Reynolds, it was the US of NA with the help of Brazil, followed by the Europeans. As far as the commercialization of space, he felt mining was okay but was dominated too much by large corporations. He thought hotels and casinos in space were just another way to make it part of the human experience.

During their conversations, Alvarez mostly smiled and nodded and gave her opinions on noncontroversial topics. Not once did she reveal she knew Jarrod McKinley, or that she was part of the SETI team that broke the Forsaken scandal, or that she had any knowledge of a new signal being sent to Earth.

However, throughout the conversation and the meals and the sleep time, in which she didn't sleep, she worried about Jarrod and wondered what was happening at Wilpena Pound. Had the last message they sent to the senders been received and did they get a response? Had there been any more threats to Jarrod's life? Had they figured out who was behind the attempted abductions? She hated being out of touch but agreed with Jarrod that, considering the data leaks at the Pound, it was better to avoid any further communications until she was on the charter plane to Wilpena Pound.

By the time the airliner was descending on its Sydney approach, Liza had decided that she liked

Josh Reynolds. He seemed very genuine, frank and honest, with hardly a negative thought in his mind.

"Well, Josh. You've made this a very pleasant trip," said Alvarez. "Perhaps we'll see you again around Sydney, if you don't spend all of your time on the beach."

"I'd love to meet you for lunch sometime," Reynolds said. "And I'd like to meet your fiancé and tell him what a lucky man his is. Can I get your cell number? Perhaps we'll both find the time."

"I'd like to," said Alvarez with a smile, "but I don't have a phone and I'm not sure where we're going to be staying." She had promised Jarrod she wouldn't use the phone in her purse until after she landed in Sydney.

"Well, I'll give you my number. If you get time, just give me a call."

Reynolds jotted his number on a piece of paper and gave it to Alvarez. She placed it in her vest pocket.

As Alvarez lifted her luggage out of the overhead, the heavyset man who had been seated two rows back got up, watching her closely. He excused himself to others as he moved forward. Some passengers were polite but others muttered that the man should just calm down and wait his turn to exit. When the man got to Alvarez, he stopped. He said nothing. Alvarez stared at the man but couldn't see his eyes because he was staring at the aisle of the aircraft. Alvarez glanced at Reynolds, gave a little shake to her head and frowned, as if to say, "What's this guy all about?"

Reynolds got out of his seat and moved between the man and Alvarez, asking to be excused as he retrieved his luggage from the overhead bin.

Deplaning almost three hundred people takes a while and it was a slow shuffle. The muscular man kept as close as he could to Alvarez. Reynolds, sensing Alvarez's discomfort, kept between her and the man.

When they reached the gate ramp and more room, Alvarez and Reynolds sped up a bit. The man increased his pace to keep with them.

On the concourse, Alvarez turned to Reynolds and said she had to go to the baggage claim area.

"Me too," said Reynolds. "We'll go together."

Baggage claim at the Sydney airport is some distance from the exit concourse and passengers pushed past Alvarez and Reynolds, in a hurry to get their bags and go through customs.

"I'm not sure what their rush is," Reynolds said. "They're just going to get in another line for customs."

"Maybe they have connecting flights," Alvarez said. "I guess you don't, seeing as you are just headed for some surfing beach."

Reynolds chuckled. "I guess that's right." But he had a serious look on his face. He noticed the heavyset man had not rushed off but was keeping pace with them, with just a few people between.

"Where are you headed?" Reynolds asked Alvarez.

"I'm traveling to the Adelaide area, but I've got someone meeting me outside the terminal. They will take me to a charter at a small airport north of Sydney."

"Wow. The royal treatment. Are you some kind of rock star, or something? Or maybe with your looks, a movie star?" asked Reynolds with a laugh.

"No, no," replied Alvarez, blushing a bit. "Nothing like that. I just need to get to the bush."

"The bush?"

"It's nothing, really," said Alvarez, as they reached the baggage claim area.

They both spotted their bags and wrestled them off the baggage carousel. Reynolds noticed that the man was standing nearby but didn't seem to be looking for his bags. He was watching them intently as he talked on his cell phone.

Reynolds and Alvarez pulled their bags toward customs and cleared with no problems. Soon they were headed for the terminal exit toward a sign that said *Ground Transportation*. The man that had been following them had disappeared.

"Well, I guess this might be goodbye," said Reynolds. "I'm going to catch a cab to my hotel."

"Well, Josh, thanks again for the company. Perhaps we'll see you again if you stay in Australia long."

"Not sure how that will go," Reynolds said. "Depends on the surf, and on how long my money lasts. When is your ride coming?"

"He should be here any moment. He had my flight number and we're right on time."

They were outside the terminal now, near the curb and they turned, Reynolds to look for a cab and Alvarez searching for a SETI vehicle.

As they turned, the heavyset man was right in front of Alvarez's face.

"Liza Alvarez?" he said with cold voice and a stare right into her eyes.

Alvarez shivered. "Yes?"

"You must come with me," the man said as he grabbed her wrist.

"Why?" Alvarez struggled to pull away.

"I am with the International Security Agency and we need to talk to you about your passport and your security clearance," the man said. "There's no time to waste. Lives are in danger."

Alvarez immediately thought of Jarrod. Had something happened to him? Was he in trouble again?

"Hold on a minute," said Reynolds. He stepped forward, trying to get between the man and Alvarez. "I've never heard of the International Security Agency. Show me some identification."

"Sir," said the man, "you need to stay out of this. It does not concern you. Move along."

"You don't have the right to just grab somebody. Show me your ID or I'll call for security and you can show it to them," said Reynolds.

"I'm warning you to move off," the man said with a snarl.

"Josh, be careful," said Alvarez.

"Careful, my ass," Reynolds said with his voice rising in excitement. He turned and started to shout, "Security—"

The man grabbed him quickly on the side of the neck and Reynolds gasped and shuddered as if he had been hit with an electric shock. Reynolds slumped to the ground as the man jerked Alvarez close to him and whispered, "Come with me. No noise. No struggles or he will die." He nodded in the direction of Reynolds.

He turned quickly and yanked Alvarez along next to him.

Reynolds struggled to clear the cobwebs as he lay on the sidewalk. People rushed to his aid, while he shouted and pointed to Alvarez and her abductor.

"Stop them! Stop them! He's kidnapping her!"

In the direction Reynolds was pointing, people saw a heavyset man push a woman into a car. The car door slammed shut and the car sped away. There was a cover over the license plate and Reynolds tried to etch in his mind the details of the vehicle.

"Black, four-door sedan, new, satellite antenna, but what make?" he said out loud. It was not anything he recognized, probably some Australian model.

"Don't go, Jarrod. Knowing Stalingwirth, this can only be a trap," said Sam Filmore.

The whole team, Filmore, Janet Brighton, Laura Henning, Jack Simington, and now Jenny Hastings, was gathered around McKinley.

"I know," said McKinley. "But, I have to go. What if Stalingwirth is telling the truth? What if there is a clue to our latest signal senders? We can't pass up any information that might be helpful."

"The bugger's lying," said Simington. "I wouldn't be surprised if the skink is working for the same people who tried to kidnap you. You absolutely cannot trust him."

"I don't trust him," replied McKinley. "That's why we are going to take precautions. But, if there is something there, I want to see it."

"Okay, Jarrod," said Brighton. "What kind of precautions do you want to take?"

"First, call Bill Rider, the rancher who lives nearby and helped us during Forsaken," McKinley replied.

He then sketched out a plan to the group. When he was done, he directed Simington to make some arrangements and he asked Jenny Hastings if she would accompany him to the launch site.

"I know it could be dangerous," he said. "You absolutely don't have to go if you don't want to. I've chosen you for a couple of reasons. First, I need an extra set of eyes, someone to see everything I see. We don't want to miss anything. Second, you are new here and Stalingwirth is not likely to recognize you or see you as a threat."

Hastings didn't hesitate.

"I'll go. It sounds interesting and I can take care of myself."

"We have about twelve hours to put this plan in place," McKinley said. "At the same time we can't ignore what's going on here. Can everyone give me an update?"

The media had been contacted and initial stories were already going online, Brighton reported. Other space agencies and major countries had been contacted and the reactions were predictable, Henning added. The space agencies all wanted to be included. Some were sending representatives, others were establishing secure communication links to give them a virtual presence at Wilpena Pound.

So far, Henning reported, most countries had been cordial and cooperative. China seemed the most aggressive, wanting to send a team of its own, not just the observers the SETI team was able to accommodate.

"Sam," McKinley said, turning to Filmore, "can we get the control center down in the Forsaken complex up and running? We could accommodate more scientists that way. If we start restricting too many people, some are going to push back, wanting to take control of this."

"We can't let China in and not invite the USNA and Europeans," said Brighton. "I know there has been a high level of cooperation recently, but the magnitude of this is bound to put on levels of pressure not seen for decades."

"If we keep it to the USNA, the Europeans and China, we should be all right," replied Filmore.

"That has to be the limit," insisted Simington. "Any more than that and we'll just be tripping over everyone."

"I agree," said Filmore. "Even though we have treaties on exploration, resource development, and commercialization of space, first contact will introduce a whole new realm of possible conflicts. Who is going to control this contact? What's going to be the point of contact for the planet Earth? We can't have every country acting as the sole contact."

"The United Space Command in Alice Springs is nearest, and it's the closest thing to an umbrella group," said Brighton. "I talked to the administrator and the commanding officer. They both will be here in a couple of hours. I suggest we have them help work out the diplomacy of this and how to put together a working team."

"Good idea, Janet," said McKinley. "You take the lead on this."

"Jack, Laura. Have we had a response to our last signal to the senders?" McKinley asked.

"None," said Henning. "It's been more than three hours and no response."

"Nothing? They didn't even acknowledge receiving our message?" asked Filmore.

"Nothing. Dead silence. Not even the standard signal we have been receiving for the past week."

"Maybe they didn't like the questions," McKinley said.

Chapter 11

Before the sun had burned its way through the red morning horizon, McKinley and Jenny Hastings were with Bill Ryder on his cattle station near the old Forsaken launch site.

McKinley gave a final briefing and then he and Hastings drove off to meet Stalingwirth.

"I'm sorry to involve you," McKinley said to Hastings. "But Stalingwirth has never seen you and it might throw him off whatever little scheme he has hatched."

"Don't worry about me," Hastings replied with a smile and a long glance at McKinley. "I know the plan. We'll be safe."

Hasting had a lean, athletic build and McKinley knew she could move fast, probably faster than he could after almost a year on the public relations tour. She played tennis, rode her bike in the outback just for fun and had been on a university cycling team.

"Just hang back until we get a lay of the land," McKinley said as they approached the launch site from a high point on a ridge.

The old launch site was mostly abandoned concrete slabs, now studded with weeds and partly covered with piles of wind-blown sand. A launch pad was sunk in the middle of the site and was surrounded by low blast walls. In the left corner was a short bunker structure with one window slot. The old control center, McKinley remembered from last year. He guessed that would be where Stalingwirth would reveal his secret.

Just as he parked the SETI vehicle, a helicopter came in low from the south, circled the launch site and sat down in the middle of the launch pad amid the weeds, dust billowing out from all sides.

McKinley looked carefully at the four-seat copter. There were only two people aboard, the pilot and someone who must be Stalingwirth.

"Good. He's alone," McKinley said to Hastings. "Time to see what his little trick is. Are we ready?"

"Ready here," Hastings replied.

McKinley stepped out of the vehicle and clambered down into the launch site as he watched Stalingwirth get out of the copter and approach.

Stalingwirth was looking at his watch.

"It's almost time," he said as the two met. "We need to go over to the bunker and be there at exactly 8:05."

"There's nothing in the bunker," McKinley said. "We checked last year."

"But," laughed Stalingwirth, "you didn't find the secret door. The sun's rays passing through that slit in the rock will reveal the door," and he pointed to a shaft of sunlight, now nearly focused on the bunker.

"Come this way," Stalingwirth commanded.

McKinley followed, staring at the shaft of sunlight now just touching the bunker.

"Over here," Stalingwirth urged.

As they reached the bunker, Hastings blasted the horn on the SETI vehicle. McKinley heard noises to his right and left. Three men jumped out of the drainage depressions that surrounded the bunker and rushed at McKinley. They were on him before he had a chance to react, strong hands gripping him by his arms.

"Stalingwirth, you snake," McKinley snarled, "what are you up to?"

"Relax," said Stalingwirth. "Just need to talk to you."

"I'm not doing any talking with these goons holding me," McKinley said.

Hastings had jumped out of the vehicle and was running toward the men.

"Jenny, stay back!" McKinley shouted.

She stopped about ten meters away.

"Jarrod, are you okay?" she asked.

"Everyone is okay," said Stalingwirth. "We're just going to have a little chat. Right, Jarrod?"

"Talk all you want, I'm not listening."

"Well, listen to this. The interest I work for wants to make you an offer. We want you on our team, the team that will make contact with the aliens."

"Got no idea what you're talking about," scoffed McKinley.

"Don't waste my time playing games," responded Stalingwirth. "We know you have received a signal from the direction of Alpha Centauri. We know you have responded and that they have responded to that.

"We also know that they have asked for you personally, although, for the life of me, I can't quite figure out why. But they think you're special. So we want you on our team."

"Whose team would that be?" McKinley asked. "The same team that abducted me at the airport, or the team that tried to kill me near Hawker? No thanks."

"That was before I was involved," Stalingwirth said. "We're taking a different approach, now. We think you would be a valuable member of the team. We have a strong lineup, good scientists, and the best technology. We can make first contact more rewarding for you than anything you'll ever see at SETI, both materially and from a scientific aspect.

"We will call the shots when it comes to first contact, so you might as well be with the winning team. We'll be very good to you and anyone you bring with you, say, the young lady over there who seems so nervous."

"Again, Stalingwirth," McKinley was almost shouting now, "who are you working for? And why should I trust you?"

"You'll find out soon enough," Stalingwirth replied with a steady calm. "Right now I just need you to come with me. Get in the helicopter."

"What about this secret you were going to reveal?" asked McKinley.

"Oh that. That was just a way to get you out here where your silly friends won't be in the way."

"And you expect me to believe anything you say?" shouted McKinley. "Forget it. Jenny, go back to the truck. We're leaving."

"I'm sorry, Jarrod," said Stalingwirth. "I'm sorry that every time we meet I have to drag you off. You'll come with us. Take him to the helicopter," he instructed the men holding McKinley.

McKinley struggled to break free but it was no use. The grip the three men had on him was like a vice and they began pushing him toward the helicopter.

A swishing sound startled the men just before a boomerang clipped one of them on the back of the head. A loud shot rang out and the two other men dropped to the ground and grabbed their guns. A flash of brown and grey shot through the air as Bill Ryder's dog Pal streaked over the edge of the launch site, Ryder close behind.

"Drop the gun," Ryder commanded, firing off another round.

McKinley was moving away quickly toward the SETI vehicle and Stalingwirth was back-peddling to the helicopter.

"Jarrod," Stalingwirth shouted. "It doesn't have to be this way. Come now or you will be sorry."

Ryder now was standing over the men. One was still rubbing his head from the boomerang blow while Pal was firmly planted on the chest of another. The third was flat on the ground with his hands out to the side.

"Jarrod," Stalingwirth shouted again as the helicopter blades began to whir. "Think of Liza. Think of what you are doing to Liza. I told you, you will be sorry."

"What?" McKinley called out. "What about Liza?"

But it was too late. The helicopter lifted off and McKinley's mind raced with fear.

Quickly he instructed Ryder and Hastings to tie up the three men as he dialed the number of Liza's phone.

She should be in Sydney, he thought, looking at his watch. By this time she should be on her way to meet the charter flight that would bring her to Wilpena Pound. The ring of the phoned echoed in McKinley's ear as he waited desperately for her to pick up.

In Sydney, the husky man checked the slumping Liza Alvarez after he pushed her into a car and injected her with a mild sedative. Her head lolled back, her mouth was slack and her breathing was slow and uneven. He checked her pulse and gave a satisfied grin.

Then her cell phone rang. He pulled the ringing phone out of Alvarez's pocket. He looked at the caller ID and smirked when he saw the name, Jarrod McKinley. He lowered the back window and threw the phone out of the speeding car. The phone burst into dozens of pieces as it bounced off the pavement.

It was a group of nine. Athrena and Conteus sat on a slightly raised platform on high-backed chairs facing a large window open to the outside where Acquaria was rising, casting a bright purple-red glow over the hills covered in a luxurious green and red mantel.

Other low-backed chairs formed a circle radiating from the two leaders. A small pedestal in the center emitted a shimmering light that flickered toward the ceiling. As the meeting participants entered the room and took their chairs, a small beam reached out from the pedestal and quickly scanned their torsos. After each scan, Athrena or Conteus nodded in acknowledgment.

When all were seated, an image formed above the pedestal. It was titled *Forgiven Project* and showed the faces of all in the group, along with their areas of expertise—political, cultural, biological, engineering, financial, astrometrics, communication, environmental, and domestic.

"Welcome," said Athrena. "We all know why we are here. There have been developments on Earth that require some decisions. You have all been briefed in the developments—the attempts to abduct Jarrod McKinley, the involvement of a third party, and the lack of a coordinated response to our message.

"The decision we make on how to proceed is critical to the success or failure of this undertaking. The options are varied. The only certainty is that we are on a path that cannot be reversed. We have revealed our existence. The question now is how to proceed so our long term goals can be realized without endangering our forces or doing too much damage on Earth.

"I would like to hear from all of you. We will begin with the political considerations. Ramus, what are your thoughts?"

"It is progressing as we thought it would," replied Ramus. "Major political powers on Earth are just learning about the signal and want to be involved. North America, Europe and China are the key players, and so far North America and China have approached the SETI team. Europe has not, but likely will in the next few hours. So far SETI has been very open and welcoming of all the inquiries. I would say the politics on Earth are, at this time, unsettled but not unstable."

"Are there any guesses at what might happen?" asked Conteus.

"I am certain there will be conflict and disagreement as to who should be the primary contact." replied Ramus. "But with SETI taking a cooperative attitude, I am hopeful there will be no unresolvable issues. Representatives from interested parties are traveling to Wilpena Pound so our communications scanning should be focused there until the situation changes."

"Good," said Athrena. "Speaking of communications, how is that going?" She turned to Bachuus.

"We remain on track," replied the woman to the left of Athrena. "Our sling points are doing their job—making response times quicker and more difficult to track. This is creating confusion at SETI, but that is not necessarily a bad thing at this point."

"Why do you say that?" Conteus wanted to know.

"At this time, we still believe caution needs to

be taken," replied Bachuus. "We are not sure of the attitude that will develop as more learn about our signal, hostile or peaceful. And besides, we know a non-governmental entity is involved and trying to communicate."

"Let us talk about that for a moment," said Athrena. "What do we know about this Galactic Mining Enterprises?"

"This company has the most highly developed technology on Earth at this time," said Temerius, the engineering team leader.

"It has been mining in the solar system for about forty years and has enough resources to develop the latest technology in communications, robotics, propulsion, and other disciplines needed for a very successful and powerful business. Its resources are much greater than SETI's and even greater than many countries on Earth."

"I also understand they have powerful political connections," said Ramus. "There is evidence of influence in Asia, Europe and North America. However, most of their influence is used only to advance their business interests."

"Why are they involved in this?" asked Athrena.

"They want our technology," replied Temerius. "It would make them more powerful and more successful, meaning higher profits and greater riches for the owners and stockholders of the company."

"Are they a danger to our mission?" asked Conteus.

"I would classify them more as a nuisance than a danger," said Temerius.

"Okay," said Athrena. "Let us carefully monitor their activities. We cannot allow them to slow us down. We need to move on. Are there any other issues that could alter our mission?"

Other members of the team had little to say and nothing to alarm Athrena or Conteus.

"It is time," said Athrena after listening without comment to team members' contributions. "How should we proceed? When do we identify ourselves? When do we reveal our mission to Earth? How do we prepare Earth for that moment? When do we reveal our mission to the Progenia citizens and do we need any special effort before we tell them the truth?"

Debate was lively but polite. Points were made about fear, protecting lives, scarcity of resources, need for water, population control, environmental degradation, unstable atmosphere and genetics.

After nearly an hour of discussion, Athrena raised her hand for silence.

"I have heard you all," she said. "Now we need a recommendation I can get approved by the Global Council."

In the discussion that followed, some wanted to continue with the present strategy. Others thought a slower pace would be better. No one sought to speed up the plan.

"I would suggest, after hearing you all, that we proceed as planned, with one exception. If we cannot get a unified point of contact on Earth, we must delay the plan until we are sure we have all points of contact accounted for. We do not want the impact of the plan to be diffused. It must hit Earth with the impact we have calculated to be most effective. Are we agreed?"

A murmur of assent rippled around the room.

"Good," said Athrena. "I will go to the council today and get approval. Ramus, prepare the communication team to formulate a reply to SETI's latest communications. They must be getting nervous."

"They should be," replied Ramus. "And I doubt they will like what they are going hear next from us."

Chapter 12

"We have to get her back," McKinley said. "I don't care what it takes. We have to find her and get her back."

"Jarrod, we don't even know where she is. The police are looking for her. We need to let them do their job," said Laura Henning.

"All we know is that she was abducted outside the terminal at the Sydney airport," said Sam Filmore. "There were lots of witnesses, especially this kid named Josh Reynolds who provided a description of the man and the car, but police have no leads."

"No leads at all?" asked McKinley.

"None. We don't know where to start looking. Police have put out an all-points bulletin for Stalingwirth but there's no sign of him," said Janet Brighton.

"We know he's behind it," said Jenny Hastings. "His goons must have been the abductors."

"He's trying to use her as leverage," said McKinley. "We need to find out who he works for. Who's desperate enough to have me on their team to go to these lengths? Who has enough money to launch these kinds of missions?"

"Must be the same people who bailed Stalingwirth out of jail," said Henning. "We tried to track it but whoever did that has enough pull to seal all the records behind the release."

"We don't have to do anything," said Jack Simington.

"What?" McKinley almost shouted.

"They want you bad," said Simington. "These skinks have killed their own people, used technology we only dream of having, and now they've used kidnapping. And it's my bet they're not done."

"Exactly," said McKinley, the tension mounting on his face. "That's why we have to find her."

"Jarrod, Jarrod. Calm down," said Simington. "They will find us. You are the ransom. They'll hold Liza until they get you. I'll bet the same guys are behind the leaks here, and based on the technology I've seen, we won't be able to find them."

"We're not just going to sit here," McKinley answered angrily.

"No, we aren't," said Brighton. "We're going use the time to develop plans for when we get that call. We can't just rely on the Sydney police. I don't think they are taking this seriously and they don't know all the circumstances of our mission and the relationships between Liza, Jarrod, the earlier abduction attempts, and Stalingwirth."

"Once they get me, what will they do to Liza?" asked McKinley. "They won't need her anymore. She'll be dead."

"That's why we need to plan this carefully,"

Brighton said. "We have to protect both you and Liza and we have to protect the integrity of our mission. We can't forget that what we are working on here is earth shattering. And you, Jarrod, are a key part of that."

"I don't care about the mission right now," McKinley said. "Liza is my first priority."

"Jarrod, you can't do that," said Filmore. "We'll have to do both at once. We have a strong team right here. We can define priorities and split them among us. You can supervise, but we'll do the work. You have to be available to both teams, but we can't risk our first contact mission by letting you be captured and controlled by someone else."

"I don't like that," McKinley replied. "I can't just sit around."

"You won't be sitting around," said Brighton. "We'll keep you very busy, but we can't risk you again. You need to be in a secure location. Like right here in Wilpena Pound."

"Not acceptable," said McKinley. "I won't stand around while Liza is in danger."

"We won't be standing around, Jarrod," said Henning. "Janet and Sam are right. If we do this smart, we can do both things—get Liza back and carry forward with our mission."

Others in the group nodded in agreement.

McKinley scowled in anger and shook his head with exasperation. "Okay."

Brighton, Filmore and Hastings were assigned to finding and rescuing Alvarez. Henning, Simington and Jim Smyth, the technician, were to lead the first contact effort. Henning said that with the help of the United Space Command and scientists coming in from the other countries, there would be no lack of manpower.

"We need to find Josh Reynolds," said Brighton. "He's the last one to see and talk to Liza. He might be able to help us."

"I'll call the Sydney police," said Hastings. "They'll have his contact info."

"Good," said Brighton. "Now let's all get busy. We have a lot of work to do."

"Jack, there's a new signal," announced Smyth as he burst into the room.

"What does it say?" asked McKinley.

"Not sure, still decoding," said Smyth. "But based on the first couple of lines, you're not going to like it."

> *More data needed.*
> *Authorization status of sender in question.*
> *Authorization status of sender required.*
> *Authorization scope of sender required.*
> *Geo-political status of sender in question.*
> *Geo-political coordination required.*
> *Present communications security in question.*
> *Communications security protocol required.*
> *Nature of source not relevant at this time.*
> *Further communication dependent on stated conditions.*

"Damn," said McKinley. "Not too revealing is it?"

"Looks like they want a lot more than we can give them at this time," said Henning.

"Why do they want this?" asked Simington. "And why won't they tell us who and where they are. I don't like this. I don't trust them."

"I think they feel the same way," said McKinley. "Where did this signal come from? Is it still moving, like the last few?"

"Yes," said Simington. "The source has shifted again. It moved another five thousandths degrees off the center line of the signal path and it is another hundredth of a percent closer to us."

"So, they're still heading this way?" said Henning.

"Appears so," replied Simington.

"What do we do?" asked McKinley. "Do we reply with our own questions again? New questions? Or do we try to answer some of their questions?"

"Based on when we sent our message and when we received this new message, I would bet they did get our last message, have considered it, and responded as they see fit," said Henning. "I don't think asking them again will help. And I don't think they're going to respond unless we answer some of their questions."

"Pushy buggers, aren't they?" said Simington.

"More like cautious, I'd say," said McKinley.

"I agree," said Henning. "But we can't answer some of their questions right now. Jarrod. They want to know who authorized you to communicate with them. I don't think they want to hear that a group of five people at SETI have authorized you to speak for planet Earth."

"And what about this geo-political stuff?" asked Simington. "What can we do about that?"

"I can see why they want to talk to one entity," said McKinley. "Having to answer to the US of NA, and China, and Europe, not to mention all the other countries that might want to respond, would very confusing, if not dangerous. We do need to speak with a unified voice as Earthlings."

"Yeah," said Henning, "but with the sad shape of the United Nations and the history of the planet, how likely is that? The best we can do right now is the United Space Command out of Alice Springs."

"How's that going? Are they here yet?" asked McKinley.

"Just arrived this morning," said Simington. "We're setting them up in admin and integrating several key operators among our staff."

"What about level seven?" asked McKinley.

"We're going to use that old Forsaken command center for other international teams," said Henning. "The Chinese and the USNA have people on the way. When the USNA learned the Chinese were coming, they sent a team. I expect to hear from Europe soon."

"Yeah, we just did," said Smyth. "They want in too."

"Okay," said McKinley. "We have the major scientific forces of the planet on board, we just need to form a politically coordinated entity."

"Not likely to happen, Jarrod," said Simington. "These scientists don't care squat about the politics. They're going to stay as close as possible to what's going on with the signal."

"Agreed," said Henning. "But, I'll talk to the team leaders and try to get some political connections going."

"That's good, Laura," said McKinley. "Also, call a meeting of all the leaders. I want to talk to them. We have to reach some kind of consensus for who will be the point of contact with, what shall we call them, the Source. Until we can get a political entity set up, scientists will have to do."

"What about the security issues?" asked McKinley. "Why do you think they're asking about that?"

"I'd bet it has something to do with all the trouble we've had," replied Simington. "The signal leaks, the threats against you, and Liza's kidnapping. Maybe someone else is trying to communicate with them."

"I think you're right, Jack," McKinley said. "What can we do? I thought we already had security in place."

"Our network is now secure," said Simington. "After the initial leaks, we beefed that up with more encryption and more firewalls. But . . ."

"But what?" asked McKinley.

"Well, it's the signal," said Simington. "We're still using the same coding and protocols the old Forsaken signal was designed with. As you know, it was designed at least twenty years ago. We didn't change it because we weren't even using it. Remember, Forsaken was a fraud perpetrated from Earth. We didn't expect to get a signal from outer space using a bogus message coding designed on Earth twenty years ago."

"What does that mean for us?"

"What it means is that anyone, other countries, space agencies, anyone with a keen interest and the means to do so, could easily intercept both outgoing and incoming signals and decode them. The signals are an open book."

"It doesn't have to be that way," said Henning. "Jim and Jack have been working on new encryption coding since the Forsaken scandal. I've been worried about this ever since the Forsaken scandal broke when I was at the Titan base command. It seemed silly for us to be listening for a signal and have no way to respond securely."

"And I've done some tests," said Smyth. "I think we can overlap this new encryption with our signal code and be okay. I just need a couple of more tests. I could check it out by sending a signal to the USC in Alice."

"Do it," said McKinley. "If it works, we can send a test signal to The Source to see if that satisfies that part of their demand. If it does, we can tell them we are working on their other demands."

"Do you think maybe they are demanding too much?" Simington again.

"Jack, I know you don't trust too many people, and I know you have good reason," said McKinley. "But right now I want to take a different attitude. Without trust, this first contact may never work."

"Okay, Jarrod. But I'm going to keep an eye out."

"Jarrod! Jarrod!" Jenny Hastings called as she rushed into the room. "Liza's on the phone!"

"Time to wake up, Ms. Alvarez."

Gregory Stalingwirth gently shook Liza Alvarez on the shoulder.

Alvarez shook her head and looked about. She was in a very plush apartment. High ceilings spread over a room filled with comfortable sofas and chairs. The walls were adorned with paintings and sculptures rested on a side table and in the hall that looked to lead to the main exit door. A large wall-mounted flat screen TV dominated the room. Off to the side was a kitchen and dining room. Two other doors were closed.

"I hope you are comfortable, Liza," Stalingwirth said. "Our men were under strict orders to not harm you in anyway."

"Forget it, Stalingwirth. Just let me go! You kidnapped me and drugged me and now you want me to play nice? Aren't you going to throw me in a cell like you did Jarrod?"

"Liza, Liza," Stalingwirth replied as softly and as quietly as he could. "You are our guest. You are very important to me, and the people I work for. We want to make you an vital part of our team."

"And what team is that?" Liza asked. "Who do you work for? Why do you want me? I'm nothing. I know nothing. I've been on a farm in Montana for the last three months. I've got nothing you need."

"Don't sell yourself short," said Stalingwirth. "You are a highly educated scientist. Your skills were tested in the SETISCOM Forsaken incident and you came through with flying colors. You have firsthand knowledge of space, signal interception and how to respond."

"Quit bullshitting me. You know that whole Forsaken 'incident,' as you like to call it, was a huge scandal dreamed up by you and your boss just to line your greedy pockets."

"I think you have misunderstood the whole effort," Stalingwirth replied. "We were trying to make contact with our brothers out there in the universe somewhere. Trying to prove the human species is not alone. To prove we are all part of God's universal plan."

"I don't buy it," shot back Alvarez. "Why have you taken me? Let me go, now!"

"Never! And just who are you working for?"

"I can't tell you that right now," said Stalingwirth. "But I can tell you that my, or our, team knows about the new signal received from outer space. We know there have been several signals. We know what the signals have said and where they are coming from. We have massive resources at our disposal and our team stands the best chance of a successful first contact. If you compare our resources with that puny little group of SETI scientists, there is no contest. We will be the ones to make first contact, not SETI. Don't you want to be on the winning team?"

"I'll never be part of your team!" snapped Liza. "I didn't trust you when you were with SETISCOM and I sure don't trust you now, and I don't trust who you work for."

"Now Miss Alvarez, let me try to assure you we are trustworthy," said a slim but well-built man as he stepped into the room from one of the closed doors.

"Let me introduce myself. Jason Ridgeway at your service. Are you comfortable? Can I get you anything? I truly want you to feel you are an important part of my team. What can I do to convince you?"

"You can start by opening the door and letting me go," said Alvarez.

"That time may come, Miss Alvarez. May I call you Liza? I want to earn your trust but you need to give me a chance."

"I don't need to give you anything. Just let me go!"

"First, please listen to me," Ridgeway said quietly, with a pleasant smile on his face.

"My team wants only to have this first contact be as successful as it can for all people. We have the most resources of any entity on Earth. Our scientists, engineers, technicians, political scientists, and business professionals have had years of making space operations work efficiently. We can do the job better than any government or any group of scientists. My team will be the one that leads the way on this, not SETI, not the United States of North America, not the Chinese or Europeans."

"Mr. Ridgeway, if you are so confident, and if you really want to earn my trust, why can't you tell me who you work for?" said Alvarez.

"I can tell you that we are a reputable global business that has done nothing in the past fifty years to warrant any kind of concern. Once you join our team, and convince McKinley to join us, all of our secrets will be revealed."

"Not good enough," said Alvarez.

"All right," sighed Ridgeway. "Let me tell you what I can do for you and your Mr. McKinley. I will place you both in positions of authority. You two will lead our team in all decisions. You will be the point of contact with our new alien friends. It will be you two who set the tone of the future of relations between Earth and whoever is out there trying to contact us.

"In addition, you will have the latest technology at your disposal. My company has the fastest spaceships ever built on Earth. We have invented and are using new forms of communication, remote surveillance, transportation, and the most modern and powerful computer system on the planet. And, we designed it and built it all within our company. When we make contact with the aliens, we will be able to enhance our technology beyond all measure. And you and Mr. McKinley will be at the point of this spear that will advance humankind's knowledge.

"Who knows were that will lead? New knowledge we can only dream about. New worlds. New frontiers in space.

"And you will be well compensated. You both will have all the fame and fortune you will ever need. Your futures will be financially, intellectually and morally satisfying, for the rest of your lives. It's a deal you can't pass up."

"Only one problem," sneered Alvarez. "You're making this offer at the point of a gun. That will never work, with me or with Jarrod. Now just let me go!"

Ridgeway stiffened. His soft, friendly body language tensed into something menacing, like a coiled snake. Then he relaxed and smiled again.

"I can understand why you are upset. And I sincerely apologize for the way you were taken. If I had been in charge of this operation, it wouldn't have happened the way it did." He shot a deadly glance at Stalingwirth.

"I don't buy it," Alvarez replied sternly. "Stalingwirth has never had an original idea of his own. He's just a gofer. I think you are behind this and I don't trust you."

Ridgeway stiffened again and a menacing light flickered in his eyes.

"Okay, Miss Alvarez, if that's the way you want it."

He stood up, grabbed Alvarez by the arm and jerked her toward him. He was stronger than he looked. He grabbed both shoulders and looked her in the eyes.

"You are now going to make a call. You are going to call your hopeless, sad little lover and talk to him. You have two choices. You can be nice and try to convince him to join us, or you can play tough and get yourself, and those you love, in big trouble. And I'm not just talking about you and McKinley. We know where your family lives in Alaska and our reach is long, swift and deadly."

"I will not cooperate," Alvarez sneered back. "Not with a snake like you."

"Very well. Then we'll call McKinley and you will say exactly what I want you to say."

He twisted Alvarez around and with one arm around her neck and one hand grasping her wrist and gave a jerk, pulling her arm up behind her until a sharp pain shot through her shoulder.

She groaned as she fought not to scream and cursed as Ridgeway pushed her to a telephone on the side table.

"We'll make that call now," he said.

"That's all? That's all to their message?" asked Conteus.

"Yes. And it seems appropriate," replied Athrena.

"Why? It is so incomplete. They did not provide the information we requested."

"No, but under the circumstances, I think it is a better response than I hoped for."

"Explain."

"It appears to be a calm, reasoned reply," said Athrena. "Even though they have not answered the questions of McKinley's authority, or who Earth's primary contact will be, they explained that they are working on that. They did not try to bluff their way around the questions. That shows some integrity and some desire to keep the communications open.

"What they did do, to satisfy one of our requests, was to encrypt their signal in an effort to make it secure. We're testing that now to see if it is adequate.

"Also, I'm encouraged that there is no sense of panic in their message. They don't seem too frightened or suspicious of our requests. That means we will be able to keep our motives secret for a time."

"Do you think that is wise?" asked Conteus. "When do we plan to tell them the truth?"

"Remember the plan, Conteus. We have been working on our strategy for two thousand years. We are not sure those on Earth can handle the truth. Even though we have done many things to ease this transition, it has not gone as well as planned. To get their cooperation they have to trust us. Trust will be paramount to the success of the Forgiven Project."

"But how long can we wait? There are forces here on Progenia Prime that think we have wasted too much time and resources on this gradual approach. They believe a more forceful and blunt approach will be better in the long run. And there are others who want to delay or quit the project."

"Now, Conteus," replied Athrena, "do not be so melodramatic. It is only a few fanatics that believe we should use force with Earth."

"Do not be so certain. I receive new reports every day that show their ideas are gaining more support with the public and with the Council. Progenia Prime does not have unlimited resources and, even though Earthlings have wasted many of the resources on their planet, we need some of what they have, and their cooperation, for the next step in the Grand Vision."

"Grand Vision is well underway and on schedule," responded Athrena with a scoff. "We will be fine, no matter what happens on Earth. And remember, a big part of the Forgiven plan is to give us the moral justification, no, the moral credentials, to continue with Grand Vision."

"Still," said Conteus, "there are forces that I worry about. Forces we will have to deal with."

"And I trust you to deal with them," said Athrena. "Keep me informed. If things escalate, perhaps we will have to take action. In the meantime, if our technicians determine the signal encryption used by SETI is adequate, respond to them, thank them for their effort and push them on the other two points— McKinley's authority and the guarantee of a single point of contact for Earth.

"If the small group of scientists at SETI cannot get Earth to cooperate, we may have to step up the timetable and nature of contact, and I do not think that would be good for anyone, Earthlings or Progenians."

Chapter 13

"LIZA, ARE YOU OKAY?" ASKED MCKINLEY as he grabbed the phone from Jenny Hastings.

"Jarrod, I'm fine. But I won't do what they want," replied Alvarez.

"Who are they, Liza? What have they done to you," McKinley asked hurriedly.

McKinley heard a voice in the background behind Alvarez say, "Okay, you've had your chance." And then another voice.

"Mr. McKinley. This is Jason Ridgeway and I'm very happy to finally talk to you."

"What are you doing to Liza?" McKinley shot back. "I want you to release her right now."

"Patience, patience," replied Ridgeway in a calm voice. "Ms. Alvarez is perfectly fine. She is our guest in a fine hotel in Sydney and her well being and comfort is our top priority. Well, maybe our second priority."

"Where is she? I demand to know."

"All in good time, Jarrod. May I call you Jarrod? I've been trying hard to talk to you since you arrived in Australia but you are a very slippery customer.

It does you credit that you were able to evade us in Adelaide and Hawker, but I suspect you had some help."

"I'll tell you what I suspect," shot back McKinley. "I suspect you and your thugs are just a bunch of murdering criminals and I have no reason to talk to you."

"Oh, but you are wrong," replied Ridgway. "I have much to offer you if you will come and join our team and help us become the first contact for your new alien friends."

"I don't know what you're talking about," McKinley replied with a stony voice.

"Sure you do," said Ridgeway. "The new signal. We know of the signals you've sent and the ones you've received. It appears they are for real this time, doesn't it?

"We know you encrypted the last signal you sent and we're confident we'll break that encryption soon."

McKinley paused, placed his hand over the phone and asked Hastings, "Did we send an encrypted signal?"

"Yes, just a half hour ago," said Hastings.

"What do you want?" McKinley asked into the phone.

"Very simply, we want you," said Ridgeway. "For some reason the aliens want to talk to you and if they think you are that important, we want you on our team."

"And what team would that be?" McKinley asked.

"It's a team that can give you much more than you will ever get working with a small group of scientists with few resources."

"Not good enough," said McKinley. "I want the name of your team, who you are working for and why it's so important that I join you."

"All that will come in time, Jarrod. Just let me say that although the company I work for has the best scientists in the world, and the latest technology, we are running into a few problems that we can't solve. We believe a good relationship with the aliens will give us new knowledge that will enable us overcome some those hurdles."

"And then you'll gladly share it with the rest of the world, right?" McKinley said with a scoff.

"What we do with that is our own business, but I assure you we will share everything we think is appropriate."

"I don't buy it," replied McKinley. "I wouldn't work for you on a bet."

"That's a dangerous bet you're making," Ridgeway replied, his voice taking on a much more stern tone.

"I'll take my chances," said McKinley, not backing down an inch.

"Are you willing to take a chance with your fiancé?"

"If you harm Liza, I swear, I will make sure you suffer."

"I'm afraid you give me no choice. If you don't want Liza to suffer, you have to come and join our team, whether you want to or not."

"No deal. We'll find you!"

"Can you find me in ten seconds?" asked Ridgeway in a deadly voice.

McKinley could hear Ridgeway walk a few steps and then heard Liza cry in pain.

"You heard that. There's a lot more where that came from and every ten seconds you delay your commitment to our team, you'll hear another cry from your beloved, until she has no more strength to cry."

McKinley paused and then he heard Liza again, this time almost a scream.

"Okay, okay. I'll do what you say," said McKinley.

"McKinley, listen, and listen carefully. I'm going to say this only once and I expect your full compliance. If you do not comply, Ms. Alvarez will be the one to suffer.

"I know you are in Wilpena Pound. In exactly twenty-four hours from now, two o'clock tomorrow afternoon, you will walk into Hyde Park in downtown Sydney and approach the Archibald Fountain there. Stand there for five minutes without talking or moving. Someone will approach you and you will go with him. Come alone and come unarmed. Do not contact the police or any other law enforcement agency. If you do, you will never see Ms. Alvarez again. Once you are on our team, Ms. Alvarez will have the choice to join you or leave the team. Do you understand?"

"If you harm Liza, I'll—," McKinley started to say, but Ridgeway had disconnected.

"What do we do now?" McKinley turned to face Hastings.

She approached McKinley and put a hand gently on his shoulder, "Jarrod, I'm so sorry," she said.

"Don't be sorry for me, it's Liza we have to worry about."

"We do. But we also have to worry about you," said Janet Brighton, who had joined them, along with Sam Filmore.

"She's right, Jarrod," said Filmore. "We can't risk you getting captured by whoever or whatever Ridgeway represents."

"We know they are absolutely ruthless," said Brighton. "Look what they did in Adelaide and Hawker. They're not beyond killing even their own people."

"And they'll kill Liza unless we do something," McKinley said. "I'm not going to let that happen."

"Jarrod, they might kill her anyway," said Brighton.

"We can't just refuse. That will be a death sentence," said McKinley.

"I agree with Jarrod," said Hastings, stepping forward. "I think I might have a plan that will give us a chance."

"What, Jenny?" McKinley asked.

"Josh Reynolds," said Hastings.

"Josh Reynolds?" said Brighton.

"Yes, I've talked to him. The police gave me his contact info. He's still in Sydney and it seems he got to know Liza pretty well on the plane and feels responsible for her abduction. He wants to help."

"Okay," said McKinley, "but what can he do. He's just one man."

"Well, for starters, he's not the police and the chances are good that neither Stalingwirth nor Ridgeway have ever seen him. They don't know what he looks like. He's a resource we can use without arousing suspicion."

"What did you have in mind?" Brighton asked. "Remember, we're dealing with killers here. Does this Josh know what he's getting into? Does he have any law enforcement experience, any self-defense skills? How can he help?"

"Not sure yet," said Hastings. "I'm not even sure what the plan will be, but I bet we can come up with something that gives us a fighting chance."

"Jenny, not so fast," said Filmore. "What can you do against a company that hires killers and has drones and remote control helicopters at its disposal?"

"We'll be in the middle of Sydney," replied Hastings. "Sydney is my home town. I lived my whole life there before going to Uni in Melbourne. We'll have the advantage there."

"Jenny, we don't know what other weapons this company has. I think we'll be outgunned no matter where we face them," Brighton said.

"Wait. I want to hear what Jenny has to say. I want to work on a plan. I'm not just going to give up. I can't give them what they want—me—and then hope they will be gracious enough to free Liza. We have to try."

"We do," said Hastings.

"We have about twelve hours before we have to fly to Sydney. Jarrod and I will devise a plan, run it by you two and get some help from Josh Reynolds."

"Okay," sighed Brighton. "Let's try."

"Damn, I don't like this," said Filmore. "But maybe we don't have a choice. I just have this terrible feeling that when it's all over, it's going to be tragic."

"Have faith, Sam," McKinley said. "Jenny's going make sure we all get out of this alive. Aren't you Jenny?" He reached out and took Hastings' hand as he looked her in the eyes.

"I'll do my best Jarrod. I really will."

Laura Henning was having a bad day. Pressure was building now that scientific and political entities around the world were taking the alien signal seriously. After the Forsaken scandal, many scientific and political leaders dismissed the first reports of the new signal, even after SETI made the official back-channel announcement.

Those who had logged the signal went back to check the details, and those who had not wanted the data from SETI. Now, after a week, they were taking it seriously and making demands.

Just as she was making headway on that front, the public announcement came out and the usual crowds began to gather outside Wilpena Pound. During the Forsaken scandal a large impromptu and unruly village formed outside the Pound. SETI was better prepared this time. Campsites had been identified, complete with streets, lights, utilities, and food vendors. She had hired a good security chief and he had made some early preparations even before that new signal had arrived. Now though, even with the head start he'd had, he was struggling to keep up.

Henning was continually surprised at how fast people from all over the world could get to Wilpena Pound. There were the usual rubberneckers, but many appeared to have come great distances and were determined to stay as long as needed to get close to any possible first contact.

As the pressure mounted, Henning contacted the South Australia police and requested their presence, partly to keep order in the camps, but more to provide security for the international teams arriving daily.

China was the first team to arrive, landing in Alice Springs at the United Space Command two days ago. The team included lead scientists, top political aides and technicians to support both groups.

Henning, with the help of Jack Simington, had made the scientific team welcome and found places in the SETI control rooms. They would work side by side until the old Level Seven could be retrofitted to house more people.

Level Seven had been the control center for the design, testing and the launch of the satellite that had sent back the fake signal at the heart of the Forsaken scandal. Simington had been tinkering around on Level Seven since SETI took over Wilpena Pound more than six months ago. He had identified systems that were still usable and those that were junk. Surprisingly, most of the equipment was still good. The software, however, was antiquated and needed serious upgrading. Simington had formed a team to get those systems online.

Henning thought the Chinese technicians would be very helpful and would dive into the project with enthusiasm. Simington estimated Level Seven would be online soon and be nearly ready to welcome the United States of North America team, which would arrive tomorrow, and the Europeans the day after.

Henning was not so sure about the political organization, but that was Janet Brighton's problem. Brighton reported that Gen. Harry Jones, commander of the United Space Command, had been a great help. His sense of organization and his political experience had been a lifesaver. Henning was glad she wasn't dealing with the politicians. She had spent the last five years on the Titan Command Base, managing just a few technicians.

Gen. Jones had established a chain of command, giving the Chinese, the USNA and Europe equal footing on an advisory panel. That panel would also include Henning, Janet Brighton and Sam Filmore from SETI. And, of course, Jarrod McKinley would act as host and titular head of the panel. The idea was that once all the panel members arrived, a meeting would formalize the structure. Gen. Jones advised flexibility because everyone on the advisory panel was answerable to a political leader in their home nation or region.

And there were some nations, such as Australia and India, that had no formal positions on the panel but perhaps had legitimate claims to be included.

Australia because it was by default the host country. India's claim was a bit more suspect. That country had no viable space program but it did have a tenuous alliance with China and it offered support services for nearly all the major space exploration companies on the planet.

Henning had found accommodations for everyone. She was getting lots of help from Brighton and Filmore, but they were more concerned about the rescue of Liza Alvarez.

In the midst of all the organization, there was still the signal to deal with. McKinley, Henning, Brighton, and Filmore were meeting to review that progress.

Per Henning, Simington's team had been successful in applying new encryption to the signal and had used it when they replied to the initial list of requirements of the Source.

McKinley's message was simple:

Working on the political organization.
World leaders gathering here now. This
signal carries new encryption for additional
security. Please advise if it is not satisfactory.

"Jarrod, don't you think we should say something else, like set a timetable for when we expect to answer the question of why you are in charge and who speaks for people on Earth?" asked Brighton.

"No," replied McKinley. "I don't want to mislead anyone and I don't want to set unreasonable expectations. We really can't answer those questions until we get some structure established."

"I think our advisory panel is a good start and about all we can do until we meet with everyone," said Henning.

"It will be tomorrow night before everyone is here. We can't do much until then," said Filmore.

"That's fine," said McKinley. "Let's see how the Source replies to our newly encrypted message and go from there. In the meantime, have we been getting any pushback from the Chinese or the North Americans?"

"Not yet," replied Brighton. "But, we have been getting some other requests."

"Oh yeah?"

"There's a small group that claims to represent the public, the common man of Earth, so to speak. They are camped outside Wilpena Pound and want to be included in any decision making, as well as to being represented.

"And then there are the Brazilians, the Indians and the Africans. Gen. Jones believes all continents should be represented. Because we no longer have a functioning United Nations, getting continental representation will be much more important."

"Those are the kinds of decisions this panel of ours will have to make," McKinley said.

"Well, so far, I think we're off to a good start, if we can find a place for everyone here," Brighton said.

"What other options are available?" asked Filmore. "Should we be looking at some kind of headquarters in Sydney, Adelaide, or even New York?"

"We can't do New York," Brighton said. "That would raise questions from the Chinese and the Europeans. They would argue for headquarters in Beijing or London or Berlin."

"I think we should propose a headquarters in Sydney," said McKinley.

"We can't do it without some financial support," replied Brighton. "We're stretched thin just keeping SETI going. We don't have funds for a whole new bureaucracy that a headquarters would require."

"Australia might be willing to fund it," McKinley replied. "It would be a feather in the cap for the country."

"Maybe," said Brighton. "I guess that's another question to put before the panel when it meets."

"Right," said McKinley. "Until then, how are we accommodating all of these people from all around the world?"

"We have quite a bit of room right here at Wilpena Pound," said Filmore. "Remember, the SETISCOM had a much larger workforce than do we. We've cut down our staff about sixty percent. We have many unused rooms. I've got a person doing an inventory. So far, even after the Chinese and North Americans arrive, we still have room for at least a dozen more people. It depends on how many the Europeans try to bring. We haven't heard yet. I understand there's a squabble between the French and Germans as to whose specialists will be on the team. No doubt the European team will be larger and more diverse than other teams."

"You mean more dysfunctional," snickered McKinley.

"Not necessarily," said Filmore. "They just have a lot more disciplines to consider. Some of the best planetary biologists and quantum mechanics physicists are from Europe."

"How are we going to feed all these people, Sam?" asked McKinley.

"We let them know they are going to have pay their own way," replied Brighton. "So far, no big arguments."

"Great," said McKinley. "And, Laura, it seems you and Jack are on top of the signal and the communication with The Source. What else can we do?"

McKinley broke the silence. "Liza, right?"

Everyone nodded in agreement.

"Jenny, what have you got? You were working on a plan."

"Galactic Mining Enterprises," replied Hastings.

"What?" asked Brighton. "What do they have do to with anything? GME has been around since the 2020s when they first started mining in the asteroid belt. I knew of them when I was in New York, but they were strictly business."

"Jason Ridgeway is the CEO of GME's Australian division," Hastings replied. "The same Jason Ridgeway who called and talked to Jarrod."

"That's hard to believe," said McKinley. "Are you sure it's the same guy? I can't believe he would use his real name when he talked to me. He's a kidnapper. He had Liza right there in the same room."

"Josh Reynolds helped me confirm it," Hastings said. "I called Reynolds and he staked out GME headquarters this morning. Around ten o'clock he saw the CEO of GME, Jason Ridgeway, meet with Stalingwirth. I'd already sent him Stalingwirth's photo. The two met at company headquarters and then went to a hotel in downtown Sydney. Josh was following them when he last reported to me."

"It just shows what money will do to you," Filmore responded. "The richest company in the world is getting pretty arrogant, thinking they can just take what they can't buy."

"They really throw their money around," Brighton said. "They always hired the top of the class at engineering schools. Always had the latest technology. They're pretty pushy."

"That's who we're going up against?" Henning said. "How do we fight all that money?"

"Jenny, do you have a plan?" McKinley turned back to Hastings.

"It depends," said Hastings. "It depends on what Reynolds finds out. I have to know where Liza is being held. How much security there is. Can we get in and out? But, I think with Reynolds' help, and I have no reason not to trust him at this point, I might have plan that will work."

"Let's hear it," McKinley said.

"You may not like it," Hastings said, looking at McKinley. "You will be putting yourself in the crosshairs of GME and the likes of Jason Ridgeway."

"Whatever it takes," replied McKinley.

"I don't like it," said Brighton. "I thought we all agreed, Jarrod would not leave Wilpena Pound. He is to stay here and lead this first contact. We can't lose him."

"If my plan works, he won't be in danger and he will never be out of contact," said Hastings.

"And what if it doesn't," retorted Brighton. "What then? I won't agree to a plan that puts Jarrod in jeopardy."

"Then we have a fall-back position. A retreat."

"A retreat?" questioned McKinley. "Does a retreat mean we abandon Liza? I won't agree to that!"

"Please, please," said Filmore. "Jenny has gone over the plan with me. I think it has a good chance of working without endangering anyone, not anyone besides Stalingwirth and Ridgeway, that is."

"Are you sure, Sam?" asked Brighton.

"Feel very confident," nodded Filmore.

"Well, if old skeptical and cautious Sam seems to think it will work, I'm willing to listen," said Brighton.

"Me too," chimed in Henning.

"Okay, Jenny. What've you got?" McKinley asked.

"Here it is," said Hastings, with a twinkle in her eye and a swish of her pony tail. "They'll never see it coming."

"Very good, that is better," said Athrena. "The response from this Jarrod McKinley seems measured, concise and honest."

"But we still do not know who we are talking to," said Conteus. "Their political organization does not nearly match their scientific knowledge. I think you know the success of our plan relies on getting the politics right. Without a united front on Earth, our plan is in jeopardy."

"It is premature to worry too much about that," replied Athrena. "We need to give them time to get their leaders together and make some decisions. We have had our plan in place for centuries and they are just learning about us. We cannot push it too fast. There will have to be a period of adjustment and education, to make them accept reality and what that means to the future of the human species on Earth."

"What if they do not accept? What will we tell them?" asked Conteus.

"They will not have a choice, will they? Once we lay out the facts, they will have to accept it. We have spent many years planting the seeds and I hope that will ease the transition."

"As do I," replied Conteus. "What is our next step?"

"We reply to their latest signal, tell them the encryption is adequate. I am a bit concerned with that mining company that seems to want to interfere. Have we responded to any of its attempts to signal us?"

"No," replied Conteus. "But there has been a development there that could be a problem. It seems they are determined attain the services of Jarrod McKinley."

"I thought we foiled their abduction plan in Adelaide," Athrena said.

"We did, thanks to our agent, but they have now abducted McKinley's fiancé. According to what we are hearing on our intercepts, they have demanded McKinley come to them or they will injure his fiancé. It is just as I feared. This whole project is going too fast. The humans on Earth are not ready. There is too much infighting, too much greed, too much every human for himself or herself."

"Very soon they will have to come together," replied Athrena. "If they do not, they will not survive. McKinley and his team, or the leaders of Earth, will have to figure out how to deal with the likes of this private company. Keep monitoring the situation, but do not interfere unless McKinley's life is threatened."

"There is another situation I am concerned about," said Conteus. "There has been more discussion between some council members about delaying this contact, or scuttling the whole Forgiven program."

"Conteus, we have talked about this before. I am not concerned."

"I think you should be. There is a group of five council members who have been meeting regularly. Now they have begun to agitate among the rest of the council. This protest is growing. They believe our measured approach is a waste of time and resources. They feel more direct action would be better."

"Who are these people?"

"The council representatives from Dorfing, Alegantria, Somilitia, Griefing and Trangilary."

"Brachus from Somilitia is involved? I thought he was one of our strongest supporters?"

"He was, for a long time. Now he is concerned that things are too unsettled on Earth and believes we should advance our schedule."

"But, Conteus, we already did, and the whole council agreed."

"Well, as we get closer to actually carrying out the plan, people get worried. They worry Earthlings will resist. They are not sure the plan will work. They want to move faster, or delay for a very long time."

"They cannot get cold feet now, Conteus. We have all agreed this is something that needs to be done now."

"They are saying we do not have to do it this way. They feel that the long term goals of the Grand Vision can still be accomplished without involving Earth. That the conflict we are likely to create on Earth is unnecessary, and perhaps too dangerous for all concerned."

"But Conteus, they are forgetting the primary motive of the Forgiven plan. That key element is something all Progenians agreed, centuries ago, needs to be seen through to the end. Without that, the rest of our plan carries far less moral authority and without that moral authority how will we have the courage to carry on? Our whole existence is dependent upon a successful execution of the plan. We do not have a choice."

"I know that," replied Conteus, "and I agree. But times have changed and people change. Sometimes convictions waiver. Sometimes short term actions are hard to justify when the rewards are so very distant. Some people cannot see that far ahead, or find it difficult to delay their gratification."

"I thought we got rid of that kind of thinking eons ago," replied Athrena. "That is how we got past our environmental and resource crises of the Platinum era. That is why we do not have any significant global conflicts. We all work together. Doing what is best for everyone in the long term."

"And it has been very successful for the last two thousand years," said Conteus. "Maybe people are taking it too much for granted nowadays."

"We need to gather, discuss this, and find a resolution. If what you say is true, there is probably more to this than just the Forgiven Project. I will speak with Brachus. Then we may have to have a council retreat to resolve this. I do not want to give up on Forgiven. We cannot afford to let our energies be diverted from the plan."

"Very well. I can help with some of the others."

"Back to Mr. McKinley and his merry band of Earthlings. What is next?"

"We will monitor the situation with McKinley's fiancé and Galactic Mining Enterprises. I will alert our agent. Besides that, the next move is up to the SETI team. They have to get the politics sorted out as to who will be a spokesman for Earth. Who will be our point of contact."

"McKinley is the key. We have to encourage them to use him. Send a message that the encryption they have designed will be adequate. In the message drop hints about how important McKinley is to the project. If he is compromised, that changes a fundamental premise of the Forgiven Project."

"It will be done," replied Conteus. He paused and gazed to the side.

"We just received a communication that the SETI team is on the move, headed to Sydney to rescue McKinley's fiancé."

"Good!" exclaimed Athrena. "What kind of trouble are they headed for? Their record of unpredictability and impulsiveness continues."

"But they do not lack courage, do they?"

"They will need more than courage to sustain themselves when Forgiven Project hits."

Jenny Hastings, Jarrod McKinley and Sam Filmore boarded a private jet at the Wilpena Pound airport bound for Sydney, unaware that they were being watched.

High above the airport, if one looked closely and knew what to look for and exactly where to look, a slight shimmering would have been noticed in the sunlight filtering through the scattered clouds.

The scene prompted the individual watching to quickly transfer the image to a wrist-band device and shut down his large monitors. Seconds later the shimmering spot in the sky was gone.

A minute later, in a suburban home in Adelaide,

the garage door opened. Nothing appeared through the open door, but small dust devils floated down the driveway and proceeded to the street. The dust devils grew in size as they moved quickly down the street toward the main highway but then disappeared, leaving just a leaf floating gently back to the pavement.

Chapter 14

The flight to Sydney took only four hours, thanks to a new ramjet personal aircraft supplied by C.R. Duncan and his company, the Australian media conglomerate which owned most of the country's newspapers and online news sites.

When they touched down at a private airfield on the outskirts of Sydney, Josh Reynolds greeted them on the tarmac.

Jarrod McKinley was taken aback. Reynolds reminded him strongly of Brad Johnson, the crew member he had lost on the Titan listening post explosion. His blonde hair, athletic build and confidant stance reassured him but also worried him a bit. Reynolds was a key part of the plan and was putting himself in some danger.

"Are you sure you want to do this?" McKinley asked Reynolds after the group traveled to downtown Sydney.

"Yeah. Dead sure," replied Reynolds.

"Let's not use that word," retorted Filmore. "It spooks me."

"Sorry," said Reynolds. "Just know I want to do

everything I can to help Liza get out of her jam. I feel I really let her down at the airport."

"Don't worry," said Hastings. "If the plan works, no one will be in danger."

"If," said Filmore.

"I have confidence in the plan," said McKinley. "We've gone over it many times and know the layout of the hotel, thanks to Josh. If everyone does their part, we'll be all right."

McKinley pulled out a large, black duffle bag and started reviewing the contents with Reynolds and Hastings.

Hastings pulled out schematics of the hotel where they knew Liza Alvarez was being held by Stalingwirth.

McKinley pulled on a leather pilot's jacket and gave an identical jacket to Reynolds. He placed a bush hat on his head, handing one to Reynolds. When the two stood side by side, it was hard to tell them apart.

Hastings gave McKinley a cell phone. "Remember," she said, "we've agreed to make the swap on the north side of the fifth floor atrium. Don't let them change the location."

"Got it," replied McKinley.

"Okay," said Hastings, "It's time to go. Jarrod, you are about a five minute walk away from the fountain in the park, right over there. Give Josh and me about a five-minute head start and then go to the meeting place. Sam, you head for the rendezvous spot and keep your ears open. If this all goes bad, call the police as we discussed."

"Is everyone ready?"

All gave firm nods and Hastings and Reynolds started toward the hotel and Filmore drove to the rendezvous point.

McKinley waited five minutes and walked slowly toward the Archibald Fountain in Hyde Park. Exactly twenty-four hours after he had talked to Jason Ridgeway, McKinley stepped off the path and stood by the fountain.

He waited. People strolled by casually. McKinley searched the faces for some sign or some sense of danger or evil. Nothing. Four minutes passed. Nothing. Five minutes, nothing.

McKinley was fidgeting. If this plan didn't work, would Liza's life be in danger? Was he doing the right things trying to save her? Should he have just given up and gone to work with Ridgeway and GME? Should he have called the police?

Suddenly a hand came from behind and grabbed his shoulder.

"Don't make any sudden moves, McKinley, and don't turn around," the voice said.

"Is Liza all right?" McKinley demanded.

"She's fine. And she will remain fine if you do exactly as you're told. You need to come with me. We've got a ride to take."

"Where are we going?" McKinley said. "I told you in my text I wanted to make the exchange at the hotel, in public, where you can't pull any of your tricks."

"Sorry," said the voice. "We're not playing by your

rules here. If you want to see your little sweetheart, come with me."

"I refuse," McKinley said with a loud desperate whisper.

"Have it your way," said the voice. "And say goodbye to Liza."

McKinley could hear the man begin dialing a cell phone.

"Okay, okay," said McKinley. "I'll come with you."

The man shoved McKinley's shoulder and they moved off in the exact opposite direction from the hotel.

McKinley reached slowly in his pocket. Hastings had foreseen this possibility and there was a backup plan. Just as his fingers grasped his cell phone, the man's hand jerked his arm, pulling the cell phone out of McKinley's pocket. He knocked the phone to the ground and stomped on it.

"You must think we're really stupid," the man said. "Nice try, but for someone so smart, that was awfully stupid."

He pushed McKinley across a curb they had come to and toward a black sedan whose rear door suddenly opened. He pushed McKinley head first into the car and McKinley literally landed on top of Stalingwirth.

"You snake," McKinley snarled. "Where is Liza?"

"Relax," said Stalingwirth. "She's fine and will be as long as you cooperate. You weren't following our orders were you? Your friends and you had some little plan cooked up, but that's out the window now, isn't it?"

As the black sedan sped away from the curb, Hastings and Reynolds, waiting near the hotel, were looking nervously at their watches. A dreadful feeling was creeping over them. Had they gotten in over their heads? Had they endangered the lives of Jarrod and Liza?

Both jumped at the sudden ringing of Hastings' cell phone. It was Filmore.

"Jenny, what's going on?" demanded Filmore. "I just saw someone push Jarrod into a big, black sedan. Shall I call the police?"

"No. Not yet," replied Hastings. "Ridgeway's obviously not sticking to the plan we agreed on. I don't know whether he saw us or not, but we're going to have to go to plan B. Can you see Jarrod's tracking device on your monitor?"

"Yes, I can," said Filmore. "But the car is moving fast."

"Can you still see the trace?" Hastings asked Filmore as she and Reynolds jumped in the SETI vehicle a few minutes later.

"Yeah, there it is, moving east, toward the harbor. Remind me of what Plan B is."

"We follow them. If it looks like we're going to lose them, then we call the police," replied Hastings.

"I doubt the police will do you much good," said Reynolds. "The way they disappeared at the airport, tells me these guys have a lot of advanced resources, and they know how to use them."

"Just stay close," Hastings said urgently to Filmore. "Speed up Sam, we need to get closer."

"I'm doing the best I can in this traffic." Filmore drove with abandon. The last thing he wanted was to put Jarrod in danger again. He was still upset at leaving him on his own outside of Hawker.

They were closing the gap. They could just spot the black sedan as it pulled off a main street and slowed to drive along a pier where a few fishing boats were tied up. The pier ended at a dock where sizable yachts were moored. Large containers were scattered about amid stacks of bundled goods and fishing equipment. A high chain link fence separated the fishing boats from the yachts at the end of the pier. A video camera monitored a padlocked gate and a large sign warned: *Stay out. Private area. Yacht owners only.*

"Get as close as you can," urged Reynolds. "Pull in between those two containers." He pointed to a spot about fifty meters from where the black sedan had stopped.

"What's your idea?" asked Hastings. "I've already sent a buzz to Jarrod's tracking device. I hope it's on so he knows we're close."

Inside the black sedan, Jarrod's mind was racing and his sense of danger was spiking. He had felt the tiny vibration in his tracking device so he knew his friends were close, but how close? He had to stall for time. He had to take action.

"What are we doing here?" he asked.

"We're going to get Liza," Stalingwirth replied, "just as we promised."

"Where is she?"

"She's close. As soon as you go through that locked gate, she will walk off the nearest yacht. She will go one way. You will go the other, to join our team and change your life, for the better, I might add."

"And what are you going to do with her? Just leave her here?"

"This is a public dock. There's a lot of traffic here and an emergency phone right over there," Stalingwirth said, pointing to the row of shipping warehouses on the pier. "She'll be fine."

"Okay," McKinley said with a sigh. "But I'm not going in that gate until she comes out and walks away. How do I know you won't just slam the gate shut as soon as I walk through?"

Stalingwirth looked around and then asked one of his cohorts, "Number 1. Do you see anything?"

"All clear, boss," replied the man.

"Okay," said Stalingwirth. "Get out of the car and stand there so our men can see you. Then they will release your friend."

McKinley got slowly out of the car. As he did he turned a full 360 degrees before he faced the yachts. As he was turning, he noticed a small flash of reflected light coming from behind a tall pile of fishing nets and buoys.

The rest of the pier was nearly empty, the only

activity being at the far end where a couple of fishing boats had just tied up.

A woman appeared from the yacht, walking slowly down the gangplank and toward the locked gate. McKinley waved and got a wave back. The woman was wearing a large-brimmed hat and he couldn't see her face.

"Okay," said Stalingwirth. "Go through the gate."

"No way," said McKinley. "I can't see her face. I don't know that that's Liza. She has to come out here. I have to see her face."

Stalingwirth signaled his guards and they went to the gate, keyed in a code and the gate swung slowly open. The woman walked through and slowly toward McKinley with her head down.

McKinley still wasn't sure. He could see long flowing dark hair like Liza's and she was the same size. But still he wasn't sure.

When she reached him, he reached up and lifted the brim of the hat. It was Liza. He breathed a sigh of relief and hugged her. When he did he whispered something quickly in her ear.

"Enough of that," Stalingwirth chided. "That will be the last hug. Jarrod, go to the gate."

McKinley gave Liza another hug.

"I said now!" Stalingwirth shouted and motioned for his guards to help urge McKinley along.

"Okay, okay," responded McKinley. "Don't worry," he said to Liza, "things will be all right. Now we have to GO!"

Still holding Liza's hand, McKinley wheeled and

started to sprint in the opposite direction of the gate. Liza struggled to keep up as McKinley pulled her toward the pile of fishing nets.

She stumbled and fell. McKinley kept running.

"Jarrod!" Alvarez cried. But McKinley kept running, grasping his hat as he ran. He dived toward the pile of fishing nets, but stumbled and fell. Stalingwirth's goons were nearly on him.

Splash!

The guards rounded the pile of nets. "Is that him?" one of them shouted.

"No. It's just a life ring," the other replied, as he looked over the edge of the dock. "He's got to be here somewhere."

"There he is! Under the nets."

They grabbed a leg and pulled out McKinley, blood smeared across his forehead and face from the fall.

"Come on, hero," one man scoffed. "Time to go. Diving across this cement pier wasn't too bright, was it?"

"Don't worry," said the other. "The blood will wash off, the scabs will come off and you'll be all pretty again."

McKinley grunted and held his arm across his face.

"Really stupid," snapped Stalingwirth, who was holding Alvarez by the arm. "What do you see in this guy anyway?"

"Jarrod, are you okay?" asked Alvarez.

"Just let her go now," mumbled McKinley.

"Go," Stalingwirth, pushing Alvarez toward the fishing end of the pier. "We've got what we came for."

He shoved McKinley toward the gate and through, pulling it closed behind them.

As Alvarez walked backward away from McKinley she mouthed the words "Jarrod, I love you."

Stalingwirth climbed back in the black sedan and the car wheeled around and sped off the pier.

McKinley was almost to the gangplank of the yacht when a young woman grabbed Alvarez by the arm and pulled her around.

"Liza. I'm a friend of Jarrod's. He's safe. We have to go now!"

As the two ran toward the SETI vehicle, Alvarez tried to get one last glimpse of McKinley.

She saw McKinley jerk away from his guards and run toward the yacht. He swerved to the left and dove off the dock between two of the crafts as bullets whizzed over his head.

"What?" she exclaimed.

"No time," said the young woman as she dragged Alvarez into the SUV.

"Jarrod can't swim!" Alvarez shouted. "He's from Montana. He can't swim."

Chapter 15

"Switch to channel two," Conteus whispered to Athrena as he leaned slightly in her direction.

The two were the only ones seated around a conference table with thirty-four seats. The monitors in front of each seat revealed the current speaker, while the head rest of each seat displayed a live picture of one of the conferees. All areas of the planet were represented on the monitors.

The view on the head rests indicated the attendee who was speaking and those who listened, or in one case, struggled to stay awake as another conferee rattled on about the history of the Forgiven Project.

"It is from Earth," said Conteus. "The SETI team is in trouble again."

"Now what?" asked Athrena as she switched to channel two. The monitor in front of her created a split screen just in time to see Jarrod McKinley break away from two men who appeared to be holding him hostage and race down a dock and dive into a harbor between two large yachts.

"Is our agent there?" asked Athrena.

"Yes," said Conteus. "If he were not, we would be receiving only audio and not the video."

"Very well. Continue to watch but leave that situation to our agent. It will protect McKinley if need be and this conference is far too important for distractions."

Conteus nodded and turned back to his monitor. He focused his eyes between the split screen and a slightly glazed looked passed across his face. He was now fully engaged in both the happenings on Earth and the conference in front of him.

Athrena switched off the split screen just as the speaker was wrapping up.

"So, citizens," the speaker concluded. "The question is, do we allow the long history of the Forgiven Project be forgotten and just abandon our efforts there or do we follow through on a plan that has been unfolding now for centuries?

"I must remind you that the Forgiven Project is just one part of our overall strategy to keep our movement alive and provide us with some of the tools needed for the successful completion of our long-term goals, the next step in our Grand Vision."

"I do not think Earth is ready," said another speaker.

The picture in front of Athrena changed to show the representative from Modail, a part of the planet that was the scientific center of their world.

"Look at the violence still going on," the speaker continued. "True, there are no major wars taking place among the nations of Earth, but the battle now has shifted to the corporations, which, in some cases, have as much power as the nations."

"I think you exaggerate," broke in Athrena. "It is true we have one mining company throwing its weight around, but generally the peoples of Earth are a peaceful bunch."

"I think you underestimate the problem," said the speaker. "This is the first real test they have had of possible alien contact. And look at the violence it is causing."

"But," chimed in another speaker. "It has been violence against them. Not us. Not the 'aliens,' as you so glibly refer to us."

"And there is good reason for that," Athrena responded. "As you know, much of the Forgiven Project has taken this into account and over the last one hundred fifty years we have been conditioning the people of Earth for this moment. I believe they are ready."

"Ready for what?" another speaker interjected. "Do you expect they will sit idly by and just watch us come to their planet?"

"It is not that simple," responded Athrena. "Our approach will be gradual. We have conditioned the Earthlings to accept that there might be other intelligent beings in the Universe besides them. Through our subtle influence and subliminal suggestions to creative people on Earth, we have used movies, literature, built a cult of UFO followers, created myths of alien landings, and more. We just have to convince them we mean them no harm; that we are here to help them join our Grand Vision. After all, it was the opportunities there and their condition that spurred us on thousands of years ago to formulate our vision and a strategy to make that vision a reality. When they begin to trust us, then we can enact our plan."

"Well I am not convinced. And neither are the people of Botanica," said a third speaker. "What can Earth contribute to our plan? They only recently began to produce enough food to feed themselves and to prevent private corporations from starving people just for the bottom line."

"I respect that thought, Heronius," said Athrena. "I feel the operative statement there is that Earth is beyond letting food be a weapon or the means to enrich the already rich. They have come a long way in the last fifty years."

"What about the way they operate in their own solar system," said another. "The private corporations dominate space. It is a commercial playground with tourism, mining and manufacturing all used to build private profits."

"True," said Athrena. "But that is changing. Look at the cooperation between nations in space exploration. That is where the conflicts used to be. I see real progress and I see signs that space corporations will be brought under control.

"I know Forgiven did not foresee moving this fast. We wanted another fifty to a hundred years. But that stunt last year that they called 'Forsaken' disrupted our plans with both negative and positive impacts.

"It brought out the worst of the fanatics, but that was put to rest. It showed the power of the space corporations, but that tide is turning. What it did do was create more interest in life in the Universe than there has been on Earth for fifty years.

"People there are again questioning whether they are alone. Whether there are others out there like them. I think Forgiven should go forward so we can show them the truth."

"And what is that truth?" questioned the first speaker.

"The truth is that Earth is part of the Grand Vision. That it has always been part of the plan. That if Earth wants to survive in the long term, they must join us."

"What if they do not want to?" asked the first speaker.

"It is our mission to make sure they do," said Athrena. "I believe we can."

"I feel there is still too much greed, envy and suspicion to allow that," said the first speaker.

"Jamis, I am truly saddened by that statement," responded Athrena calmly. "We must give the people of Earth the benefit of the doubt and work with them to make this happen. To do that we must first be united. And we have been united for thousands of years. We, as a people, are doing what is morally right. We must continue our mission."

Athrena paused and looked around at the monitors on the back of the seats. All eyes were on her and there were many nods in agreement. This was the time, she reasoned.

"I call for a vote of confidence in the Forgiven Project," declared Athrena. "Shall we carry on with our mission? All in favor mark accordingly."

She watched as green lights flickered on, showing agreement. Some went on quickly, others hesitated. Soon, all lights were on. Thirty-two green lights, no red lights, and two blue lights. The final tally was thirty-two in favor, none voting against, and two not casting votes.

Jamis and Heronius, the two most outspoken conferees, had not voted. They represented two critical segments of the planet, Technology and Botanics.

"The project goes forward with thirty-two yes votes, zero no votes and two non-votes," Athrena said. "Jamis and Heronius, may I come to your sectors and visit with you about your concerns?"

Both conferees nodded in ascent.

"Very well," said Athrena. "I will see you later."

As the monitors around the table flickered off, Athrena turned to Conteus.

"This is trouble," she said. "This is the first time in a thousand years we have not had unanimous support for the Forgiven Project."

"I am worried," said Conteus. "It is an indication there is trouble stirring on the planet."

"We must work harder to win them to our side," said Athrena. "Forgiven must go on. Speaking of trouble, how is Jarrod McKinley doing?"

"I last observed him disappearing in the harbor," replied Conteus. "Our agent is searching, but there are many more from the mining company looking for him. I fear he is either going to drown or be captured by GME."

"Tell our agent that cannot happen. If we cannot control this situation, do you know what that will do for support here for Forgiven?"

"It will be dead," replied Conteus.

"Let us hope that is not McKinley's fate."

Chapter 16

Janet Brighton was having trouble. Accommodations at Wilpena Pound were filling up fast. Scientific and diplomatic teams from around the planet were flooding into the complex. The Chinese and United States of North Americans had arrived a couple of days ago and were settled, although there were some complaints about the rooms (too old) and the communications (too slow).

Now the European teams were here and raising a fuss about having to take what was left. Brighton explained all the facilities in the complex were the same. The only spaces larger and more luxurious than any other were the executive suites that had been occupied by the Rev. Christopher Larchmont and his assistant Gregory Stalingwirth, the leaders of the fraudulent Forsaken project. Those suites had been locked and the SETI team stayed in the two-room units similar to those that everyone else occupied.

McKinley, Brighton and Filmore agreed the luxury suites would only be used by visiting dignitaries, if there were any. Up to this point, the need had not arisen.

However, now some of the diplomats were eying the suites and wondering why they should not be housed there. Brighton was firm. Maybe if the King of the United Kingdom paid a visit, the President of USNA, or the Chinese Premier, but no one of any lesser stature would be allowed in the suites.

A bigger problem for Brighton was finding room for everyone. The European delegation was twice the size of the Chinese and USNA delegations, and India, Japan and the African Congress also wanted space. Decisions would have to be made that Brighton didn't think she should make.

"I don't want to be the one to tell the Indians or the Japanese they can't be here," Brighton said to Laura Henning. "And the Africans want in too."

"Well, I think we could send a few of the diplomats home," said Henning. "The scientific teams are more important. Every diplomat seems to need two assistants. I don't think we need them."

"Hmm," said Brighton. "Perhaps that's true right now when so many scientific questions are unanswered. But, if we're going to put together a united front as a planet, we'll need all the diplomacy we can get."

"Okay, but can't we limit each diplomat to just one assistant?"

"We can make the recommendation. But I don't know how to enforce it."

"I think the best we can do is to get the delegations from those we invited together and have them set some ground rules," said Henning.

"That might work. But there are still requests coming in from all over the world. Indonesia wants in, South America has no representation. The Russians say they deserve a place."

"Not everyone can be here," said Henning. "We might have to double up in our single rooms just to get the major players here."

"There are the cells in Level Seven," said Brighton with a laugh.

"Sure," said Henning with a chuckle. "Like the one room, bare walls, iron beds and no windows cell that Jarrod was locked up in by Larchmont. Don't think that will work."

"Just kidding," replied Brighton. "But we will be out of room very soon and I don't want to be the person who upsets someone who could do us damage."

"Our first meeting with the major delegations is this afternoon. Shall we address the issue then?"

"Okay," said Brighton as she answered the phone on her desk.

"Hi, Jack. What's going on?"

A serious frown spread across her face and her eyes widened with alarm.

"When? How bad is it? Have you told anyone else?" She listened for a minute.

"Just a moment. Laura is right here. Let's not say anything else on the phone. We don't know how deep this goes."

She paused again, "Yes come right up to the office. And tell Smyth not to mention this. We don't want a panic."

"What's going on," asked Henning as Brighton hung up the phone.

"Jack says we have had another leak."

"Was the signal compromised?" asked Henning.

"He doesn't think so, but he's not sure and it could be worse than that," said Brighton. "It appears someone has hacked into our internal servers and has been reading our internal memos and emails."

"How could that happen? We took the internal system offline," said Henning.

"Jack thinks it's an inside job," said Brighton. "Maybe someone from the Chinese or USNA delegations. Or maybe someone from SETI. Jack can't be sure right now."

"It might be a mole from Galactic Mining Enterprises," said Henning. "They seemed to know about our plan to rescue Liza."

"If that's the case, because of our recording system, everything we've been saying could be going straight to GME."

"That's dangerous," said Henning.

"Yeah," said Brighton. "What have you heard from Sydney?"

"Last I heard Sam, Jenny and Josh were following a signal from a car that had picked up Jarrod and was heading for the docks."

Jack Simington burst through the door.

"It's worse than I thought," he said. "Damn those buggers at GME. They must have access to our system and that means we've got a mole and have had one for some time."

"Why," asked Brighton. "What's happened now?"

"It's Sydney," said Simington, holding up his cell phone. "Sam called from the dock. There's been an exchange and they've got Liza."

"That's good news then!" said Henning.

"Yeah," said Simington. "But there's also been gunfire and now both Jarrod and Josh are missing!"

Jason Ridgeway slammed the sat phone down on his desk, cursed and punched the intercom.

"Riley. Get in here!" he demanded.

A tall, tanned and lean man in his early forties came through the door. He was wearing a tight fitting two piece gray athletic suit that accentuated his muscular build and his quick, fluid moves. On his right side a bulge under the suit top hinted of some kind of weapon.

"Stalingwirth has bungled it again," fumed Ridgeway. "He's lost the Alvarez woman and McKinley got away before we could grab him."

"What now sir?" asked Colin Riley.

"Stalingwirth has failed three times now and he knows way too much about our strategy, our people and our technology. He needs to disappear."

"Temporarily or permanently?" asked Riley.

"Don't care. And I don't want to know. I just want him out of the way where he can't hurt us."

"I'll make arrangements," said Riley.

"And I still want McKinley," said Ridgeway. "Our

plan will not work without him and the stakes are way too high to quit now."

"I'll contact our contractors," said Riley.

"No," said Ridgeway. "I want you and your men to handle this."

"Sir, I must caution you that it will be much harder to protect you and the company if our men are involved."

"I'm tired of failure. I'm tired of working with amateurs. I want this taken care now and I want it done right. I have people to answer to and they're not going to take failure much longer. They want McKinley and we, you, are going to deliver him."

"What's the plan, sir?" Riley asked.

"That's up to you," said Ridgeway. "Use any force you need. Use all the resources available to you. Just get it done."

"What's the status?"

"Stalingwirth just called. He and his team are at the docks. The SETI team has this Alvarez women and McKinley dived into the bay to escape his men. Get down there as fast as you can. Mop up this situation and then get a bead on McKinley. You have two days to deliver him to me and the company."

"That's not much time to come up with a plan."

"That's all the time you've got," snapped Ridgeway as he turned back to his desk.

"Yes sir," Colin Riley replied and with a quick turn headed for the door.

Colin Riley was worried. True, the contractors and Stalingwirth had shown remarkable incompetence in the apprehension of Jarrod McKinley. But McKinley had also shown an uncanny knack for evading very concentrated schemes to capture him. Whether it was luck, or skill, McKinley had something that set him apart. This would not be as easy as Ridgeway made it seem.

But Colin Riley had battled many worthy adversaries in his life. He had been team leader on one of the last Special Forces strike forces before the USNA had demilitarized. He had captured the worst of the world's terrorists, undercover agents from the fading Russian empire and, more recently, he'd been able to compromise wealthy executives protected by huge security forces.

One man, aided only by a few untrained and unskilled friends, should be easy prey. But for some reason, Riley could sense an uncertainty about this mission.

"Okay," Riley said as he received the report and climbed into a two-passenger black helicopter. He would have to move fast to find McKinley and he needed to enact another plan to protect the company. He would need another level of clearance. He pulled out a secure satellite phone and punched in a fourteen-digit code.

A computerized voice came on the phone asking for a confirmation code. He typed in another fourteen-digit sequence. "Authorized," said the computer.

"Speak," said a human voice on the other end of the connection.

"Agent 43 needs authorization 0088," Riley said.

"Justification required," responded the voice.

"Refer to transmission 401," said Riley.

After a moment of silence the voice said, "Authorization granted. Sending authorization code."

Riley saved the code in an encrypted file on the phone and sighed in relief. Now he was on his own with the backing of the company. He had authorization to use all company resources, not just those in Australia. His authorization granted him one more clearance—to make sure that whatever happened was not traceable to company headquarters, even if it meant dealing with Mr. Ridgeway.

As his helicopter bore down on the Sydney docks, Riley was already formulating his plan to capture Jarrod McKinley. It would not be subtle and the small group of SETI scientists would have little defense. He smiled to himself as he thought of the surprise he was about to unleash on Jarrod McKinley.

All he had to do now was find him.

A half hour later two simultaneous explosions rocked Sydney. One happened just off the dock at the Sydney pier, and the other on a main street leading from the bay. A large yacht went up in a huge fireball and began sinking as shrapnel fell into the water. On the streets of Sydney a dark limousine was blown into the sky in a ball of flames and came to rest on its top. The blast shattered windows of the sleek skyscraper that housed Galactic Mining Enterprises.

Jarrod McKinley surfaced slowly at the edge of the dock. He could hear Stalingwirth barking out orders on the dock just above him and beyond the pile of fishing nets and containers. It appeared the impromptu deception had worked. When he launched himself behind the fishing nets where he'd noticed the flash of light, Josh Reynolds was waiting for him.

Reynolds noticed the abrasion on McKinley's face and used his hand to transfer a bit of McKinley's blood to his own face and pointed to the water. "Dive," he ordered.

McKinley didn't have time to question Reynolds, even though he was not a good swimmer. He could hear Stalingwirth's goons hot on his heels. He jumped off the dock and went feet first into the water. He heard another splash just before his head went under.

Now he stayed as still as he could and listened carefully. Stalingwirth was buying it. He thought Reynolds was him. He heard Stalingwirth order his men to grab Reynolds and then order him through the gates into the docks where the yachts were moored. A few second later he heard men shouting, a splash and then gunshots.

"Where is he?" one of the guards shouted. "Find him. There'll be hell to pay if he gets away again."

McKinley wanted to help, but what could he do? Reynolds was on his own now. McKinley was more worried about Liza Alvarez. Was the switch made? He could see nothing and could only hear the confusion near the yachts.

He looked the other way down the dock and then remembered his sense of danger. He had been ignoring it during the rescue attempt, knowing danger was going to be all around him. He realized now that might have been a mistake. Maybe he could have sensed Stalingwirth's change of plans. Now he tried to focus that sense.

Danger emanated from the yacht end of the dock. The other way seemed safer and he saw a ladder reaching up from the water about a hundred meters away. Using his hands to cling to the edge of the pilings and stay afloat, McKinley worked his way quickly but silently to the ladder. He started climbing but stopped as he heard a noise above him. No sense of danger. He was only an arm's length from reaching the dock when a head pushed over the edge.

"Hurry! Hurry!" It was Sam Filmore.

"What happened? Where's Josh? Did we get Liza?"

"No time for questions," said Filmore. "We've got about two seconds to get out of here."

Filmore pulled McKinley onto the dock and pushed him toward the SETI van.

"Get in," he ordered. "We have to go."

The back door swung open and Filmore literally pushed McKinley through the opening.

McKinley was sprawling on the floor when he was grabbed by a pair of hands.

"Jarrod. Jarrod. Thank God." It was Liza.

"Are you all right?" said McKinley as he climbed into the seat. "Did they hurt you?"

"I'm fine," said Alvarez. "How about you? I was worried. I know you can't swim."

"Didn't have to," said McKinley. "There were plenty of handholds. Where's Josh? I heard a splash, some gunfire. Where's Stalingwirth? He's going to be pissed."

"Josh is in the water," said Jenny Hastings, looking back from the front seat. "Stalingwirth's limo is leaving the dock."

"We should stay," said Alvarez. "Josh tried to save me at the airport. Now this. We can't leave him."

"Josh volunteered for this," said Filmore who was swinging the van around and accelerating off the dock toward the street. "We can't wait. If we do we endanger you and Jarrod, and the plan was to save you. To get both of you out the clutches of Stalingwirth. As soon as he finds out his plan went bad, he's going to be searching for you again."

"But Josh . . ."

"I'm sorry Liza," said McKinley. "Sam's right. After we get away from here and make sure we're clear, we can send someone to find Josh. We have to remember what our primary mission is—the signal."

"You and your damn signal," Alvarez barked back. "It's going to get us all killed."

"Liza," said Hastings as she reached back and put a hand on Alvarez. "I'm sorry, but I agree. It's not nice. Maybe not even right. But this is the way it has to be. Jarrod is safe. We have you back. We need to get back to Wilpena Pound where we'll all be safe. I hope Josh will be okay. He's young and strong."

The SETI van was well away from the dock and headed to the private airport and the jet waiting to take them back to Wilpena Pound when a police cruiser with lights flashing and sirens blaring raced past them in the opposite direction, headed toward downtown Sydney.

Two large plumes of smoke were rising in the skyline. From what Jarrod could estimate, one was coming from downtown and another from somewhere on the bay.

"What the hell," swore McKinley. "I hope that's not . . ."

"Keep driving Sam," said Hastings. "We need to get to the airport."

"Oh, Josh." said Alvarez with a whimper.

Josh Reynolds felt a lot safer once he entered the water. During his college days in California he spent a lot of time on the beaches, surfing, long-distance swimming, and working as a lifeguard. Part of his lifeguard training was swimming out into the ocean and pulling people to safety.

Now it looked like all that training was going to come to good use, just to save himself. He dived deeper as he heard bullets zinging through the water. The guards who had been manhandling him, and one on the yacht, were firing randomly. They didn't know where he was. He swam under the yacht to the stern, grabbed a quick breath, dove under again, and headed out into the bay.

He was very skeptical of the last-minute plan devised by Hastings as they drove on to the dock.

But when the deception worked, when he was mistaken for McKinley and herded toward the yacht, he thought there might just be a chance. The only problem was, the plan ended once the exchange was made. He was truly on his own now. There had been no plan to rescue him. No mention of where or how he would find the people from SETI. He had only a few contact numbers, the name of a mysterious space facility somewhere in the outback, and names of people he had met only once, just a few hours earlier, written down on a slip of paper.

Would they wait around for him? Unlikely, he thought, knowing that Jarrod McKinley was the top priority for a secret project not shared with him. They didn't really need him now.

But there was Liza. He couldn't stop thinking about her. He believed the switch had worked. The last thing he saw was Jenny Hastings taking Liza by the arm and dragging her back to the van.

He had lost his hat when he dived into the bay, but he was still wearing the heavy jacket that had been part of his disguise. It weighed him down, making swimming hard and slow. He dove again and stripped off the jacket, letting it sink. He started to swim again, but realized all of the contact information was in the jacket. He sucked in a big gulp of air and dove. The jacket was sinking fast. He pushed hard, straining every muscle. He was gaining on the jacket, but not fast enough. He pushed hard again and reached out. He missed by inches. His lungs were about to burst. He stopped, turned up and reached for the surface, slowly exhaling as he went. He exploded through the surface, gasped for air and quickly ducked under again. Slowly he peeked above the water line. He was about two hundred meters from the yacht and could see the crew launching a small boat to mount a search.

He dipped under the water and began swimming hard again. He wasn't sure how wide the bay was but it looked to be at least a mile. Not too far for a swim, he thought, but not one I'm used to doing when killers are searching for me.

Now he was truly on his own. All the contact information had gone down with the jacket. He started repeating in his mind the names and places he had heard that morning—Jarrod McKinley, Sam Filmore, Jenny Hastings, something called SETI, some mysterious space facility called Wila-something, and . . . Liza Alvarez.

Maybe he should just forget it. He was in Australia for a surfing holiday, he reminded himself. And there was school, a career, a future, and . . . Liza.

Reynolds surfaced and looked back. The small boat was searching the area about the docks, weaving in and out around the yachts. They didn't think he would swim out into the bay, heading away from land. He continued swimming, but when he felt the shock wave of an explosion, he surfaced.

The yacht that he would have been on went up in a huge fireball that took a couple of other yachts with it. The men in the small search boat were lucky, they had been a few boats away and were only knocked flat. The crew of the yacht? A sickening feeling crept over Reynolds. This was a deadly business. Was he now a marked man? Did he have any safe haven? He didn't even know where the SETI team had gone.

The thought gave him an additional adrenalin rush and he swam faster. This bay was probably not a safe place. After a few more minutes of swimming underwater he surfaced. He figured he was far enough away from the dock now that he could swim on the surface. And the people who were looking for him had their own problems.

He swam using the freestyle stroke that had led to several records in his competitive swimming back in California. The other side of the bay was closer than the docks he had left.

He heard a rumble, and looked up to see a black helicopter swing low over the docks. It circled the yacht that had exploded and hovered over the little search boat. Moments later shots rang out and the men in the boat slumped and disappeared into the boat. A large blast from the helicopter sank the boat. Reynolds swam like crazy.

The black copter moved slowly up and down the water near the docks. It was looking for him, Reynolds was sure. As the copter made each pass it moved further out in the bay, closer and closer to him. He was in a race now. Could he reach the shore before the copter made a sweep over him? What was it using? Sonar? Radar? Infrared? It was probably something that could spot him no matter where he was. Reynolds swam harder. The copter crept closer and closer. After each pass, it seemed to narrow the search pattern. It was almost as if they could see his trail in the water.

He was starting to feel a strong sense of vulnerability. Alone in the water. No place to hide. He tried to sprint, but he was becoming exhausted. He was getting close to shore now and estimated he would just make it. A horn blared loudly to his right. A large speedboat was on top of him. He was too exhausted to dive so he pushed hard to move. The speedboat swerved just as it was on top of him, the propeller missing him by inches. Luckily he was on the shore side of the boat as it roared past. The wake of the boat pushed him to the shore and his speed increased markedly. He was going to make it.

Reynolds lunged to the beach, gasping for breath and rolled over on his back. He could see the black helicopter getting closer. It was still making sweeps, but very narrow in scope and coming quickly his way. He looked around for cover. He must be in some kind of a public park. He noticed a path, some tables, and wide swathes of mown grass. No place to hide.

He jumped to his feet and ran toward a cluster of trees about a hundred meters from the shore. As he took shelter under a tree, he searched his surroundings for better cover. If the helicopter pilot could follow him through the water, a heat signature on land would be easy.

He spotted a tunnel out of which a small stream flowed. It must be a stormwater drain, he thought. He ran to the entrance but found a heavy steel grate blocking it. He grabbed the grating and pulled. It moved just a bit and he pulled again. No use. It was too solid.

Reynolds grabbed a large piece of driftwood and pried on the grate. He got a corner loose and pried some more. He glanced back toward the beach. The helicopter had reached the shore and was now pointing directly into the park in his direction. He slipped behind the grate into the tunnel. He would either be hidden or trapped.

He breathed a sigh of exhaustion. There wasn't much more he could do.

A quiet rustle just outside the tunnel made him turn. A figure dressed in black leather approached, holding some kind of scanning device that illuminated his footprints!

Each footprint seemed to glow as they led the figure directly to him.

When it reached the grate, the scanning device was swept forward and showed his footprints leading right to him.

Reynolds looked back in the tunnel. It was black as a moonless night and he had no light. He inched back trying to feel his way. He ran into a brick wall. A smaller hole and another grate blocked his way.

A small blast rocked him. The grate fell away and Reynolds was bathed in light.

"Okay, Mr. McKinley," a strong male voice said. "Your little run has ended and your escape plan has failed."

"Don't know what you're talking about," responded Reynolds. The man had on a helmet with a black visor. It was impossible to see a face.

"You can make it easy on yourself and easy for me," the man said. "Come voluntarily or come after a little shock."

"No," said Reynolds.

"Have it your way, McKinley," said the man.

A sharp pain like a thousand pin pricks assaulted Reynolds before he collapsed in the dark tunnel.

"Damn," said the man. "Now I've got to carry this piece of crud."

He dragged Reynolds out of the tunnel, past the grate and onto a grassy area near where the helicopter was parked.

He rolled Reynolds over so his face was in full sunlight. He grabbed a photo out of a pocket and stared.

"Shit," was all he said.

He turned quickly, ran to his craft and a minute later the rotor wash was blowing debris as the helicopter lifted off and headed out over the bay.

A few minutes later Josh Reynolds shook his head. It felt like it was going to fall off. He tried to open his eyes but quickly closed them against the blinding sun. He tried to turn away from the sun and realized he was lying on the grass. He was still wet and now muddy from the tunnel. The last thing he remembered was a blinding flash and sharp pain. He had a gash on his right hand and he felt bruised on his back and shoulder.

He rolled over, got on his hands and knees and was

about to get up when a hand pushed hard against his back.

"Stay on the ground," a voice said. "Hands behind your back."

Reynolds started to protest, but he was pushed down, his hands grabbed and jerked behind his back and his wrists pinched as a pair of handcuffs clicked ominously.

Athrena stepped from her craft to the moving sidewalk inside the transport terminal in Agrillia, provincial capital of Botanica, one of the seven provinces on Progenia Prime. As she looked out the windows she was glad to be here. Agrillia was the center of the planet's agricultural network that kept the planet, and some its colonies fed with good, wholesome, natural food. Lush fields were bustling with automated crop tenders, harvester, tillers, and planters.

Centuries ago Progenia Prime's scientists had learned how to manipulate the climate so growing conditions were generally more than favorable for this part of the planet. True, they had not fully mastered the natural cycles. There were still storms that caused destruction, flooding, killing frosts, and scorching droughts, but with a whole planet at their disposal, the agronomists were able to put all the land to the most suitable use—fruits in one part, grains another, animal grazing in another, fiber production in another.

The move back to natural products also had occurred centuries ago. Athrena had learned in early childhood education that the synthetic products that scientists once had thought would be the answer to satisfy demands also had unintended side effects such as cancers, birth defects, early dementia. Natural was a better way and with the whole planet being coordinated and supply chains running smoothly and without political bias, everyone on Progenia Prime had all the healthy food and fiber they needed.

Agrillia was the most suitable area for plant growth, hence the brilliantly green and lush fields she was seeing. With proper husbanding and working toward long term production rather than short term gains, the land tenders had been achieving this level of production for generations.

She would have to congratulate Heronius on the continued good work of his department and of the people of the Botanica province.

But she wasn't here to offer congratulations. She was on a mission to convince two leaders of the value of continuing the Forgiven Project. Heronius and Jamis had not voted against the project, but they had abstained. It was a sharp warning signal that trouble could be brewing and she wanted cool the simmering discontent.

For generations, policy on Progenia had been governed by consensus, accomplished by careful crafting of policies after taking into consideration the needs, wants and desires of everyone on the planet. Almost all policies were approved unanimously. She reminded herself that the Forgiven Project had been approved unanimously too, but that was more than four thousand years ago and leaders had changed, opinions evolved and perspectives altered.

Jamis, provincial leader of Modail, the technology province, and Heronius from Botanica, were among the most influential leaders on the planet, and for good reason. The food and fiber and technology that had saved the planet thousands of years ago, were the bedrocks of present stability and the hope for the future. The Grand Vision could not be completed without their support and, Athrena was convinced, neither could Forgiven. And Forgiven was a key to completing the Grand Vision. Now she had to convince Jamis and Heronius. She would meet with them face to face.

Leaving the transport terminal in an air car, she punched in the coordinates to Heronius's office and reviewed her strategy to convince the leaders to continue with Forgiven. Besides the moral argument, she didn't have many strong justifications for continuing. Could Earth offer new technology? Not really. In fact, most of Earth's technology was far inferior to Progenia Prime's. Did Progenia Prime need the food or water of Earth? No. Progenia Prime was doing just fine feeding itself and Earth was still struggling to balance its nutritional needs with its production capabilities.

But there was one thing on Earth not found on Progenia Prime and Athrena needed to convince Jamis and Heronius that if they could only capture that element, the success of the Grand Vision would be greatly enhanced. In addition, there was still the moral consideration. And that was strong.

She was warmly greeted in Heronius's office by the two leaders. Athrena complimented Heronius on the beauty of his region.

"Beauty translates into production," he replied.

She complimented Jamis on his latest achievement, a further reduction of the time-shrinking differential in the sling point network.

"A long way to go, still," Jamis replied with a smile and slight nod.

"Gentlemen, we all know why we are here, so we might as well get right to the point—the Forgiven Project. I was hoping after some discussion we might come to agreement on the issue."

"I am very willing to listen," Heronius said.

"As am I. Are you?" said Jamis.

"Certainly," replied Athrena. "That is why I am here. I have often stated the case for Forgiven. Our history with Earth, our motives to continue, our moral obligation to ourselves, the advantages it will create as we go forward with the Grand Vision. I would like to hear what your concerns are. Heronius?"

"I have concerns about the sustainability of our food and fiber system if we are going to take on the population of Earth. They do not seem to have control of their production, which barely is able to adequately feed their planet. They have not fully endorsed natural food and fiber and integrating their system into ours would be difficult. They are still practicing too much of a depletion economy, not sustainability. They are seriously depleting some of the most fundamental resources, water and soil nutrition."

"I agree with your assessment Heronius," replied Athrena, "but I think they are making progress on those fronts and Forgiven never envisioned we would supply resources to Earth, quite the contrary."

"But I worry that when they learn of our standard of living, they will feel quite impoverished by comparison. Especially some of the poorer regions. Earth has had trouble in the past by not balancing resources."

"I agree with Heronius," said Jamis. "The same can be said for technology. The planet has not balanced the benefits of its present technology. What happens when they see what our advanced technology can do?"

"Again, it was never the intent of Forgiven to give Earth our technology. Instead we intend to take what we want of theirs and let them deal with the consequences. We might show them what is available, whether they like it or not. What they do with it is up to them. Remember one of the fundamental tenets of Forgiven, we do not help them, they have to help themselves."

"That is what concerns me," said Jamis. "They have a hard time helping themselves. By that I mean that it seems the people of Earth are only out for themselves. Each trying to be the first, be the best, be superior to everyone else. Do we want to get involved in that?"

"Consider what you just said," replied Athrena. "Can we not take advantage of that? Is not that spirit something we can use? That ambition, that desire to be first, to push the envelope, to stretch the limits of their capability. Do not we need some of that right now? That spirit?"

"Perhaps," said Heronius. "But, can we control it or will it bring the destructive competition we have witnessed on Earth for centuries?"

"I will remind you of two factors," Athrena said. "If we compare the progress of Earth toward a higher technology and a higher standard of living with that of Progenia Prime, Earth's timeline moved much faster. They have been in the modern age just under two hundred years and they are already exploring their solar system. It took Progenia Prime nearly a thousand years of modern civilization to achieve the same.

"Second, Earth is still a long way away and we control access to our system, to the universe. We can control what gets back to our system and to those already part of the Grand Vision."

"You must admit, Athrena, Earth has had a little help along the way," said Jamis. "They did not do it all on their own."

"True, but with so LITTLE HELP FROM US THAT THEY believe they did it themselves," replied Athrena. "And what help they had was balanced by some of the re*striction*s they faced. They had a much tougher system than we had here. Some parts of that planet are very gentle, but much of it—the deserts, the vast oceans, the polar caps—we have never had to face here."

"Perhaps."

"Remember our commitment when we launched this project," continued Athrena. "We decided we wanted to bring Earth into the fold, so to speak. That meant a long period, more than a century, of educating the people of Earth. Besides a few scientific hints along the way, we had to point them to answers to major questions we knew the species would have. What are the stars? Why are they up in the sky and we are down here? Are there others like us up there, in the sky? Knowing of their curiosity and their mental abilities, we knew they would develop some of their own theories. It was our mission to guide them in the right direction."

"I would say we had only marginal success there," countered Jamis with a scoff.

"True, the hints of extra terrestrials we supplied sometimes were taken to the extreme," said Athrena. "But overall, the books, the movies, even those silly video games over the years brought a general acceptance that there was other life in the universe, and some of it might be similar to that on Earth."

"There are still many people on Earth who do not believe that," said Heronius. "And many who very much still fear what is out there."

"And perhaps with good reason, if they truly understood what is to be discovered in nearby star systems," added Jamis.

"We believe there are many more willing to accept an approach by us, extra terrestrials. And we have taken more direct steps to try to get that message across. That is why right now is a good time take a few steps forward with the project, although it is a little sooner than we planned."

"What steps?" asked Jamis.

"We have agents posted to help, when help is needed," replied Athrena. "One of our agents is monitoring the situation and can intervene."

"That is one agent," said Heronius, "Can that really help?"

"We have others besides the one on scene and we have additional resources."

"You are talking about the blending project, are you not?" asked Jamis.

"I cannot be specific. But things have fallen into place regarding that."

"How likely will they be to fall out of place?" asked Jamis.

"We have actively been working on this project now for more than two hundred years and things have now aligned to where we believe this is the right time to move forward. If not now, it might be another hundred years, and I am sure you do not want to delay the Grand Vision for another century. I know all of the excellent work you both have done on the Grand Vision and I know you both want to move forward on that."

"But with Earth in tow?" said Heronius.

"No one over the centuries of this plan has ever seriously questioned that premise," said Athrena. "Are you now questioning generations of a moral obligation?"

"No, but . . ." Jamis trailed off.

"I know there are risks. But would we have progressed as far as we have without risks? Remember it was the original risk that put us on this path. Can we abandon our long held principles because risk makes us uncomfortable?"

"If you put it that way," muttered Heronius.

"I suppose not," agreed Jamis.

"Thank you for understanding. I appreciate your willingness to listen and I will do all I can to ensure Forgiven does not manifest the problems that concern you both. Can we agree to go forward?"

Jamis and Heronius nodded and rose to shake the hand of Athrena.

"You will have the support of Botanica," Heronius said.

"And Modail," said Jamis.

"Please make your support known to the others," Athrena requested as she left the capital building.

Jamis and Heronius stood together, talking quietly and at times shaking their heads in frustration. After a few minutes of conversation they nodded, shook hands and left the room in opposite directions.

Athrena, back in the air car heading to the transport terminal, signaled Conteus.

"We have agreement," she said, when she made contact. "This should smooth the waters a bit to continue."

"Very good," replied Conteus. "Now if we could just control things a little better on Earth."

"What now?" Athrena asked with a sigh.

"It is Jarrod McKinley. In and out of one crisis

after another. I fear those Earthlings will never get organized."

"Is he still safe?" asked Athrena.

"At this moment," replied Conteus. "But our agent reports a new and more dangerous threat is bearing down on the SETI team. He says . . . wait. There another signal from the agent."

There was a short pause and then Athrena could hear Conteus swear into the phone.

"I must go," he said urgently. The attack is on."

"On McKinley?" asked Athrena.

"Who else?" said Conteus as he signed off.

Chapter 17

The SETI team's van pulled onto the apron of the private airstrip outside of Sydney. It stopped near the sleek private jet provided by The Age and the team began to board.

"Jarrod," said Liza Alvarez, "We should wait for Josh. He risked his life to save yours. Don't you care about that? Can't we wait until we hear he is safe?"

"How are we going to hear, Liza?" responded McKinley curtly. "We don't know where he is. Did he get away after he dived in the bay? Did he get caught in that blast we saw? He didn't even have a cell phone. We've called Sydney police. They're on the lookout for him. That's all we can do. I'm sorry if Josh is hurt. He seems like a nice young man. But, he knew what he was getting into and he knew the risks. We were very clear with him. Sam, Jenny, we all warned him, but he wanted to do it."

"He was doing it for me, Jarrod," Alvarez said.

"I know he cares for you," said McKinley. "I guess I didn't realize how much you care for him. Remember Liza, you're part of this program too. I need you. We've been in this together since the academy, the

Titan mission, the Listening Post, and Forsaken. You know just as much as I do about everything. We are a team. A team critical to making this new contact work."

"Josh was part of the team too," Alvarez shot back. "We can't just leave him so fast. Please wait a few minutes, at least."

"Okay. We'll wait fifteen minutes. If the police find him they'll call."

"Bad idea," Jenny Hasting replied when McKinley told her of the plan to wait.

"We have saved Liza and prevented GME from grabbing you. That was the plan and I don't want to risk your life again," Hastings grabbed McKinley's arm.

"We need to get you back to Wilpena Pound."

"I agree," said Sam Filmore. "Besides, I just got a call from Janet at Wilpena. There's been another leak, internal. Someone inside the Pound knows what we're planning. That probably means they know we're right here, at this airport, preparing to fly back to Wilpena. We have to leave now."

"We'll wait another ten minutes." McKinley eyed them with determination. "I promised Liza. I think we're safe here right now. I don't sense any danger and I—" He paused, looking in all directions.

"Jarrod, what is it? What's coming?" asked Hastings.

"Danger," said McKinley. "From above."

"Everyone on the plane, now," ordered Filmore.

"Hey, you said we could wait," Alvarez said to McKinley.

"Sorry, but we have to go. Something bad is coming and it's coming fast," said McKinley.

"There it is!" yelled Hastings, pointing to a small black helicopter that was rapidly approaching from the direction of Sydney.

McKinley grabbed Alvarez by the arm and half pulled and half pushed her up the stairs into the jet.

Hastings quickly pulled up the stairs and latched the door as the pilot taxied the jet toward the runway.

"Faster," said McKinley who had taken a seat just behind the pilot. "It's almost on us."

"I'm doing the best I can," said the pilot. "We need a few more feet for the takeoff." He turned the plane off the taxiway and onto the runway.

As the jet maneuvered, the helicopter whizzed by them, turning in a sharp, acrobatic move. By the time the jet was lined up for takeoff, the helicopter was hovering just a few feet in front of the cockpit window.

The pilot of the helicopter, dressed in black with a black helmet and visor, moved his hand up and down, motioning to the jet's pilot to shut down.

"Keep moving," ordered McKinley. "He'll get out the way. He doesn't want to crash anymore that we do."

The pilot pushed forward on the throttle and the jet began to move.

The black helicopter moved out of the way but slid to the left and turned so he was traveling parallel to the jet as it began to increase speed. The helmeted pilot in the copter was still motioning vigorously for the jet to shut down.

"Take off," McKinley said to the pilot. "He can't stop us."

The jet began to accelerate quickly as the pilot pushed the throttle full forward. Suddenly McKinley's sense of danger spiked. The helicopter pilot was pointing a large weapon at the jet.

"What the—," McKinley tried to say before a blast enveloped the cockpit of the jet and sparks flashed from the instrument panel and the engines died. The jet was now coasting, but traveling nearly at takeoff speed.

"We're dead," shouted the pilot. "We'll never make it!"

The pilot pulled the manual brake levers and the tires started smoking as the plane hurtled toward the end of the runway.

"We're going too fast," the pilot said. "I can't stop. We're going to overshoot. Brace for impact."

McKinley rushed back to the passenger compartment.

"Everyone brace for impact," he shouted as he strapped into a seat next to Liza.

The jet, tires screeching, began to slide sideways down the runway. It smashed through warning lights near the end of the runway and chopped off barricades at the end of the pavement.

When it hit the dirt the wheels dug in and the plane swung violently to one side. The wing slammed into the ground, crumpled but not broken. The plane rocked back to its wheels and came to a stop upright.

McKinley jumped out of his seat and rushed to the cockpit. The pilot and copilot were shaking off their daze and checking instruments.

"Thanks for that," McKinley said. "We're all okay in the back."

"Get out!" shouted the pilot. "Get out of the plane fast. We're leaking fuel. Our tanks must have been punctured."

McKinley raced to the passenger compartment where Hasting was working on the door.

"It's jammed," she said.

McKinley grabbed the door release and pulled as hard as he could. It didn't budge.

"Let's both pull," said Hasting.

Even with both straining as hard as they could, the door release wouldn't move.

"Jarrod!" shouted Liza, looking out a window. "The fuel. It's leaking!"

"Move," shouted the pilot, who pushed aside McKinley and Hastings.

He grabbed an axe from the emergency compartment and took a violent swing at the door release. It popped open.

"Now, all of us!" he shouted.

The pilot, McKinley and Hasting pushed at the door. It must have been twisted in the violence of the stop because it was still jammed.

"Harder!" shouted the pilot. "It's the only way!"

Slowly the door started to move. As it opened a crack, McKinley could see spilled fuel in a long trail back toward some of the landing lights on the runway where sparks were flying. The sparks reached the fuel and it began to burn. The blue-white flame grew larger along the fuel trail. Now the fire was burning rapidly along the trail to the plane.

"Push! Push!" shouted McKinley.

The pilot grabbed the axe and began prying as McKinley and Hastings pushed.

Slowly the crack between the door and plane's frame widened. The fire in the fuel trail was getting closer quickly.

"There aren't any stairs so we have to jump," said the pilot. "Women first."

Hasting squeezed through the door and leapt to the ground, a drop of a few feet.

Alvarez was next and she stumbled to the ground as she landed. Hasting pulled her out of the way as Filmore almost landed on top of her. McKinley was next and shouted for the others to run as the fire in the fuel trail was just a few inches from the plane.

The copilot jumped and ran followed by the pilot. When the pilot hit the ground, McKinley was there to jerked him up hard. They both sprinted away from the plane.

They ran to the others and turned just as the plane's fuel tank exploded in a ball of flame.

The small group from the plane shielded their faces before staring back at the sleek jet provided by *The Age* as it was engulfed in flames.

Then they heard it. The deadly swishing of rotor blades. They turned and looked directly at the black helicopter hovering behind them.

"Everyone on the ground. Now!" boomed an amplified voice. A burst of gunfire just above their heads emphasized the point.

McKinley remained standing as everyone else hit the ground.

"You too, McKinley," the voice thundered. "On the ground."

McKinley sank to his knees, but stayed upright.

"All the way down! Now!" and another burst of gunfire ripped the air.

McKinley lay down.

The helicopter landed and the black-robed pilot got out with a weapon in his hand.

"Everyone except McKinley stay flat on the ground," the helmeted figure ordered. "McKinley, you're coming with me."

"No!" shouted Hastings. "He's not going anywhere!"

"Your choice, McKinley," said the gunman. "I don't need any of them. You come peacefully or they all die." He fired a burst from the weapon.

"All of you, stay where you are. Do as he says," McKinley said to his friends.

"McKinley, on your knees, hands behind your back," the black figure ordered.

McKinley complied as the sharp bite of plastic ties pinched his wrists.

"On your feet. Walk to the copter. We're leaving," said the gunman as he jerked on McKinley. "You've got a date with some very special people."

He fired another burst over those lying on the

ground and shouted, "Stay where you are and be thankful that you're alive."

As they walked around the helicopter to the door and out of sight of those still on the ground, the copter's pilot noticed a slight shimmer in the air to the right and rear of the helicopter. He heard a faint hum just as a narrow beam struck him. He collapsed to the ground.

A second later a tall figure stepped out of the shimmer, walked quickly to McKinley and snipped off the plastic ties.

"Go quickly," the figure said. "He will awake soon. The EMP blast that stopped your jet is just a minor weapon in their arsenal. This is the work of GME. They will not stop unless you stop them."

"Thank you, again," said McKinley. "Who are you?"

"You must get back to Wilpena Pound. Things there are deteriorating on all fronts. You are needed."

"What about GME?" asked McKinley. "How do we fight them?"

"Later," said the figure. "I must leave."

He took several steps away from McKinley, turned back for a last look, took a step up and disappeared into the shimmer. A whooshing noise and then the shimmer was gone.

"What happened," shouted Hastings as she rounded the helicopter.

"It was our friend again," said McKinley as the rest of the team joined them.

"Everyone, run for the hanger to our van. We've got to get away before this guy comes around and we've got to get back to the Pound. There's trouble there."

They sprinted toward the hanger as emergency vehicles pulled out of their bays. At the same time the SETI van at the hanger headed toward them, passing the emergency vehicles.

As the vehicle screeched to a halt, Josh Reynolds stuck his head out the window and shouted, "Get in! Let's get out of here!"

"Oh, Josh! You're alive," cried Liza as she rushed to the van and threw her arms around Reynolds' neck.

"Get in the van," ordered McKinley as he pulled Alvarez away.

"Josh. Great to see you. How'd you get here? What happened," asked Hastings.

"Police picked me up in a park," Reynolds said. "Just about the time they got me, they also got your message to bring me to this airport to meet you. I got here just in time to see your run in with the copter guy.

"From what I've seen at the bay and when he found me, we're all lucky to be alive. Hey, where's the other guy? I saw someone else out on the runway."

"What happened?" asked Alvarez. "We saw an explosion."

"We can all share details later," said McKinley. "Right now we've got to get back to the Pound."

As the van raced toward the terminal, McKinley was on the phone setting up another flight to Wilpena Pound. Filmore was on the phone with Janet Brighton at Wilpena Pound.

"Jarrod," Filmore said as he pulled McKinley aside. "Make it a fast plane. Things are going crazy at the Pound."

"What's happening?"

"Mostly it's just the political stuff. We need to be there for the first meeting of all the principals. They're waiting on you."

"That's all?"

"No, one more thing. You know we have a mole, right?"

"Yeah."

"Well, now it appears we have sabotage on our hands. The Pound is now on emergency power and Jack tells Janet he suspects more than just routine failure."

"Come on," replied McKinley. "We've had power outages before. That's an old system."

"Jack found a suspicious code in the power control command module. It's got the same signature as the leak that gave us away."

"Damn," said McKinley. "GME."

Janet Brighton and Laura Henning were doing their best to ease the concerns of the diplomats and scientists at Wilpena Pound. Serious questions were being asked by many of the delegates. Commander of the United Space Command, Gen. Harry Jones, was standing nearby in support of the two SETI team members. His stature seemed to deflect some of the toughest questions.

"Where is Jarrod McKinley?" the USNA representative wanted to know. "I've heard he's run off on some adventure that has nothing to do with the signal."

"What is the latest signal? When do we plan to respond?" asked the science leader from the European delegation.

"And now this power outage!" exclaimed a Chinese diplomat. "I question whether your team has the leadership and the resources to be in charge of this situation."

"Gentlemen and ladies," Brighton responded. "Mr. McKinley is on his way here and should land within the hour. Our regular power has been restored and an investigation will determine the cause of the outage. I'm asking for your patience. We will answer all your questions at our first conference set for just under two hours from now.

"In the meantime, here is an agenda for the meeting. We need to answer some fundamental questions about how we Earthlings are going to manage this situation and respond to the signal.

"You will see in the notes provided that the signal senders, whom we are now referring to as the Source, are asking for certain guidelines to be established before communications proceed. A few are technical, which we've already complied with. Others are political and will require some discussion and the reaching of a consensus.

"Please take time before the meeting to think about the questions posed and how we will deal with them. I want to have an open and full discussion of all relevant issues. Thank you very much. Now, please excuse us. Ms. Henning, the General and I have some things to attend to prior to the meeting."

As the three left the room, they gathered in the hall and took a collective sigh of relief.

"The natives are getting restless," said Jones.

"I don't blame them," said Henning. "Things are a bit chaotic right now."

"We need that meeting to go well," Brighton said. "We have to find a way to reach a consensus on the leadership issue. The Source was not ambiguous. They want the point man to be Jarrod."

"I'm not sure that's going to be possible," said Jones. "I'm especially worried about the Europeans. They have too many conflicting interests to even reach consensus in their group."

"We need to get past that hurdle," said Brighton. "If we don't, this entire mission could go up in flames."

"I'm more concerned about the entire complex going up in flames," responded Henning. "Jack is very worried that the saboteur could do more than just shut down the power. Especially now with Jarrod escaping the latest abduction attempt by GME."

"Do we have any clues as to who the mole is?" asked Jones.

"Jack thinks he's narrowed it down to a few suspects but he's still digging, with the help of your men, General."

"Laura, check with Jack. Get the latest," Brighton said.

"Harry, can you go back into that room and try to calm some nerves? They all seem to have great respect for you."

"I'll do what I can," Jones said.

"As soon as Jarrod lands we'll meet with him briefly before the meeting and try to present a united front. Now is a critical time for the success of our first contact. Can we keep this thing moving forward, or not?"

Brighton went back to her room as the other two set out on their missions. She wanted to be able to quickly update McKinley when he returned and there were details of the conference to be settled. As she was studying her notes and making calls to support staff, she was interrupted by the intercom.

"The McKinley party has arrived, Ma'am," said the voice.

"Good," she responded. "Ask Jarrod and Sam to come to my room and tell Laura and Gen. Jones to meet us here."

The next half an hour might be the most important of my life, Brighton thought. No. Not true. The conference after the next half hour will be. Time was flying and Brighton was not at all sure she was keeping up with events.

Half an hour later, she was even more uncertain. McKinley seemed tired and distracted after the events in Sydney.

"We have to go in there and show them we know what we're doing," said Brighton to the SETI team. "We've all been in this from the beginning and we all know how important this moment is. We are united and we know what we have to do. The question is, can we unite those in the conference. The Source wants to see a united front on Earth with one spokesman. And they want that spokesman to be Jarrod. Can we do that?"

"I know what they want," McKinley said curtly. "I just don't know if we can convince all those politicians."

"We have to try, Jarrod," Henning responded. "And if you are going to be our spokesperson, I think you need to lead the discussion. They're not going give you control unless you show you can take it."

"And what about the leak, or the sabotage, or whatever is going on with the power outage? What do we tell them about that?" McKinley asked.

"I think we need to tell them the truth," said Henning. "We know we had an intrusion of our network. We think it's someone on the inside working for someone on the outside. We're tracking it down now and Jack thinks we'll find the culprit soon. If it is someone from any of the delegations, it will give them reason to be nervous. If it's someone from GME, we can enlist the help of the teams from the different countries to ferret out the saboteur."

"Okay, Laura. I'll let you handle that discussion," McKinley said. "I'm going to have enough trouble on the other topics."

"Think about the options we discussed," said Brighton. "Think about everything you've gone through since this started. Dig deep, Jarrod. We need you now."

"I'm not ready," said McKinley. "Liza is still worrying over that Reynolds kid and I wanted to have her next to me."

"No time for that," said Brighton. "We meet in fifteen minutes."

"I'm telling you I need more time," McKinley said through his teeth.

"All right," said Brighton. "Laura, Harry and I will start the meeting. We'll say you and Sam need time to clean up from the Sydney trip and that you will join us in half an hour. We can spend that much time just giving them the background of the Forsaken scandal and the details of the new signal."

"Not enough time," said McKinley.

"Sorry Jarrod. I can't stall them any longer."

"She's right," said Filmore. "It's now or never, Jarrod."

"But—," McKinley started to protest.

"Go now," ordered Brighton, "and meet us in the conference room in half an hour. Thirty minutes."

McKinley mumbled to himself and half stumbled out of Brighton's room and down the hall to his room.

Brighton looked at Gen. Jones as the others left her room. She held up both hands, winced and shook her head. Now she was concerned the conference was going to be the biggest disaster of her life, not the most important moment.

She took a deep breath, gathered her notes, and headed for the conference room.

Jarrod McKinley entered his room and collapsed on his bed. This was going to be impossible, he thought. I'm exhausted. I've been thinking only of how to save Liza, how to escape GME, and how to stay alive. Now they want me to take control of some of the most prominent diplomats and scientists in the world? Impossible!

He clasped both heads behind his head and closed his eyes. No good. A little sleep was not going to help.

He got up and went to the bathroom. Maybe a good hot shower would relax him. He turned the water on as hot as he could stand and stepped in. Again he put both hands behind his head and closed his eyes.

In his mind's eye the figure of the tall man in the shimmering craft at the airport appeared. The figure seemed to reach out and put a hand on his shoulder. The feeling was so real he jerked back and opened his eyes. His nerves jangled. He closed his eyes and focused his mind on the man. Again the figure appeared and this time held out his hand, as if offering a hand up, or a hand to lead the way.

McKinley kept the man in his mind as he shut off the shower, dried, slipped on a bathrobe, and walked to his bed. He lay down and, with the man still hovering nearby, closed his eyes.

He began to feel a sense of calm. The images started to change. Strange scenes blurred together and raced forward. It was as if he was standing on a tall hill and in the valley below a chain of events began unfolding. It made no sense to him. Chaos followed by order. Disaster followed by recovery. War followed by peace. Poverty followed by prosperity. Famine followed by bounty. What was happening? McKinley didn't understand. But he felt a strong sense of promise, possibility and reality.

As his vision began to slow McKinley saw himself on that hill now. The tall thin man was behind him. Gently, he touched McKinley on the shoulder. When McKinley turned around, the man smiled and pointed up and to the left. McKinley looked up. He could see nothing. He looked back at the tall thin man with a question on his face. But this time he saw a tall, slim woman in a tight fitting, one piece suit. Her angular face and almond-shaped eyes were friendly. Behind her were others, a multitude, shifting in and out and blending with one another. In the background a slow, whirling scene shifted between strange new planets, stars and galaxies.

The woman smiled, pointed at him and then stepped forward and beckoned him to follow. A strong sense of calm enveloped McKinley. Now, instead of a set of uncontrollable events whirling around him, he was in control and people were supportive, following his lead, all working toward a common goal as they strolled further up the hill.

McKinley jumped at the sound of a loud buzzing. It was the intercom.

"Jarrod. Where are you?" asked Brighton. "It's been forty minutes. We're all waiting."

McKinley sprang from the bed. He felt completely rested, energized even. And he was confident. He knew what had to be done and he knew how to do it. He pulled on his clothes, brushed his hair and headed toward the conference room.

It was early morning on Progenia Prime. The rays of Acquaria pushed aside the constant dusk of Progenia and the luxuriant greens, purples and rose shades of the planet were coming to life.

Athrena was pleased with herself. After meeting with Jamis and Heronius, the two members of the council who had abstained from the Forgiven Project vote of confidence, she had gotten their endorsement for continuing the program.

True, it was not an enthusiastic endorsement, but she believed it would be enough to allow her to move forward. The project was at a critical stage. Although events on Earth had prompted them to advance the timetable of the project, to reverse now would surely be a disaster. It would cause profound suspicions on Earth and ruin the element of surprise that was at the heart of the strategy they had devised to ensure success.

Her communications console chimed and she turned to the console and said, "Reveal."

A small three dimensional figure appeared, floating just in front of the console.

"Conteus. Good morning. What can I do for you this *fine* morning," said Athrena in a pleasant manner.

"Good morning," replied Conteus. "I do not want to worry you on this fine morning but I am still hearing a simmering of discontent about the Forgiven Project. I have heard from two more council members who are concerned with the path we are taking. They believe that pushing up the project is creating more risk than they are willing to accept."

"Who would that be?" asked Athrena. "Is it still Jamis and Heronius? I received their endorsement just two days ago."

"No. It is Mattrixx from Alegantria, our energy province, and Acquius. I expect they have been talking to Jamis and Heronius. They are making the same points about why going forward now is not advisable.

"Acquius, for example, does not believe the people of Earth will take kindly to what we have in mind for the water on their planet."

"Nonsense," snapped Athrena. "Our plan for the water on Earth should not be threatening at all, if we follow the strategy set out in the plan."

"Perhaps," replied Conteus, "But that is from our point of view. And there is the energy strategy. We could be finding a lot of resistance to our plan for energy on Earth."

"Why," asked Athrena. "Our energy plan can easily be absorbed by Earth."

"I also believe it can," said Conteus. "The question is whether Earth is ready for it. Whether they will accept it or fight us to stop this integration."

"Conteus," said Athrena, with a sigh. "Are you beginning to question the project? I thought we were together on this. You know it is more a matter of messaging than implementation that will make the Forgiven Project successful. We have to convince the people of Earth that what is about to happen to them will be a benefit to everyone—the people of Earth, the Progenians, and the others. We must convince them that a peaceful acceptance of what is about to happen to them is the best, no, the only way for the people of Earth to move forward. For them to realize their destiny."

"Athrena. My belief in Forgiven is as strong as ever. I just thought you should know there are still some who question the timing of the project. They are saying just another hundred years might make a big difference. It would give Earth time to be better prepared for such an evolution."

"One thing we have learned over the last five hundred years is that Earthlings respond better to challenges," said Athrena. "Look at all the major jumps they have made in politics, science and technology when faced with crisis. I do not believe they will fail this latest test.

"And we must not forget that what we are doing here is trying to correct a long string of bad decisions we made beginning almost ten thousand years ago. A few thousand years ago we made a moral commitment to rectify those lapses in judgment. That is what Forgiven is all about."

"We all know that," replied Conteus. "But is this the right time?"

"We made that decision just a few months ago when we decided to respond to the Forsaken scandal.

We decided that event created a new awareness of Earth's effort at first contact, a new desire for contact, and a new acceptance of what that contact might be. And since that time SETI has been working hard to make first contact seem possible again. The council decided it was time to launch the final stages of the project. We cannot stop now."

"We could," replied Conteus. "If we just stop communicating, it will simply be considered by Earth as another false signal."

"And what would that do?" asked Athrena with an edge to her voice. "Provide more discouragement to the people of Earth? Give them another excuse to not prepare for what will eventually happen to them? Create more distrust of the public entities such as SETI and play into the hands of the mega businesses such as GME? I do not think that to be the wisest of moves."

"Calm yourself," replied Conteus. "I told you I believe in Forgiven. I am just trying to relate some of the concerns I have heard."

"And I do appreciate that. What can we do to get some enthusiasm back for the project?"

"I would suggest an informal retreat," said Conteus. "No vid-conferencing. No formal agenda. No formal rules of order. Just everyone gathering to allow an open and free discussion. Let us make it a holiday for everyone. Get them in a good and sharing mood and remind them that working for the betterment of all has been the keystone to our success and will be the key to the success of the Forgiven Project."

"A splendid idea." said Athrena. "Go ahead and set it up. Perhaps by that time we will have some better news from Earth. Perhaps Jarrod McKinley will have conquered some of his demons and taken control of things on his end."

"I hope so," said Conteus. "I have been in contact with our agent on the scene and he reports McKinley is struggling. His confidence is not high right now and he needed to be rescued again from GME. That distraction and his emotions over a female have kept him from focusing on the signal."

"He is key, Conteus. What can we do?"

"I have authorized the agent to make a slight intervention. To make some intrusions that might guide McKinley. They are to be subtle, but profound."

"I hope they work," said Athrena.

"We will know soon," responded Conteus. "McKinley is about to make his case in front of Earth's leading diplomats and scientists that have gathered at Wilpena Pound."

"If he does not emerge as the leader of this group, it might play into the hands of those on Progenia Prime who think we are moving too fast."

"Ironic, is it not? That the success of this project might rest in the hands of one Earthling?"

"He is more than just a normal Earthling," replied Athrena.

"But is he enough?" Conteus asked.

"For the sake of those on Earth, let us hope so," said Athrena.

"Pray to our Gods," replied Conteus.

"Really?" queried Athrena, with a little scoff. "Where did that come from?"

"Just an old, old saying," said Conteus.

"Well, I hope McKinley is not reverting to such nonsense."

"I doubt it. But right now he is probably questioning what he might see as some kind of divine guidance."

"Let us just hope he thinks he just had a dream and that it gives him the confidence to be successful at his meeting at Wilpena Pound."

"If he does not, we might all be having nightmares."

Colin Riley was still trying to figure out what happened at the airport. His attempt to stop the jet carrying the SETI team had worked to perfection. His EMP cannon had disabled the jet, he had grabbed McKinley and was about to board his helicopter when things went blank.

The next thing he remembered was awakening to find all SETI members gone and emergency crews fighting the fire that had engulfed the jet at the end of the runway.

It had taken strong talk and significant pulling of strings to get the incident commander to allow him to get back in his helicopter and leave.

Now he was studying the video taken by the cameras on his copter. What he saw scared him. He was taking McKinley to the helicopter when a beam of light struck him. He watched himself slump to the ground unconscious. The beam seemed to appear out of nowhere. After rerunning the video several times, Riley detected a slight shimmer near the helicopter just before the beam flashed.

What happened next surprised him even more. A person stepped out of the shimmer, talked briefly to McKinley, then stepped back into the shimmer and disappeared. By slowing the replay he could tell it did not disappear, it just moved very quickly, faster than anything he had ever seen.

Cloaking technology! Riley knew the theory and had seen lab demonstrations. In fact, his company, GME, was the leader in developing a cloaking device and had been able to make it work on a large variety of objects, some as large as the attack helicopter he was using. However, making a cloaking device work on a moving object was something GME had not been able to do.

Riley knew immediately that GME's effort to control first contact through McKinley was the right strategy. Someone had used that technology to help McKinley. And, Riley speculated, this probably was not the first time. That's why McKinley had escaped previous abduction attempts. It meant McKinley had access to, or at least exposure to, advanced technology not available to anyone else on Earth. Controlling McKinley and first contact would give GME access to that higher technology and give it a strategic advantage, not only in mineral extraction, but perhaps in many other areas where it could influence policies and political power.

Riley filed his report. His superiors were not happy his abduction attempt had failed but were pleased with the additional intelligence he had provided. They also approved his new plan.

There would be no black helicopters, no EMP weapons, no brute force. He would join assets already in place and converge on McKinley when he was most vulnerable, where he thought he was safe, where he would have let down his guard.

Riley peeled off his black uniform and dressed in a casual pair of slacks, a loose fitting T-shirt and a photographer's vest. He loaded some of the vest pockets with camera gear—batteries, memory cards and a flash. He put his pistol in one of the larger pockets.

He grabbed a second flash attachment that had a slightly different appearance. He pushed a button and the prongs of a stun gun popped out. He retracted the prongs and put this "flash" in another pocket. He then selected another battery, one that hid a syringe.

His last piece of equipment was a camera, which he slung over his shoulder. After gathering up a small clothing bag, he looked around his apartment, flicked off the lights, and smiled as he closed the door behind him.

Four hours later Riley parked his jet on an airstrip in the outback of South Australia. He thanked the driver of the golf cart that had picked him up and driven him to a large white tent with a banner reading: *Media Credentials.*

"Hi," he said cheerfully to the receptionist. "I'm here to cover the hottest story on the planet."

The receptionist scanned a list, checked his identification, marked off his name, and handed him a packet of information.

"Mr. Means," the receptionist said after finding his name. "So, the mining industry has finally decided this is a story worth covering?"

"Sure thing," Riley said with a laugh. "Might as well join the party."

"Great. Your pass is all in order. You can catch the bus at the back of the tent."

"Thanks, doll," Riley said as he walked out of the tent. He reached in the packet and pulled out the pass and draped it around his neck. The pass, swinging on his neck as he walked toward the bus, stated in large print, *George Means, Photographer, International Federation of Mining Companies, Full Access, Wilpena Pound.*

Chapter 18

Jarrod McKinley entered the conference room at Wilpena Pound at a slow, casual pace, an electronic tablet in his hand and a smile on his face.

He sat next to Janet Brighton. Sam Filmore was on his left. Laura Henning was to the right of Brighton. The four occupied a center portion of the long conference table that had been expanded to accommodate all the delegates. Behind McKinley sat Jenny Hastings and Gen. Harry Jones from the United Space Command.

Delegations consisted of political and scientific representatives from China, the United States of North America and the European Union. China had four delegates. The USNA had four—one from the continental US, one representing its territories, and one each from Canada and Mexico. The European Union had eight—four each from northern and southern Europe. Behind each delegate, sitting around the room, were assistants and security personnel.

"Briefing go okay?" McKinley leaned over and whispered to Brighton.

"Not bad," said Brighton. "But there will be some questions."

"Delegates," McKinley said as he leaned forward and looked around the table. "I want first to apologize for being a bit late. And I want to thank you all for participating so enthusiastically and cooperatively. Without the efforts of all of us, meaning all of us on this planet, we may not be successful in what will be one of the most significant events in our history.

"The future of our planet, our people, our cultures, could well depend on how we deal with this opportunity. I know you have all had a chance to study the agenda, to hear the briefing from our team, and to raise some questions. We will get into the agenda later, but right now I'd like to hear any other questions or concerns. I will do my best to answer as many as I can."

Hands shot up around the table.

"I'm sorry, but I don't know many names right now. I assure you as the days unfold I will get to know all of you well. Would the gentlewoman from China please go ahead?"

With that the questions began.

"About the signal. Our scientists agree with your conclusions as to approximate source and content but we have two questions. Why does the signal appear to change locations slightly and to be getting closer? The other question is: Who will be formulating responses?"

"To be honest," replied McKinley, "we don't know why the signal moves. We hope you all can help answer that. As to the responses, to this point our SETI team has reached a consensus on responses. He motioned to include those next to him. Up to this point our responses have largely been governed by requests made by the senders, whom we have taken to calling the Source, such as requests for encryption and specific information from us. You have all seen every response that has been made. I would hope we can have a similar method of consensus building from this council to formulate future responses."

More hands were raised.

"Is there a danger from the senders of the signal, or the Source?"

"Not that we know."

"Who is interfering with SETI operations and what about the attacks on SETI personnel?"

"We have no concrete proof but we believe that Galactic Mining Enterprises is involved."

"What do they want?"

"They want me to work for them to make first contact so they can take advantage of new technologies that might be revealed."

"Is there proper security for the operation at Wilpena Pound?"

"We feel secure and the United Space Command is bringing extra security personnel. We also have upgraded our cell phones with secure, more powerful communication devices that we can link with others and that are tied into the internal communications of Wilpena Pound."

"What do we tell the public?"

"We believe, just as we have been forthright with all of you, that the public needs to know everything we know."

Finally, the question McKinley had dreaded in the past, but now was eager to answer: "Why does the Source insist there be a single spokesperson for Earth and what makes them ask for you?"

"I am not sure as to the motivations behind those requests. I can't answer for the Source," McKinley said. "I can, however, imagine many reasons why they want a single spokesperson. First, just the logistical aspect dealing one point of contact instead of dozens, or hundreds, will greatly simplify first contact.

"But more than that, a single point of contact implies a united Earth, a planet that is fully supportive of any first contact effort, a planet ready to take the next step in its evolution. What this next step will involve, we don't know, but it is likely to require using the combined resources of the planet to make it successful.

"It just makes sense to have a united Earth reaching out to the Source."

"But why you?"

"Again, I can't presume to speak for the Source. I can just tell you what I've been through, not only during this past year but for the past few weeks, and what I see for the future."

McKinley drew a deep breath and outlined his experience with the Forsaken scandal, his recent escapes from the abduction attempts, and even his encounters with the tall thin man in the shimmering vehicle. He could tell his audience was verging on the edge of incredulity, perhaps even outright disbelief. He pushed on.

"Through all of these experiences there has been a strong sense of moving in a new direction. Not just going from one place to another, but moving to a different plane. A strong sense of moving upward to something better and moving with a helping hand.

"Look at all the progress mankind has made over the last few centuries. The advance of our civilization has depended on our spirit of adventure, our new technologies, and our willingness to work for the betterment of all, not just a favored few.

"Every time the Earth has floundered, it is because we have lost sight of that. When we work for the benefit of a few, a single individual, a single subset of society, a single business interest or a single country, we become involved in conflict and often violence.

"We've made major progress when we work together. Look at what we have accomplished. No longer do we have a need for the armies of the United Nations. We now put our resources into the UN agencies that strive to better the conditions of our populace.

"Our food and energy production and distribution have made great strides but more can be done. The health and education of the people on Earth has made leaps forward compared to the first part of this century. How have we done that? By working together. By realizing that a healthy, well educated, and prosperous population means benefits for all.

"Our future depends on more of the same. But, as we know, we have reached some roadblocks. Roadblocks of a physical nature. We are limited to our solar system. For centuries our frontiers were limited by mountain ranges, oceans or energy sources. We have overcome most of these roadblocks and I strongly believe we can overcome our remaining roadblocks on Earth and in the solar system and beyond. And I believe we can overcome them faster with the completion of a successful first contact.

"What new technologies are waiting for us? What new frontiers will open up? New energy sources, a solution for the barriers of the speed of light? I don't know.

"But I believe! I believe we are only limited when we refuse to trust in the promise of the future. I believe mankind is on a grand journey and will complete this journey easier and faster by going there as one people, with favoritism shown to no one, and with the helping hand of the Source.

"I don't know why they have asked for me. But I believe they mean to help, not hurt; to guide not push; to include not to enslave.

"One thing I promise is that even though I may be the single point of contact, I will not attempt to make decisions on my own. Any decisions made will be made by this council or another entity that you believe is more appropriate.

"It's time for our species to take another big step, no, a leap forward to fulfill our destiny. To not be satisfied with being inhabitants of one small planet but citizens of the universe. It's time to take our place among the stars!"

With that McKinley made a slight nod with his head and sat down.

There was a silence in the room. Then one of the delegates from Europe rose and began to clap slowly. Others looked around and then began to stand. Soon all were on their feet, applauding. Brighton, Filmore, Henning and Jones joined them, all standing, clapping, and smiling at McKinley.

McKinley remained seated and Hastings reached forward and touched his shoulder, "Great job, Jarrod. I believe in you," she said.

"Council, I move Mr. McKinley be named leader of this council and represent Earth to the Source," said the lead delegate from China.

McKinley stood.

"Thank you for that," McKinley responded. "But I do not accept. This council needs to be the leader. This council can represent the people of Earth. I will be the single point of contact but we need consensus leadership."

"I amend my motion to say Jarrod McKinley will be the single point of contact with the source and report to this council," said the Chinese delegate.

"I second the motion," said the delegate from the USNA.

The vote was unanimous in favor of the motion.

McKinley began moving around the table, shaking hands and gathering names. He was hit with an uneasy feeling. A sense of danger was beginning to creep into the back of his mind. He struggled to crystallize the feeling, but it was fragmented by his effort to memorize the names of the council members he was greeting.

When he finished he turned to address the delegates.

"I want you to know that I appreciate your vote of confidence," said McKinley. "Not so much a vote of confidence in me, but a vote of confidence in the people of Earth. A vote of confidence for our spirit of adventure. A vote to continue to push the boundaries of our frontiers. A vote to continue to build a better future for all of the people of Earth as we begin this new era of exploration.

"Now I believe Ms. Brighton has an agenda to get through."

Brighton began to address the unfinished business of what to do about unrepresented areas of the world; how to accommodate other countries at Wilpena Pound who wanted to be involved; whether to locate another office in Sydney or Adelaide; how to fund the operation; what role the United Space Command would play; and, finally, how to combat the intrusions of Galactic Mining Enterprises.

All the time, McKinley's sense of danger was growing. He turned to talk to his security chief.

Just as the delegates decided the best approach to GME would be a face-to-face meeting with the conglomerate's board of directors, personal communication devices began buzzing around the room, including his security chief's.

McKinley looked quizzically at his security chief, his danger meter now at a high level.

"It's Jack," said the security officer. "We thought it would be best to link all the security chiefs together on one line so we all know what's going on."

"Good," said McKinley as he clicked on his device. "What's happening, Jack?"

"An intrusion," he heard Simington say. "I hope I'm reaching all of the security chiefs."

Around the room the heads of security from all the delegations responded affirmatively.

"Gentlemen and ladies," said Simington. "Please put all your personnel on alert. We've had an intrusion."

"What system this time?" asked McKinley.

"No system. It's a physical intrusion. Someone has breached access points in two restricted areas. We're sending teams out now."

"How many people?" asked McKinley.

"Not sure," said Simington. "Could be two or twenty. All security chiefs are requested to send all available personnel to the security office on the third floor. Make sure they are armed and ready."

McKinley clicked off and looked at the SETI team.

"Someone breached our physical security," he said.

"GME?" asked Brighton.

"Not sure, but we have initiated a code red."

McKinley turned back to the conference table where delegates were in hurried discussions with their security chiefs.

"Ladies and gentlemen. We've had a security breach of a physical nature. Someone or something has accessed two restricted areas of this complex. Security personnel report to the security office. For the rest of you, we're going into lockdown. You all will be confined with me in this room until the situation is resolved."

"Who is it?" demanded one of the delegates.

"We'll soon find out. Could be anything. An alarm malfunction, wildlife or something else."

McKinley turned to Brighton and said quietly, "My bet is on GME."

"The man in the black helicopter?" she asked.

McKinley nodded grimly and sat down.

"Anyone have any playing cards?" he asked cheerfully, trying to suppress his growing sense of panic.

The rest of the delegates were not smiling.

Athrena and Conteus were standing side by side welcoming delegates to a mountain resort on the shores of a shimmering purple lake high in the Aracius Range of Progenia Prime.

The planet of Progenia Prime was divided into seven major land masses connected by a series of shallow seas and broad rivers. The land masses were large, covering more than sixty percent of the planet. The mountain ranges were small and tangled, showing the effects of billions of years of erosion and very little recent geological trauma, such as earthquakes or volcanoes.

The interiors of the land masses tended to be gentle and consistent. There were no expansive deserts, no polar ice caps, no vast impassable jungles. Instead, a mild climate and gentle topography well watered by meandering rivers and streams made most of the planet very hospitable and productive.

Some isolated regions were inhabited by only a few beings—rugged individuals who were willing to put up with a lack of modern conveniences such as auto transport and instant communications in exchange for a more quiet existence.

The Zarius resort in the Aracius Range was in the middle of such a region.

Athrena had chosen the resort specifically for that reason. She wanted the delegates to relax and not be harried by their everyday lives. She hoped to take the edge off of what Conteus reported was a simmering discontent with the direction of the Forgiven Project.

Managers of the resort had prepared well. Food, drink, soft music and flickering video displays greeted the seven delegations as they arrived. There was no security; there wasn't a need. Security had not been needed at these kinds of meetings for centuries. Conflicts, when they arose, were resolved by negotiations conducted in a spirit of cooperation and compromise.

After waiting a respectable time after the last delegation arrived, Athrena tapped her glass with her long fingernails, creating a gentle chime.

"Thank you all for coming," she said. "I know you all have very busy schedules in your regions and had to disrupt those schedules for this meeting. Let us all relax for a day and enjoy this magnificent resort. I know that I, myself, do not visit here often enough.

"This will be a very informal gathering. I do not have an agenda to follow. The only goal here is to get back on track with the Forgiven Project. I know some of you have concerns. I hope when we leave here you all will be once again enthusiastic about the project and carry that enthusiasm back to your regions."

"All of you know about recent developments with the project," added Conteus. "And you have all been on this council for many years. You have been strong supporters and we hope to show you that support is still warranted, even though our timeline has been accelerated."

"That is the problem," said Heronius. "I worry that Earth is not ready. The level of political and economic development on Earth is still primitive. I doubt they are ready for the changes they would experience under Forgiven."

"True," said Athrena. "There will be major changes required once our plan is fully implemented, but Earth has made progress the last fifty years. There is much less violence than in the early part of this century and much more cooperation in the areas of political governance and scientific exploration. The evolution of their United Nations and their United Space Command are just two examples."

"What about our resources?" asked Jamis. "I worry this project might divert some of our resources that are now committed to our Grand Vision."

"The acceleration of the Forgiven Project should not affect our resources to any significant level," responded Conteus. "Earth has done a good job the last fifty years with its food production and distribution. They will not need our help there."

"And with their off-world energy development, they now have most of the energy they need to be successful," added Athrena.

"What they need is some of our technology so they can more efficiently utilize their renewable resources," said Conteus. "They are still too much caught up in extracting and expending their finite resources. They have not yet bought into the notion of Reuse Infuse Accommodate Leverage, or RIAL, that we on Progenia Prime endorsed thousands of years ago."

"There are strong competitive forces that are profiting from their present system," replied Jamis.

"Yes, there are," said Athrena. "And those forces appear to be the biggest impediment to going forward. On Earth a for-profit energy conglomerate controls virtually all of the major energy production and supply chains. I expect that as the project develops, the political leaders of Earth will see that the goals of Galactic Mining Enterprises and the people of Earth do not coincide and that appropriate measures will be taken."

"Is there the political will and power to do anything?" asked Heronius.

"It is too soon to tell," replied Athrena. "Our agent on scene reports that the actions of GME are getting more aggressive and violent. I would hope the political leaders would put a stop to it."

"And if they do not?" asked Jamis.

"We do not wish to intervene," said Conteus. "But we can if we must. Our agent has made limited interventions to protect the life of Jarrod McKinley.

At this time, our agent's connection to us is unknown. And it will remain that way until it is appropriate to reveal it."

"How can you be sure?" Heronius prodded. "If Earth suspects intervention, will that not create distrust and opposition, perhaps violent opposition, to our plan?"

"Nothing is certain," responded Athrena. "And at some point our connection will be revealed. After all, is that not the ultimate goal of Forgiven, to bring Earth into the fold, whether they like it or not. But if we are successful, we can make this seem like a good thing for Earth while at the same time fulfilling our goals in the Grand Vision."

"I worry that we are dealing with an unstable civilization," said Acquius. "Earthlings are not far removed from wars of all kinds—religious, genocidal, political and environmental. It took us on Progenia Prime nearly a thousand years of peace and cooperation before we were able to launch even the first steps of this project, to say nothing of the Grand Vision."

"And we have learned much over those years," said Athrena. "Earth can benefit from our knowledge, or they can refuse us and suffer the consequences.

"Gentle souls," Athrena said with a sigh. "I understand all of your concerns. But it was that silly Earthly scandal they called Forsaken that gave us a unique opportunity to advance the Forgiven Project schedule. We believe Earth has never been more ready to face the challenges of the universe than it is now.

"Our plan is to go slow. To reveal our plan gradually. To allow those on Earth to absorb the impact of this project and what they will learn. Just facing reality may be a shock too great for them to handle. And agreeing to our conditions that will allow them to move forward may not be acceptable to them.

"We always knew it would be a risk. Would they accept the reality of their existence? Would they accept their fate? What Forgiven offers could propel them into the future at a rate that is too fast for them to handle.

"I doubt one hundred years, or two hundred, will make a difference. I believe now is the time to test Earth. If they pass the test it will be all the better for them, and for our Grand Vision."

"And if they do not pass?" asked Jamis.

"We withdraw," replied Athrena. "Earth is still locked into its solar system. At the present rate of their technological advance, it will be centuries before they have an impact outside of their system.

"Gentlemen and ladies. I believe we have an opportunity right now to put right, to make amends, to correct a long ago mistake. We must make the effort or the moral underpinnings of our Grand Vision will collapse and that effort will fail.

"We will proceed with caution. We will maintain a position that can be reversed if Earth fails to comply. We must make them realize that failure to comply could be much more catastrophic than to accept the terms we will offer in the Forgiven Project."

"As long as we maintain a fail-safe position, I am willing to go forward," said Heronius.

"I would agree," said Jamis. "But, I would request one condition."

"And what is that?" asked Conteus.

"We want another person to be privy to daily activities and plans," said Heronius.

"Is there an issue of trust here?" asked Athrena, glancing quickly at Conteus.

"No. Not of trust," said Jamis. "Of communication." He indicated those around the room who nodded in agreement. "We sometimes feel we are not fully aware of the latest events. For example, what has happened to our request for a single Earth representative?"

"We have tried to keep you all informed," replied Conteus. "Our request to Earth for a single representative has not been complied with, as of yet. We did receive communication that there would be an effort to comply but apparently getting agreement on the issue required more diplomatic efforts than we anticipated."

"You see, this is just what we are talking about," said Jamis. "I believe it imperative that every detail, even if it seems insignificant, be passed on to the entire committee. Another person could assist you in that effort."

"That is no problem," said Athrena with a smile. "We would welcome the help. Would not we Conteus?"

"Of course," replied Conteus. "Who wants to join us with this little headache?"

"I will," said Acquius, as he raised his hand.

"All agreed, then," Athrena said. "We proceed with the Forgiven Project with caution. We maintain a fail-safe position in case Earth does not comply. When we all agree moving forward will cause more damage to our Grand Vision than it will cause on Earth, we will suspend the project."

As they went around the room voicing their agreement, there was a noticeable sense of relief among the delegates and they began to enjoy the food and drink and the view from the mountain top lake. As the delegates chatted and said their goodbyes, Conteus pulled Athrena aside.

"We have more news from Earth," he said quietly.

"Acquius," Athrena called out. "We have news."

"As you know, our communications from Earth are about four and a half hours delayed but we are getting reports from our agent that there was another abduction attempt on Jarrod McKinley."

"What has happened? Is he safe?" asked Acquius.

"Yes. It is a complex story in which the SETI team rescued McKinley's fiancé but then was attacked as they were headed back to Wilpena Pound. It required an intervention."

"Was our agent revealed?" asked Athrena.

"He said he was very careful," replied Conteus. "He believes he revealed himself only to McKinley but he cannot be sure."

"Who was the attacker?" asked Acquius.

"A new player from GME," said Conteus. "Our agent had to disable him but reports he was very competent and has a higher level of technology than we have seen before. He says he doubts he was deterred."

"Are there any other communication to us from the SETI team?" asked Athrena.

"No," said Conteus. "But all the players appear to be gathering at Wilpena Pound so we may soon have an answer to our representative question."

"What do we do about this GME agent?" asked Acquius.

"Nothing," replied Athrena. "That is an issue that Earthlings have to resolve. We cannot solve all their problems. We may step in if we have to."

"I hope they are up to it," said Conteus.

"Jarrod McKinley has the capability, I am sure," said Athrena. "My question is when is he going to realize it?"

"It better be soon," said Conteus. "I fear they have not heard the last of GME."

Colin Riley was sitting in the public relations room at Wilpena Pound. He wiped a tiny droplet of sweat from his temple and smiled. He had just taken his seat in the room when two security officers hurried past.

Things had been set in motion for his latest plan to capture *Jarrod McKinley. It was going to be a delicate operation to extract McKinley from* this mostly underground complex. He had spent the last two hours casing the complex and contacting his asset. GME had taken precautions six months ago by inserting the asset and those steps were paying off. Without his inside asset, the assault on this complex would have been much more difficult.

As more security personnel rushed by, he smiled again. He was willing to be patient. He was going to be more careful after his failure in Sydney. Failure was something he was not used to. It wouldn't happen again.

With his press credentials and his fake name of George Means, he had been able to wander about much of the Wilpena Pound complex. He had seen all of the top floors, the administration, base operations, living quarters and the shared access eating and recreation facilities.

He had even been allowed to see the main control room where scientists from around the world were analyzing the signal from the senders. He noted the separate areas for signal reception, encryption and transmission. With teams from countries that still had space programs vying to be part of the effort, there was a sense of chaos. People wandered to and fro and many just stood around waiting for something to do or some place to work.

In the disorganized environment, it was easy for him to contact his inside asset and share his plans to spread confusion and alarm throughout the base. In the height of this confusion he would grab Jarrod McKinley and escape Wilpena Pound.

When he and his partner breached two secure areas and the alarms sounded, he hurried back to the press room. He watched as security people headed to the security office. Soon, he was sure, teams would be dispatched to the areas where alarms had indicated there was an intrusion. He had breached a door on the fourth floor. His asset was on the sixth floor. This would draw security teams to those areas, spreading *the thin force across the complex.*

In the press room, he was only two doors away from the conference room where McKinley was waiting. It was time to make his move.

Jack Simington and his assistant Jill Sanders had just finished composing their message to the Source when Simington's secure comm device chimed.

"Simington here," he said. "Hope this is important. I'm right in the middle of something."

He listened for a moment and cursed quietly to himself.

"Okay, investigate immediately and make sure we're in a Code Red in lockdown," he said into the device. "Yes. A lockdown. I'm not taking any chances. Not after what happened in Sydney. I'll call McKinley and the security people with the delegations but then you know what to do. I've got to finish a job here."

"What's going on," asked Sanders as Simington signed off.

"Not sure yet," Simington said. "Two alarms that indicate a physical breach of the complex. Could be an alarm malfunction. Maybe not."

"Do you need to go?"

"No. Let me make a call and then we've got a signal to send. This could be the signal that allows first contact."

When Simington finished his call, he turned to Sanders.

"Okay, what have we got?"

"Our message is simple," Sanders said. "It says: Jarrod McKinley now authorized as single point of contact for communications. But I think we should ask them for something."

"What?"

"We need to know who we are talking to. What do we call them? We should have a name, something."

"According to the notes from the meeting, Jarrod announced that the SETI team leaders have been referring to the senders as the Source," Simington said. "It appears that the council is calling them the Source now, too. I suppose this is as good a name as any, until they identify themselves to us."

"Well, we need to keep the dialogue going. We've got to generate a response from the Source. So far it's all been one way. They demand, we respond. I feel like we're too compliant. We need this to be a two-way communication, not just answering to dictates from some unknown Source."

"I agree but it's not our place to initiate such a policy," responded Simington.

"But Jarrod has been so distracted with keeping one step ahead of GME, he hardly knows what's going on. Does he even know that the signal has moved again? The replies to our signals have shifted another two degrees. And the last response only took nine hours.

"That means the time delay has gone from about four and half days to four and half hours each way. Does that mean it's closer? We don't know. I would hate to think something is coming our way and we don't even know what, or who, it is."

"I fully sympathize," said Simington. "That means it could be as close as the outer planets of our solar system, even though our base at Titan and our satellites have not detected anything."

"And now this security breach. That's going to set us back again. Jarrod and the council are not prepared to carry on this conversation with the senders. We need to advance this communication."

"Well, we can't ask them a direct question. That would violate the single point of communication they have demanded."

"Why don't we construct the message like a memo? Let's say:"

> To ?
> From Jarrod McKinley and SETI
> Worldwide Council
> Jarrod McKinley now authorized as single
> point of contact for communications between
> Earth and ?
> We await your response.

"No. I don't think so," said Simington. "That's too simplistic. I can't go along with that. We need to stick to the original message, with the added, 'We await your response and wish to proceed with further communication.' "

"All right, there it is," said Sanders as she finished typing, with Simington looking over her shoulder at the screen.

"Hit the send button," said Simington.

"I hope they give us a clue as to who they are," said Sanders. "I want to know to whom I am talking."

"You and the whole world," said Simington with a scoff. "Now, let's find out about this security breach."

Chapter 19

Jarrod McKinley's comm device trilled after he had been in lockdown in the Wilpena Pound conference room for about fifteen minutes.

"What have you got, Jack?" he asked.

"We've had two physical breaches, one on the fourth level and one on the sixth level," said Simington.

"What happened?"

"Can't say for sure. I can only say that someone opened two doors that shouldn't have been opened. It was not an alarm malfunction."

"Who did it?"

"It's a bit puzzling and concerning," replied Simington. "Both areas were very out of the way locations, down the ends of long hallways and out of sight of the security cameras so we couldn't see what caused the breaches.

"We have cameras at the other end of those hallways but there are blind spots. Whoever opened those doors had to know things about the security system that could be known only by someone who was in the building. And, there had to be two people involved. One person could not have caused both breaches."

"So we do have a mole or two," said McKinley. "We have people in this building who are working against us."

"I'm afraid I would have to agree," said Simington.

"We need to find out who it is," said McKinley. "Do we have the resources for a complete forensic examination of those doors? Can we check for fingerprints, try to collect DNA samples?"

"I've got people collecting samples and checking for fingerprints," replied Simington. "Getting those things checked against databases is another thing. We'll have to send samples to Adelaide electronically. It could be a couple of hours. Right now we're conducting a search and checking inventories to see if anything is missing."

"What would they have access to through those doors?"

"That's another strange thing," said Simington. "The door on Level Six leads to a dead-end storage room containing mostly junk and few items of any value. The door on Level Four leads to an emergency exit stairs. Those stairs lead to the surface but the surface exit is still closed and the access is well covered by security cameras which detected no movements."

"Sounds to me like we have someone who is probing our security, trying to learn more about it, testing our responses," said McKinley.

"There's another possibility," said Simington. "They may be creating a diversion. We just rushed all of our security to those two levels and now we have them searching for people we haven't even identified."

McKinley could feel the fine hairs on the back of his neck begin to tickle. His sense of danger began to spike.

"A diversion for what?" he asked.

"Who knows?" replied Simington. "I've put extra security in the control center to protect the computers and analysts. I've got security heading for the top floor to protect the main entrance. We're getting stretched a bit thin but we're in lockdown so I'm hoping the rest of us will be safe."

"Okay, Jack. Thanks. Just to let you know, I am sensing more danger, and it seems very close. Keep searching."

When McKinley clicked off, he noted other delegates were receiving the same report from their security staff.

He gathered Sam Filmore, Janet Brighton, Laura Henning, Jenny Hastings and Gen. Harry Jones around him and explained the situation, including his sense of danger.

"I'm worried," Hastings said. "Every time you've had that feeling, you have been in danger."

"I know," McKinley said. "But we're in lockdown and I don't think I have to worry."

There was a sharp banging on the conference room door.

"Stay here," said Hastings as she held back McKinley, "I'll check this out."

Before he could protest Hastings was on her way to the large double doors. She braced her foot and one shoulder against the door as she cracked it open.

"It's Liza and Josh," she said as she looked back towards McKinley.

"What? Let them in!" said McKinley.

As the two squeezed through the door another man behind them pushed his way in.

"George Means," he said. "International Federation of Mining, United Minerals Magazine. Sorry I was in the hall when the lockdown happened. I've been looking for a place to go. Can I come in here?"

McKinley's sense of fear was spiking again.

"Jenny, check his credentials. Hold him by the door."

"Let me help," said Josh Reynolds as he cast a quizzical look at Means.

"Liza, what are you and Josh doing here?" McKinley asked as she came up to him.

"We were in the cafeteria when the lockdown happened and then a few minutes ago we got a call from a security officer saying you wanted to talk to us."

"Me? I never asked anyone to send for you. I've just talked to Jack and he didn't mention it."

McKinley watched as Hastings examined Means' press credentials while Reynolds questioned him. Reynolds turned and walked quickly towards McKinley.

"Jarrod. There's something wrong. I think I recognize that voice. It sounds just like—"

Before he could finish, Colin Riley in one smooth motion spun Hastings around and put a neck lock on her. He pulled a pistol from his pocket and fired a shot into the ceiling before placing the pistol against her temple.

"Everyone, hands in the air! All of you, or this young lady will die."

McKinley hesitated.

"I mean everyone, including you, McKinley," said Riley. "Now, all of you take your comm devices and put them on the table."

As they complied, Riley waved his gun at McKinley and ordered him to grab a trash can and put all the comm devices in the can.

"Bring the can here, McKinley," ordered Riley.

He pulled a flat disk out his pocket and threw it in the can. A small flash sparked and a white hot flame started melting the comm devices.

"Now, we're going to walk out of here," Riley said. "McKinley, you will lead our little parade, just a few steps in front of this pretty little miss. If you try to run or anyone tries to stop us, she will die."

"You don't need to do this," McKinley said. "It's me you want, just leave Jenny here."

"Jenny is it?" Riley replied with a sneer. "I don't think so. Given your history, Mr. McKinley, I think you'll be much more cooperative if you think you're protecting someone. No. The three of us are going to walk out of here without a problem or at least two of us are going to die."

"One of them will be you," sneered Josh Reynolds.

Riley laughed.

"I should have shot you in Sydney, pretty boy. You're such a waste! Get on that intercom over there and tell those amateur security people out there what's going on and have them stand down."

"Why don't you have your accomplice do that?" asked McKinley.

"You really do want to hurt this sweet little thing, don't you?" Riley scraped Hastings' forehead with the barrel of the pistol. A trickle of blood emerged.

"Now, let's go," he ordered. "You're going to open that door and we're going to walk down the hall and take the elevator to the ground floor. If I see so much as one of these rent-a-cops reaching for a weapon, little Jenny will die."

"Okay, okay," said McKinley. "Josh, do as he says. Have Janet back you up when you talk to Jack."

He opened the conference doors and the three made their way to the hall and started for the elevator.

"George, or whatever your name is, I know you're working for GME. This whole scheme of me going to work for them is insane. I'm of no value to anyone. What's the point?"

"I couldn't care less about reasons or motivations. I have my orders and an unlimited budget to get it done. You must be worth something. Keep moving."

As they reached the elevators, McKinley saw security people coming down the hall. They had their hands on their weapons but had not drawn them. He waved them back and pushed the elevator button.

Moments later, the elevator door opened on the ground level where five security guards were poised. McKinley recognized two of them from the security details from the USNA and China. They had all backed off and had no weapons drawn.

"Okay. We're doing fine here," said Riley. "Walk slowly out the front door and down the steps to the driveway."

As they approached the driveway, the security people followed without taking any action. A SETI SUV pulled up. The driver had a black baklava pulled over his head, although he was wearing a SETI uniform and had a SETI security badge.

"So you're the mole," McKinley said to the driver. "Feel real proud about betraying your friends and workmates, do you?"

The driver did not respond.

"Get in," Riley ordered. To the driver, he said, "Drive to the airport. My jet is at the far end of the apron near Hangar B. Go. Now!"

The driver stepped hard on the accelerator and the wheels of the SUV spun gravel as it lurched around the circular driveway and through the SETI gates.

Quickly a SETI security officer pulled up in another SUV and Jack Simington, Josh Reynolds and Liza Alvarez piled in. It matched speed with the SUV carrying Riley and his captives but maintained a safe distance.

When the SUV carrying the gunman and his captives pulled up next to the sleek private jet Riley had flown in on, he ordered the driver to handcuff McKinley and Hastings together and he pushed them to the steps of the jet.

"Go on. Up the stairs," he ordered.

"Let Jenny go," McKinley said. "You've got me. She's of no use to you now."

"Maybe. Maybe not," Riley said. "I like the insurance she provides. Plus, I like looking at her."

"Let her go!" McKinley yelled.

"Get in!" Riley shouted, raising his pistol over Hastings' head. "You want me to make her bleed some more?"

McKinley grunted and started up the stairs, pulling Hastings with him. When he reached the top, he stopped.

"Keep going," Riley ordered.

When Hastings reached the top step, Riley ordered them to halt. He turned to the driver of the SUV.

"Driver. Colin Riley thanks you for your service. GME sends its regards."

He pulled the trigger and the driver fell with a bullet through his forehead.

Riley pushed Hastings into the cabin of the jet as McKinley tried to come back to see what had happened.

"Jarrod," she gasped. "He just, he just, he shot—"

"Get in there and sit down," ordered Riley. "It's time to go."

Riley quickly handcuffed the pair to a seat and raced to the cockpit.

From his window, McKinley saw the SETI SUV pull up beside the dead man. Reynolds and Alvarez jumped out and examined him. Jack Simington, standing next to them, was on the phone as the jet began to move down the apron toward the runway.

A few minutes later McKinley watched Wilpena Pound fade away down below as he wiped blood from Hastings' forehead.

"What now, Jarrod?" as she leaned close to him.

Janet Brighton and Sam Filmore struggled to restore calm in the conference room.

"You call that security?" questioned the USNA representative. "If one man can walk in here and abduct our leader, how safe are the rest of us?"

"And why are we still in lockdown?" one of the European delegates demanded to know. "We should be out there helping, or making sure the rest of our teams are safe. It's apparent you can't provide security for anyone here."

"And what do we do now that our single point of contact has been taken?" asked the Chinese delegate. "I was impressed with Mr. McKinley, but it's obvious his plan has a serious flaw. Who is our contact now that McKinley is gone? I think the SETI team is ill prepared to handle this situation. And I'm not talking about just this abduction. I'm talking about the whole first contact plan. We need to revisit our last vote."

"Ladies and gentlemen, please be calm and patient," pleaded Brighton. "We have seen much more difficult situations than this. Jarrod is very resourceful. I'm sure he will be back to us soon. Recall the dangers and difficulties he has overcome in the past year. Not just here but also on the Titan listening post and the

Titan base. He has to this point defeated all of his adversaries and I'm sure he will again. Let's wait for a progress report."

The phone on the conference room table rang and Brighton answered. After a few seconds of discussion she turned back to the group.

Her report that McKinley, Hastings and the abductor had escaped didn't sit well.

"Please, please," she said over the talk of others. "Please, let's all sit down and discuss this."

"We need to do more than discuss this," said Chin Lieu, the Chinese delegate. "We need to take some action. We can't function like this and we can't sit back and just respond to these attacks on McKinley, SETI and this effort of first contact."

"I agree completely," said Brighton. "Let's talk."

"The first thing we need to do is make sure Mr. McKinley and Ms. Hastings are safely returned," said the USNA delegate.

"I disagree," countered one of the delegates from Europe. "The first thing we need to do is chose a different single point of contact."

"That will not work," said a different European delegate. "The Source made it clear they want McKinley."

"Well, he's not here now is he?" scoffed the other European.

"This plan relies on one person? Ridiculous," said another European.

"There is a simple solution," Lieu responded calmly. "McKinley remains our single point of contact, in person when possible, in absentia when not. We choose two more people who can receive messages for McKinley, but in his name."

"Please explain," said Brighton. "We don't want to work a deception when dealing with the Source. This has to be a totally honest relationship. We don't know where any of this will lead but we don't want to start by being deceptive. We don't know their capability to monitor what we do. Will they be able to tell if Jarrod is not personally involved?"

"Let me remind you of what McKinley himself said," responded Lieu. "He said he would not make decisions on his own. He said he would leave that up to this council. I think having two people working with McKinley to make sure communications are not interrupted falls within that same philosophy and spirit."

"Perhaps," said Brighton. "But we must give McKinley every chance to be that point of contact."

Henning interrupted. "Just to let you know, we did send a message to the Source announcing the decision this council made about Jarrod being the single point of contact. That message was sent by Jack Simington in operations. And it was sent while Jarrod was in this room."

"See?" said Lieu. "How is what I proposed any different?"

"It's different because McKinley gave his approval to send the message," said the one of the Europeans.

"But did he approve the exact text? And did he push the button to send the message?" asked Lieu.

"There was a nondescript ending to the message that Jarrod did not see and he did not push the button," said Henning.

"Technically, then, he was not the first point of contact," responded Lieu.

"What happens when the Source says they want to communicate directly with McKinley?" asked the delegate from USNA.

"We can deal with that demand if necessary," said Lieu.

"And who would those two other people be?" asked the USNA delegate.

"I would be happy to volunteer," said Lieu with a smile.

"And why you?" asked one of the European delegates.

"Well it was my idea."

"Just because you said it first doesn't mean anyone of us could not have come up with the idea."

"All right, everyone," said Brighton. "Let's work together on this. I would suggest that we expand Lieu's idea to include four people. From SETI we have McKinley. We should then have one from each of our delegations, China, the USNA and Europe. Who those people are can be up to the delegations."

"I would go along with that," said Lieu.

USNA and the Europeans nodded in agreement. Most also said they would have to report the situation to their central governments.

"Okay," said Brighton. "Jarrod McKinley will still be our single point of contact but three other people will be authorized to accept messages when he is not available. We must be certain to make that clear to the Source and we must give Jarrod every chance to be personally involved in the communications."

"What happens if the Source doesn't accept this plan?" asked Henning.

"We'll cross that bridge when we come to it," said Brighton. "Now, we have other issues to discuss and we have a situation update from Gen. Jones."

"We are tracking the jet that carries McKinley and Hastings," Jones said. "We immediately notified all law enforcement agencies and the United Space Command security has mobilized. The jet is heading south. It's final destination is not certain. It could be Adelaide, Melbourne, Sydney or anywhere else depending on its fuel. Based on the type of aircraft and the fact that it flew from Sydney to here and did not take on extra fuel before departing again, we believe it must land at a distance no further than Sydney. But it could land anywhere on a private airstrip or commercial field.

"We're tracking it with radar and GPS and we are shadowing it with a chase plane carrying Jack Simington, Liza Alvarez and Josh Reynolds. We are certain it cannot escape. What we will do to rescue the hostages, is not certain. We're working on plans and a rapid strike force also is following the aircraft. What we can do will depend upon where the plane lands and what kind of resources the abductor has."

"What about overall security?" asked Lieu. "Now

that others of us are more involved, are we in more danger?"

"Possibly," said Jones. "I have reassigned more security personnel from the United Space Command in Alice Springs to this facility. In addition, I have put in an urgent request to USC members to provide additional resources. I think within a matter of hours this facility will be more secure and within days our Alice Springs command center and branch facilities in other countries will be more secure.

"We don't know how far this assault will go. Is it just Galactic Minerals Enterprises or something more? And, are they just after McKinley and the SETI program or will they try to sabotage space programs all over the globe?"

"I believe this is a targeted attack," said Sam Filmore. "Since the first cyber attack and the attacks on McKinley, including the release of Gregory Stalingwirth from prison, every piece of hard evidence points back to GME. No one else."

"Then we need to go after GME," said Lieu.

"What do you mean go after?" asked Brighton.

"The first order of business is to send a delegation to GME and demand to know what is going on," said Lieu.

"We must order them to stop this interference," said the USNA delegate.

"How to we do that?" asked Brighton.

"Right here in this room we have representatives of at least sixty percent of GME's customers," said Lars Johannson, the lead European delegate. "Some of us have personal relations with some of GME's board members. Others have ties to some of GME's largest contractors. We can cut them off."

"What if they cut off their supply of natural resources?" asked another European delegate. "You forget that GME probably controls at least sixty percent of the supply of rare elements, fossil fuels and inert gases."

"There are other companies that could help fill that gap," said the delegate from the USNA.

"Yes," replied Johannson. "Companies in North America, no doubt."

"Please, everyone," said Brighton. "We must work together on this. I believe going to GME is essential. We need to try to reason with them to stop this interference. If they will not, we must be united to have any chance at stopping them. I know there are still a lot of independent political and economic interests in all of the countries we represent. We must impress on everyone that we, and by that I mean the people of Earth, must act together. If we continue to bicker and fight among ourselves, how can we be expected to live up to the challenges of first contact.

"We don't know what kind of challenges they might be. If this is contact from another civilization, what do they want? Do they want peace and do they want to help us, as Jarrod thinks, or do they have something else in mind? Do they want our resources, our water, our people?

"We don't know. But whatever it is, we need to be united. I would hope we can convince GME of the same thing. If we can't, we can discuss other strategies at that time. Now we need to go in the spirit of goodwill and cooperation."

"You mean like the goodwill and cooperation we just experienced," scoffed one of the European delegates.

"I agree with Brighton," said Lieu. "We must be gentle but powerful. The most effective power we can have is to be united. If GME sees a united front around the globe, they will have no choice but to comply."

"I also agree," said the USNA delegate. Most of the others nodded in agreement.

"Okay," said Brighton. "I will set up a meeting with GME. It will likely be held in GME's Sydney's office. It will probably be a few days before their leadership can get here from New York."

"Right now we have a signal to think about," said Henning. "We sent our signal about an hour ago. Based on the latest information on the time delays, we don't expect the next signal any sooner than about eight hours from now. That gives us time to organize our new structure and be ready to receive the signal. I would like to brief our selected delegates on some the technical details of our signaling procedure."

"Perhaps eight hours will give us enough time to get McKinley back here," said Lieu.

"I wouldn't count on it," replied Gen. Jones, who had just hung up the conference room phone. "The latest report is that the plane is still in the air, heading toward the Grampians Range in Victoria. We don't know where it's going.

"We're close by. The strike force has now caught up to the chase plane. We'll be ready when it lands. But it will be dark in a couple of hours and that will hurt any rescue attempts."

From the minute he and Jenny Hastings were handcuffed to the seat of the jet that they now knew was being piloted by a man named Colin Riley, Jarrod McKinley searched for a way out.

His right hand was cuffed to Hastings. His left was cuffed to the armrest of one of the captain's chair seats on the left side of the cabin. Hastings was not cuffed to her seat. On the opposite side of the cabin, two chairs faced them and a bar and lavatories were to the rear of the plane.

Riley was alone in the cockpit with the door open and he occasionally glanced back or stepped back to check on his captives. The plane appeared to be on auto pilot for much of the time.

McKinley didn't mind if Riley had little to say because he was working over how to free Hastings and himself. He was certain Riley would kill Hastings the minute she was of no use.

McKinley tested the handcuff on his left wrist. It was tight. The other end of the cuff went through an opening on the left arm of the chair. He pulled quietly and then harder on the left cuff. The armrest seemed solid.

He turned to Hastings.

"Jenny, I'm so sorry I got you into this. You don't deserve this."

"It's not your fault," Hastings said. "I stepped up to that door."

"But he wouldn't be here if it wasn't for me," McKinley said with a nod toward the cockpit.

"I am sensing extreme danger, Jenny, deadly danger. We need to get out of here. Is your cuff tight?"

"I have some slack," she said. "But I don't think I can slip it off."

"Do you have anything on you that we can use as a tool?"

"Not really, just a small pocket knife."

"Let's see."

Hastings' knife was a tiny Swiss Army knife with one blade about two inches long as well as a tiny scissors and a nail file.

"See if there's anything on this arm rest that we might be able to weaken," McKinley said.

Hastings stood up and leaned closely over McKinley, brushing him slightly, to exam how the handcuff was attached to the seat.

"Nothing," she said. "I don't see any screws, no breaks in the upholstery."

"Hey! Sit down back there!" Riley shouted. "It's no use. You won't be going anywhere until I say so." He laughed a little and turned back to the cockpit.

McKinley jerked on the armrest again. Nothing budged.

He took Hastings' little knife, twisted his left hand around and poked at the armrest. It was solid. He looked around the cabin. On the wall near the exit door hung a fire extinguisher and an axe. They were on the opposite wall and were attached with quick release mechanisms.

At the same time Hastings was fiddling with her handcuff. She could slip it partly over her wrist but her thumb prevented her from slipping it off completely.

"Jarrod, I think if I dislocate my thumb, I might be able to get this cuff off."

"Wait. Not yet. You might need all the strength you have in that thumb. We have to be sure he doesn't get us off this plane. If we work together, it will be hard for him to drag both of us off. Look at that exit door. Check out the placement of the extinguisher and axe. How close can you get to them?"

"If we both were out of our seats and stretched, I could reach the axe."

"He's not going to allow that. Not now."

"What are you thinking?"

McKinley looked around the cabin again.

"I'm working on it," he said. "Keep thinking about that axe and think about how we are cuffed together. We don't know what's going to happen when we land. Will he take us one at a time, or together? Work over some scenarios in your mind to be ready for anything."

"Got it," Hastings said and she began looking around the cabin, measuring in her mind the distances between the cockpit and the seats, the seats and the exit door, the bar and the lavatory, the lavatory and the exit door. Her eyes kept coming back to the axe and extinguisher. She tried to envision how the quick release worked.

McKinley spotted something under the seats on the other side of the cabin. It appear to be a strap to secure items to the seats. One end had dropped down to the floor.

He motioned to Hastings. Then he whispered, "Check this side. Is there a strap under these seats?"

Hastings reached below the seats they were sitting on.

"Yes."

"See if you can loosen the strap."

"There," said Hastings after a few minutes.

McKinley, looking across the aisle, could see the strap was attached to the bottom of the seat, but with one arm cuffed to the chair's armrest and the other to Hastings, he could do nothing to reach the strap under his seat. He noticed a quick-release buckle, but couldn't get to the one on his seat.

A plan was forming in his mind.

"Jenny," he said as he grabbed her hand and looked her directly in the eyes.

"I am sure that we have to stop this guy before we get off this plane. If we don't, there is a good chance that one or both of us will not survive. I've got a plan but it's going to require some quick action and a lot of precision."

"I'm ready, Jarrod," Hastings said.

"I estimate we'll have about two minutes during the landing when he will have to watch the runway.

We might have a chance then. Here's what we're going to do."

Athrena clicked off the holovid and turned her chair toward the large window in her office when her comm device buzzed. It was a Forgiven Project technician.

"Very well," she said. "Send it to me and then ring Conteus and Acquius. Have them come to my office."

She had been reviewing Forgiven Project historical documentation looking for holes in the plan, for anything that might go wrong, and searching for actions Progenia Prime might take to counter unexpected events. One thing she was sure of, something would happen that would require nimble moves on their part to keep Earth in line.

It would not be easy for Earth to accept what it was about to face. Knowing Earth's history intimately, the biggest worry Athrena had was the independent nature of the human species. During the last fifty years there had been many developments on Earth that showed a willingness to combine resources and efforts for the betterment of everyone on the planet. But, there was still a strong streak of individualism which manifested itself in many ways, strong private corporations being the most pronounced.

Being part of a master plan, having behaviors dictated to you, drawing limits around individual choices, had been both the strong part and the weak part of humans. On one hand it had done much to ensure the survival and advancement of the species on the planet, but on the other hand, the lack of cooperation and the competitiveness had caused untold conflicts to slow progress. She was sure there would be resistance on Earth to the Forgiven Project. How much and what to do about it would be a major issue as the plan moved forward.

Another big issue, she believed, would be the ability of Earthlings to accept the story behind Forgiven. She would have proof. She would be able to show them the truth. But often, as she knew from studying Earth, truth was not accepted.

"We have another signal?" said Conteus as he entered the office.

"Yes, and it is good news."

There was a quick knock and Acquius entered.

"Acquius. Welcome to your first taste of what we are dealing with here with the Forgiven Project," said Athrena.

"I welcome the chance," said Acquius.

"Earth has agreed to our conditions," said Athrena. "Jarrod McKinley will be our single point of contact as we move forward."

"What does that mean exactly," asked Acquius. "Will this one person speak for all of Earth? Given Earth's history, I am reluctant to accept this acknowledgement on face value."

"We made no demands other than a single point of contact," said Conteus. "What happens after we relay messages to McKinley had not been outlined. We do know that a group of delegates from all the regions of Earth with major space programs were with McKinley before the message was sent. We assume there was agreement among those delegates."

"Please remember, Acquius, this is just the first step," said Athrena. "What this gives us is one person to communicate with. We will make do with that until we find the situation unworkable.

"What we need to do now is to review our response as outlined in the plan, get agreement from the whole council, formulate the message, and send it back to Earth."

"As I understand the plan, we do not, at this time, reveal who we are or what we want on Earth."

"That is correct," said Athrena. "The changes Earth faces when the project is in full force may not be easy to accept. There will have to be a gradual revelation of who we are, of where we come from, of the project, and of the fate of Earth."

"That is why the single point of contact is so important," said Conteus. "We believe Jarrod McKinley has the insight and temperament to relay this information in the most benign way possible."

"A prolonged communication of mostly mundane information will build a level of trust, perhaps, between us and McKinley," said Athrena. "We are hoping he then will impart that sense of trust to others around him and that will filter down to leaders around the planet and from there to the general populace. We want acceptance from everyone, not just the leaders, before we present the ultimate plan for Earth. It could mean the difference between success and failure of the project."

"And of the Grand Vision," said Conteus.

"Yes," said Athrena. "Now, let us review the 'script' and determine what we want to say to Earth."

Within the hour, the message to Earth from Progenia Prime had been formulated and sent out to project conferees for approval. A half hour later, approval had come in from everyone.

"Now do we send it?" asked Acquius.

"No," said Athrena. "We wait a day. The waiting will build a level of anticipation with McKinley and those around him. We do not want them to think we are too anxious to get the communications going."

"Keep them guessing?" asked Acquius.

"Not exactly," said Conteus. "We just want them to be the ones eager for the next message. If we respond too fast, we might look too aggressive."

"It might make them more suspicious," added Athrena.

"Suspicious? I did not see anything to be suspicious of," said Acquius.

"Remember who we are dealing with," said Athrena. "Earth's history is not one built on trusting your neighbors."

"And now they are facing possibly the biggest and most unknown threat they have faced," said Conteus.

"But do you not believe that our messages will raise that level of suspicion? We will ask for details they may not want to reveal if they believe we are hostile."

"Perhaps," said Athrena. "But this will test their resolve to make first contact. They know there is some risk. Are they willing to take that risk, not knowing if we are friend or enemy?"

"But we are not—"

Athrena's comm device buzzed.

"Speaking of enemies," she said to Conteus and Acquius after she clicked off, "Jarrod McKinley is in trouble again with his primary foe."

"GME?" asked Conteus.

"Yes."

"Why do we let one private company interfere with this?" asked Acquius.

"It is a problem for Earth to solve," said Athrena. "If they cannot bring this entity in line, what will they do faced with the Forgiven Project?"

"What is the status of McKinley?" asked Conteus.

"Unknown."

Chapter 20

Jarrod McKinley felt the jet beginning its descent after three hours of flying. For the last hour he and Jenny Hastings had gone over the plan they hoped would free them from GME agent Colin Riley.

Riley had visited them many times during the flight, letting the autopilot direct the jet. Based on what he had said, McKinley was sure that doing nothing would mean the death of Hastings and his transfer into the bowels of GME, where any kind of escape would be doubtful. They had to make their move as soon as the plane landed and before the doors were open.

Their plan relied on Riley being distracted for a few minutes during the landing. McKinley had tried to imagine all contingencies: Riley leaving him in the jet while he disposed of Hastings, Riley taking the two of them out of the plane still handcuffed together, Riley just shooting Hastings where she sat. They would have to act fast and aggressively the instant Riley was within reach. From what he had seen and heard of Riley, he was a highly trained professional killer.

"Are you ready?" he asked Hastings.

"Ready."

The descent was more rapid now and McKinley was certain Riley was looking for a place to land. He could see they were still over a sparsely populated country, but he had no idea where. Based on the three hours flying time from Wilpena Pound they could be in New South Wales, Victoria or South Australia. Where ever they were, the only visible lights were those of small towns and scattered rural stations and settlements.

As the plane banked, McKinley spotted the lights of a larger town, still just a small city. They were not near Sydney, Melbourne or Adelaide, McKinley guessed. He wondered why Riley was setting the jet down in such an isolated area. His sense of danger began to rise.

"Well, folks," said Riley as he came out of the cockpit and sat in one of the seats opposite them, "are you ready to take the next step? I want you to behave like you have the last couple of hours. No dramatic escape attempts. No trauma and we'll all live through the next few hours."

"You won't get any trouble from us," said McKinley. "Not much we can do handcuffed together and to this seat. Don't you think you'd better attend to the landing? I wouldn't want to die in some stupid plane crash."

Riley chuckled. "Amazing technology these days. Did you know this plane and this private airfield are equipped with the latest GPS and radar guidance systems? The nice thing is that when the pilot has special guests to attend to, such as you two, he can just let the plane land itself. Hell, it will even taxi right up to, and inside, our special hangar. I only have to give you the special attention you deserve."

"That's nice," said Hastings with some resignation in her voice.

"I just want to make sure you two are safe and secure for the final few minutes of this flight. You are precious cargo, after all," he said looking McKinley in the eyes.

"Well, this precious cargo has to go to the bathroom," said McKinley. "Counting the conference I was in at Wilpena Pound and this flight, it's been about five hours and I can't hold it much longer."

"You'll have to hold it a bit longer," said Riley. "Wait 'til were in the hangar. I'm not separating you two until we're safely inside."

"So you want to present us to your bosses with soiled pants? That won't be too cool."

"Not to worry. It will be a while before you see my bosses. We've got some processing to do first."

"Processing?" asked Hastings.

"Never mind," said Riley. "We're landing now."

McKinley shot a grim look at Hastings. She looked back and reached her fingers to his where their wrists were connected with the handcuffs.

He squeezed her fingers three times and looked away.

The jet glided smoothly to a landing and braked hard.

With Riley still sitting across from them, the jet turned off the runway and taxied toward an apron and a single large, new hangar.

"Ladies and gentlemen. Welcome to Bendigo. Or I should say, the Bendigo region. Please remain seated with your seat belts fastened until our plane has come to a complete stop," Riley said with a malicious laugh.

The jet steered itself to the hangar and turned toward a pair of large double doors that were starting to open.

"Almost there," Riley said looking out the window.

McKinley feverishly stretched the fingers of his left hand, trying to unlatch the storage strap under the seat, but he couldn't reach it.

Hastings looked at him. A sense of worry was creeping into her normally confident demeanor. She raised an eyebrow and nodded slightly. She mouthed a word and turned back before Riley looked at them again.

McKinley nodded. They were now committed to the most risky escape alternative they had envisioned.

Just before the plane stopped, they both stood up, hands still cuffed together and McKinley's left hand cuffed to the armrest.

"I said to stay seated," ordered Riley just as the autopilot put the last touch on the brakes to bring the plane to a full stop.

Hastings lurched and fell across McKinley, knocking him back into his seat. Her right hand dove under the side of his seat as she splayed out on top of him.

"What did I tell you?" Riley barked. "Stand up little miss pretty. Get back in your seat."

Hastings wriggled about, but didn't get up. She struggled to get her feet under her.

"I said get up," shouted Riley and he grabbed her shoulder and pulled. Hasting still laid on top of McKinley and Riley had trouble pulling up her dead weight.

"Stupid woman," Riley grumbled and he pulled her again. This time he was able to turn Hastings and he jerked her, half fallen, back into her seat.

"Now sit there while I get this door open," ordered Riley.

McKinley looked at Hastings as she righted herself in her seat. She tensed and stared back at him. He nodded slightly.

Riley opened the door and swung down the exit stairs.

"Okay, you two. We're going to do this just like before. Down the stairs together. Just like one happy family. McKinley, you will go first and little miss Jenny will follow."

Riley released McKinley's left hand from the handcuff that had attached him to the seat. He backed off and grabbed Hastings and jerked her to her feet.

"Now you, McKinley. On your feet. It's time to go."

McKinley's sense of danger was skyrocketing. It was palpable and it was changing. He recognized the rage building in him. He had experienced it before on Titan. He knew this time it was being caused by an immediate threat to his life, or perhaps the life of Hastings.

He had been attacked in a hangar on Titan by a man who intended to kill him. That man barely escaped with his life. McKinley now let that rage build, focusing it on Riley.

He remained seated.

"I said get up," ordered Riley. "Do you want me to hurt little miss pretty?"

"You're going to kill her anyway," said McKinley. "Why should I help you do that?"

"Okay," sneered Riley. "If that's what you want."

Riley reached into his pocket and pulled out his pistol. He pointed it at Hastings' head.

"Now. Get up!"

With a shrug of resignation, McKinley started to rise. In one fluid, lightning quick movement, he rose, jerked hard on Hastings and swung his left arm at Riley.

The thick black baggage strap snaked instantly around Riley's pistol hand and McKinley pulled as hard as he could. Riley dropped the pistol and staggered to his knees as McKinley jumped on his back, pulling Hastings with him. He wrapped the strap around Riley's neck and began to pull as hard as he could.

Riley was gasping but struggling. He lurched forward and pulled McKinley and Hastings with him. As he was falling he reached for the pistol but Hastings had also seen it and kicked it down the aisle of the aircraft.

Riley was trying to turn now, so he could fend off McKinley. McKinley's eyes were blazing and he pulled harder on the strap around Riley's neck. He smashed a knee into the side of Riley and pushed hard toward the floor as he continued to pull on the strap.

Riley was reaching for his boot. He grabbed a knife and swung it toward McKinley's leg. The knife went deep into McKinley's thigh and McKinley screamed but the rage was in control and he jerked harder on the strap. Riley was turning blue but not giving up. He pulled the knife out of McKinley's thigh and raised it to swing again.

Hastings lunged for Riley's knife hand. She couldn't stop the swing but redirected it and Riley stabbed himself. He let out a groan and slumped, his last resistance gone.

McKinley was still pulling hard on the strap.

"Jarrod, Jarrod. He's done. He's done. You can stop now!" Hastings shouted.

McKinley didn't hear her. All he could see was that the man on the floor of the plane was trying to kill them.

"Stop! Stop, Jarrod. He's better to us alive," Hastings urged.

McKinley didn't respond.

"Jarrod," Hastings said louder. "He's dying!"

She slapped McKinley hard across the face with her free hand.

"Enough," she said. "We've got other problems. There are people coming."

McKinley jerked back and sank to his knees. The

rage faded, his vision cooled, and a look of recognition returned. He swept his eyes around the cabin. Riley was motionless on the floor of the plane, but was still breathing. McKinley's leg was bleeding badly and now the pain began to throb. His face hurt where Hastings had slapped him.

"Look outside Jarrod. Someone's coming."

Three men were running toward the plane. Two were carrying automatic rifles.

"Get the door up!" McKinley shouted.

Still cuffed together, they jerked on the exit stairway and it began to slowly raise. The men were almost on them now, their rifles pointed at the plane.

They saw Riley unconscious on the floor of the plane and began to fire their weapons. Bullets glanced over the top of the door opening as McKinley and Hastings ducked.

The door swung back across the opening, bullets lodging in the metal. Hastings latched the door and turned back to McKinley. He was staggering now on his wounded thigh.

"Jenny, grab that strap and tie Riley's hands behind him."

Hastings pulled McKinley along as she did as he instructed.

"Now let's get these handcuffs off," he said.

Outside of the plane people were shouting.

With handcuffs off, McKinley sank to the floor.

"You in the plane!" a voice from outside called. "Give up now. You're in a hangar. The doors are closing. You're not going anywhere."

"What are we going to do, Jarrod?"

"We've got Riley," said McKinley.

"I don't think that matters much," replied Hastings. "GME seems to treat all of its people as very expendable."

"I don't know. I don't know," sighed McKinley. The rage was gone and he was exhausted.

Hastings put an arm around him.

"It's okay, Jarrod," she said softly. "You saved us. You saved me. I'd probably be dead now if you hadn't taken down Riley."

"You in the plane. You have two minutes to open that door before we blast it open. Come out now if you want to come out alive."

"We might still be dead," McKinley said.

"I have faith in you, Jarrod." Hastings bent to him and kissed him on the lips.

He was startled, but soon relaxed and returned the kiss, wrapping his arms around her.

"One minute," shouted the voice outside.

"They're headed down," said Jack Simington in the chase plane.

"Where are they going?" asked Josh Reynolds.

"Not sure, but they're close to the town of Bendigo," said Simington. "Bendigo is one of Australia's earliest mining towns. All the mines have been dormant for at least a century but GME has built a regional research facility there. It's all been very hush-hush. They're good at keeping secrets."

"What kind of research?" asked Liza Alvarez.

"They say it's to support their space mining operation," said Simington. "But that could mean a lot more than just mining techniques. Their biggest problem is getting back and forth to their space mining locations, Mars, the asteroid belt, Titan. Time is a big problem for them. They waste a lot time and energy just getting to the mining locations and getting their raw materials or refined product back to customers on Earth.

"It's been rumored they're experimenting with teleportation, time warps and other unproven technologies."

"That would explain why they so desperately want the help of the aliens," said Reynolds.

"Perhaps," said Simington. "Perhaps they're looking for something else. Or they're just greedy buggers and want to keep any new technologies for themselves."

"Jack. I'm sensing something is going wrong on that plane carrying Jarrod," said Alvarez.

"What do you mean? Can you sense danger as Jarrod can?"

"No. Not really," replied Alvarez. "But I know Jarrod thinks he is in big trouble."

"Yeah, I would too if I'd been snatched by that GME thug," said Reynolds.

"It's more than that," said Alvarez. "Jarrod is sure getting off that plane will mean the death of someone, perhaps Jenny."

"You're just guessing," said Simington. "We don't know what GME's planning."

"It's more than a guess," insisted Alvarez. "It's almost like he's talking to me. We've been together a lot over the past few years, and we know a great deal about how the other person thinks. Sometimes we finish each other's sentences."

"It happens," said Reynolds.

"But this is more. I've never experienced this before. Even on Titan, or last year when we were battling Larchmont. I can hear Jarrod."

"Must be the stress," said Simington. "Stress will do strange things."

"Jack," Alvarez almost shouted. "Listen to me. We have to get closer and we have to act fast. And call that quick strike team. Jarrod's and Jenny's lives are hanging in the balance."

"Okay," said Simington.

He ordered the pilot to close the distance between the chase plane and the plane carrying the hostages. He called the strike force team.

"Looks like they're making a landing approach," said Simington. "Bendigo it is."

As their plane touched down, Simington could see the aircraft carrying McKinley and Hastings had cleared the runway and was turning into a large hangar where the huge double doors were sliding open. The GME jet slid through the doors and came to a stop. A minute later the door of the plane swung open and the exit stairs dropped down. Then nothing.

Simington thought he noticed movement on the plane but no one appeared at the door. Another minute passed. Nothing.

GME personnel were spotted walking toward the plane. Three men. Two of them carrying automatic rifles. They were shouting and running. Now they were firing their weapons. The door of the plane swung closed against the glancing bullets.

Now a fourth man rushed to join the GME team. He was carrying explosives and a large weapon that looked like a rocket launcher.

As Simington's plane reached the taxiway, he knew they were going to be too late. The doors of the hangar had closed. There was no way they could get in that hangar before something very explosive happened to the plane carrying McKinley and Hastings.

"Liza, I'm sorry," he said. "We're not going to make it."

Alvarez pressed her face against the window trying to get a glimpse. All she could say was, "Damn, damn."

Josh Reynolds put an arm around her shoulders.

She stayed pressed against the window.

Janet Brighton, Sam Filmore and Laura Henning were in the Wilpena Pound infirmary. Laid out on an exam table was the body of the man Colin Riley had shot as he had made his escape with Jarrod McKinley and Jenny Hastings.

"Who is it?" Brighton asked.

"It says here he was Dennis Wright," said Henning as she looked at a personnel folder. "He's been with us for almost a year. He was hired as part of the sanitary crew but his work had been exceptional and he had been promoted twice since."

"Promoted just enough to give him access to the whole compound," said Filmore.

"His background is sketchy, but clean. There is no indication he ever worked for GME or any other industrial company."

"If he's been here almost a year that was before we received this new signal," said Brighton. "That means GME must have reached in and recruited this man."

"Or they were way ahead of us and planted this man here while we were still in chaos during the Forsaken scandal," said Henning. "It says here he was hired by Stalingwirth."

"But Stalingwirth wasn't working for GME until they bailed him out of jail," said Brighton.

"And we vetted all of the old Forsaken personnel after we took over," said Filmore. "We cleared the recent hires with clean backgrounds, believing they would have no allegiance to Larchmont or Stalingwirth."

"Well, this guy didn't. He had an allegiance to GME, apparently," said Brighton.

"We weren't even looking for that," said Filmore. "GME wasn't even in the picture."

"We wouldn't have seen it, even if we had been looking," said Henning. "There's no hint of it in his file."

"Question is, what should we do now?" said Brighton. "We don't know if there are any more moles in Wilpena Pound. And now that we have added all these people with the delegations from Asia, Europe and the USNA, how secure are we?"

"That's what we would like to know," said Chin Lieu, as the leader of the Chinese delegation entered the room with the delegation leaders from Europe and the USNA.

"We are just hours from this event happening," said Brighton. "Our security chief and Gen. Jones have already launched an investigation. We should have some answers soon."

"We are concerned that 'soon' is not sufficient," replied Larry Mitchell, the USNA delegation leader. "We've all been in contact with our home governments and I must tell you concern over this operation is reaching the highest levels. I worked hard to convince my government not to send in their own security personnel here to take over."

"I also had some hard explaining to do," said Lieu. "My government has given me an ultimatum. If things don't stabilize here within the week, they will vote on whether to take direct action."

"What does that mean?" asked Brighton.

"It means our governments are very wary of having a bunch of scientists deal with such a momentous event as first contact with an alien species," replied Lars Johannson, the European delegation leader.

"It's more than just the small security issues we are facing here," said Mitchell. "There are also economic, military and sociological questions. Surely you don't expect this group to provide those answers for the planet."

"No, I don't," said Brighton. "This operation is only the first step. The team we have here, with all of your teams included, is composed of the best minds in the fields necessary to determine the validity of this signal. If, after we exchange a few responses with The Source, we determine the signal is valid, we always expected we would ask for help to find the most appropriate path forward."

"Our governments need to know that," said Lieu.

"Not tonight they don't," said Henning.

"I agree," said Filmore. "It's midnight. We are right in the middle of a crisis threatening one of the key elements of this project, namely, McKinley. We need to resolve this before we get into the politics of this."

"It can't wait much longer," said Mitchell. "I've got some very concerned, very powerful people pulling at me."

"Okay, let's all relax," said Brighton. "We've all had a stressful day and we need to get some sleep. We'll deal with this tomorrow. We'll deal with this after we get our staff back safe and sound."

"When will that be? Can you be sure?" demanded Lieu.

"I can be sure of one thing right now," said Brighton with a glare. "Sam and I are in charge of this facility. With the help of Gen. Jones, our security team is doing a sweep and locking things down. Besides making sure we are secure, Gen. Jones will ensure our orders are followed. Now, it's time to say goodnight, ladies and gentlemen."

"I don't think that response will satisfy my people back home," said Lieu.

"Nor mine," said Johannson.

Trying not to show her exasperation, Brighton breathed a deep sigh and turned to the delegates.

"Listen. I didn't mean to be so aggressive. But right now our priority has to be two people whose lives could be in danger, McKinley and Hastings. And we have to determine whether GME has placed anyone else in this facility who could do us harm. I would hope you all agree on that?"

Lieu, Mitchell and Johannson all nodded.

"Okay then. Let's gather all the conference delegates tomorrow afternoon at two, or today, I guess. We'll hope that by that time we will have better news about McKinley and Hastings and some evaluation about our security. Can I count on all of you to try to ease the concerns of your governments? Just work with us for a while. Can you?"

The delegates nodded in assent.

"Sam, Laura," Brighton said after the delegates had left the room, "we need to get some sleep. There's little we can do here except worry. We should all plan to meet at noon tomorrow, uh today, before the two o'clock meeting. This thing is getting out of control."

"Always knew the politics would be harder than the science," said Filmore.

"I never thought much about the politics," said Henning.

"Everything is political," said Brighton.

"Everything would be a lot easier if Jarrod were not under attack," said Henning.

"Probably wouldn't solve the politics," said Filmore.

"No, not all of it," said Brighton. "But Jarrod has a way of uniting people. A way of making people believe in him."

Filmore's comm device buzzed.

"It's Simington. The plane carrying Jarrod and Jenny just landed in Bendigo and pulled into a GME hangar. They're close. But maybe not close enough."

Athrena, Conteus and Acquius were reviewing the message they planned to send to Earth. After sending their draft message out to all of the Project Forgiven counselors, there was only one small change.

"Heronius wants to change one word in the message," said Athrena.

"Our draft message read:

Acknowledged.
Jarrod McKinley will be the single point of
contact between Earth and this location.
Jarrod McKinley will agree to message
protocols which will be sent shortly.
Jarrod McKinley should be the only
person to see all initial messages.
Please affirm this is acceptable.

"Heronius wants to change the word should to must."

"Why the change?" asked Acquius.

"Remember we are dealing with many languages," replied Athrena. "First there is the translation from Progenian to English. Earth still has many languages and Heronius believes the more definitive 'must' is preferable if what we are trying to do is get a consistent message to all of Earth. We do not want the people of Earth arguing over semantics."

"I can see this causing problems," said Conteus. "This order precludes even technicians from seeing our initial messages. I am not sure that will be possible, given what we know about how humans tend to organize their workforce."

"There is a way to do this so we do not give them any option," said Athrena. "When we establish message protocols, we give McKinley an encrypted code that only he will have and that code could change with each message. When Earth receives the message they will not be able to read it until McKinley puts in the code. We would have to trust McKinley not to reveal the code to others."

"Given the lack of security and the leaks the SETI team has experienced, I am not sure that even if we trust McKinley, we can be sure only McKinley will read our messages," said Acquius.

"I share your concerns, but with what we are going to reveal about our plans, it is vital we have a single source of messaging," said Athrena. "Earth will have a hard time accepting the truth and the fate of their planet. We do not want different interpretations of our messages being debated and fought over."

"I feel we should change *should* to *must*," said Conteus. "If they do not agree, or cannot do this, we stop communication."

"I agree," said Acquius.

"We will send the message in twelve hours," said Athrena. "Given the four and a half hour transmission time, that will put the message to Earth more than a day from their last message to us. I hope the delay will arouse their curiosity and their eagerness to keep the communication going."

"It might also give them a chance to get McKinley back," said Conteus. "Our agent reports the latest confrontation with GME is coming to a head."

"Has he had to intervene?" asked Athrena.

"Not yet. But it is uncertain whether McKinley will be able to save himself."

"And what about GME?" asked Acquius.

"There is still no resolution there," said Conteus.

"I hope Earthlings understand the gravity of the situation," said Athrena. "Dealing with GME is a major obstacle for them. Compliance and unity on Earth will be required to ensure the success of this project. Earth must get on board with the plan or the Grand Vision also will be jeopardized, or at least delayed."

"Time is on our side," said Conteus. "We have waited more than five hundred years for this moment. If things do not align, we can wait another hundred years."

"Windows of opportunity come only so often and I truly believe this is one of those windows. The time is right. The right people, Jarrod McKinley and SETI, are in place. We do not want to pass up this chance to make it work," Athrena said.

"This only works if McKinley can become more stable," said Conteus. "As we reveal details of the plan, he will be fully occupied trying to distribute the message. He will have significant public relations to do."

"Yes," said Athrena. "He should be able to handle that part of it. He has spent the last eight months traveling around the planet promoting SETI's mission and has built a strong following that believes first contact is possible and is a good thing."

"But will he buy into the Forgiven Project?" asked Acquius.

"We believe he is the best person on Earth right now to accept the truth and to carry the message," said Athrena. "His background, his genetics, his demeanor. All are working in our favor."

"We believe all he needs is to be able to apply all of his time and talents to the mission," Conteus said. "Pieces of the puzzle often just fall into place. We think that is what has happened here for McKinley, for the Forgiven Project and for Earth."

"But he cannot be effective if he worries about being constantly in danger," said Athrena. "That is why the GME issue is perhaps the biggest roadblock facing Forgiven."

"Why not take action against GME?" asked Acquius.

"Earth needs to decide on its own that unity and

compliance is necessary," said Athrena. "If we start forcing compliance, the defiant nature of Earthlings will surface all over the planet. We cannot force this at the initial stages. We need cooperation in the beginning if we are to have any chance of success."

"Leaders on Earth need to get the cooperation of GME," said Conteus.

"Now would be a good time to start," said Acquius.

Chapter 21

Jarrod McKinley was recovering from his fight with GME assassin Colin Riley. His rage had faded and Jenny Hastings had helped him rip off his pant leg and wrap the knife wound in his thigh.

"You in the plane," a voice from outside shouted. "Your time is up. Come out now or we will blast the door open."

"Jenny, move away from the door," McKinley said. He grabbed the legs of Riley, still unconscious, and dragged him toward the cockpit. At the same time he waved a hand in front of the window, trying to signal those outside.

"Jarrod, you can't give up," said Hastings. "Not now."

"Not giving up, stalling. Get another strap and tie up Riley's legs. I don't want to have to worry about him when he wakes up."

Hastings pulled out another strap from under the seats and tied Riley's legs. He was beginning to stir.

"Wake up Riley," McKinley ordered. He slapped Riley in the face. "Unless you want to die, you'd better wake up and call off your dogs."

Riley shook his head no and gave McKinley a big smirk.

"Grab him," McKinley ordered Hastings.

Together they were able to prop Riley up enough so he could be seen from outside.

Riley looked out and shook his head no, trying to signal his team to go ahead with its plan to breach the plane.

"It's not working," said Hastings. "They're still setting up the explosives and that rocket launcher."

"Just a few more seconds," said McKinley. "We just need a few more—"

A blast rocked the plane and the GME team in the hangar swung around to face the hangar doors, now bent open at an odd angle. They tried to fire their weapons but a withering assault from the oncoming Special Forces team cut them down. It was over in a matter of seconds.

McKinley and Hastings watched the GME men fall and the Special Forces team rush to secure them. Three of the four were dead. The fourth was severely wounded and a paramedic immediately applied first aid.

"You in the plane," shouted the Special Forces leader as he turned to the jet. "You are surrounded by United Space Command Special Forces. Release the hostages and open the door."

McKinley and Hastings crowded to one of the windows and waved. They carefully opened the door and held out their hands to show they had no weapons.

"We're okay," said McKinley as he pushed a bound Riley to the door.

Hastings released the stairs and a moment later Special Forces troopers had grabbed Riley and pulled him out of the plane.

Once McKinley and Hastings were on the ground, a paramedic immediately began to examine McKinley's wound while another questioned Hastings.

"Captain, hold this man and make sure he is secure," said McKinley. "His name is Colin Riley. He's extremely dangerous and we need to take him back to Wilpena Pound for questioning."

As some of the troops secured Riley, others fanned out to secure the area. Alarms blared and lights flashed throughout GME's Bendigo complex. Other troops pushed open the big hangar doors as another airplane rolled up. The door on the plane opened, the stairs dropped and Liza Alvarez jumped out and ran toward McKinley.

"Jarrod, are you okay?" she asked as she threw her arms around his neck.

McKinley staggered a bit on his wounded leg.

"I'm all right," he said."

"Are you sure?" She stepped back and reached down to touch his leg.

"I'm fine. I'm told it's just a flesh wound."

Josh Reynolds was right behind Alvarez. He stopped and hesitated when Alvarez embraced McKinley.

He turned to Hastings. "Jenny, are you all right?"

Hastings nodded her head but didn't take her eyes off McKinley and Alvarez.

"Jarrod. Are you okay? Looks like you've lost lots of blood." It was Jack Simington.

"I'm fine, Jack."

"Jenny. You okay?"

"Yeah. I'm fine. Jarrod took all the punishment."

"We need to get Jarrod back to Wilpena Pound's infirmary and check that wound," said Simington. "What do you want to do with him?" he motioned to Riley.

"His name in Colin Riley. I believe he can be of use to us," said McKinley. "I've asked Special Forces take him back to Wilpena Pound. We'll decide later how to use him."

As McKinley and his party moved toward the SETI plane, he stopped.

"Jack, we need to search that jet Riley was piloting. Look for anything tying it to GME."

"Okay. Josh, Liza, come with me," Simington said.

"No," said McKinley. "Take Jenny. She knows the layout."

When McKinley and Alvarez were seated on the SETI plane, he turned to her and gave her a big embrace. "I knew you were coming," he said.

"I knew you were in trouble," Alvarez replied. "It was almost as if you were calling for me, or maybe calling for help."

"I wasn't speaking it out loud. But I sure was thinking it. I was thinking especially about you. Calling for you."

"I tried to tell you we were coming. I tried to say it in my mind."

"I heard you. Just before Special Forces blasted the hangar door open, I could almost hear you say, 'Two seconds, Jarrod. Hang on for two seconds.' "

"That's exactly what I was thinking. I could see them getting ready to breach that door. What's going on here, Jarrod? How are we communicating?"

"It's probably a combination of the power of the stress and wishful thinking."

"I don't think so," said Alvarez. "I've had hints of this before. It started on the farm in Montana."

"Why didn't you tell me?"

"It didn't seem real, at the time. And it wasn't important."

"It's very important, Liza. We need to explore this some more. Just like this sense of danger I've been developing. Maybe it's something we can enhance."

"If we have time," replied Alvarez. "Things have been crazy since I've arrived in Australia."

"It will get better, Liza. I'm going to make sure of that. This thing with GME will stop, and soon. I'm not going to let one mining company derail our first contact."

"Jarrod, they're not just a mining company. They are the largest mining and resource corporation in the world and one of the largest private corporations left in the world's economy. They have strong ties to many, many powerful politicians."

"I know. But we have the proof now. They've tried to kidnap me twice and probably were going to kill Jenny. We have one of their assassins. We have one of their planes. I think we have some leverage."

"I hope so," said Alvarez.

Simington, Reynolds and Hastings climbed aboard the SETI plane.

"It's clean," said Simington.

"What?"

"Yeah," said Hastings. "Jarrod, there's nothing on that plane to tie it to GME. And there's nothing on that plane to tie it to Riley, or Riley to GME."

"We have Riley," said McKinley. "And we did land at this GME facility. GME is stamped all over this place. We'll see if we can get Riley to talk."

"I wouldn't bet on it," said Reynolds. "That guy's more of a killing machine than a man."

"Let's get back to Wilpena Pound and see what we can do," said Simington as he moved to the cockpit to give instructions to the pilots.

"Thanks, Jack," said McKinley. "I want to thank you and everybody. It wasn't looking good for me and Jenny. And thanks, Jenny. Thanks for being with me. You helped us escape."

"It was you, Jarrod," said Hastings as she reached out and touched his arm. "You came up with the plan. You took down Riley."

"I couldn't have done it without you." He squeezed her arm back.

"Jarrod. You need to rest now," said Alvarez, as she pushed closer to McKinley.

She got a blanket for McKinley and glanced sharply at Hastings.

Colin Riley cursed himself as he regained his control. He could hardly believe what had happened. Being overpowered by two civilians and tied up like a common criminal and handed over to a Special Forces team. Now he had to find a way to free himself from this team and get back to business, capturing Jarrod McKinley.

Having his arms strapped behind him and being surrounded by troops, locked in an airplane and flying at nine thousand meters over the Australian outback, didn't stop him from reviewing his options.

He was sure he could find a way. He'd been in tougher scrapes than this and prevailed. He immediately identified some weak points in his confinement and began probing. This wouldn't be the last time he tangled with McKinley.

The morning after the security breach, at ten o'clock, after about four hours of sleep, Janet Brighton and Sam Filmore sat on one side of a table in a small room at the Wilpena Pound SETI complex.

Across from them was the first of the five suspects on their list of possible moles. They had narrowed the original list of fifteen staff members down by eliminating those that Brighton, Filmore or Henning could personally vouch for. They had also called Jack Simington on the plane that was carrying McKinley and Hastings back after they had been rescued from Riley. Simington had vouched for only one other person. Others working at the compound didn't have the kind of access the mole had demonstrated from the leaks that had occurred or the security breaches experienced just before Riley had grabbed McKinley and Hastings.

Their goal was to discover whether Dennis Wright, the SETI security guard killed by Riley during the abduction, was the only mole and the only security threat. They had promised to meet the council delegates at two that afternoon with an update. It would be good news that McKinley and Hastings were safe and that Riley was in custody. What they wanted, desperately hoped for, was that Riley and his partner were the only threats.

Their four questions were simple and direct.

"Are you working for some entity to spy on the SETI complex?"

"Did you know Colin Riley or Dennis Wright?"

"Have you released any information about SETI's First Contact mission to any outside source?"

"Do you have any reason to sabotage the SETI mission?"

Each person being questioned had half a dozen sensors attached to various spots on their head and body and each session was being recorded and analyzed by a facial monitoring program to detect dishonesty or incomplete answers.

By eleven they had interviewed all the suspects and found nothing suspicious. Gen. Jones had been monitoring the facial monitoring and was with them now.

"Well, that's good news," said Filmore. "I think we can report to the delegates we have plugged our security leak. Wilpena Pound should be safe now for everyone working here."

"I'm satisfied that those we have interviewed are not the problem," replied Brighton. "I'm not sure there won't be problems in the future. There are still people working here that we didn't include in this sweep. And what about all the new people arriving with the delegations? Are we safe from future threats?"

"We will broaden the scope of our sweep to include others, such as minor security staff, maintenance and custodial personnel and SETI leadership," said Jones. "One good thing about your operation up to about two weeks ago, is that you had a small staff of around thirty."

"Do you really think we need to question the leadership team?" said Brighton.

"Everyone on Wilpena should be questioned," replied Jones, "including me and my staff. I want to eliminate all SETI people as suspects. That should give the delegates a sense of security."

"What about the staff of the delegates?" asked Filmore. "That European delegation must have close to twenty people on it."

"We can't start questioning their staff unless they agree and we certainly can't question them until we're sure about our own staff," said Brighton.

"I agree," said Jones. "We have to be one hundred percent sure all SETI people are loyal before we question others."

"Okay. You might as well get started on me," said Filmore. "We'll ask Jarrod and the others when they get back."

"They'll be here in about thirty minutes," said Jones. "They're starting their descent now."

"I'll go after Sam and then we'll get Laura to agree to be questioned," said Brighton. "That way we'll have only Jarrod, Jack and Jenny and we'll have the whole team by the time of our two o'clock meeting with the delegates."

"What about Liza and Josh?" asked Gen. Jones.

"I see no need," said Filmore. "They've only been here a day or two. They haven't had time to do anything."

"All right," said Jones. "I will be questioned after Henning. My assistant after that. Then we have only the minor staff, the low risk people that will not have been questioned by the time of the meeting."

"Great," said Brighton. "Ready, Sam?"

"Ready."

Colin Riley was prepared as the plane began its descent to Wilpena Pound. By the time the plane reached a safe altitude at which he could launch his escape plan, he would be about one hundred fifty kilometers from Wilpena Pound.

If things went as planned, he would hit the ground about one hundred kilometers away from the complex, far enough that he might have a chance to escape detection from any ground forces the limited security team at Wilpena Pound could launch. The strike force team on the plane he was on wouldn't be a factor.

Riley was being held in the back of the small strike force plane. His hands were bound behind his back by thick plastic straps. He was being guarded by two troops in full combat gear holding automatic rifles. In the front of the plane another fifteen troops had taken off their helmets and bullet-proof vests and had placed their weapons in flight-secure receptacles. They were laughing and joking with each other.

Riley estimated the plane had been flying at about nine thousand meters altitude and would be passing the six thousand meter level soon.

In a split second when his two guards looked briefly at the other troops and shared a joke, Riley tucked his legs through his arms and maneuvered his hands to the front of his body, and attacked.

Before anyone could react he disabled both guards. He grabbed the weapon of one of the guards and opened fire on the troops. In three seconds, seventeen Special Forces troopers were either dead or wounded so badly they were unable to respond.

At the first sound of gunfire the bullet-proof door to the cockpit had slammed shut and locked.

Riley grabbed a trooper's knife, cut the plastic handcuffs and reached for a parachute. One of the troopers made a move to respond but Riley put a bullet in his head. He turned and shot the other disabled guard who was starting to stir.

The plane stopped descending and Riley could feel it start to climb.

He looked for oxygen, but found none. No matter, he thought, with a confident smile.

Riley grabbed a pistol and magazine and shoved them in his pocket. He attached an automatic rifle to the straps of his chute and a magazine for the rifle went in a second pocket. The knife he used to cut the plastic straps was tucked in his boot. He tightened the chute, opened the cargo door, took a deep breath and jumped.

Jarrod McKinley and his party were met at the door by Brighton when they arrived at Wilpena Pound.

"You want all of us to take the truth test?" he asked.

"Not Liza or Josh. But you, Jack and Jenny," replied Brighton as she explained the reasons.

Jack Simington grumbled a bit, but said okay.

Jenny Hastings protested.

"Jarrod, why do I have to take this test? It's demeaning and haven't I shown you enough loyalty? I've been with you at the old Forsaken launch site, in Sydney and now on this damn plane. I've risked my life for you. Isn't that enough."

McKinley put his arm around her shoulders and pulled her aside. When they were a few steps away from the others, McKinley put one hand on each of Hastings' shoulders, turned her gently to him and looked directly in her eyes.

"Jenny. I know you are loyal to me. I'm aware that you've stood strongly beside me and probably have saved my life at least once. For that I am, and always will be, very grateful. And I trust you without question. I've trusted you with my life. This truth test is just a formality we must all go through to put the delegates at ease and make sure they trust SETI. Without their trust we can't move forward."

"If you really trusted me, if you cared for me at all, you wouldn't make me do this."

"I'm not going to order you to take the test, Jenny. But I'm asking. There's nothing to be afraid of. I know you'll pass with flying colors. Just like others on the team who have already passed. You're a valuable part of the team and I want you to stay on the team. I feel much more confident of success when you're near me."

Hastings smiled a bit and her shoulders sagged just slightly.

"If you want me to, Jarrod. I'll do it for you. Just you. But I don't like it."

"Thanks Jenny. Janet will get you set up."

By the time Brighton escorted McKinley and Hastings to the testing room, Simington had taken the test and passed.

"Stupid questions, stupid machines," was all he said.

"Thanks for your support," Brighton chided as Simington walked away grumbling.

McKinley was next. It was over in less than five minutes.

Hastings appeared nervous when she sat down and the sensors were attached.

To the first two questions, there was no reaction.

On the third question, "Have you released any information about SETI's First Contact mission to any outside source?" there was a noticeable blip. She was clear on the last question.

"Jenny. We need to ask you a couple of follow up questions," said McKinley.

McKinley, Brighton and Filmore were all sitting across the table from Hastings.

"I haven't done anything to compromise SETI, I haven't," said Hastings defiantly.

"The *third question, Jenny," said Brighton. "You showed some hesitancy. You weren't being completely honest. Or maybe you misunderstood the question."*

"Have you released anything about our mission that was not public information?" asked Filmore.

"We've all talked about the mission," said McKinley. "We're trying to be very public about this. But there must have been something."

"It's nothing. It's not important," Hastings said, now slumping back in her seat.

"Please tell us, Jenny," said McKinley. "Like I said before, I want you on the team. You have many skills and your enthusiasm and energy are great assets."

"And I want to be on the team," Hastings said, leaning forward and looking at McKinley. "I want to keep working with you."

"Tell us then," said Brighton firmly.

"It's private," she said with a quick cold glance at Brighton.

"It can't be," said Filmore. "Jenny we're all friends here. We work closely together. We can't have secrets. Who did you tell and what did you tell them?"

"It was just one text," said Hastings as she *slumped back in her chair again. "One text I sent to my mother. Maybe there was something in that."*

"We need to see that text," said Brighton.

"It's personal and it's private. It's to my mom, okay?" said Hastings, again being defiant.

"I'm sorry," said Brighton firmly. "But who knows who your mom might have shared that text with? We have to see the text."

"Jenny. Can you show me?" asked McKinley.

"If I have to. But only you."

McKinley looked at Brighton and Filmore.

"Is that okay? If I look at the text will you take my judgment on whether it might have compromised SETI?"

Brighton and Filmore nodded.

"Good," said McKinley. "Janet, Sam, please leave the room. Turn off the monitor and the cameras. This will be private. Okay, Jenny?"

"All right," she said looking down and slumping even further in her chair.

"Can you show me?" McKinley asked when they were alone in the room.

Hastings pulled out her personal communications device. She flipped through several texts until she found the right one.

"Here it is, " she said, looking longingly at McKinley.

> *Mom, I need your help. I'm in trouble here. Oh, the job's great! I love it. The trouble is I think I'm in love with my boss. Well, he's not really my boss. It's Jarrod McKinley. I would do anything for him. He has been in mortal danger fighting this giant corporation the last couple of times I've been with him. I know it's dangerous but I don't care. I just want to make sure he's safe. I would jump in front of a moving car to protect him. I would take a bullet if it would save him. I would die if anything happened to him.*
>
> *But, Mom, he's already got a girl friend. He's engaged. And I don't think he knows how I feel. Right now he's fighting Galactic Mining Enterprises, the giant corporation trying to capture him. He is vital to this first contact mission. He's the only one the aliens will talk to. What do I do, Mom? Do I tell him? Will he even care that I love him? Help!"*

McKinley looked at Hastings and slumped in his seat.

"Jenny," was all he said. He scrolled up to see a reply from Hastings' mother. All it said was, "Be honest. Tell him."

The text was dated the previous day, just prior to the lockdown.

Hastings was still slumped, looking at the floor, her hands on the table. McKinley reached across the table and gently put one hand on top of Hastings' hands.

"Jenny, please look at me."

Hastings rose a bit in her chair and looked McKinley in the eyes.

"I'm not sure what to say," McKinley whispered. "I think you're a fantastic person. You're smart, athletic, enthusiastic, and all the things I want and need from a person working beside me."

"But you don't love me."

"Jenny, we've only know each other for a few weeks now. I do have some feelings for you and I knew you had some feelings for me, but . . . why didn't you tell me?"

"How could I? You don't love me."

"I'm engaged to Liza. I love her. We love each other. We've been together now for about five years. With school, the Titan Mission, the Forsaken scandal, we've been through a lot."

"But you kissed me on the plane."

"I did. And I admit I liked it. But I was responding to you and I was exhausted and emotionally wired."

"You don't even like me?"

"Jenny, I like you very much. I enjoy your company. I think you're great."

"But you don't love me."

"Maybe if I wasn't engaged, if there were no Liza, maybe we could have something. Right now you and I are just friends and I hope it stays that way. I meant what I said. I want you and need you on this team. You have a lot to offer."

"I don't know. I don't know if I can work so close to you and just be your friend."

"I hope you can, Jenny. The next few weeks are sure to be full of surprises and situations where I will need your intellect, your strength, your commitment. I want you to stay. Can you do that for me? For the mission?"

McKinley now had both of his hands wrapped around Hastings' hands and gave them a gentle squeeze.

Hastings straightened up, brushed her hair back with one hand and dabbed at a tear forming under one eye. She gave a brave smile.

"I'll do it for you, Jarrod. Not the mission, you. I'll be here for you. Ready when you need me and if Liza falters one inch, I'm moving in."

"Good. That's settled then. I'll tell the others you're to be trusted and still a strong member of our team."

Even though the recording devices and cameras had been turned off, the observation window to the interview room was still open and Alvarez and Reynolds had been among those watching McKinley and Hastings.

When she saw McKinley grasp Hastings' hands and watched Hastings gazed longingly at McKinley, Alvarez tensed and leaned a little toward the window. She didn't say a word but exchanged a glance with Reynolds, who placed a hand gently on her shoulder.

She looked at him briefly before quickly staring back into the interview room.

Brighton and Filmore were in the conference room at a quarter to two when the delegates and their entourages began filing in. USNA delegates, assistants and security personnel were first, followed by the Chinese.

McKinley and Henning joined Brighton and Filmore. Gen. Jones sat behind them and Hastings beside him. McKinley gathered them all around him.

"I had a long talk with Jenny," he said. "She's fine. It was a text she sent to her mother. She mentioned a few things about me and the project. But it was nothing we haven't shared with all of these delegates," and he tilted his head to indicate others in the room.

"Are you sure?" asked Jones.

"Positive," said McKinley. "Like she said. It was personal. It was private. Nothing anyone else needs to know."

"Okay," said Brighton. "If you're satisfied, I'm willing to go with that. Just know that you are now responsible for her. If there's a problem it will be on you."

"I trust Jarrod," said Filmore. "If he says Jenny is okay, I'm okay."

"Me too," said Henning as she glanced back at Hastings.

Hastings showed no reaction.

The European delegates had started filing into the conference room. There was some milling about and a persistent chatter among all the delegates. Brighton could tell they were worried.

"Ladies and Gentlemen. Please take your seats. We have a lot to discuss." Brighton stayed silent until everyone was seated and had turned their attention to her.

"Now, I've got good news and I've got some not so good news." Brighton spoke in as light a tone as she could without being too trivial.

"The good news you can see here. Mr. McKinley and Ms. Hastings are back with us."

A few claps and exclamations of approval came from the delegates.

"Some other good news is that we have screened all relevant SETI personnel, including everyone you see in this room, and found everyone is trustworthy and loyal to SETI and this mission."

"And the bad news?" asked Chin Lieu from the Chinese delegations.

"The abductor, a man we believe to be named Colin Riley and to be a GME operative, has escaped."

A chorus of questions erupted around the room: "How?" "When?" "Who failed this time?"

"I will let Gen. Jones brief you," said Brighton.

Jones walked to the head of the table and at his voice command a large screen came alive and a video began playing, showing the strike force approaching the hangar in Bendigo. Nothing was kept from the delegation. Every moment had been recorded, right down to the escape of Riley from the strike force plane.

"As you can see from this video, we are dealing with a highly skilled operative," said Jones. "It's obvious he's had special training and is very deadly. It's amazing that Jenny and Jarrod managed to overpower him."

"How did you?" a delegate asked McKinley.

"We surprised him," said McKinley. "Jenny was a great help. One of us alone couldn't have managed it. I think he thought we were nothing to worry about."

"Where is Riley now?" asked another delegate.

"We don't know," said Jones. "We don't even know if he is alive. As soon as he started shooting, the pilots put the plane in a steep climb. A jump without oxygen at that altitude is highly dangerous. He would have had to hold his breath for some time in a free fall to get to a safe altitude. Our plane circled the area and spotted an open parachute but couldn't tell if the body hanging from it was alive or dead. We've launched a search and recovery team but a cloud cover obscured the suspected landing site."

"When will we know more?" asked Lieu.

"Our teams should be on site momentarily."

"I've got another bit of bad news," said Brighton.

"Our team searched the plane Riley was flying and found no connection to Galactic Mining Enterprises. We can't prove he was working for GME."

"But we still highly suspect GME is behind all these abduction attempts, don't we?" asked the USNA delegate Larry Mitchell.

"Yes we do and I believe we still need to confront GME," replied Brighton.

"I agree," said McKinley. "It all points to GME. Everything we've seen and heard during the last few days leads directly to GME. What Stalingwirth told me. What Liza was told by GME executive Ridgeway in Sydney. They aren't trying to hide their intentions."

"When are we going to meet with them?" asked Lieu.

"Not sure," said Brighton. "We've been in crisis mode the last twenty-four hours. We'll try to set that up today."

"I would like to help," said Lieu.

"Thanks. I might take you up on that," said Brighton. "We should get that set up for tomorrow if possible. Now, there's another matter."

"More bad news?" sneered Lars Johannson, leader of the European delegation.

"Not at all," replied Brighton. "Just an update on the signal. As you know, we sent a signal to the Source after we agreed Jarrod would be the sole contact. That was about twenty-four hours ago and we have not received a reply. I'd like Laura to fill you in."

Henning explained that recent activity had shown sending a message and receiving a reply normally took about nine hours, four and half hours each way.

"We don't know the mechanics behind the way that happens," said Henning. "It might be that some of the earlier responses from the Source were pre-programmed as auto responses, meaning they were not waiting for our signals before sending theirs. Many of their signals were very formulaic and could have been sent before they received our signals. In cases where it appears they responded to our questions, the time lag has been longer. But in those cases, the responses were still within certain windows. We have never had to wait longer than twenty-four hours."

"So, what does this mean?" asked Mitchell.

"We're not sure," Filmore responded. "We'll just have to wait. It could be anything. Perhaps they didn't like our last response. Perhaps they've decided to break off communications."

"I doubt that has happened," said McKinley. "I believe strongly this communication will continue. Perhaps they have had to consult with a council such as this one to decide on their reply to us." As McKinley finished he could see Gen. Jones move to the edge of the room to take a call.

"We must be patient," said Brighton. "Besides, we've got to deal with GME and with all the other decisions we, as a council, need to make."

"What kinds of decisions?" asked Lieu.

"What do we call ourselves? What do we do about Africa and India, who both want delegations here. How are home governments responding and how do we assure them we have everyone's best interests in mind? And more," said Brighton.

Gen. Jones stepped forward.

"We have our first report from the landing zone where Riley went down. There is no sign of him. The chute is on the ground, Riley is gone. There is an indication he commandeered a vehicle and left the area."

"Great," said Johansson. "We have a killer on the loose."

"I assure you we are doing our best and we have reinforcements arriving as I speak. Wilpena Pound and Jarrod McKinley are safe," said Jones.

"Sure," scoffed Johannson.

"Let's work on some of the issues we can tackle," said Brighton. "What do we want to call this council?"

As the discussion began, Brighton leaned over to McKinley.

"Jarrod. You don't need to be here. Take Jenny out of here and you two get some rest. You need to be sharp when, or if, that next reply comes in."

"It'll come," said McKinley. "But yes, I could do with some rest. I'll let you deal with this bureaucratic stuff."

Brighton turned back to the conference table. After a few minutes she spoke.

"Okay. We've all agreed. When the next signal comes in, The SETI World Council will be ready to evaluate and respond."

Chapter 22

Jarrod McKinley had been asleep for about eight hours when the chime sounded on his room's intercom system.

While he struggled to keep his eyes open and gather his senses, it chimed again. He rolled over and tapped the intercom button.

"Yeah?"

"We have another signal," said Laura Henning. "And again, it's directed specifically to you."

"What does it say?"

"I'd rather you come to the signal center and see for yourself."

"Is it urgent?"

"Not really."

"Okay, I'll be down in half an hour or so. Has anyone else seen the message?"

"Just Jack. He agrees you need to see this before anyone else gets a look."

"Really? What do our scientific friends from the other delegations think about that?"

"They're not too happy. Please get here as soon as you can."

"Be right there."

Fifteen minutes later McKinley walked into a contentious scene in the signal center. Not only were Henning and Simington there, but crowded around the now darkened screen where the signal had arrived were technicians from the Chinese, USNA and European delegations. Larry Mitchell, lead delegate from the USNA had just arrived and was pushing through the crowd.

"What do you mean we can't see the message?" he demanded.

"I didn't say you couldn't see it," said Henning. "I just want Jarrod to see it first."

"Why? What's so important? I won't stand for this. We're all partners in this. You asked us here. We deserve to see all the messages."

"And you will," interjected McKinley. "We are all in this together. We're not trying to hide anything. Please just give me a minute with Laura and Jack."

He sat down in front of the screen. Henning and Simington stood behind him, blocking the view of the others.

McKinley turned on the screen and read the message.

"No problem," he said after a second or two. "Have a look." He motioned for Mitchell to approach the screen.

"This is impossible," said Mitchell after he read the message. "How can they expect you, one person, to be the only one to see the messages? This creates a big bottleneck. You can't monitor this screen twenty-four hours a day. If you're not here, who sees the messages? And why should it be just you?"

"All good points," said McKinley. "I will share this message with everyone. We can discuss it at the council. I'm sure the Source has their reasons, some seem apparent, some might not be. We, as a council, have to decide if we are going to comply with their wishes."

"You mean their orders?" said Lars Johannson, the lead European delegate who had just entered the signal center.

"It's all a matter for the council to decide," said McKinley. "I told you, I'm not going to make the decisions for this council or this planet. I'm only serving as a conduit for these signals. Laura will print a copy of the signal for everyone and we'll discuss at our next council meeting. I'll get Janet to schedule a meeting as soon as possible, probably later today. I'm going back to bed." He glanced at a clock on the wall. "It's still early enough for all of us to get a few more hours of sleep, have some breakfast and still make a mid-morning council meeting. Janet will message you all when a time is set."

By ten o'clock delegation members were gathering for the council meeting. As usual, Brighton, McKinley, Filmore and Henning were seated together on one side of the table. As soon as Brighton called the meeting to order, protests and questions flew in from all directions.

No one seemed happy with the dictates of the senders. Technical staff, even Laura Henning, did not want to be cut out from monitoring the system for signals. Many were concerned that they could be deceived about what the message said if multiple people were not able to see the signals as they came in. The political leaders were most upset.

"How can we trust one person to accurately portray the message?" asked Lars Johannson. "How do we know that one person will not interpret the message to favor his country, his team, or his friends?"

After allowing a free-flowing discussion for nearly an hour, Brighton held up her hand, asking for order.

"I respect all of the opinions I have heard here," she said. "Let me assure you, the SETI team that you see right here has no other interest than making sure this first contact is as accurate and honest as it can be. We have no hidden agendas. No special interests to answer to. No one behind us pulling strings. We are here only to facilitate this first contact between Earth and whoever is sending these signals. To emphasize this, I will tell you that this team," she indicated those next to her, "has not even discussed this signal among ourselves. I'm sure we all have our own opinions, just as I'm sure none of us are trying to shape this signal in any way.

"I am also sure Jarrod McKinley has given it a lot of thought and I'd like to hear from him."

"I fully understand your concerns," said McKinley. "But I also believe I understand why the Source has made this request. It's the same reason they want a single point of contact. They want to be sure messages they send are not being interpreted in different ways.

Imagine translating their thoughts and ideas from whatever language they use into the many languages we use here on Earth. If we have different language users translating the same message, we are bound to get some different interpretations. For this to work, we all have to speaking the same language.

"Having one person get the first look at all the messages ensures that person's interpretations will be consistent. There should be no question as to what has been said."

"How can we trust you?" said Johannson.

"There is a way," McKinley responded as he pulled some papers from a stack in front of him. "I've spent the morning outlining a system that will guarantee that I cannot change the message once it is received. It also sets up a system of alerts and a schedule for me to review the messages. I won't have to be at the terminal twenty-four seven. Please have your science teams review this to make sure it will work and is acceptable to all your leaders."

"What if we choose not to comply with the requests of the Source?" asked Mitchell.

"That's your choice," replied McKinley. "But I don't see that we have many options. If we want to keep the communications going, I think we have to agree to their conditions. And I don't think this condition will be the last."

"What do you mean?" prodded Johannson.

"As the message says, the Source is going to establish protocols if we agree to this condition. Who knows what these protocols will be."

"When do we, as Earthlings, start making our own demands?" pushed Johannson.

"That's up to this council," said Brighton. "We are here to establish the validity of this communication, to direct it in positive ways."

"We all have many, many questions," said Chin Lieu, leader of the Chinese delegation. "Who, or what, is the Source? Where are they? What do they want from Earth? Are they friendly?"

"I understand," said McKinley. "I see discovering the answers to those questions as the primary mission of this council. That's part of confirming the validity of the signal. Is it real? Who is sending it? Is there any danger to Earth? Once those fundamental questions are answered to the best of our ability, we can begin to ask the truly interesting questions. What kind of planet do they live on? Have they ever been here? Do they know of other intelligent life in the reachable universe? These are exciting times but if we don't keep the communication going, none of this will happen. I would recommend that we comply with their request. I vow to interpret all messages as honestly as I can and to pass on those messages immediately."

"I want the European science team to review your proposal," said Johannson. "If we find it acceptable, the Europeans will agree to the conditions."

After another few minutes of discussion, the other delegates affirmed they would do the same.

"Great," said Brighton. "Now, is there anything else we should put in the message to the Source?"

Hands shot up all over the room. After considerable

discussion, it was agreed that it was time to ask the senders some questions.

The message, which would be sent at the end of the day, read:

> *The SETI World Council agrees that*
> *Jarrod McKinley will be the only person to*
> *see all initial transmissions from your source.*
> *He will be responsible for the interpretation*
> *and distribution of such messages. To make*
> *this communication more formal, how should*
> *we address our messages to you? What*
> *should we call you? Where are you located?*

"This is good," said McKinley to Brighton and Filmore. "Now what are we going to do about GME?"

"I've scheduled a meeting for tomorrow at their Australian headquarters in Sydney," said Brighton. "I'm going to need more info from you and Jenny about the evidence you think you have that GME and Riley are connected."

"And don't forget to get a statement from Liza," said McKinley. "She actually saw Ridgeway and was held as a hostage by him."

"Taken care of. Larry Mitchell and Chin Lieu will join Sam and me for the showdown. We've got to get them to back off."

"Good luck with that," scoffed McKinley. "And see if you can find out what happened to Riley. He has a lot to answer for and I know he is, or was, working for GME. We're going to file a complaint with the national police accusing him several counts of murder, abduction and attempted murder."

"Our evidence connecting him to GME is thin so don't count on too much on that front."

"Just hoping for everything I can get," replied McKinley. "I would finally like to be able to concentrate on communicating with the Source."

"Wouldn't we all," chimed in Henning.

Athrena, Conteus and Acquius sat in a small conference room overlooking a purplish-green sea. Gentle waves lapped against rocky cliffs and the sandy shore of a public beach. It was nearing the third apex of the day and Progenia Prime residents were enjoying the brightest star shine they would see for the next thirty-six hours.

Citizens strolled walkways and stopped for lunch or a drink at rest points with tables and interpretive signs that explained the nature of the flora and fauna of the landscape.

Behind the shoreline and walkway were connections to a transport corridor that guided automated personal mobility vehicles to convenient stops nearby. These vehicles came and went as directed by voice commands of the travelers. Beyond this coastal transport corridor the tall glass buildings of the city rose, dissected by more transport corridors that led to convenient stops in the city and then a regional transport hub where larger vehicles made regular regional and planetary-wide trips to other population centers.

The system hummed with the efficiency and precision of a collective effort that had been in place for more than a thousand years. Workers could be seen at various points making repairs and upgrades to the system.

"Did you have a good trip?" asked Athrena. "I know we do not often meet in Griefing region, but I thought we needed to be near our capitol Athenia as we consider this last message from Earth."

"The message does not seem that difficult," said Acquius. "The Forgiven Project Team should be able to answer the questions the Earthlings ask."

"Normally, I would agree," replied Athrena. "But there have been some developments that concern me. Someone on the council has been speaking to politicians on the Planetary Council and questions have been asked."

"Some want to know if we will have the resources needed for Project Forgiven while continuing to complete the Grand Vision," added Conteus.

"What they do not realize is that when we assimilate Earth, some of the resources of Earth will be used," said Athrena. "I want to be able to talk to those on the planetary resources committee and assure them of that. I know we could have used our vid conferencing, or even personal telepathy, but sometimes there is no substitute for a face-to-face conversation."

"Who is raising questions?" asked Acquius.

"It does not matter," said Athrena. "We will meet

with the committee before we respond to the latest message from Jarrod McKinley. Now that the SETI council has agreed to our message protocols, some real communication needs to begin. And I want the endorsement of the resources committee as we go forward."

"We have a few minutes before we see the committee. Let us review our presentation," said Conteus.

The three huddled at the table while the souls of Progenia Prime were enjoying the amenities of the planetary capitol as the well-oiled system hummed along.

As Athrena led her trio into the committee room she spotted Heronius.

She nodded and gave a friendly smile. He nodded back, not smiling.

"Chair Alexia," said Athrena after they sat down. "It is a pleasure to have the opportunity to speak to you and your committee today."

"Welcome." Alexia was from the Botanica region of Progenia Prime. She was tall by Progenia standards. Her jet black hair curled on top of her head, and her dark bronze skin gave her a commanding presence.

"What do you and the Forgiven Project Team wish to present?"

"It has come to our attention there are questions about the resources needed for Forgiven," said Athrena. "We are here to assure you that the resources used have been budgeted for and any additional resources required will be appropriated from Earth.

We believe now is the time to make these assurances because our communications with Earth are about to take a new and more direct and critical nature."

"How so?" asked Alexia.

"We have agreement with Earth on message protocols and now is the time for questions and answers. Soon it will be time to reveal to Earth who we are. From there we will begin to explain the Forgiven Project and how Earth fits in to the Grand Vision.

"Once we establish a foundation with Earth and they accept the reality of the situation, it will become necessary for them to begin using their resources."

"And what makes you think Earth will accept this reality?" asked Alexia. "As I understand the situation on Earth, they barely have adequate resources and many of them are controlled by private entities."

"True," replied Athrena, "but when we provide them with our technology, private control will become unnecessary and resources will become more than adequate for Earth's needs."

"What makes you think that even then they will want to share?"

"We have spent the last one hundred years grooming the population of Earth to believe in other life in the universe. We have the evidence to show that Earth is part of a much larger family. When they see that connection, we believe they will want to join that family."

"I am well aware of the work done on the Forgiven Project and I have reasonable confidence the project will be successful. But, there are others who are not sure." Alexia gave a quick glance at Heronius before saying to Athrena, "Do more to convince this committee."

Athrena sighed and glanced briefly at Conteus and Acquius before turning her gaze to Heronius. She began a narrative that clarified the Forgiven Project and the strategy that had been adopted almost a thousand years ago.

After two hours of explanations, questions and answers, Alexia signaled for silence. She glanced around to her committee members and shot a quick stern look at Heronius.

"Athrena, Conteus, Acquius, thank you for your thoughtful and comprehensive explanation of exactly where your project is at this time. The committee sees no reason that you should not proceed. However, I would ask one consideration. I would like to be included on your monitoring panel. Do you have room for one more?"

"Most certainly," responded Athrena. "We would welcome your wisdom and insight."

"And my political connections," chuckled Alexia.

"True," said Conteus.

"Very well. I expect to be updated daily and I will make every attempt to be there personally when at all possible. When we adjourn this committee meeting, I would like to work with you on the response to Earth's latest message."

"Certainly," replied Athrena. "We will complete our response before we leave Athenia."

"Excellent," said Alexia. "I will see you in the

conference room shortly as our committee has other resource questions to resolve."

"I feel that went well," said Acquius as he, Athrena and Conteus left the conference room.

"I hope that satisfies Heronius," said Athrena. "He seems to be questioning us at every step."

"Heronius will be fine now," replied Acquius. "He knows where the power lies. As one of the primary managers of resources on the planet, he was just covering his bases. Now that Alexia has endorsed Forgiven, we will have no problems with him."

"I hope so. Now let us get started on this response to Earth."

By the time Alexia joined them, they had a response drafted that primarily asked questions and only tangentially answered Earth's questions. Many of the questions they asked, they already knew the answers to.

"Tell me why we are asking these questions." asked Alexia.

"We are trying to start a conversation," said Conteus. "We ask simple questions, they respond. It builds trust."

"What if they feel threatened by the questions?" asked Alexia.

"We hope they do not," said Athrena.

The message read:

> *Message protocols agreed to.*
> *Security codes for Jarrod McKinley follow.*

Encryption codes were entered, followed by the main message:

> *Our message to you comes from the*
> *second planet orbiting the third star of the*
> *Alpha Centauri complex.*
> *Address messages to FPT.*
> *More information will follow.*
> *Questions:*
> *Who controls Earth's natural*
> *resources?*
> *Which entity makes political decisions*
> *for all of Earth?*
> *What percentage of Earth's resources is*
> *spent on military defense?*

"That is all we want to say right now?" questioned Alexia.

"Remember. We are trying to get a conversation going that will test the level of trust," responded Athrena.

"Well. Let us see how it works," said Conteus as he sent the message to the Forgiven operations center and told operators to wait twenty-four hours before sending the message to Earth.

SETI World Council representatives felt a little intimidated when they saw the Galactic Mining Enterprises headquarters in Sydney. The glass and steel skyscraper dominated the Sydney skyline and there were well positioned guards everywhere.

"I guess this is our welcoming committee," grumbled Larry Mitchell as he went through a security scan.

"Pretty normal stuff," replied Janet Brighton.

"Not really," said Chin Lieu. "We don't even do this in Beijing anymore."

Brighton, Sam Filmore, Lieu and Mitchell had been kept waiting for almost an hour after they had arrived at the office building to confront the company about its aggression toward SETI and Jarrod McKinley.

When the elevator arrived on the sixty-fourth floor the group was escorted to a conference room that looked out on Sydney's rooftops, with a stunning view of the Opera House, the Bay Bridge, and Port Jackson Bay.

Already seated on one side of the table were five GME executives, three men and two women. Others stood nearby ready to assist, or were they there to intimidate? Two appeared to be younger executives, two appeared to be security people and one appeared to be ready to record the proceedings.

The eldest of the seated GME executives must have been at least in his eighties. His wrinkled face seemed out of place when compared to his erect posture and his steel-blue eyes that shone out brightly. He motioned for the SETI group to be seated and when they complied, he made a signaled to one of the security personnel. Doors on the conference room clicked loudly as locks slipped into place. Room-darkening shades dropped to cover the large windows. The conference room lights brightened.

"Do not be alarmed," said the GME leader. "These measures will help us concentrate on the issue at hand. We have been briefed."

"And who might you be?" asked Brighton assertively. "Perhaps introductions are in order?"

"I am Randolph Turnbridge, GME CEO," the leader responded. "The others at the table represent GME operations or divisions around the planet. We know all of you, Brighton, Filmore, Mitchell, Lieu. Frankly, we're surprised there's so little authority represented in your group. None of you speak for any political entity from around the planet. You're just a bunch of scientists. I want you to know it has been with considerable expense and time wasted that we have assembled this leadership team to listen to your petty complaints. Let's get this over with. We have better things to do."

"We have all been appointed by our governments," responded Mitchell curtly. "We have all the political backing we need."

"We represent the majority of the industrial nations of the world," added Lieu. "And we all have connections that you do not want to test."

"We'll see," replied Turnbridge. "Get on with your complaint."

"If you've been briefed, you know your company, or your operatives, have been actively trying to abduct one of the SETI team," said Brighton. "You have kidnapped the fiancé of our team leader, you attempted to abduct two of our team right out of our Wilpena Pound operations center. Your actions are criminal and we demand they be stopped."

"Nonsense. You have no proof," shot back Turnbridge.

"Perhaps. But you might ask Mr. Ridgeway over there," Brighton nodded to one of the young executives standing off to the side, "why he was holding Liza Alvarez in this very city. And you might want to talk to your head of security at your Bendigo complex about the men we killed or injured when we rescued two of our team. And you must be curious why Gregory Stalingwirth, a known accomplice of the infamous and convicted felon Rev. Christopher Larchmont, was in your employ until his vehicle was blown sky high after another abduction attempt. Don't be too smug, Mr. Turnbridge. We have documented evidence to back up all these claims."

"You might also want to know that we have reviewed your contracts and that at least sixty percent of your products are going to countries or companies in which we have strong political connections," added Mitchell. "We can pull some strings."

"I am not the least concerned," Turnbridge replied. "And we can test your evidence in court, if that's where you want to go. As for Mr. Stalingwirth, your assertion is nonsense."

He made a motion to one of his security people and a side door opened and Stalingwirth stepped into the room.

"We can refute your other claims just as easily," he said smugly.

"Perhaps I can put this in a different light," said Sam Filmore. "We know why you are interfering. Your Mr. Ridgeway made it very clear. You hope your company will have exclusive use of any new technology that may be discovered if and when our first contact bears fruit. You may think you can control us. But do you really believe you can control who the aliens will share their technology with? Why not be part of this global effort instead of trying to dominate it?"

"This company did not get where it is by sharing its company secrets," replied Turnbridge. "We don't think we should start now."

"If you continue to pursue this course of action, we will be forced to use all the economic, political and military resources at our disposal," said Brighton. "We are not going to let one greedy company ruin the biggest moment in the history of Earth."

"We also have considerable resources, Ms. Brighton. Some of a very military nature. Please don't try to scare me."

"I'm not trying to scare you or threaten you. I'm just stating facts and reality as they exist right now, today, not tomorrow or some distant point in the future."

"As you know, Jarrod McKinley is essential to our first contact effort," said Filmore. "We want him left alone until first contact is established. What happens to any new science we discover will not be up to us anyway. If there are choices to be made by people of

Earth, it will be up to the politicians, not this group of scientists."

"That is why GME wants to be in front of this," replied Turnbridge. "If there's anyone I trust less than scientists, it is politicians. This company didn't get where it is today by letting others make critical decisions."

"We would like to have your cooperation," said Brighton. "But make no mistake, this first contact mission is going forward according to our plan, not yours. We will use all of our resources to ensure that."

Turnbridge glanced up and down the table at those sitting next to him. He motioned to one of his security people and the doors unlocked and the blinds began to raise.

"Let the games begin," was all he said.

Colin Riley was piloting a stolen single-engine airplane on his way to Sydney but his mind was working overtime. His boss was going to be upset. He had used extensive resources in his effort to abduct McKinley and had failed. He had to come up with a plan that would convince his boss to let him try it again. If he didn't, he would be expendable and he knew what that meant.

He had easily penetrated the Wilpena Pound complex earlier because security was not expecting it. Even though he had fully scouted out the complex, getting inside wouldn't be possible again. He was sure security would be tightened and reinforcements added.

The plan he was formulating now would take a different tack. The key would be in finding a way to compromise the entire SETI operation so much that if first contact were going to be made, GME would be the only viable option left to whoever was sending the signals.

The plan was gelling in his mind by the time he landed on the outskirts of Sydney. He found a public communications portal and put in a call.

A brief conversation left him even more concerned. His boss didn't want to talk to him. He was given orders by someone else to continue to headquarters and surrender to the corporate security team. He knew what that meant, debriefing first, then an uncertain future. His plan had better be convincing or he was a dead man. He decided not to go directly to security. He had some additional planning to do.

It had been two days since the unsuccessful meeting with GME in Sydney and Jarrod McKinley was getting worried. First contact, as envisioned by the SETI team seemed to be unraveling.

There was disagreement on the SETI World Council as to what the next steps should be to rein in GME. Some wanted to turn up the pressure on GME by going to political and economic leaders around the globe. Others wanted to take a more defensive position by beefing up the security forces at Wilpena Pound and shadowing McKinley with multiple guards twenty-four seven. The council couldn't agree and a stalemate was stalling any decision.

As for the signal, Lars Johannson, leader of the European delegation, was not happy with the plan McKinley had set up for message reception and distribution. He didn't trust McKinley to be fair.

McKinley had to come up with a better plan. He needed to find a way to convince everyone that his interpretations would be correct. Just as he thought he had come up with a solution, his alarm chime sounded. It was the special chime he designed to let him know a new message from the Source had arrived.

He signed off from his tablet, enacted the security code, and turned the tablet off before heading for the operations center.

The first thing he saw when he signed into the terminal at the message center didn't make sense. He was looking at the letters *RUJM* with a short, bright line moving up and down next to them. He sat there, puzzled. Laura Henning and Jack Simington, along with representatives of the other delegations, were outside a screen that had been set up. They could not help him.

He stared at the screen. He reached up to touch it. The bright line glowed a little brighter. He put his thumb on the screen and let the line move up and down over it. Immediately new words appeared: *ACCESS APPROVED.*

New words: *RECORD DATE TIME.*
He typed in the date and time.
New words: *MESSAGE ACCESS CODE*
and then THIS CODE IS *1234.*
He typed in *1234.*
New words: *MESSAGE PROTOCOL.*

A set of instructions displayed on the screen. The instructions included the log in procedure he had just figured out and the explanation that each time a message was sent a new access code would be included. Then the words: *MESSAGE FOLLOWS, HIT RETURN.*

McKinley hit the return key on the keyboard and a message scrolled over the screen. He smiled as he executed a copy and a print command. He then typed in a command to save and time/date stamp the message. Then he executed another command and the message was sent to all delegation leaders.

Now we have something to work with, real information, he thought. Some of it would raise eyebrows, he was sure, but it was a start.

He signed off the message computer and headed to the conference room. Already his message alert was pinging that there was an emergency meeting of the SETI World Council to review and respond to a new message from "FPT from Alpha Centauri."

He was grinning from ear to ear when he entered the conference room ten minutes later. He was the first one there.

After another ten minutes Jarrod McKinley was

not smiling. He was being bombarded from all sides about the content of the message.

"What is FPT?" Chin Lieu of the Chinese delegation wanted to know.

"And which star is the third in the Alpha Centauri system? The location is too general," complained Lars Johannson.

But it was Larry Mitchell of the USNA delegation who was most concerned.

"What do they mean, 'Who controls our resources'? What do they want with our resources? And what are they talking about? Do they want our water? Our nuclear energy? Our orbiting solar farms? I don't like the question."

"And I don't like the question about how much we spend on defense," Gen. Jones added. "Next they're going to ask for our military command structure. Are they probing planetary defenses? By controlling our resources and our defenses, they could leave the planet helpless."

"And why do they need to know about our political decision making process?" Lieu asked. "Do they want to infiltrate that too?"

"Let's all take a deep breath," said McKinley. "I understand your concerns, but we might be over thinking this. Perhaps this is just a conversation starter. Just something to get a dialogue going. If we examine the questions, they are very general. We can answer in a general way without compromising any concerns any of you may have."

"Yes," said Brighton. "I agree with Jarrod and

think we should go over each point to see what, if any response we wish to make. The important thing is, they are talking to us. Do you realize what an Earth shattering event this is? We are having a dialogue with someone else in the universe. It's a moment we've all dreamed of."

"It's the 'Earth shattering' part that I'm worried about," responded Mitchell. "I need to report this to USNA leaders."

Johannson and Lieu nodded in agreement.

"I have no problem with that," said McKinley. "I think we must keep our national governments completely informed. I would just ask you to wait until after we've fully discussed this and had a chance to reach a consensus among this group."

Delegates nodded or muttered a reluctant agreement.

"Let's start with the location," McKinley said. "Laura, do you have any ideas?"

"They said the third star in the Alpha Centauri system," responded Henning. "As you know, the three stars in that system consist of two stars similar to our Sun and one brown dwarf. Each has a different level of brightness. If they say it's the third star, I would take that to mean it's either the brightest or the brown dwarf."

"But," interjected Lieu, "It also could be either the one with the largest diameter or the smallest."

"Yes," said Henning. "Or it could be the newest star or the oldest. We don't know for sure. But other things we know about that system can help us make an educated guess. Over the last seventy years we've been searching for planets around stars. The Alpha Centauri system, being the closest to our Solar system, has been thoroughly studied. Researchers are positive there are no habitable planets orbiting either of the bright stars. There's just nothing orbiting those stars that appears habitable by any life forms that we know.

"The brown dwarf is another matter. It's harder to detect anything orbiting that star because of the dim light it emits and its small size. We know that planets are discovered by the gravitational wobble effect they have on their mother stars.

"Finding a planet around the brown dwarf of the Alpha Centauri system is complicated by the light being emitted from the two larger stars of the system. Given that we haven't seen habitable planets around the two larger stars and that we can't be sure about the brown dwarf and that the Source says the third star, I would bet the farm the planet is orbiting the brown dwarf."

"Sounds reasonable," said Mitchell. "Now what is 'FPT'?"

"No way to know that," said McKinley. "We will have to ask them."

"What about the resources question? How to we answer that?"

"With the truth," said McKinley. "We can tell them the truth without giving away any secrets."

"I suggest our response goes something like this," said Brighton.

> *Earth's resources are controlled primarily by regional or continental political governing bodies, numbering in the dozens. A few privately managed entities control the refinement or processing of some resources.*

"What if they want specific names?" said Johannson.

"And what about GME? That company has tremendous control over a large amount of energy resources." asked Mitchell.

"GME controls mostly off-world resources," said Brighton. "FPT asked about Earth's resources. They can ask the question again if they want specifics. I think this answer will let them know we are willing to communicate."

"I agree," said McKinley. "Now what about the military defense question?"

"We need to answer that without giving away any details," said Gen. Jones.

"But we need to answer honestly," said McKinley. "We're not sure how much they know already. Perhaps they're testing our ability to be honest with them."

"We could say it this way," Sam Filmore said.

> *The percentage of Earth's resources allocated for defense purposes is primarily established by regional or continental political entities as they determine necessary. These entities have formed alliances to fully protect their interests. Some local political*

entities have established their own military systems to serve their own purposes.

"I would change the second sentence to say," said Lieu.

These entities have formed alliances to fully protect the planet and their own interests.

"I like that," said McKinley. "And I think we can drop the part about local militias."

Others nodded in agreement.

"Now, how do we answer the governance question?" asked Lieu. "No one body or person makes decisions for all of Earth."

"Again, with honesty," said McKinley.

"How about this?" said Johannson.

People on Earth do not answer to any single ruler. Each country or region has its own governance.

"Honest, but a little blunt," said McKinley. "And don't forget about the United Nations."

"The United Nations?" scoffed Johannson. "That organization has been irrelevant for fifty years."

"True, it's not what it used to be," said Mitchell. "But it still does manage aid and health programs and it serves as a mediation council when needed. We're just lucky we haven't needed it to mediate regional military conflicts like it did during the first quarter of this century."

"How about this?" said Brighton.

> *Earth has a United Nations council which helps mediate global or regional political issues as needed or requested. However, each country or region governs itself.*

"I would go with that," said Johannson.

"Great," said McKinley. "I'd like you all to relate to your political leaders our discussion and our decisions. I don't think we've endangered Earth and I'm sure these are answers we can give that will carry the conversation forward with FPT, whoever or whatever that is. Now. What do we want to ask?"

Suggestions for questions flew around the table: What is FPT? What do you call your planet? Are you humanoid? What do you want from Earth? Do you have a military establishment? Have you ever been to Earth? How many times have you been to Earth? Are your intentions peaceful? How can our communications travel back and forth so fast? What new technology can you share with us?

McKinley held up his hand and asked for quiet.

"Good," he said. "We all have a lot of questions and I'm sure there are many more. I believe we should keep them short and limit them to just a few, let's say three for this time."

After much discussion, the delegation decided on four questions:

> *Are your intentions peaceful?*

What do you want from Earth?
Are you humanoid?
When can we see you?

Henning wanted to add one more:

Does your planet orbit the brown dwarf
of the Alpha Centauri system and what is it
called?

The group opted to cut the humanoid question to add Henning's.

"Okay," said McKinley. "I think this council is doing a great job and you all should be proud to be part of this historic moment. I'm very optimistic that we are about to cross a threshold that will make us members of a much larger community than we ever imagined, a community of the stars, of the universe.

"Please let Laura know when you've heard back from your governments so we can send our message. If there is trouble, let me or Janet know."

As McKinley pushed back from the table and got up to leave, Jenny Hastings approached.

"Jarrod. I'm so happy. You handled that very well and I'm so excited. What can I do to help?"

"Thanks Jenny. But it was a cooperative effort. I'm almost as happy about how the council worked together as I am about our communication with 'FPT,' whatever that is."

"Yeah," said Hastings. "I'd really like to know who we are talking to. Can I help there?"

"Not sure what you could do, Jenny. We've got lots of people helping."

Hastings' shoulders sagged a bit before her eyes steeled and she looked McKinley straight in the eye.

"Don't shut me out Jarrod. I want to help you. I'm going to find out who, or what is behind this 'FPT.' There must be some record of transmissions from that planet orbiting that brown dwarf."

"Jenny. That's going to be almost impossible. Do you realize how much data you would have to sift through?"

"Yeah, I do. But if that's what I have to do to stay part of this team, to stay near you, I'm going to do it."

"Okay. You have my full support. I'll get Laura and Jack to set you up with your own equipment. And stay in touch. Let me know how you are doing."

"Don't worry about that," said Hastings with a smile. "I'll be a real pest."

As McKinley and Hastings walked out of the conference room they were smiling and joking about Hastings' impossible assignment.

Liza Alvarez happened to be waiting in the hallway.

"Jarrod," Alvarez called out sharply. "We need to talk."

"Right now, Liza?"

"Yes, now. Please come with me," she said with a quick glance at Hastings and turned to go down the hall.

"See you Jarrod," Hastings said.

"See you," he said as he turned to follow Alvarez.

Colin Riley was taking a beating. Not physically, but the scolding by Randolph Turnbridge was worse than physical torture. After having blown his one effort to grab Jarrod McKinley, Riley knew his future with GME, and perhaps his life, was on the line.

Making it even worse, the snot-nosed kid executive Jason Ridgeway was standing nearby acting as if he had done nothing wrong, even though he had blown the first three attempts to abduct McKinley. And standing next to him was Gregory Stalingwirth, even more incompetent than Ridgeway. Were those two the best Turnbridge could find?

"You tried twice and failed," scowled Turnbridge. "Why should I trust you this time? What makes you think you can succeed?"

"Once," replied Riley. "The first time in Sydney I was just cleaning up the mess made by junior over there." He nodded at Ridgeway.

"But you failed," replied Turnbridge.

"I had about thirty minutes to plan that one," replied Riley. "I would have had him but an entity with high tech intervened."

"Yes. I saw your report. But your attempt at Wilpena Pound also failed and I saw no mention of high tech intervention there. You just blew it."

"I admit I under estimated McKinley and some of those around him. I can assure you I won't do that again."

"Mr. Turnbridge," said Stalingwirth. "I must speak up for Mr. Riley. I have had several encounters with

Mr. McKinley and I have to say there is something special about him. He seems to always be at least one step ahead of our plans. Almost as if he can see into the future."

"Silence," Turnbridge shouted at Stalingwirth. "You're lucky to be standing here at all. If you hadn't stopped for coffee after one of your failed attempts, you'd be ashes by now. Just know at this moment you are much more a liability than an asset."

Stalingwirth shrank back into the shadows.

"Okay Riley. You tell me you have a plan. I want to hear it. You've got one more chance to prove you belong at GME. Let me hear what you have in mind."

"I'm going to need more resources," said Riley.

"Let me hear the plan first," said Turnbridge.

"I've tried to do this quietly by myself and with just a few resources. Like a surgeon using a scalpel to go after a cancer by myself. It's time to put away the scalpel and get out the chainsaw."

"Colorful words, Riley. What do you have in mind?"

"My plan will work like this," said Riley.

After a few minutes Turnbridge held up his hand.

"Stop. Can you guarantee GME will not be implicated?"

"Absolutely. I'd bet my life on it."

""You just did," said Turnbridge. "And take Stalingwirth with you. If this thing goes up in flames all I want to see is two piles of cinders—one for you, one for Stalingwirth."

"Are you sure?" asked Athrena. "The Progenia Prime Plebeian leadership want to get involved?"

"Yes," said Alexia. "I spoke to the Supreme Plebeian myself. There appear to be questions about Earth's stability, politically and militarily."

"*Now* there are questions?" asked Conteus. "We've been studying Earth since its modern civilizations began. We know all there is to know."

"But we don't know how Earth will react to our presence," said Alexia. "Some Plebeians believe Earth's response to our questions are evasive and defensive and show the likelihood of a splintering of the political entities and an escalation of their military readiness."

"But the Forgiven Project Team has been running this program for a thousand years," replied Athrena. "We have an excellent record of predicting the responses from Earth. Each time we have taken an action on Earth, their responses have fallen well within our predicted outcomes. We know what they are thinking and what they will do. We know what we are doing."

"I'm not saying you do not," said Alexia defensively. "And neither is anyone on the Plebeian assembly. But now that contact has begun, our expeditionary forces commanders are providing input. They want to be ready for all contingencies."

"And they should be," said Conteus. "However, if all goes as planned, their role will be quick and easy.

We do not expect Earth's resistance to be significant no matter the source, whether from individual countries or even a coordinated planetary defensive strategy. I am not worried about that."

"I do not believe that anyone on Progenia Prime is worried about the final outcome of our first contact with Earth," replied Alexia. "We just want it to be as painless and inexpensive as it can be."

"Painless for us or those on Earth?" asked Athrena.

"For all of us," replied Alexia.

"Very well," said Athrena. "We will include the Plebeian leadership. I hope it does not slow down our progress. Right now we must decide how to respond to Earth's questions and determine what our next questions will be."

"I believe Earth answered our questions satisfactorily," said Acquius. "The answers were general in nature but not untrue. I am sure they have their own reasons for being cautious with their answers. They do not know our motives. Who we are? They do not even know what kind of creatures we might be. We must remember this is their first contact with anything not from the planet Earth."

"All right," replied Athrena. "Our next message must give them a reason to trust us. It is important to keep building that trust until we finally reveal the reality of the situation. That will be hard enough for them to accept."

"I do agree with that," said Alexia. "But we must include the Plebeian leadership. They have to approve our messages from this point."

"Very well," said Conteus. "Let's get started."

"I reluctantly agree," said Athrena.

"I as well," said Acquius.

The four Progenians poured over the answers to their questions that they had received from Earth, as well as the four questions Earth had asked them. They drafted four new questions to Earth before focusing on how to answer Earth's questions. Several attempts later the answers were condensed to a few words.

"I do not believe these answers will be very satisfactory to those on Earth," said Athrena.

"Perhaps not," replied Alexia. "But I believe these are the kinds of responses that will win the approval of the Plebeian Assembly and the expeditionary forces."

"But I feel it will just raise more suspicions on Earth," said Athrena. "We are supposed to be building trust."

"Building trust is a complex process," said Alexia. "Part of that is testing the truth. Let Earthlings pass a few more tests to see if trust is deserved."

"But creating suspicions will not reveal the truth or build trust."

"And the Forgiven Project does not contemplate one hundred percent trust from Earth before it is enacted and carried to completion," said Conteus.

"We must go out of our way to earn the trust of Earth," said Athrena. "Even more, we have to understand their reactions and their motives. Otherwise we will not get Earth to accept reality and not only will Forgiven fail, the Grand Vision also will suffer."

"Trust is a two-way street," retorted Alexia. "The Plebeian Assembly leader was clear on that. Not having that trust could be disastrous, especially for Earth."

"Very well," said Athrena. "If we have no choice, I would agree to our answers and our new questions."

"Excellent," said Alexia. "I will send these off to the Plebeian leaders and then we will send them to Earth."

It was all over in a matter of minutes. The Plebeian leader signed off on the message, but instructed them to wait twenty-four hours as they had with the previous message. Alexia gave the okay and Conteus signaled the project operations center get the message ready to send.

Athrena and Conteus huddled on one side of the room while Alexia tried to busy herself with resource committee affairs on the other side. Acquius was on his vid communicator, nervously talking to Progenians in his home district.

It would be about twenty-nine hours before Earth received the message. Subconsciously they braced themselves for the response that would not get back to Progenia Prime for at nearly three days, not counting the time Earth would have to take to analyze the message and draft a response.

There would be a lot of pacing until that time.

Chapter 23

"LIZA, IT'S NOT LIKE THAT. There's nothing going on between me and Jenny," Jarrod McKinley said to Alvarez as they sat in his quarters.

"Why is she working so close to you?" Alvarez responded. "She's been at your side every day since I've been here. And from what I'm told she's been your shadow ever since you got to Australia."

"Who have you been talking to? And why have you been going behind my back? Don't you trust me? Liza, we're engaged to be married."

"It doesn't matter who I've talked to. And it's been more than one person. Josh can see it. I can see it. There's something going on."

"There's nothing going on. We just work together. I like and respect Jenny, but I have no feelings for her. Liza, I love you."

"But Jenny loves you. It's obvious to me and to Josh. We saw you talking to Jenny in the interview room. We saw you holding hands. What's going on?"

"Were you spying on me, Liza? That interview room talk was supposed to be confidential. I promised Jenny."

"We weren't spying. We were just looking for you. And what else did you promise Jenny?"

"Jenny has been a good member of this team. I told her I wanted her to stay on the team."

"What else do you want from her?"

"Nothing. I told her you were my fiancé, my true love. If you don't believe me, I'll prove it to you. You can join my team. We can work together. We need to work together. Liza, I love you, not Jenny."

"You don't need to do me any favors, Jarrod. But know we will be watching you."

"We? You mean you and Josh? I noticed you've been spending a lot of time with him. Why is that, Liza?"

"He's new here. He doesn't know anyone else."

"Come on, Liza. How long has he known you? One airplane ride and a couple of days? You can't tell me he's following you around for nothing. And he risked his life for you. You can't see it, can you? Josh wants you as much as Jenny wants me."

"Jarrod, you're being ridiculous."

"Prove it, Liza. Get away from Josh and come and join my team. I do need you."

"So I can be part of your harem? I don't think so. You can work with Jenny!"

Alvarez stood up, whirled around and walked out of the room, ignoring McKinley as he called to her.

A day later McKinley was at his desk trying to write a letter after failing to talk to Alvarez again. He had tried to contact her numerous times to no avail. And there were no responses to his messages. He had seen her with Josh Reynolds and called out to her but she turned her head and walked away with Reynolds.

He now resorted to writing her a letter the old fashioned way—putting pen to paper, both of which had been hard to find. He wanted to pour out his feelings for Liza, while at the same time making a rational argument for why they should work together. He hadn't been successful, as attested by the pile of crumpled papers on the floor. He was running out of paper when his door bell chimed. He hoped it would be Liza.

It was Janet Brighton.

"What do you mean, you're worried about India," McKinley said when Brighton gave him the news.

"It's just very strange," said Brighton. "India and the African coalition have been lobbying hard to get delegations here at Wilpena Pound. India has been pointing out how it now has the world's largest population and should not be excluded from the SETI World Council, even though its space program collapsed twenty years ago.

"On the other hand, the African coalition has been saying that even though its space program is still in its infancy, it represents a continent that has shown the world's largest economic growth during the last fifty years, with projections showing it will soon be a worldwide economic powerhouse."

"So? We've heard those arguments before and aren't we about to make room for both of them anyway?"

"Yes," replied Brighton. "But I just got a message

from the Indian delegation. They're no longer interested. They don't want to be on the council and they don't care if their scientists are here or not."

"Did they seem angry?"

"No. Just the opposite. They seemed almost smug. I think they're up to something. I just wish I knew what."

McKinley paused, feeling a niggling suspicion. He focused his senses.

"Let's keep asking questions," he said to Brighton. "This does seem strange and I don't like the feeling I'm getting. Check with some of the other Southeast Asia countries to see what you can discover. We need to know what's behind this."

"Will do," said Brighton. "I'll keep my feelings to myself until I discover something more definite."

"Good. Hey Janet, can I ask you something personal?"

"Sure."

"Have you talked to Liza? Have you seen her around, hanging out with Josh?"

"I haven't talked to her. I think she mostly stays in her quarters. The only time I've seen her with Josh is when you're around. If you're in the operations center, they seem to turn up close by. Same when you're going to and from the admin center. What's going on?"

"Nothing, really. Thanks a lot Janet."

"Is there anything I can do?"

McKinley was about to say no and then he paused.

"Ask her to be on the team. Get her involved. That's

always been my idea. But now she seems reluctant. Maybe you could get her interested."

"I'll give it a try," said Brighton. "What is she supposed to be doing?"

"She's my backup. With her experience on Titan and the fight against Larchmont and Stalingwirth, she knows more about this whole story than almost anyone else, maybe even more than the core team members. I need her to bounce ideas off of."

Brighton agreed and said her goodbyes.

McKinley sat back down at his desk. He wrote a simple note:

> *Liza,*
> *We need you on the team. Janet will give*
> *you your assignments.*
> *Miss you.*
> *Love, Jarrod*

He sealed the envelope and put it on a table next to the door. On his next trip he would deliver it to the admin mailboxes.

His special chime sounded, announcing another message from FPT. It had been too long and he'd been worried the vague answers in the last message SETI had sent hadn't been accepted.

He rushed out the door to the message center. The envelope was still laying on the table as the door slammed shut.

SETI World Council members were not happy with the message. They didn't like FPT's response to the questions they had asked, and they were even more upset with the new questions from the Source.

McKinley tried to help Janet Brighton keep things under control.

"I know the answers to our questions are cryptic and may raise more questions than they answer," said McKinley. "And I, too, have concerns over their new questions, but let's take one thing at a time. Let's look at the answers they gave."

"It's all riddles," retorted Chin Lieu, from the Chinese delegation.

"Perhaps," replied McKinley. "Let's see.

"The first question was: *Are your intentions peaceful?*

"The answer is: *Intentions reflect destiny.*"

"Exactly," countered Lieu. "What does that mean? Our destiny, their destiny? Is it good or bad for us, for them? Does that mean we have no choice? I don't like it."

"Nor do I," said Lars Johannson, the European delegation leader. "We should be looking and the worst case scenario. We need to be ready for anything."

"Let's not panic," said Sam Filmore. "I would assume this species has a broader perspective than do we, here on Earth. They probably know what first contact leads to."

"The domination of Earth," said Johannson.

"No," said Filmore. "The growth of the human species from a planetary existence to being a family member of the universe."

"Or slaves of the universe," countered Johannson.

"There's no reason to be melodramatic," said McKinley. "We need to keep talking to them. I don't see anything here to make us that frightened. I see it more as another test. They want to know how we are going to react."

"I would react by putting our military forces on alert," said Johannson.

"I think that's a bit of an overreaction," said Brighton.

"As do I," said Filmore.

"Let's look at the next question," said McKinley.

"Our question was: *What do you want from Earth?*

"Their answer is: *Spirits live, die.*"

"This is nonsense," said Larry Mitchell. "Whose spirit? Why is it dying?"

"Again, I see it as a threat," said Johannson.

"Perhaps," said McKinley. "I am a bit baffled by this answer, but I see no direct threat."

"Perhaps it's religious in nature," said Lieu.

"Maybe they are talking about capturing our souls," said Johannson.

"Lars, don't you think that's a bit silly?" asked Brighton.

"Who knows?" said Johannson. "It could be something totally alien to us. No, it's bound to be something alien. These things are not from Earth."

"Everyone, please calm down," said McKinley. "I see no direct threat from this answer either.

"Now for question three. *Does your planet orbit the brown dwarf?*

"Their answer is: *All equals one*."

"Again, not an answer," said Johannson. "They're being deceptive. I don't trust them."

"It does seem we have reason to be cautious," said Lieu.

"Perhaps they did answer the question," said Laura Henning, who had lobbied for that particular question to be asked. "*All equals one* could mean the orbit around the brown dwarf also indicates their planet orbits the other two stars in the Alpha Centauri system as it tags along with the brown dwarf."

"Let's go on to the last question," said McKinley.

When can we see you?

Their answer is: *Time is relative*."

"True enough," said Filmore with a smile.

"But still not an answer," insisted Johannson.

"One thing you have to admit," said Filmore. "It's gotten us thinking. Forcing us outside of our normal perspective. Loosening up our minds a bit."

"I agree with Sam," said McKinley. "That's my take on all of this. This first contact is a new experience. It is our destiny, and with the right attitude and spirit we will become one with other species of the universe at a time that is right, a time that is now. I don't see it as a threat. I see it as a promise. An exciting journey that our alien friends can help us fulfill."

"Hopeless romantic," scoffed Johannson. "You attitude could leave us dangerously exposed."

"You may be right," said McKinley. "I believe we need to be positive, but cautious. I would advise our political leaders to start taking initial steps to be ready for all possible outcomes, but not to the extent that we become paranoid. I still see no direct threat."

Others voiced similar opinions and it was clear Johannson was in the minority. The SETI World Council now had to deal with the new questions from FPT.

There were only four and they were cryptic and simple, but puzzling.

"It seems to me these questions are again designed to test our trust," said McKinley. "Nearly everyone in this room could find reason to be alarmed, so we should all stay cool."

Define military alliances, how many are
    there?
Most abundant resource?
Strongest religious movement?
Are you ready to say goodbye?

"Again they're probing our defenses with their first question," said Johannson.

"Let's be realistic," said Mitchell. "Anyone who reads our media knows the answer to that. It's no great secret."

"Yes," said Filmore. "If they can send this message, they can monitor our media and know this answer."

"Regarding the second question, it depends on who you talk to, how you count resources," said Lieu. "Solar energy, nuclear, off world, water? We are a water planet after all."

"Precisely," said McKinley. "A question that could have more than one correct response. Nonthreatening."

"Not the way I see it," replied Johannson. "They are still probing our strengths, our weaknesses."

"I see the third question as a tough one," said McKinley. How do we measure that? What counts as a movement. Why do they want to know?"

"Probably want to steal our souls," quipped Johannson with a chuckle.

"Perhaps they want to know if their religion, if they have one, will conflict with ours," said Filmore.

"I was thinking kind of the same thing," said Lieu. "What if their belief system is contrary to the basic building blocks of our major religions. An afterlife, a heaven, reincarnation. Shaking the foundations of our faiths could be very disruptive."

"I agree," said McKinley. "But again, I'm wondering why such a question? Back to Sam's point, if they can communicate with us they probably have been monitoring our societies and know a lot about our religions. Probably another question to make us think, make us ponder our existence."

McKinley pivoted to the last question. "I know the fourth question has us all very curious, or troubled."

"I am very troubled by this," said Mitchell. "Who needs to be ready to say goodbye and what are they saying goodbye too? Are we talking individuals? Masses of our population? Are we supposed to be ready to leave Earth or just die?"

"And how do we answer this?" said Lieu. "It seems to be a question for an individual but other questions have been about Earth in general."

Again it was Filmore who came up with a new idea, his years of looking for extraterrestrial life coming through. "Are they asking Earth if we are ready to say goodbye to our isolation from the rest of the universe? Are we ready to join a universal family? Are we ready to accept a new reality?"

That plausible thought seemed to set people at ease, give them a reason for the question.

"Okay," said McKinley. "We need to carry on this conversation to come up with answers and a new set of questions. We must concentrate on keeping our answers simple. Let's come up with new questions for the Source. This time, let's make them a little more probing and aggressive. It's time for us to push them, to test their trust levels."

"Agreed," said Johannson. "We still know little about who or what is behind this entity they call the FPT."

"I agree that it's time to take the next step," said Filmore. "We need to meet this FPT, or whoever is behind it."

"Great," said Brighton. "But I think we should take a break. We've been at it for more than two hours. I'd like to adjourn and get together again tomorrow morning when we're all fresh and have had a chance to digest our discussion." Hearing no dissention, she gaveled the meeting closed.

As McKinley was leaving the conference room he

saw Brighton and Gen. Jones huddling in the hallway. There was concern on Jones's face.

"Not yet. We're not prepared. I can't guarantee his safety," McKinley overheard Gen. Jones telling Brighton.

McKinley probed his sense of danger. There was nothing specific. He was safe for the time being, but it seemed a haze was building on the horizon.

On his way to his room, he passed the cafeteria and noticed Liza sitting by herself. He turned to go in just as Josh Reynolds appeared and sat down next to her.

McKinley swore to himself as he remembered the letter he had forgotten to deliver. He walked to his room, not thinking about what was troubling Brighton and Jones.

Colin Riley stood in the background and watched as others worked to set up a scenario that would allow him to reach his goal of bringing Jarrod McKinley into the clutches of GME.

He'd had little respect for Gregory Stalingwirth until the last few days. Stalingwirth had no backbone and wilted at the first sign of trouble. His loyalty was suspect and Riley didn't trust him any further than he could see him.

What he did admire was Stalingwirth's rhetorical skills. When presented with a plan, Stalingwirth could sell it very skillfully, probably the result of selling the Rev. Larchmont's bogus Forsaken program. That program, until exposed by McKinley, had operated for almost twenty years.

Now Stalingwirth's diplomatic skills were being put to the test. The diplomats across the table from Stalingwirth were hesitant.

"Why should we take this course?" the lead diplomat asked. "What advantage will it be for our country, our people?"

"You country has been locked out by SETI," replied Stalingwirth. "You have not been allowed at Wilpena Pound. You are not going to be involved in this first contact effort. We have looked at the evidence and your country could benefit more than any other from being on the ground floor when first contact is made."

"Why do you say that?"

"We know from our sources that when first contact is made many new technologies will be made available that could help your country," said Stalingwirth.

"Technologies that will help you feed your out-of-control population. Technologies that will aid you in bringing your space program back on track. Technologies that will give your nuclear program a boost to make it superior to those of your competitors."

"Why should we align with your sponsor?" the diplomat asked. "What makes you sure that you can deliver all these new technologies?"

"Our plan is simple," replied Stalingwirth. "When we are done, not only will we have Jarrod McKinley working with us, the entire SETI effort will be under our control."

"Your plan may be simple," the diplomat responded,

"but you've given us few details and asked for a lot of support. We are concerned our position will be worse if the plan fails."

"Our plan will be successful," retorted Stalingwirth. "Our sponsors have vast resources at their disposal and by far the most advanced technology of any entity on Earth. We have demonstrated that by the manner in which we transported you all to this conference."

"That was impressive," responded a lesser diplomat. "I didn't even know there was a workable supersonic magni-lev transport system."

"Our sponsors have the only one," responded Stalingwirth. "And other technologies we possess may interest you—cloaking systems, advanced encryption, first generation warp drives—it's all yours if you join our cause. And that's before we gain access to the new technologies of the aliens."

"Such as?"

"There will be many," assured Stalingwirth. "We have seen and heard some remarkable details. The kind that suggest technologies for creating force fields, instant communications across star systems, faster than light travel. The limits are boundless. These technologies could make your country a world power, give it the place it deserves."

"My country is still concerned with its role in this plan. If we participate, we could be risking our current good standing in the world community."

"Good standing?" scoffed Stalingwirth. "Is that why you have been excluded from Wilpena Pound? Is that why the world has put sanctions on you until you rectify your resource allocations among your population? Is that why your nuclear program is under constant monitoring to prevent expansion? Good standing? Is seems to me the world has had you under its harsh thumb for quite some time. You could break that hold by joining forces with our sponsor and gaining control over the new technologies bound to come to Earth via this first contact."

"We also are concerned your plan will put us in direct conflict with the SETI World Council and with other countries."

"It will not put you in conflict with other countries," responded Stalingwirth. "And it's our opinion the SETI World Council needs a little conflict. That self-appointed body needs to be reminded there is a real world out here, one that is not going to ruled by a tiny group of scientists."

"We still don't feel comfortable with a violent course of action," said the diplomat.

"Let me go over the plan again," said Stalingwirth. "Your role will be primarily one of support. Our sponsor will do the heavy lifting."

As Stalingwirth reviewed the details of the plan, Riley became more confident. He was sure that he now had the power to carry off his plan. SETI would soon see that the only choice for going forward with first contact would be to align itself with the players in his plan. And the way this alliance was constructed, GME would be invisible. There would be no way to connect his actions to GME, if the one weak link was eliminated.

He smiled as Stalingwirth finally gained the approval of the diplomats around the table. They would recommend their country join forces with The World Cooperative for First Contact. They assured Stalingwirth that approval would be forthcoming within the week and that full cooperation would be offered.

"We're in," Stalingwirth said to Riley after the diplomats left.

"Here's a list of their military leaders with whom you will coordinate. You can start planning your mission as soon as we get word of approval."

"Good," said Riley. "Nice job, Greg. You handled that well."

"Just doing my part for the future," Stalingwirth replied. "A future I consider very promising."

"When we get back to Sydney I'm going to be heavy into planning so don't contact me until you get the approval. Then come directly to me. I will have a new assignment for you. Until then, talk to no one about this meeting or this alliance."

"Will do," said Stalingwirth with a smile.

Riley was smiling too. Things were falling into place. He would deliver SETI to GME without anyone knowing GME was behind the effort unlit it was over.

The World Cooperative for First Contact was his front but he would be in control through his operatives who had no idea who he was or who he worked for. It was funny to him how easily people could be swayed with just the tiniest promise of power and influence.

Even more amusing was the fact that all of those

he had promised power and influence to would have neither. He would be pulling all the strings and no one would know what his real motives were.

No one, that is, except for Stalingwirth. That's why there would be one last assignment for Stalingwirth. One that he wo*uld not like.*

Janet Brighton gaveled to order the SETI World Council. It was the morning after the long discussion about the latest questions from FPT.

Delegates greeted each other and joked about the food in the cafeteria and shared stories about their exploration of the Wilpena Pound region. Several had taken hikes through the Pound crater and had observed abundant wildlife that included kangaroo, dingo, galah and cockatoo, and dozens of other native Australian species.

"Morning all," said Brighton. "It's good to see such a positive mood. Let's carry that forward through this meeting. There have been no major developments since we met y*esterday, but this is one issue of which* you need to be aware. India has decided it does not wish to join us here."

"For what reason?" asked Larry Mitchell.

"No reason given," replied Brighton. "They just said it was not now in their best interests."

"Probably couldn't afford it," said Chin Lieu. "They've been having trouble lately, economy, resource allocation, civil unrest."

"Not sure," said Brighton. "But we have the request from the African Council. They still want to be included."

"I move we include the Africans," said Mitchell.

Everyone agreed and Brighton gave word to Laura Henning to have the SETI admin team send the invitation to the Africans.

"Now on to the important issue of the day," said Brighton. "How do we respond to the latest questions from FPT?"

"And what questions do we have for them?" chimed in Sam Filmore.

"Yes," said Brighton. "Let's tackle the answers first. To refresh our memories, here's the list of questions again:"

> Define military alliances, how many are
>   there?
> Most abundant resource?
> Strongest religious movement?
> Are you ready to say goodbye?

"Military alliances are all recorded at the United Nations," said Lars Johannson. "Let them research that information. And why are we being asked to define an alliance? That's pretty fundamental."

"You know, Lars," said Jarrod McKinley, "I agree with you."

"It's about time." Johannson smiled.

"Seriously," said McKinley. "The more I study the questions, the more I'm convinced they're asking questions to which they already know the answers. We should be cryptic in our answers, if not b*lunt. Why don't we just say:"*

Alliances on record at United Nations.

"Sounds good to me," said Johannson.

"Great!" said Brighton. "That was easy. On to question two."

Chin Lieu spoke up. "This is an easy one—people. Our people are our most valuable, if not abundant, resource. Without people nothing none of the resources could be utilized.

" 'People are our most valuable resource.' I like it," said Mitchell.

"Me too," said McKinley.

After unanimous agreement, Brighton moved to question three."

"That one is not quite so easy," said Lieu.

"True," said McKinley. "Three major religions, and many minor ones, are based on the concept of a god, everlasting *life*, and a place called heaven somewhere 'up there.' But many are based on doing good deeds on Earth to earn some type of reward in the afterlife, a good reincarnation, a longer life, a reward to those that survive you."

"And we can get into a big discussion about which is the stronger," said Filmore.

"If we boil it down to the essence don't we get the Golden Rule?" said Johannson. "Be good to your neighbors, do unto others, and you will be rewarded."

"Can we say this?" asked McKinley. "No predominate religion but we look to our gods in heaven to judge us by our goo*d deeds.*"

*"Not true for all religions," repli*ed Lieu.

"But for most, I'd wager," *said McKinley. "Look at all the temples and alter*s now and in prehistory *that point to the sky. The Egyptian pyramid*s, South American temples, European cathedrals, temples in Asia."

After considerable discussion, the council decided to go with the answer suggested by McKinley, with a small change.

> No dominate religion but we look up to
> our gods to judge us.

"Now for the final question and perhaps the toughest one," said Brighton."

"I'd like to make a suggestion," said Sam Filmore. "I don't think any of us want to say goodbye to everything in the way this question implies. But, I think most of us would be willing to say goodbye to the isolation of Earth if it means new opportunities in space. I would hope we are willing to cast off our superstitions, our prejudices, our narrow thinking that life on Earth is all there is. Wouldn't we all be willing to say goodbye to the past in exchange for the excitement of exploring the universe?"

"Sam. Now you're the hopeless romantic," said McKinley. "I agree with your sentiment. But how do we answer the question?"

"I don't agree so much," said Mitchell. "I'm not willing to say goodbye to this existence, no matter how imperfect, without the promise of something better. Who knows what's out there? Could be a real mess."

"I second that," said Johannson. "Why say goodbye to what billions on Earth have created for what might be, and I emphasize might be, a chance for a few on Earth to explore and experience the new things in space?"

"Lieu said, "Why not respond with this."

Goodbyes must mean something better for us.

"How about this?" added McKinley.

Goodbyes are acceptable if our future is better.

The final response was:

Goodbyes acceptable for a better future.

Following a little give and take, the council agreed to all the responses.

"Okay," said Brighton. "Let's all take a lunch break and meet back here in an hour to go over the new questions we have for FPT."

As Brighton and McKinley were walking out of the conference room, Gen. Jones approached.

"Nothing too serious," he said. "Just wanted to inform you that a group of campers outside of Wilpena have organized and they wanted to be recognized. They call themselves the World Cooperative for First Contact."

"What do they want?" asked Brighton.

"Nothing, really," replied Jones. "According to security, they just want to be recognized. And they want a certain section of the camp designation as their world headquarters."

"Who's behind this?" asked McKinley, a small niggling of caution rising in the back of his mind.

"It's one of the long-time campers," said Jones. "Security tells me he's been here since the days of the Forsaken scandal. He seems harmless enough and has never caused trouble."

"Why does he want recognition?" asked Brighton.

"Just so he can claim a part of the camp his and so he can fly a homemade flag."

"I don't see any harm," said Brighton. "Tell him he has our recognition."

"Shouldn't we take it to the council?" asked McKinley.

"We'll let them know," said Brighton. "But the council has more serious things to deal with rather than every crackpot who wants some attention. Jarrod, want to join us for lunch?"

"No thanks," said McKinley. "I'm planning on having lunch with Liza. And I've got to meet Jenny to see how her work is going."

"Still trying to mix business and pleasure, I see," chuckled Jones.

"Not funny."

"Sorry," said Jones.

"Jarrod. I have talked to Liza and given her a job. I asked her to start right away," Brighton said as she looked at her watch. "She's going to shadow you. I hope it goes well."

"Shadow me?" said McKinley.

"Well, it's just as you said. She has the background on this like no one but you. She can help you."

"Okay. But then I'm going to have her with me when I talk to Jenny about her work."

"Will that be a problem?"

"I hope not."

After a pleasant lunch McKinley broke the news to Alvarez.

"Now I've got to meet with Jenny about the assignment she's taken on."

"Okay," she said. "I'll just tag along."

"As you wish," McKinley said, his voice becoming more tense.

They found Hastings in the special work module Jack Simington had set up for her. She was munching on a sandwich and had a bottle of water and an apple nearby.

"No lunch break?" asked McKinley.

"Not really. Been pretty much twenty-four seven since I started," replied Hastings, directing a cool glance behind McKinley at Alvarez.

"Liza is joining me," McKinley said. "Janet thinks there's something to be gained by her shadowing me. Liza has been in on this since the beginning, as you know."

"Know all about it," responded Hastings with a noticeable chill in her voice.

"Hi, Jenny," said Alvarez warmly.

"Liza," nodded Hastings.

"How's it going? This search for the impossible," asked McKinley.

"Not that impossible, as it turns out."

"What did you find?" asked Liza.

"What I found out, Jarrod," said Hastings, ignoring Alvarez, "is that there are some common traits to the signal we're getting from Alpha Centauri."

"What kind of traits?" asked McKinley.

"From the very first signal, even before the encryption, right up to the latest signals that have more content and are coming faster, there is a common wave pattern and sequence. I programmed an algorithm to search for those commonalities in previous SETI archives.

"I discovered there has been a long series of such signals over many years."

"How can that be?" said McKinley. "SETI has been searching for radio signals for decades."

"They were disguised. Sometimes they appeared to be gamma bursts from stars. Or they were cluttered with random radio noise. Often, years and years passed between the signals."

"How far back did you go?"

"SETI only has records back to the sixties and many of those records are incomplete, with the change from private to government and then back to private operations."

"Any idea what the signals contain? Are there messages in the signals?"

"I can't tell. It's too soon. But I do know that if I apply the same rules we use to receive the present messages, I get nothing. If they were sending messages with the signals, they weren't to any modern day humans."

"Who would they be sending them to?" asked McKinley.

"I have no idea, but whoever or whatever they were, they weren't using our technology."

"Good work, Jenny. I'll report to the council what you have found."

"Not yet, please, Jarrod. Give me a couple more days. Maybe I can make more sense of what I've found. Now that I've isolated these signals, I can try to find out their relevance."

"Okay, Jenny. Please get in touch with me as soon as you find out anything new."

"Will do, Jarrod," Hastings said, smiling at McKinley.

"Well, it was a little icy in there," Alvarez said to McKinley as they were walking down the hall outside of Hastings' workplace.

"Give her some time," McKinley asked. "She has to get used to seeing us together."

"And you have to get used to having me next to you," Alvarez replied,

"Already am," McKinley said as he put one arm around her waist.

Alvarez did not smile, until she saw Josh Reynolds walking down the hall.

"Hi, Josh," she said cheerfully.

"Hi, Liza. You okay?"

"I'm okay."

"Can I help in anyway?" Reynolds asked.

"You know, I think Jenny Hastings could use your help," replied McKinley.

"Jenny?" asked Reynolds.

"Yeah," said McKinley. "She's been stuck in operations for a while and I think she could use some company."

"Really?" asked Reynolds, looking back and forth at McKinley and Alvarez.

"Really." responded McKinley as he guided Alvarez down the hall.

Reynolds shook his head in wonder and moved down the hall the other way toward where Hastings was working.

"What was all that about?" asked Alvarez.

"Nothing. Jenny just seems to need some company right now."

"Now that she doesn't have you?" Alvarez responded with a tiny smirk.

"Something like that," McKinley said, placing his arm around Alvarez again.

As they walked down the hall McKinley's sense of danger was simmering. He started thinking about what it could be.

"It'll be okay," said Alvarez.

"What?"

"That source of danger you're thinking about. I'm sure it's nothing."

McKinley looked knowingly at Alvarez.

"This is one reason we need to stay together," he said. "We can help each other."

"Right now I think we should find Gen. Jones and see what's going on," said Alvarez.

They began walking with a new sense of urgency and turned quickly down a hall where a sign pointed to *Security*.

"What do you think is the delay?" Alexia asked the other three Progenians on the Project Forgiven leadership committee.

"It has been more than three days since we have had a message from Earth. I understand that previous responses have come much faster."

"That is true," replied Athrena. "Perhaps they are having some debate on our answers to their questions."

"They probably are also debating our questions," said Conteus. "We did ask some probing, but vague questions."

"Maybe they are becoming frightened, or are reluctant to continue the communication," said Acquius.

"I doubt that," said Athrena. "They have been very eager in the past and Jarrod McKinley is now safely at their operations center. I suspect that they are feeling more confident and just want to take time to make sure the communications continue and are as meaningful as possible."

"I am asking because our Supreme Plebeian is taking more of an interest," said Alexia. "He is still getting pressure from some on the assembly to justify the continuation of the Forgiven Project at this time. Heronius is still concerned that the resources of Progenia Prime will not support both Forgiven and the Grand Vision."

"Heronius has always been a worrier," said Acquius. "Before the last phase of the Grand Vision he raised the same issues."

"And with justification. I might add," said Alexia. "You recall the struggles we had regulating the rhythms of the planet to get our resource production in line with our needs, to say nothing about giving us surpluses to begin the Grand Vision."

"But we solved that basic issue nearly a thousand years ago," responded Conteus. "I do not see that as a problem."

"It is just that kind of thinking that created the original problem," said Alexia. "That is the reason we are sitting here debating how to handle the Forgiven Project."

"I beg to differ," said Athrena. "The issues that created the need for Project Forgiven were far more complex than just resources. And, for land's sake, it is not just a thousand years ago, it is more like four or five thousand years ago."

"True," said Alexia. "But I think time has made many of us forget what it was like in the interregnum and how hard it was to get beyond that period. Reading the history records cannot give us an appreciation of just how hard it was to recover. And resource control was hit the hardest and had the longest period of recovery."

"I agree," said Athrena. "But I also know that Heronius does not fully appreciate the resources that we will harvest from Earth. What we gain from Earth should easily offset anything we expend to complete Forgiven."

"We need to gain the confidence of Heronius," said Acquius. "I have worked side by side with him for years and I know he is not going to let this go until he is convinced the project will not hurt what he is responsible for, the supply of resources."

"Very well," said Athrena. "Let us bring Heronius here to discuss this issue and explain exactly what we expect to gain from Earth and what Progenia Prime will need to supply for the Forgiven Project and the Grand Vision."

"I would think he would know that," said Alexia.

"It has all been explained in the documents," said Conteus. "Perhaps Heronius just needs to hear it again, from us, in person."

"And to have his ego stroked," chimed in Acquius.

"Maybe there is a problem with the resources on Progenia Prime that we do not know about," suggested Athrena.

"As chair of the Plebeian Resource Committee, I think I would be aware of resource issues," replied Alexia.

"Perhaps Heronius is hiding something," said Conteus.

"His ego could be getting in the way of the truth," said Acquius. "He does not like to admit anything is troubling him, or that there is anything he cannot control."

"Another reason to bring him here for a discussion," said Athrena.

"Yes," said Alexia. "I do not want any surprises on the resource front. Especially if it affects the Grand Vision."

"And Forgiven," said Athrena.

"Speaking of which," said Conteus. "We had an alert from our agent on Earth. The one in Australia. He is concerned. Things are unusually quiet around the SETI complex. There have been no recent threats against SETI or Jarrod McKinley."

"That is good news, is it not?" asked Alexia.

"Given the track record of McKinley. Any quiet time will soon become very loud and dangerous," said Conteus.

"Is there any evidence of trouble?" asked Athrena.

"Nothing concrete," said Conteus. "But our agent has detected some energy shifts that he finds ominous."

"From what source?" asked Athrena.

"Nothing defined as yet. They are coming from multiple sources and directions and seem to be coalescing on Wilpena Pound. He has asked for permission to bring in additional resources in case the situation gets out of hand."

"Very well. We need to consider allowing other agents to provide assistance," said Athrena.

"What resources do we have available?" asked Alexia.

"We have adequate resources on Earth," replied Athrena. "The bigger question is whether we want to use them. Using such resources would likely reveal us to people on Earth. That, I am afraid, could raise the level of suspicion and paranoia about us to Earthlings."

"And that could jeopardize the Forgiven Project," said Conteus.

"Perhaps that could also save Forgiven," said Alexia.

"Explain," said Athrena.

Alexia described a scenario that had the other committee members worried. It would be a real gamble. It could either advance Forgiven by years or it could ruin any chances of the project ever being a success.

By the end of the discussion the issue was left undecided but precautions would be made to cover this new contingency. Heronius would have to be convinced of the plan. The agent in Australia would be given the okay for additional resources. The project would be advanced if needed.

It left the committee as unsure as it had been in decades. One of the uncertainties was that Earth had not responded to Progenia Prime's last message. The biggest uncertainty was that they had the feeling they were losing control. The control was shifting to Earth.

Earth. Where there was still a lack of central

control. Where the spontaneous and unpredictable nature of the species extended well beyond individuals to countries and private power centers.

Earth. Where the first impulse was a primitive urge to use power to resolve issues. Still a far too dominate trait.

Earth. Where the very strongest traits of the species still were also its weakest.

Earth. Where events were on a collision course.

Jarrod McKinley was concerned.

"Janet doesn't think it's anything to be concerned about," Gen. Jones told McKinley and Liza Alvarez.

"I disagree," said McKinley. "You say there has been heightened activity in the camp just outside the Wilpena Pound gate?"

"Yes. A new banner has gone up on part of the camp. It's touting something called The World Cooperative for First Contact. The organizer is a hanger-on from the old Forsaken scandal days."

"I remember him," said Alvarez. "He was considered a crackpot last year."

"He seems a bit more organized as of late," said Jones. "He's got a new flag, and he's segregated about half of the camp, claiming it belongs to the 'Cooperative.' He's pushed others out of that part of the camp. He's also put up some new tents and we've seen new people joining him."

"Anything ominous?" asked McKinley.

"Not really," said Jones. "Just a lot of loud music and twice a day proclamations that the time has come for salvation for the human species. How we will be saved by first contact."

"Sounds like the same old crackpot," said Alvarez.

"I'm not sure, Liza. General, keep a close eye on the camp. We don't want to miss anything. We've got to get back to the council meeting to compose some new questions for FPT."

"Do you think we should tell the council?" asked Jones. "Janet doesn't want to bother them with what she thinks is a trivial matter."

"I don't disagree at this point," said McKinley. "It's just a feeling," he said mostly to Alvarez.

By the time McKinley and Alvarez sat down around the council table, McKinley had changed his mind. There had been another small wave of danger float over his mind. He had squeezed Alvarez's hand and she had nodded in understanding.

He marveled at how fast their minds had been syncing since she had joined him. She was becoming a real part of the team, almost a part of him.

When he explained the situation to the council, no one seemed concerned.

"We see that in America, too," said Larry Mitchell. "Nuts are coming out of the woodwork everywhere."

"In China as well," said Chin Lieu. "People are looking for something new. Some will grasp at anything."

"We saw a lot of it here last year," said Brighton. "I think it's more of a nuisance than anything."

Everyone was far more concerned about new questions for FPT than about some ragtag protestors outside Wilpena Pound.

McKinley eased back in his chair and let Brighton take over the meeting to compose the new questions.

When it was over, he was happy. The council was onboard with his strongest wishes, to push first contact to fulfillment. The questions were more than just questions.

> *Eager to meet you, set time and place.*
> *Can we travel to you?*
> *Earth ready for travel, exploration. Where*
>   *are we going?*
> *Our images included, please provide*
>   *yours.*

The questions were a bit pushy, McKinley agreed, but he believed they also tried to begin a conversation among equals. Earth didn't need to submit to every wish by these aliens without making some demands of its own.

Some on the council worried about the provocative nature of the questions, but most agreed it should be the next step.

If Earth was looking to become a member of the universal family, it needed to start acting the part, not the part of an awestruck toddler.

After the council meeting ended, McKinley and Alvarez walked to the observation deck on the ground level of the Wilpena Pound complex. From there they could see the brilliant streaks of the gold and red sunset lighting up the rocky ridges of the Wilpena Pound crater.

They also had a view of part of the camp outside the compound gates. Lights were on and loudspeakers blared. There was a riotous atmosphere throughout the camp. Off to the eastern edge there was more activity than usual. McKinley noticed several large trucks entering the camp and moving toward that area. The area of The World Cooperative for First Contact.

"Look," he pointed out to Alvarez.

A heightened sense of fear was creeping up on him.

He looked at Alvarez. She stared back with a solemn look on her face.

Danger was coming, he could sense it like he could see the darkness creeping westward as the sun set. He knew he had to probe that darkness.

Chapter 24

"No, Liza, not right now," Jarrod McKinley said to Liza Alvarez as they huddled in the dark near the main gate of Wilpena Pound. "I don't know what's going to happen. It could be very dangerous."

"All the more reason I need to be next to you," she said. "My job is to stay by your side. I can help detect danger."

"Yes, you can. But you can do that by staying inside Wilpena Pound while I go into the camp. If you sense danger, tell me. Reach out to me by thinking it. We know that works. We've practiced it enough now."

It had been two days since McKinley and Alvarez had stood on the observation deck watching the activity in the camp. The activity in the area occupied by The World Cooperative for First Contact had increased steadily but they had been unable to make out precisely what was going on. More tents had been erected and a high canvas wall now surrounded the entire World Cooperative section. McKinley had asked Gen. Jones for some aerial surveillance but Jones had given it a low priority.

McKinley decided he would undertake a reconnaissance mission on his own to discover what was going on behind the wall. He had not told Janet Brighton or Jones about his mission. He knew they would not approve and they didn't seem concerned anyway. Brighton had dismissed his concerns and Jones was busy organizing the security reinforcements that had been arriving from around the world. Wilpena Pound was beginning to look more like a military compound than a scientific institution.

McKinley also knew they would not want him to risk his personal safety. He was key to the first contact and since he had been safely in Wilpena things had been going smoothly. The SETI World Council was functioning effectively. Delegations had been able to gain approval from member countries for the actions taken regarding the signal and the preparations for first contact. SETI staff maintained a high level of coordination with other delegations from around the world and all the scientific teams were working well together.

But McKinley could sense danger growing and part of it was coming from the camp, he was sure. He had waited for two days until there was a new moon and the night sky would be at its darkest. He also had studied the camp, looking for ways to avoid the lighted areas and get as close to The World Cooperative as he could.

Now he was at the Wilpena gate and telling Alvarez to back him up by waiting and watching from the observation deck. They had been practicing their communication, thinking thoughts to each other. They weren't sure exactly how it worked for them, or how far it would reach, but they had it down. All they had to do was think about each other and then say something to themselves and the other would sense it. A line of sight helped, but was not necessary.

"Okay. I'll wait until I see you on the deck and then I'm going out," McKinley said.

A few minutes later he could just make out Alvarez on the observation deck and he sensed her thought: *All clear. You can go now.*

He slipped out of the gate, hesitated a moment and then ran crouched low to a large Wilpena Pound welcome sign.

Still clear.

He sprinted to grouping of large garbage dumpsters set up to serve the camp.

Go!

Now he was inside the camp's western edge, sliding in and out of the shadows of tents set up by individual campers. He had about a hundred meters to get to the wall dividing the camp between the general population and The World Cooperative.

Stop! Someone's coming!

He crouched low. Two campers strolled by as McKinley dropped and flattened himself on the ground.

All clear.

He kept moving. Only one row of tents was positioned between him and the large canvas wall. It was too high to see over and he began looking for an opening.

All clear to the wall.

McKinley sprinted the last few meters to the wall and tried to flatten against it. It was soft and pliable but opaque. He could hear sounds of machinery and the clanking of metal. Someone was assembling something.

He started moving along the wall, searching for an opening. He rounded a corner and could no longer see the Wilpena Pound compound.

Jarrod, are you okay? The signal seemed weaker.

McKinley sent his thoughts to Alvarez. *I'm good but still can't see inside. Heading toward a small slit in the canvas just ahead a few meters.*

Someone's coming toward you from this side. Jarrod, get out of there!

McKinley looked for cover. There was none. He stood up tall and walked casually.

"You! Stop!" a burly man shouted as he rounded the corner and saw McKinley.

"What are you doing here?"

"Just out for a walk," replied McKinley.

"Walk somewhere else. This is World Cooperative territory."

"Thought this was all a public campground. What's with this crazy wall?"

"None of your business. Now get out of here. Back to your side of the camp." The man he pulled up his jacket to reveal a sidearm.

"Okay, okay. Don't panic, man. I'm going."

As he backed away he heard a strange clicking sound. A hard sound of metal on metal. It sounded familiar, like the latch of a gate closing, but more solid, harder. He desperately wanted a look under or through that canvas wall but he wasn't going to get it. The stocky man followed him back around the corner of the wall toward the public area of the camp.

"Now keep going. And keep your nose out of our business."

McKinley walked to the camp and into the first row of tents. The guard watched for a minute and then turned to continue his round. McKinley ducked behind a tent and crouched in a shadow.

> *Time to come back, Jarrod.*
>
> *I really want a look under that canvas. Something's going on that we need to know about.*
>
> *Not possible. I can see another guard. They're increasing their security.*
>
> *All the more reason to find out what's going on. Can't you sense the danger growing?*
>
> *A little, maybe. My danger alert isn't as strong as yours. You're more attuned to that.*
>
> *I need a look. We've got to know.*
>
> *Let's tell Brighton and Gen. Jones. They can decide. I don't want you risking your safety. That's not your job here. You're our ambassador for first contact, not some special ops covert agent.*

I'm going to try again.
If you do, I'm coming with you.

McKinley watched Alvarez leave the observation deck.

No. Okay, I'm coming back.

A few minutes later they were together behind the Wilpena Pound entrance gate. Alvarez sighed in relief. She had fulfilled the most important part of her assignment from Brighton—to keep McKinley from doing something reckless.

"We'll go to Janet and Gen. Jones first thing in the morning," said Alvarez. "We'll convince them to investigate. The general can just go out there and see what's going on."

"I hope that's not too late," McKinley said.

As they walked back into the Wilpena Pound complex and to the observation deck, McKinley's feeling of danger was growing. Storm clouds were brewing in the northwest. Flashes of lightning stabbed the dark. And McKinley's danger signal was growing blacker by the minute.

The activity behind that canvas was also growing. They could see flashes of light, sparks flying.

"They're welding something," McKinley said.

"Yes."

"We can't wait until the morning. We need to see the general now."

McKinley and Alvarez turned in unison and walked quickly inside the Wilpena Pound complex.

It was mid day on Progenia Prime. Acquaria was high in the sky and the brightness made the green and purple hills around the Project Forgiven headquarters shimmer and sparkle.

Heronius was resisting attempts by the Forgiven leadership to convince him that now was the time to bring the project to fruition.

"It is not that I do not believe the moral and ethical rationale for the Forgiven Project. I just do not believe it will work at this time. And it is not all about resources," said Heronius.

"What are your concerns, then?" asked Athrena.

"I do not believe Earth is ready to take part in the Grand Vision. The Earthly species has not reached the maturity necessary to sacrifice what is required to take part."

"It should be little sacrifice," said Athrena. "That is what we want to explain to you. This program will be no sacrifice to either Earth or Progenia Prime. It will benefit both."

"Tell that to those on Earth who we conscript," said Heronius. "They might see it as sacrifice. They might want to have a choice. And what about uncontrolled individualism? It is difficult to see Earthlings being able to bend to our will for the needs of the Grand Vision."

"We understand your concerns," said Alexia. "But we believe we are making good progress. Earth's answers to our last questions show a growth in their understanding and a willingness to cooperate."

"But have not we been gentle so far?" asked Heronius. "We have not asked the hard questions. We have not demanded anything from Earth. The Grand Vision will require more. And what about the conflict swirling around this SETI group? Have they resolved that?"

"Not entirely," said Conteus. "There appears to be cooperation from most governments around the world but the private sector is still exhibiting self interests that could damage our efforts."

"Exactly," said Heronius. "Leaving Earth to settle its internal disputes will not work. Their history is one of continuous conflict. Why would they act any different now?"

"They have much to gain by working together with us," said Alexia. "They will see that when we explain."

"And if they do not see it our way?"

"Then we will have to convince them," said Athrena.

"With force. Which will expend resources that would be better used in the Grand Vision. Exactly my point."

"We do not anticipate using force," said Athrena. "Based on their growing understanding, their questions and answers, we think they are ready."

"What is our fail safe?" asked Heronius.

"We abandon Earth," said Alexia.

"Again?" scoffed Heronius.

"We hope not," said Athrena. "We are ready to reveal our reasons for the Forgiven Project."

"If that does not work?"

"We cut communications. With their level of technology and even with them knowing who we are and where we are, it would take them hundreds of years to reach us," said Conteus.

"Look at it this way," said Acquius. "If we are successful with Forgiven, we can take the next step in the Grand Vision within a few years. If not, it could be decades, maybe more."

"Acquius is right," said Athrena. "With Earth's resources, the Grand Vision will be greatly enhanced. Is not that worth a little risk?"

"Perhaps," said Heronius reluctantly.

"You will support us, then?" asked Alexia.

"I will not oppose you," said Heronius. "But I reserve the right to speak out at the first sign of failure."

"You always have that right," said Athrena.

"Begrudgingly given," scoffed Heronius.

"Thank you. We welcome your cooperation."

"Indeed," said Heronius.

All four of the Forgiven Project leaders shook Heronius's hand and wished him well.

"We need to accelerate our timetable," said Athrena after Heronius left the room. "Heronius is not on board and will cause trouble at the first sign of difficulty."

"Agreed," said Alexia. "What can we do?"

"We need to give Earth something that is a bit more concrete. Based on their questions, they are ready, but they are getting impatient. It is time to give them information that will go part way to satisfying their curiosity. Knowledge to prepare them for this contact."

"Yes," said Conteus. "Data that will be encouraging and give them even more reason to work together before contact is made."

"Is not that what is proscribed in the reveal program?" asked Acquius.

"Yes," said Athrena. "But we need to compress the reveal schedule and combine steps one through fifteen into what leads directly to step sixteen."

"But sixteen is the riskiest step and if we are not careful it will destroy our whole project," said Conteus.

"I do not think we have many options, considering the stance of Heronius and what is a dangerous situation on Earth," said Athrena.

"Are our agents on Earth ready?" asked Alexia.

"They are ready for the worst," said Conteus.

"Very well," said Alexia. "I will tell the supreme Plebeian we are ready to launch reveal."

"Good," said Athrena. "It is now up to us to craft a message that explains our plan and encourages Earth without causing them distress or to ready their defenses."

"I just hope they are ready," said Acquius.

"As do we all," said Alexia with a deep breath.

Colin Riley was ready. He had just one more puzzle piece to be put in motion.

"You deserve the honor," he said to Gregory Stalingwirth.

"With everything you've put up with, it should be you who gives the final signal. It should be you who is there to see SETI put back in its place. Put back to being a tool for powers that have a higher purpose envisioned."

"But I'm not sure why I have to be there," Stalingwirth said with uncertainty.

"Because it's where you belong. Wilpena Pound was your operation for decades and you were kicked out, humiliated and nearly landed in jail. Now you can reclaim what is rightfully your place. Back in charge at Wilpena Pound."

"But I could go there after."

"No. You need to show some leadership. If you want to take command, you need lead the way."

"But it sounds dangerous."

"Not to worry. We have experienced commanders leading each move. When their job is done, you will be able to walk right in. And, we don't really expect much resistance to the forces we have marshaled. Wilpena Pound doesn't have the defenses. They will fold when they see what they're up against."

"Perhaps. But McKinley has a record of fighting back, as you know."

"But he's not really in charge at Wilpena Pound. The council will not be willing to risk a confrontation of the kind we will present. Council members would all have to get approval from their governments. By that time, it will be too late. We will make our move."

"Okay. When do I go?"

"After dark. We'll take you in by stealth aircraft to get you in place by tonight. This is going to happen soon."

Riley gave Stalingwirth some last minute instructions and then directed him to the operations center where he would prep for the evening flight. He then called the flight commander.

"Yes, I'm certain," Riley told the commander. "He is a spy. He pretends to be on our side but we think he's still working for SETI and has undying loyalty to Wilpena Pound. Why else would he insist on going there. He's no good on the battlefield. He'll just betray us."

After listening to the commander, Riley was insistent.

"Yes. I want it done. Just make it look like an accident."

He hung up and smiled. The last loose end, the link to GME, had just been tied off.

He made one more call.

Forces that had been moving around southern Asia all week now began to coalesce. They all were heading to the outback of South Australia. To a large natural bowl shaped landform named Wilpena Pound, but which the aboriginals called Ikara, which means "meeting place." Perhaps the soon-to-be site of Earth's first contact with intelligent life from the universe?

The red ridges of Wilpena Pound were just catching the first rays of sun when Jarrod McKinley and Liza Alvarez finally got to see Gen. Jones.

They described what they had heard in the public campground around the enclosure of The World Cooperative for First Contact. They explained that activity was taking place behind the large canvass wall that boded ill. The sense of danger McKinley felt had been growing and the sounds of assembly and construction had them fearing the worst.

"I can't help feeling that they're building something to harm Wilpena Pound," said McKinley.

"Like what? We have the gate and most of the perimeter well guarded. Our troops are highly armed."

"But only with handheld weapons," said Alvarez.

"If they are building heavy weapons of some type we could be in danger," added McKinley.

"As head of security, you have the authority to go out there and see what's going on," said McKinley. "Just go take a look. It could be nothing. They could be building a spaceship to greet the aliens like the nutters they are, but it could be more. We should find out."

"All right," said Jones. "I'll go out there after my morning briefing with Janet. She should know about your concerns anyway."

Just as they were leaving Gen. Jones, McKinley's personal alarm sounded. There was a new signal from the aliens.

"Got to go to operations. Another message," he said to Alvarez.

Ten minutes later McKinley was at the signal terminal. The fingerprint scanner authenticated him and he punched in his new security code.

He read the message, a longer one this time, and took a deep breath. As he reread the message a large smile spread over his face. He punched in the commands to time-stamp and distribute the message to all delegations, most of whom would still be asleep, he was sure. Then he buzzed Brighton.

"Janet. Good morning. Have you seen the message?"

"Not yet, Jarrod. Just getting ready for the day."

"Look at it now, please."

It took a few minutes before Brighton spoke again. "My God, Jarrod! Is it really going to happen?"

"Looks like it. How fast can we get the council together? They've all been sent the message."

"One hour. I'm sure everyone will want to meet right now."

"Good. I want our team to meet in half an hour. It's important that we're all together on this. Now is not the time to show any disagreement."

"Half an hour it is. See you soon."

On the northern coast of Australia, a warning sounded from a radar station. There had been a blip where there should not have been one. It was quick. It was only one. The radar operator shrugged his shoulders and went about his morning reporting. He had seen these kinds of anomalies before and wrote it off as a random radar ghost.

Overhead, a pilot in a jet fighter had just been chastised. He had, for less than thirty seconds, broken the height on the flight pattern, the height that might expose them to radar detection. He dropped down again and matched his speed to the three attack helicopters that were heading to the outback of South Australia.

"Ladies and gentlemen," said Jarrod McKinley after Janet Brighton had turned the council meeting over to him, "it appears as if we are on schedule for first contact.

"You've all had time to read the new message from the Source, who we now know call themselves Proximians. I know you haven't had time to do much but read the message but we, the SETI team, thought it was best to meet as soon as possible to assess all of our reactions."

There was a murmuring of agreement.

"We have taken the liberty of sending this message to our government," said Larry Mitchell of the USNA delegation. "We've had no response yet."

All the other delegate leaders, with the exception of the newly seated African delegation, indicated they had done the same.

"Our government will want a representative from the premier's office here," said Chin Lieu, from China.

"As will the European Union," said Lars Johannson.

"Let's take a deep breath," Brighton said. "I want Jarrod to go over the message. Let's take some time to weigh the implications of the message."

"First, this message is much different from earlier messages," said McKinley. "It's not brief. It's in a friendly conversational tone. They answered some of our questions. They do want first contact and they set a time frame. I'll go over it one by one.

"Our first statement was: *Eager to meet you, set time and place.* They responded:"

Proximians also eager to meet Earth. We will initiate contact at 0730 GMT at Wilpena Pound on Earth day 329.

"Using standard measurements, that means three days from now at four-thirty in the afternoon. Our second question was: *Can we travel to you?* Their answer is:"

We can assist. Will take some preparation on your part. Plans provided on first contact.

"Our third question was: *Earth ready for travel, exploration. Where are we going?* Their response is:"

Many destinations accessible across the galaxy. You may choose.

"Our fourth question was: *Our images included, please provide yours.* Their response is:"

All will be revealed at first contact. We are all Proximians.

"There it is," said McKinley. "I'm open for questions."

An awed silence filled the room, as if each attendee was taking a deep breath and contemplating a day that most thought would never come.

Sam Filmore broke the silence. "Interesting that they would say 'We are all Proximians.' I would take that to mean they are humanoid, or human-like."

"Perhaps," said McKinley. "But we should be prepared for something different, or be prepared to see nothing at all. We don't know what form their contact will be.

"We have a lot of work to do," he said. "Our new friends, the Proximians, don't say how they will initiate contact. We have to keep our minds open to many possibilities. I assume it will be remotely, but they may arrive here in the flesh. We need to alert all nations not to be alarmed if something strange appears in the sky. That means going public. We don't want the public to panic."

"And we need to get as many of the leaders of the world's countries here as we can," said Brighton. "It won't be easy and we need to be sure not to exclude countries that could impact this mission. Even countries not represented here."

"Even India?" asked Lieu.

"I would recommend it," said Brighton. "And we need someone from South America, Indonesia and Russia."

"We can't have the whole world here, we don't have room," said Filmore.

"We're going to have to make room," said Brighton. "We might have to move the first contact meeting to Sydney."

"Not Sydney," said McKinley. "We've had too many close calls there. Sydney presents too many variables. We can't control the situation. We have to do it here."

"And we should enlist our media friends to get this first contact on a worldwide broadcast," said Laura Henning.

"I suggest Janet creates working committees on this council to ensure all tasks are completed," said McKinley. "We have only three days."

Brighton went to work creating committees and doling out assignments in a room that overflowed with high spirits. A strong sense of working together permeated the council meeting room.

McKinley motioned to Liza Alvarez to come with him out of the room. As they walked out Jenny Hastings, who had been sitting in the back of the council room, approached.

"Jarrod. I've got some more news on my research into the signal," she said.

"Can it wait, Jenny?" McKinley asked. "We need to move quickly on this new information and old signals probably don't mean much."

"I think they do," Hastings replied. "There's a pattern that's continued right up to the present time. It makes a difference. It's something we all need to be aware of before first contact."

As they walked down the hall to the media room to see how that room might be used for first contact, Josh Reynolds waited for them.

"Jarrod and Liza, I believe you should listen to what Jenny has found," said Reynolds.

"We will when we get time," replied Alvarez curtly.

"Now would be a good time," said Reynolds.

"Give us two hours," said McKinley. "We'll talk after lunch."

"Okay," said Hastings. "We'll be in my operations office."

"Sure, Jenny. And, Josh, thanks for helping—"

McKinley's sense of danger, which had been simmering all morning long, suddenly spiked.

"There's something going on. You feel it?" he said to Alvarez.

"Just slightly," said Alvarez. "What is it?"

"I don't know. But we've got to find Gen. Jones, fast."

As they turned down the hall towards security, an alarm sounded. They started to run.

Gen. Jones, McKinley, Alvarez and several guards were standing on the observation deck looking out at the gates of Wilpena Pound and the campground beyond.

There was a large, noisy crowd pushing against the gate.

"What do they want?" McKinley asked Jones.

"They demand to be let in and to be a part of the SETI World Council," said Jones.

"Are they dangerous?" asked Alvarez.

"We've looked over the crowd and there don't seem to be any arms. Just signs and that man with the large bullhorn."

"There must be a threat or I wouldn't sense such danger," said McKinley.

"That guy with the bullhorn has given us ten minutes to let them in or they claim they will force their way in," Jones said.

"Can they do that?" asked Alvarez.

"Not with what they've got," said Jones.

"It's behind the wall," said McKinley. "They got something behind that canvas wall. General, I think you'd better sound the lockdown alarm and reposition all your resources toward the front gate."

"Calm down," said the general. "We're heavily armed. They are not. We've got reinforcements coming in from the United Space Command in Alice Springs. Should be here within a half an hour."

"It won't be soon enough," said McKinley. "We've got less than ten minutes. We need to protect our operations and the people inside."

"I'm telling you . . ." The general paused. As he listened to his comm device his face turned red.

"That was the reinforcement convoy," he said. "They've been hit by some kind of aerial assault. Two dead, all vehicles disabled."

He spoke into his comm device and two seconds later a siren sounded for the lockdown. Steel curtains rolled down over the windows of the visitors' center and large steel panels slid across the gates of Wilpena Pound.

Two seconds later the canvas curtains dropped and McKinley saw three large artillery guns. Two were pointed at the gates and one directly at them on the observation deck.

"You've got four minutes," said the man with the bullhorn.

Two armored personnel carriers rolled out of The World Cooperative compound taking positions to the left and right of the crowd that had gathered behind the man with the bullhorn.

Confusion was settling in among the crowd. It was apparent that many of the onlookers had no part of this standoff. People began to scatter. A few of them, instead of scattering, ran to positions behind the armored personnel carriers. They pulled assault rifles from under their coats and pointed them at the gates.

"Two minutes," said the man with the bullhorn.

"We need to get inside," said Jones. "My men will take up positions here. We're going to call their bluff. I can't see them firing those artillery guns. They're not that crazy. Besides, most of Wilpena Pound is underground and nothing but an armed assault can breach our defenses and they don't have enough men."

"I'm not sure," said McKinley, and he point to the northwest.

Two helicopters and a jet fighter were approaching fast.

"One minute," the bullhorn blared. He was now the only one standing in front of the gate. He looked back to one of the APCs and waited another thirty seconds. Then, just as the helicopters swung around to hover nearby and the jet roared overhead, another voice, this time from inside the armored personnel carrier.

"Jarrod McKinley. Open the gate. I don't want to have to destroy Wilpena Pound. This is your last chance."

The voice was familiar to McKinley. He was sure who the owner of that voice was.

"No way, Stalingwirth. You're not getting back in Wilpena Pound."

He and Alvarez scrambled for the door of the observation deck and reached the visitors' center just as the first artillery gun fired a direct hit on the gate. The blast ripped a small hole in the gate, killing two security guards. Guards on the observation deck opened fire on the artillery guns but the operators were well hidden. Others at the gate pulled away wounded men under covering fire.

Troops began rappelling out of the helicopters and advancing, waiting for the next artillery shell to fully breach the gate. Jones ordered his troops to fire on them but their fire seemed to be deflected by some sort of invisible shield. Jones crouched behind the observation deck wall as he directed other security guards to reinforce the gate.

"No need to do this," said the voice from the APC. "Just let us in."

Gen. Jones responded this time by ordering his guards on the observation deck to fire on the APCs. They took out three or four of the men hiding behind the vehicles but were immediately met with withering fire from the troops on the ground and from the attack helicopter. In an instant the guards on the deck were cut down. Jones was hit in the shoulder and slumped behind the wall.

Looking through a slit in the steel curtain over the windows of the visitors' center McKinley observed the troops advancing and saw a second shot from the artillery gun blast a gaping hole in the gate.

The third artillery gun was redirecting its aim, away from the observation deck and directly at the window he was peering out.

"Run!" shouted Gen. Jones as he struggled to get inside.

"Jarrod, we've got to go!" cried Alvarez.

McKinley was pulling against her, still looking out the window. At the instant he thought he saw the artillery crew pull the trigger, he saw a shimmer and an explosion at the end of the barrel of the artillery gun. He staggered back, arm over his eyes, sure the end was near. But nothing happened. No blast smashed the window. No gaping hole appeared in the wall of the visitors' center. The silence was shocking as no more shots rang out.

The only sound assaulting his ears was a repeating buzzing noise.

He ran to the window. Those troops that could, scattered. The others lay motionless on the ground. The artillery guns were silent. One was bent like a large hand had grabbed and twisted it. The barrel of the gun that had fired at the visitors' center was shattered, shredded and peeled back, as if a cover had been placed over the barrel. The APCs were steaming and silent, the troops behind them blanketing the ground. A driver was slumped out of one of the windows. One helicopter lay crumpled and burning on the field. The other spun around in an attempt to escape, but another buzz disabled it and it spiraled down. The fighter jet had disappeared.

Out in the campground people peered out of their tents, pointing to three different locations above the Wilpena Pound visitors' center.

McKinley threw open the door and rushed to the observation deck door. He knew immediately what had happened. He didn't know how but he was sure of one thing.

It was time.

McKinley heard a voice in his head: *Jarrod McKinley, deploy your security forces to neutralize the attackers. The stuns will dissipate in eight minutes and thirty-one seconds.*

McKinley thought he recognized the voice but he didn't waste any time.

"General," he said as he helped the general to his feet, "the attackers are just stunned, except those your forces may have shot. Get your security out there and detain them. We've got eight minutes."

Jones looked at McKinley with a quizzical stare but nodded and immediately ordered his forces to comply. They rushed through the gate and rounded up the stunned troops and poured into the camp looking for more attackers. They had neutralized everyone within seven minutes.

McKinley, Alvarez, Hastings, and Reynolds waited on the observation deck staring at three spots in the sky above the Wilpena Pound visitors' center. Three shiny orbs pulsated, seeming to fade in and out of view.

When the last of the attackers had been detained and the security forces signaled all clear, the orbs began to change.

The shimmering faded and within each orb a spacecraft became visible. Each was about the size of the trailer of a tractor-trailer long-haul truck standing vertically. At the top of the craft appeared to be a clear bubble with a figure inside. A metal band encircled the vehicle, merging with the ends of the inner rectangle which had rounded edges. A pulsating light flashed around the band.

Again, McKinley heard a voice in his head: *Jarrod McKinley. We respectively request permission to land in the Wilpena Pound secured area.*

McKinley responded with his mind as he pointed to a clear area inside the compound to the right of the observation deck: *Granted.*

"General, they're going to be landing over on the recreational fields," he told Jones.

As each craft moved slowly to the landing area it began to rotate. The main rectangular body of the spacecraft rotated to land horizontally. The metallic ring adjusted to align itself with the ground and the cockpit bubble traveled from the end of the spacecraft body to the center.

The machines made no sound. Only when the spacecrafts neared the ground could a slight movement of the debris directly under the crafts be detected. When all three had settled on the field in a slight semicircle, the lights that had been circling the metal bands slowly faded away.

By this time all of the leaders of the SETI World Council were on the observation deck. They had been joined by a cadre of news media, their cameras recording the landing of the craft.

A deafening silence settled on the area like a fog creeping over the land.

No words were spoken on the observation deck. The security forces holding the attackers under detention stood silently, watching. Outside of Wilpena people from the campground cautiously approached the gate where security guards held them back as they simultaneously kept eyes on the three craft. Some campers climbed up the ridges on either side of the gate, hoping to get a view.

"What do we do now, Jarrod?" asked Brighton.

"We wait."

McKinley received another message: *Jarrod McKinley. Do we have permission to exit our vehicles?*

Yes.

Please bring your leaders and gather in the semi-circle.

"Why do they want us down there?" asked Lars Johannson after the group had assembled. "It seems a bit exposed."

"We needn't be concerned, Lars," said Larry Mitchell. "If they wanted to hurt us, they could have done so a long time ago."

"Still. I'm taking my weapon," said Gen. Jones.

"Don't think it matters," said McKinley. "Let's go."

McKinley counted ten in the group—all the delegate leaders representing regions or nations of Earth, Gen. Jones, and the SETI team of himself, Brighton, Filmore and Henning. At the last minute he motioned Alvarez to join him. Then he saw Hastings in the background, still holding the report she wanted to present. He signaled her to come along.

The group of twelve walked slowly out of the visitors' center and toward the spacecraft.

McKinley was in the lead with Gen. Jones and Brighton right behind. McKinley signaled for Alvarez to join him in the front.

When they reached a point where there was a spacecraft to each side of them and one in front, McKinley signaled everyone to stop.

Jarrod McKinley. I will now exit my craft. Please advise your friends not be frightened.

"Okay, everyone. The door of the spacecraft in front of us will open. There is no danger."

They watched in wonder as a light slowly began to flash on the body of the spacecraft. It formed a rectangular pattern on the side of the spacecraft. The flashing increased in frequency until it was a solid line and then it went black and the frame of a doorway was outlined.

The leisurely opening of the door gradually revealed the silhouette of a tall human-looking figure. Without hesitation it walked briskly down a ramp that extended to touch the ground several meters in front of McKinley.

McKinley recognized the man immediately. It was the same man who had saved him before, once at the Adelaide airport and once in Sydney.

"It is good to see you again, Jarrod McKinley," said the man as he reached down to shake McKinley's hand. McKinley was a full six feet tall but this man stood a good five inches above him. He was slim but muscular, had a slightly angular face, what looked to be a well-tanned skin, dark hair and slightly almond shaped eyes.

"Very good to see you again. And thank you for your assistance today. What may we call you?"

"I am Jaso," replied the man. "I am an agent for the Proximians you have been communicating with."

"I still have many questions," said McKinley.

"I am here to help answer them. Now is the time.

First, allow me to introduce my fellow agents, who also will answer questions."

The doors of the other spacecraft opened and two Proximians walked down their ramps. One was two inches taller than Jaso, with lighter colored hair, round eyes and fair skin. The other appeared to be female and was easily as tall as Jaso, with closely cropped curly dark hair. Her skin was a rich bronze color that glimmered with flashes of blackish purple.

"I introduce Herculium and Delia," said Jaso, motioning first to the male and then the female. Both nodded politely. We Proximians have just one name, chosen by ourselves when we reach equilibrium, which we will explain later."

"Let me introduce to you our team here at SETI," McKinley responded. "Leaders from our world governments are on their way as we speak."

McKinley led the three Proximians through the SETI group. The three seemed right at home, shaking hands, exchanging smiles, nodding with acceptance.

When it was done, McKinley paused and faced Jaso.

"What now?" he asked.

"We are prepared to answer your initial questions," Jaso replied. "But the full message from Proximia would be better delivered when your world leaders arrive. Is there someplace we may begin?"

As they gathered in the council conference room, McKinley asked Jaso if there could be a media representative present.

"I know how important it is to satisfy the curiosity

of your public," Jaso said. "But I also do not want to cause undo concern by inaccurate information being distributed. In the presence of media, my answers may not be as candid."

"C.R. Duncan is our most trusted media representative," said McKinley. "He has treated us fairly throughout all of this, even during the Forsaken scandal."

"That was a bit of a challenge, wasn't it?" responded Jaso, with a smile.

"You know about that?"

"Oh yes. That is the main reason we opened communication with you."

"You mean with Earth, with SETI?"

"No. With you, Jarrod McKinley."

"I don't understand."

"Just another question to be answered in time."

"When?"

"When the time is right."

"A man of riddles, are you?"

Jaso smiled and the projection was one of humor and friendship.

"It will not be long now. However I am not the one to bring you the truth. The truth will be revealed to all your leaders, but the story is a long one with many twists in the road and the answers will only bring more questions. And the questions and answers may be hard to understand. It will take time. Patience will be one of your final tests, Jarrod McKinley. For you and all of Earth."

"Well, let's begin," said McKinley.

McKinley first called for C.R. Duncan to join them in the council conference room from the media center. Others in the media protested and were assured everyone would have equal access, but through the eyes of Duncan.

Duncan was not awed by Jaso.

"Do you want to censor what I report?" he asked suspiciously.

"Not at all," Jaso replied. "I ask only that you report what I say accurately with no sensationalism."

"This is sensational," replied Duncan.

"I am sure it seems that way to you. I only ask that you report the facts with no speculation and no assumptions of what might come."

"Why? What is coming?"

"Nothing to be concerned with. But I can only answer simple questions at this time. The full story of our first contact must wait for when all the world leaders are gathered."

"Why?"

"It will be apparent when it happens. I cannot answer."

"Cannot or will not."

Jaso smiled pleasantly and replied, "You will understand."

Duncan sighed as he agreed to Jaso's conditions. Just the facts.

Three Proximians now sat at the end of the council's conference table. A camera had been set up in the corner and Duncan was on the side close to the Proximians.

Around the table, the SETI World Council delegates took their seats and their entourages spread out along the walls. The number of attendees had swelled when several of the scientists and technicians had been invited to attend.

McKinley nodded to Jaso to begin.

"First. I must apologize for the theatrics outside," he said. "We had no intention of making our introduction so dramatic. Unfortunately, circumstances required us to take extraordinary actions to prevent a less desirable condition from developing. We regret any injuries and deaths we may have caused. You will find that those who were stunned will fully recover. It was not possible to prevent the deaths and injuries of those in the aircraft that were disabled.

"I will make a few opening remarks and then open it up to questions. As I told Mr. McKinley, answers to many of your questions will have to wait until your government leaders are assembled. I will answer all I can.

"We," indicating the three aliens, "are Progenians. We come from the only habitable planet in the Alpha Centauri system, orbiting the star you call Proxima. For that reason you may call us Proximians, if you wish. We are agents of those with whom you have been communicating. We have been tasked with ensuring the success of this first contact. It is very important that Earth and Progenia Prime, or Proximia, have a successful and beneficial relationship. Our jobs here have been to make sure that certain people, Mr. McKinley for one, can continue to work toward this end.

"Our spacecraft utilize light displacement arrays, to become invisible when necessary. Our floatation capabilities are made possible by a gravitation-neutralizing generator. The tool used in the confrontation outside was a focused auditory immobilization wave.

"Our crafts are mostly electronics and hardware. Each one only has the capacity to carry a small automated terrestrial transport, a small amount of cargo, and up to four passengers. Your scientists and engineers are welcome to examine our technology."

There were murmurs of excitement around the room.

"I will now try to answer your questions."

"But you haven't answered any of the important questions," C.R. Duncan jumped in, not waiting for the others. "Why are you here? Why do you want first contact? How long have you been here? What else have you done here that we don't know about? Are your intentions peaceful? Do we on Earth have anything to fear from this contact? Sir, don't you realize the absolutely traumatic conditions this will create among our nations, our populace?"

"Of course we do," responded Jaso with a friendly smile. "I can assure you our intentions are peaceful and you have nothing to fear. Other than that. I cannot answer your more general questions. We have a process that we intend to follow for the good of all concerned."

"When will this process begin and how long will it take," asked McKinley.

"The process will begin when we can address the leaders of your countries," replied Jaso. "The process will take some time. That time cannot be determined by me, or even the Proximian leaders of this project. That will depend on your leaders."

"Why?" It was Duncan again.

Jaso smiled and looked at Duncan and then back to the conference table.

"That word, why, seems to be a favorite among you, does it not? I can only say there are certain realities that are coalescing at this moment that need to be accepted or rationalized by the people of Earth before we can move forward with first contact."

Nervous murmurs echoed throughout the room.

"Do not fear. It is not any kind of a physical threat to you."

"What kind of threat is it?" Duncan interjected.

The three Proximians looked at each other intently.

"That is all we can say at this time," Jaso said. "We will now conduct tours for those who wish to see our spacecraft. And each of us will work with your scientists and engineers to explain more of our technology, such as our near light speed travel, or NLST, engines, and our sling-point time displacement modulators. Thank you for your attention."

"But we have more questions," said McKinley.

"Surely you do," replied Jaso. "But they must wait for the reveal."

"The reveal. What is that?" said Duncan.

"That is when we reveal to your world leaders the reality of this moment in your long history." With that, the three Proximians rose and walked out of the room.

The mumbling in the room became a loud buzz.

Jenny Hastings grabbed McKinley.

"Jarrod. I think I know what he's talking about."

"What?"

"It's in the signals I've been studying. Part of it anyway. You need to know this, before the reveal."

"Why?"

Hastings smiled. "Man's favorite word, says Jaso. Trust me, you need to know. It will help you understand."

"Shouldn't we tell the others?"

"I don't know if they will believe it. I've got no solid proof, just some hints."

"Some hints about what?"

"Why they are here. What they are doing. What they want."

"Well?"

"I hope I am wrong."

Chapter 25

Jarrod McKinley and Liza Alvarez stood next to Janet Brighton as they watched the final modifications being made to the Wilpena Pound Visitors' Center. It was the largest room at Wilpena Pound and would be the site of the reveal.

In the last three days the center had been stripped down to the walls. All of the displays, the gift shop, the small auditorium, and other trappings had been removed. In their place a seating area capable of holding one hundred people had been fashioned. A small stage occupied the front of the room, and a sound system had been installed. In addition, the conference room had been altered to become a secondary auditorium to handle the overflow crowd. Audio and video links connected it to the visitors' center.

"With one hundred seats we will have just enough room to hold the SETI World Council and the leadership teams coming in from around the world," said Brighton.

"How are you going to assign seats?" asked McKinley.

"Well, about forty countries or regions are being represented and each representation will get two seats in the visitors' center," Brighton replied. "The others will have to be in the conference room. We've also put large TV monitors on the observation deck and two near the main gate. Plus we will have the live TV feed which will go out worldwide."

"I hope that will be enough," said Alvarez.

"It will have to be," said Brighton. "We're using all the space we have here."

"Any reaction from governments around the world?" asked McKinley.

"They are all concerned about security," said Brighton. "Most are bringing in their own security teams. Several advance teams arrived yesterday. Large camps are being set up outside the Pound gates. The moods of the political leaders range from eager anticipation to paranoia. All are very anxious."

"Gen. Jones seems to believe the immediate security threat from forces outside Wilpena Pound have been eliminated," said McKinley.

"Did he find Stalingwirth?" asked Brighton.

"No. He did find a remote broadcasting system in one of the APCs. Stalingwirth was never here. That voice that sounded so much like Stalingwirth could have been his voice, or someone else, but it didn't originate from anywhere around here."

"So where is Stalingwirth? And what about Colin Riley and GME?" asked Brighton. "I'm still convinced GME is involved. They didn't seem like they were going to give up."

"Jones has issued an alert for both of them. He found no sign of Stalingwirth and no evidence of Riley or GME in the camp, on any of the attackers, or the in equipment. But I agree. I think GME was behind this attack. They were going all out to control this first contact."

"Not surprising," said Alvarez. "Just look at what we've learned already. Even though we are still trying to understand it, it's clear the Proximians have solved a few things technologically that will free us from the bounds of Earth."

"Yeah," said McKinley. "Like how to neutralize gravity. How to travel at ninety-five percent the speed of light and have our communications travel even faster than that."

"Yes," said Brighton. "The scientists in the compound are calling for experts around the world to get here to help them understand all of this. I guess GME was right, this technology will fundamentally change how we travel in space; how we explore the universe."

"And now it will be for the benefit of all humans, not just one company," said Alvarez.

"I certainly hope so," replied McKinley. "I hope the reveal goes over well and that the leaders of the world will cooperate to make this a positive for all Earth's people. I'm afraid others might try to dominate, try to control the situation for the benefit of their country or their region."

"That would only be human nature," said Alvarez.

Brighton's comm device buzzed and she held it to her ear.

"The President of the USNA has arrived," she said. "The first of many. Others are inbound and I've got to go. Jarrod, you said you wanted to talk to me about the work Jenny has been doing. Can you give me a quick overview? I've got a few minutes."

"Jenny has found that there has been a pattern to certain radio signals over the years that have characteristics that match the signals we've been receiving from Proximia," said McKinley. "If she is right, the Proximians have been sending signals to Earth since well before we invented radio signals."

"I'm not surprised, given their advanced technology," said Brighton.

"Nor am I," responded McKinley. "But that's not the most interesting part. We can't tell what the signals were about, the code is entirely different. But the timing of the signals is curious. At almost every stage of significant activities on Earth, there is a burst of signals."

"How so?"

"Our records only go back to about 1960 but there was a burst of signals when our space programs started, another with the first moon landing, again with the Mars settlement, when the Mideast War ended in 2045, when SETISCOM established the Titan Listening Post, when we started mining the asteroid belt, and when the last nuclear weapon was destroyed in 2060."

"What does this all mean?" asked Brighton.

"I think it means they've been watching us," said Alvarez.

"Perhaps," said McKinley. "I'm hoping the reveal will shed some light. It will certainly give us some more questions for our visitors."

"We should tell the others," said Brighton. "Everyone needs to know this."

"Not yet," McKinley said. "Jenny is not done with her research. We can probably ask better questions when she is finished and has shared her findings with other scientific teams."

"Okay," said Brighton. "Keep me informed. I've got to go meet the President of the USNA."

"Jarrod," Alvarez said after Brighton had left the room. "I've got to tell you something. It's something I've put out of my mind recently but this study by Hastings got me thinking about it again."

"Okay, Liza. What is it?"

"Something your father told me."

"My father? What's he got to do with this?"

"I can't tell you here. Let's go to your room. I'm not sure what it means. It might not mean anything. But I know I don't want anyone else hearing this."

"Liza?"

"Not here Jarrod. In your room, please."

Colin Riley was afraid, more afraid than he had ever been. Failure was not something he was used to. Whether it was during his time in Special Forces or the time he had been working for GME, he had always worked from a position of overwhelming power. If his opponent showed force, he applied more force. If his opponent showed advanced technology, he found ways to defeat it.

But now he had been beaten by a force he could not overcome. Even with GME's newest technology in the shielding of his helicopters and robotics to assemble his armaments at Wilpena Pound, everything had been wiped away in an instant by the aliens who had more advanced shielding and superior cloaking of their airships.

He didn't understand the weapons they used but his one contact who got out of Wilpena Pound reported the sighting of alien spacecraft. One thing he was certain of, GME would not be happy. He had failed in his mission, again. The company was not one to abide failure. He was sure the attack on Wilpena Pound could not be tied to GME. Gregory Stalingwirth's body would be found in the outskirts of Adelaide with no link to GME. There was nothing on any of the personnel or equipment at Wilpena Pound that could be tied to GME. But it was still failure and GME would be looking for him. He would have to go underground, disappear. Yet, even as he made his plans to become invisible, he still searched his brain to find a way to get back into Wilpena Pound. He was not finished with Jarrod McKinley and SETI.

Athrena was awakened by the persistent buzzing of her comm device.

"Yes, Conteus. What is it?"

"We have had to activate Protocol 43 of the Forgiven Project," said Conteus.

"What is the status of Jarrod McKinley and the SETI team?"

"All is secure but it took direct and visible intervention from our agents."

"How many agents?"

"Just three. We have others on standby."

"Do the Earthlings know about the others?"

"No. Agent Jaso has been very discreet. We have no need to reveal our other agents at this time."

"Was it GME?"

"Yes. But it is no longer an immediate threat."

"Good. Protocol 43 requires immediate reveal. Are we ready?"

"Yes. The political leaders of Earth are now gathering at Wilpena Pound?"

"Will they all be there?"

"All that matter. Enough so our plan should have the desired impact."

"Now all we have to worry about is whether they accept what they hear."

"Yes. Do you want me to notify Alexia and Acquius?"

"No I will do that. I also will notify Heronius. He needs to know what has happened. When will the reveal happen?"

"In one day, Earth time."

"I wish there were a way to monitor it in actual time. I am very eager to see how Earth accepts its new reality."

"Yes, that would be desirable. Our time lag is still about four hours. It is not going to be easy for some, I am very certain."

"We can only hope."

By the morning of the fourth day since GME's attack on Wilpena Pound, Gen. Jones was nearing mental and physical exhaustion. There had been vast changes around the complex. The Proximian spacecraft were still parked on the fields outside the visitors' center. A small area around the craft had been cordoned off, although Jaso, the lead Proximian, said he was not concerned. Gen. Jones thought it helped control foot traffic as there had been mobile housing units placed in the open space around the craft to house the delegations arriving from around the world.

A constant flow of people moved between the housing units and the entrance to the Wilpena Pound complex. They stopped to stare at the spacecraft and the groups of scientists going in and out. The three Proximians were mostly out of sight, being occupied with showing the scientists around their ships and explaining the science behind the cloaking, the anti-gravity generator, the near-light-speed travel and the time displacement modulator.

They endeavored to explain the science but each time they answered a question, more questions were raised. It was becoming clear that additional specialists were needed who might aid in the understanding how these technologies worked.

Outside the gates, the public crowd was growing fast. Cars streamed over the highways traveling to Wilpena Pound. The proliferation of private aircraft flying over the area forced Gen. Jones to call in military air traffic controllers to prevent collisions. People lined up outside the gate for the chance to enter the complex and walk by the spacecraft. Occasionally, when one of the Proximians was outside their craft, the line would stop and people would call out to Jaso, Herculium or Delia. Their images had been broadcast enough that they were recognized. The Proximians always waved and smiled but didn't talk to the people in line, or respond to those who wanted to go inside the spacecraft, or those who volunteered to travel with the aliens.

The mood was mostly celebratory, festive and good natured. Every once and a while someone would shout threats or sound fearful. Others in the crowd, however, quickly put them down and Gen. Jones had been surprised how little his beefed up security had been needed.

The biggest problem, by far, was coping with the thousands of people arriving outside the gates of Wilpena Pound. There was constant activity to increase the size of the campground and its support facilities. More vendors for food and drink had been contacted and were on the way.

By eleven thirty on the fourth morning, the last delegation from the worlds' governments arrived—

the Russians. The president, premier and all of the cabinet members were present, along with the leaders of their legislative assemblies and all of the top military leaders. Their entourage was easily twice as large as any other country.

Gen. Jones thought this was appropriate considering that the Russians, under the twentieth century Soviet Union, had been first into space and had the longest continuous space program. Their technology, although sometimes not as advanced as other countries, had always been among the most reliable. In the last fifty years, however, the Russian space program had been more dormant than usual, although there had been rumors of new developments coming and of research that would push the country back to a leadership role in space exploration.

The Russian delegation was so large it had arranged to set up its housing outside Wilpena Pound, near the airport. Several large cargo planes landed with modular housing and communication units that created a separate village near the airfield.

As the Russian technicians set up the village a Russian limo delivered the President and his entourage to the Wilpena Pound Visitors' Center.

Everyone was now in place for the reveal.

Gen. Jones breathed a sigh of relief. He would be more relieved when this show and tell was over and all of these high security risk people left.

At four that afternoon, Janet Brighton scurried to get everyone in place. The last minute addition of the large Russian delegation had forced her to change the seating in the Visitors' Center. Instead of being part of the crowd seated in the front row, the SETI team members and the SETI World Council lead delegates would now sit on chairs to the side of the stage. She was worried that this position would restrict their view of whatever Jaso was about to show.

Jaso assured her it would not matter. He seemed at ease and confident as he made minimal preparations for the presentation. He brought with him only a large bag and small container about the size of a shoebox. He said he needed no sound system, no screen, no other aids to assist him. He assured Brighton that with a few specifications from the audio-visual team at SETI and the broadcast companies, his presentation would be automatically picked up and distributed to all, at the center and around the world.

He also seemed unconcerned that stragglers were still filing into the Visitors' Center at 4:35 p.m., breaking the announced deadline for his reveal.

At 4:45 on November 24, 2089, Thanksgiving Day, Brighton asked Jaso to tell the world what First Contact would mean to the human species and the planet Earth.

Jarrod McKinley sat with the SETI team on the side of the stage and took a deep breath. He reached over and took Liza Alvarez's hand. Her story about what his father had told her had him more nervous than he should be. Were his father's story and his speculation and conclusions even true? If they were, would it be part of the reveal Jaso was about to present? And if they were, would it make a difference? If they weren't, how could he find the truth, and would that matter to his future and to the future of mankind?

"I am Jaso," were the first words of the Proximian. He spoke with no visible microphone or any other assists but his amplified voice and his image were projected to the overflow conference room and the broadcasting systems set up in the Visitors' Center.

"I and my fellow Progenians, Herculium and Delia, are here as part of a long-planned project to initiate first contact with you, Earth," Jaso said as the signal was beamed around the world. "I am using the word Proximian because that is the name you know our star by. As our program continues, our leaders will be using the word Progenia, our name for our star.

"Because of the imminent threat to your SETI team four days ago, we intervened to keep our project intact and to ensure this first contact will be beneficial to as many of the peoples of the Earth as possible. I humbly apologize for any deaths that may have resulted and for any damage we might have done. Let me assure you we used the minimal force that was available to us that would be effective in eliminating that immediate threat.

"At this time I will activate a visual and auditory presentation that explains this Proximian project and what its objectives are. This presentation was developed by our project leaders on Proximia. Unfortunately, there is no direct, real-time communication with that team, although I assure you they know I am about to make this presentation and they are monitoring this day, albeit with a four-hour time lag. The name of the project will become apparent shortly and I ask that you listen to and view the entire presentation before I accept questions from those in attendance here.

"Much of what you will see and hear may seem impossible to you, but let me assure you it is all true. Many of the questions you will have will need to be answered over a length of time. If we have your permission, we will make other Proximians such as me and my colleagues available to help answer those questions. As time passes, and again with your permission, other Proximians may arrive on Earth to help.

"We will also have questions for the people of Earth. Proximia does not expect immediate answers. Time is not a concern. The questions we have for you can be answered soon or much later. It is up to you.

"But now is the time to reveal the Forgiven Project."

The lights dimmed as Jaso touched the small box on a table in front of him. A large holographic image rose from the box, giving everyone in the room a clear view.

The first view was from overhead, like from a

very high-flying aircraft or an orbiting spacecraft, of a planet that shimmered with small but abundant oceans. As the view descended, low mountain ranges and vast continents with abundant forest, plains, croplands and cities began to appear.

As the view came closer, the vegetation took on more subtle colors, predominately green but with streaks of purple and violet. Then the voice began.

"Welcome to those on Earth from Progenia Prime. We come in peace with a spirit of cooperation, reconciliation and a longing to be friends."

The view began to zoom in on a city and a building that stood near the shore of an ocean. A room, a person and, finally, a face appeared.

"I am Athrena, lead coordinator of this project. This is Conteus. There are many others now and throughout our history that have worked on this project, the Forgiven Project. It is a project that we initiated because of actions we took nearly ten thousand years ago. It is a long story and will seem unbelievable to many, if not all, of you.

"I beg your indulgence. I will tell the story in the broadest of terms. In the succeeding time, whether days, months or years, we will do our best to answer all questions and turn doubters into believers. At the end of the story, our motives will be clear, and we hope you will join us to help fulfill our objectives.

"But first, I, and all of Progenia Prime, beg your forgiveness. We abandoned you at a time when you needed us most and as a result you have endured a long, long road to reach where you are at this time.

"Let me explain. Ten thousand years ago, Progenia Prime, orbiting the brown dwarf star in the Alpha Centauri system that you know as Proxima, was a planet that had conquered most of its obstacles as far as war, feeding our people and advancing our science. We began looking to the universe to explore. At that time we were still traveling through space in real time. We discovered Earth was the closest habitable planet to us and began to explore.

"We found a wild place with a violent geology, widely variable plant life and extremes in climate, compared to Progenia. We also found a planet with a rich and diverse animal life. Evolution had done a good job on Earth. Many of the species we found on Earth were only existent on Progenia in our fossil record. None were exactly the same but many were similar enough to show there was a grand design in evolution.

"Among the vast array of animals were human-type species of several types. Many of the species were primitive and many appeared to be on the way to extinction. Because of this, and because the population of these human-type populations on the entire planet of Earth was less than one hundred thousand, we decided to send colonists to Earth. We called it Project First Seed. We intended them to be the first of many on Earth. Also, we were certain we would find other habitable planets in our region of our galaxy.

"In the year 87400, in Progenia Prime's recorded history, we sent seven colonial expeditions to Earth. Colonies were to be established in what you call

Northern Africa, the Indian Subcontinent, Australia, North and South America, and Europe. The travel time of the trip from Progenia Prime to Earth was more than fifty years in Earth time, so it was a one-way trip for our colonists. They had limited supplies but all of the latest technology from Progenia to help them establish small, but workable societies.

"Each colony was composed of one hundred fifty beings and enough supplies to be self-sufficient for up to four years. Resupply ships were to be launched from Progenia Prime within a year of the initial launch to make certain our colonies would receive the help they needed to become permanently established while they learned to adapt to, and adopt, their environments on Earth.

"The colonists had a strict no-contact policy regarding the existing intelligent species on Earth. There was to be no contact, none, until the evolutionary progress and compatibility had been fully studied and reported to Progenia. We did not want to interfere with, or displace, any of Earth's indigenous populations.

"Unfortunately, as always seems to happen, things did not go as planned. First, the colony bound for Australia never reported. We suspect something happened on the trip to Earth that disabled the spacecraft. There were never any reports that it landed successfully. We mourned their demise, but we had factored in such a possibility. Other colonists arrived safely and established colonies. Over all, they found the environment hospitable, with the exception of violent weather they experienced. The dangerous animal life, the large predators, did prove to be more of a challenge than we expected." There were chuckles from the crowd. "But they were able to control that problem.

"The biggest issue, however, was not on Earth. It was on Progenia Prime. At that time we had extended our technology and our resources to the maximum point just to launch Project First Seed. This caused political dissention on our planet and several factions withdrew their support for the project. In addition, we did not have our energy and resource delivery systems as refined or reliable as we needed and suffered shortages of energy and of some basic food and fiber.

"In short, after one resupply mission, we could not continue supporting Project First Seed. The guilt was overwhelming, but the public and political resistance was even greater. Some asked why we should sacrifice our well being on Progenia Prime to support a small group of colonialists on a world far away that most of our people would never see and never hear from again.

"As the controversy grew, political factions developed on Progenia Prime. Those factions became more strident and they began to hoard more and more of what was needed for Project First Seed. In the end, there was even armed conflict, which only destroyed many of the technological and industrial capabilities vital to any space travel, let alone trying to get back to Earth and to support our colonies.

"There was limited radio contact over the early years, but back then a radio message took four and a half years to go one way. We did send some small missions to Earth to assess the colonies and to assure them help would be on the way after we resolved our conflicts on Progenia and rebuilt our space program. Unfortunately, after about ten decades even those limited missions were ended. We lost contact with Earth. One hundred years turned into one thousand years with no contact with Earth.

"After two thousand years, we finally resolved our conflicts on Progenia and began rebuilding our technology and industry. A sad irony was that through our war period, as you have experienced on Earth, our technology advanced rapidly. Our developments included stealth technology, new kinds of weapons, shielding, and very advanced propulsion systems. Once we had rebuilt our resource system and our industrial capacity, we were able to again look to the stars and into our galaxy searching for new places to explore. Even though our planet at that time was well balanced, meaning resources were balanced with the needs of our population, there was that burning desire to explore. We longed to see what was over the next horizon. To keep pushing ourselves to do more.

"And then the subject was raised of our colonies on Earth. A topic that hadn't been discussed for nearly a thousand years. It was now four thousand years since the first colonists had landed on Earth and at least three thousand years since last contact.

"A small mission, just one spacecraft, was sent to Earth. They visited all the colonial sites and found either remnants of settlements or no signs at all of the colonies. Some places that had been lush grasslands were now deserts. Some former colonial sites were now covered by seas. Some mountainous areas had been obliterated by geologic activities, earthquakes, volcanoes, landslides.

"What they found was a population that was much more widely dispersed and much more abundant than had been apparent at the time of the first colonial settlements.

"That population had physical characteristics nearly identical to those of Progenians but there were differences depending upon where on Earth those populations were located. We have always had more than one race of Progenians, but on Earth the varieties are much more pronounced. Studies were done. It was apparent that Progenian colonialists had mixed with the existing population in almost every area of Earth.

"It was also apparent that the colonial system had collapsed and that Progenians had had to rely on their own devices to survive. The Progenian technology had all disappeared. Communications systems were nonexistent. Any type of internal combustion had disappeared. There was no metallurgy or science being practiced, and no medical knowledge. Civilization as we knew it, and as we had brought to Earth, had disappeared. But there had been much advancement in the indigenous populations since we first arrived ten thousand years ago. Agriculture was well established. Cities were being formed. Fire was being controlled.

"They also found remnants of the colonies scattered among the existing populations. There were signs some artifacts had survived but instead of being used as intended, myths, legends and belief systems had been built up around them. One of our artifacts that was a communications module was referred to as the Ark of Covenant, but even its existence was more myth than reality. Drawings on cave walls depicted spacecraft, space suits and higher powers coming from the sky. Monuments, such as the pyramids around the world, astrological stone works and landing strips on high plateaus showed there was a mythological memory that stretched back to our colonies.

"A long debate ensued on Progenia. Should we come back to Earth? Should we bring our advanced technology to a planet that was surely advancing on its own? Many on Progenia had an extreme feeling of guilt. We had sent our people here and had abandoned them. Now when we had the capacity to help, they believed we should do so. Others believed Earth should have a chance to forge its own future without our interference, the right of self-determination. Others thought it would be an interesting experiment to see how Earth developed. Would they discover some of the elemental truths in physics and other sciences and advance on the same path as did Progenia Prime?

"We decided not to come back immediately. We would observe this hybrid civilization growing on Earth. When the time was right we would come back to Earth. We would offer our friendship, our help, and welcome them back to our family. For the last four thousand years, the Forgiven Project has been working toward this day. The day when you learn of your heritage.

"The path has not been easy. It has been hardest on you, the people of Earth. Your unique environment and genetics have presented many obstacles not found on Progenia Prime. We never envisioned it would take four thousand years for this day to come. Even though the civilizations on Earth were making great progress, certain hurdles were slowing you down. Hurdles of science, culture, religion, war, and resource development slowed your development.

"It was only at the beginning of your eighteenth century that we began to see the progress that would lead to this day. A few hints to just a few people on Earth helped your scientific progress accelerate. Medicine began to develop.

"By the beginning of the nineteenth century we were further encouraged. You, the people of Earth, were starting to develop the science you would need to advance rapidly. Unfortunately, much of that science was used in war. Armed conflicts, while advancing technology, slowed the cooperation among nations and societies, reinforced nationalism, propped up the separation of linguistics, sharpened the division of religious ideologies.

"It was not until the beginning of your twentieth century that we on Progenia thought there might be hope for the Forgiven Project. When, after your First

Global Conflict, your leaders formed the League of Nations and we saw a general acceptance on Earth that war was not the answer to every dispute, we decided to initiate phases of the Forgiven Project to build a path to this day.

"We began by building on that seemingly inherent knowledge on Earth that the heavens are the source of power, of life, of everlasting promise. We encouraged the idea that there was other intelligent life in the universe through literature, art, and the sciences. But more hurdles remained. The Second Global Conflict, the development of a nuclear weapon and the creation of huge nuclear arsenals, and the further hardening of religious and territorial disputes all slowed the progress of the Forgiven Project.

"But it hardly slowed the progress of you on Earth. You kept pushing your boundaries. You kept alive your hunger to explore. You built space programs, launched rockets, began to explore your solar system, landed on other planets, worked to advance your resource and energy efficiency. You were developing along the lines of Progenia Prime. You were following in the footsteps of your ancestors, but you did not know it. And some of what we attempted did not work. We tried to reinforce the idea of intelligent life in the universe. We visited Earth and gave you signs there were others about.

"Unfortunately, some of our actions led to many misconceptions. The biggest was that any alien life form would be dangerous. The second was a common thought that even if there were human-like aliens, they could not be trusted. Another was that aliens were abducting humans and conducting experiments. That did not happen, although there were some attempts to study how compatible this hybrid Earthly Progenian, you, would be with the home species. Let me assure you now, we are all Progenians, Proximians, if you wish.

"By the time you had reached the outer planets of your solar system, your listening posts around Saturn and the mineral exploitation of asteroids and planetary moons, we knew it was time to bring the Forgiven Project to a close. To bring you home and make you part of your family. The only question was timing. Your public had become disillusioned by unfulfilled tales of life in the universe and the unsuccessful attempts to find life. It is ironic that the failed scandal of the Forsaken project by SETISCOM was the trigger to convince us now was the time. That scandal, which your Jarrod McKinley exposed, revitalized the interest among your public. They were now on board. They wanted to make First Contact.

"That brings us to this day. Forgive us. Forgive us for abandoning you after Project First Seed. Forgive us for waiting so long to come back. Forgive us for letting you struggle to advance to this day, although we believe your struggles made you strong, stronger in some ways than we on Progenia Prime. You have that curiosity we have lost, that desire to explore that has become mundane to us, that spirit of adventure that we struggle to maintain.

"And that brings us to our one request. We want you, the people of Earth, to join us in our Grand Vision. We need you. We need your spirit, your bravery, your enthusiasm. We need your people to join our teams who are traveling throughout the galaxy, exploring new regions every year, establishing other colonies on other planets. When Project First Seed failed on Earth, we withdrew for thousands of years. But as our resources and technology advanced and we decided not to interfere with Earth, we began looking for other places to explore. Our Grand Vision.

"With our sling point compression of time and space, distances are not the problem they were when we first came to Earth. We have established a dozen colonies in other parts of the galaxy. We want you to join us in this adventure. We want you to be part of the Grand Vision. We want to welcome you home.

"This concludes our presentation. I know you, the leaders of Earth, will have many questions, as will your religious leaders and your people. Please ask our agents anything you wish. They have been authorized to answer questions fully and honestly, whether they are about our technology, our planet, our history, our history on Earth, our motives, or our requests of you.

"Do not feel pressured to answer our requests. If you wish to join our Grand Vision, a process will be established to determine who and how many will be recruited, enlisted and trained for our missions. Our agents will distribute devices that can be taken to your public for repeated presentations of this program you have just seen.

"Thank you. And again, we ask you to forgive us for our past actions and we invite you to join us for an exciting journey to fulfill our Grand Vision."

Silence draped over the room as the lights returned to normal. All sat staring at the space where the presentation had been flickering moments before.

Jaso returned to the center of the stage. He said nothing but held a large cloth bag in his hand. Slowly a murmur spread throughout the crowd. Members of the SETI World Council began chattering among themselves. The Wilpena Pound SETI team huddled together. World leaders spoke with their deputies and assistants.

McKinley walked to the stage to stand beside Jaso. Jaso showed him the bag. McKinley motioned to Liza Alvarez, Jenny Hastings and Josh Reynolds to come forward.

"Ladies and gentlemen," McKinley said, and then louder, "May I have your attention, please. My name is Jarrod McKinley. Please, give me your attention for a minute."

Hastings and Reynolds raised their hands. Slowly the crowd quieted and turned to face McKinley.

"We have all heard a story that many of us will have a hard time believing. Jaso has provided the devices," he pointed to the bag, "promised for distribution of this program. SETI staff will now distribute them to you. I think we all need time to consider what we have seen. I would suggest we adjourn so we can talk among ourselves. We can meet here again to decide how to proceed. There are many issues that need to be discussed, the first of which is what our reply will be to Progenia Prime. Are we ready to join them in their Grand Vision?"

The murmur of the crowd of leaders rose to a loud roar as some raised their hands to be heard, others stood, and some just began to try to speak above the others.

By this time Brighton had led the SETI World Council delegates to the front of the stage.

"Ladies and gentlemen," she said several times before the crowd quieted. "Mr. McKinley is right and this council agrees." Others on the council nodded in agreement.

"As your appointed delegates for First Contact, we would like your permission to continue to act in that role. We realize there are many questions to be answered by the Progenians and by us. Questions about how we, this council, you as leaders, and the planet will respond. We ask you all to take the rest of the day to consider all the ramifications of what we have learned today and to think on how to proceed.

"The council and the SETI team will be on this stage tomorrow morning at eight to begin that process. What direction it takes will be up to you and your citizens. We should not rush this, but begin to take the first steps. Can we get your agreement on this first step?"

There was again a murmur in the crowd and then a few began to agree, "The USNA agrees." "Russia will as well." "The African Union will assent." Others followed suit.

Brighton turned to McKinley, still on stage.

"Thank you all for your cooperation," he said to the crowd. "I believe we are about to embark on a new phase in the life of our planet. We are about to begin our journey through the stars. We are going to take our place in a family of explorers of the likes we have never known before. Tomorrow we take that first step."

A solitary figure was seated in a dark corner of a bar in the Dowry Quarter in Sydney. He had been sipping rye whiskey while watching the single TV screen that usually aired Aussie Rules footy or a cricket match.

When McKinley finished, Colin Riley smirked, thinking, *not if I can help it, you won't.*

Four and a half hours later on Progenia Prime, Athrena let out a large sigh. Now the hard part would begin.

In Agrillia, the provincial capital of Botanica on Progenia Prime, Heronius was fuming. This was a disaster, he thought. He vowed to do all he could to stop this insanity. And he needed a new plan. He could not hide his secret forever.

At Wilpena Pound Jarrod McKinley dialed his father on the farm in Montana. It was about five in the evening at Wilpena Pound. In Montana it would be about noon the day before and his father was probably having lunch in the farmhouse. Liza had told him an amazing story about his mother. He wanted to confront his father. Was it true? What did it mean? Why hadn't his mother told him?

Appendices

Appendix # 1

The Alpha Centauri Triple Star System, as Known by the People of Earth

Alpha Centauri, also known as Rigil Kent or Toliman, is the closest star system to the Solar System at 4.37 light years. It consists of three stars, Alpha Centauri A, Alpha Centauri B and a small and faint red dwarf, Alpha Centauri C (better known as Proxima Centauri because it is the closest star to the Sun) that is probably (but not certainly) gravitationally bound to the other two.

To the unaided eye, the two main components appear as a single object forming the brightest star in the southern constellation Centaurus and the third brightest star in the night sky, only outshone by Sirius and Canopus.

Alpha Centauri A has one 110 percent of the mass and 151 percent the luminosity of the Sun. Alpha Centauri B is smaller and cooler, at 91 percent of the Sun's mass and 45 percent of its luminosity. Proxima is at the slightly smaller distance of 4.24 light years from the Sun, making it the closest star to the Sun, even though it is not visible to the naked eye.

The Alpha Centauri Triple Star System, as Known to the People of Progenia Prime

Alpha Centauri A is known as Acquaria, Father Sun. Alpha Centauri B is known as Alphine, Mother Sun. Proxima is known as Progenia, Child Sun. Progenia Prime orbits Progenia.

The orbits of all three suns and the orbit of Progenia Prime means there is always some starlight on all parts of the planet, protecting it from extremes in temperatures. However, the star shine is not enough to cause extreme heating. It has also affected the way Progenians view their existence and how their religions were formed. Pre science populations honored three gods, based on their stars, Acquaria being the source of life, Alphine being the caretaker of life, and Progenia being the inspiration for future life. Post science populations discontinued regular worship of these gods and realized that science was the key to progress and success in all aspects of planetary life. However, many on Progenia who look for faith still refer to their "Gods."

When the Progenians contact Earth they allow themselves to be called Proximians.

Appendix #2

Progenia Prime

The only habitable planet in the Alpha Centauri (AC) system, Progenia Prime orbits the brown dwarf star known locally as Progenia. Progenia Prime is bathed constantly on all sides by star shine from the three stars of the AC system. That has created a lush environment and a moderate climate nearly perfect for abundant life.

The planet's land mass covers about sixty percent of the planet. The seas are shallow and small compared to Earth's oceans, but there are many more of them. This has a tendency to moderate the climate. There are breaks in the landmasses that allow for good circulation between seas. Mountainous regions are scattered throughout the planet, but the mountains are gentle, similar to the Appalachians in the eastern United States or the Snowy Range in eastern Australia. Only two active volcanic regions exist on Progenia Prime, one in the province of Dorfing and one in the province of Modail.

Early civilizations found survival easy because of the moderate climate and topography. This also created conditions more conducive to cooperation than conflict. When one group of Progenians needed resources, there were plenty to share from other populations. Part of the planet was able to develop more food and fiber than they needed, another more metallurgy or energy than they needed. An easier time fulfilling basic necessities led to rapid development of civilization and formal education. This accelerated the progress of science and technology.

Social, cultural and political systems were built on sharing abundant resources and learning better ways to use them. Progenians believed cooperation was better than conflict and built their reward systems to emphasize this. The only exception was when they first started interstellar exploration and stretched their resource thin. Then there was profound political conflict and some minor armed conflict. They quickly realized, however, that armed conflict was one of the biggest wastes of resources so they reverted to tried and true practices of cooperation and collaboration.

Progenia Prime is composed of seven regions equally represented in a planetary Congress that sets policy, goals and make laws when necessary. It resolves disagreements between regions and enforces existing policies. There is a planetary security division with armed forces that can be deployed when collaboration and compromise do not work. Since the beginning of the interstellar age, the force has been primarily concerned with planetary defense and supporting missions needed to carry out the Grand Vision.

The seven regions of Progenia Prime are:

1. Botanica is focused on food and fiber production, many large production facilities and land for growing crops.
2. Modail is the primary location of science and technology, dominated by cities hosting research facilities and factories producing the latest technological devices.
3. Dorfing is primarily a mountainous pastoral region with a small population and many animal herds.
4. Alegantria is a region primarily of energy production and research. Energy production is all sustainable—wind, solar, ocean currents, and geothermal.
5. Somilitia has a small population concerned mostly with the study of cultural and traditional values.
6. Griefing hosts the planetary capitol, Athenia, and has a dense population that fills bureaucratic offices needed to run the planet.
7. Trangilary hosts major universities and schools of higher education, although most regions have their local educational systems including schools of higher learning.

About the Author

Richard D. Bangs was born in Havre, Montana, and raised on a farm fifteen miles from the Canadian border north of Inverness. He attended elementary school at a one-room school near the farm, graduated from Inverness High School and earned a degree in Journalism from the University of Montana. He worked on newspapers for thirty years in Wyoming, Montana, Colorado, and Australia as a reporter, columnist, editor, and publisher. *Forgiven* is a sequel to his first published novel, *Forsaken: Searching for God's Fingerprints*. He is retired and lives in Littleton, Colorado. He spends his time working for non-profits, writing and riding his bicycle.

www.ingramcontent.com/pod-product-compliance
Lightning Source LLC
Chambersburg PA
CBHW032155180726
48284CB00001B/55